Praise for Chris Bohjalian's

The Light in the Ruins

An *O, The Oprah Magazine* "Must-Read Book"

A *Kirkus Reviews* Best Book of the Year

A *Good Housekeeping* Best Book of Summer

"At the heart of a good novel is a good story, and this story is a doozy. Bohjalian expertly weaves together a tale of how [WWII] split Italy between the people who willingly collaborated with the Germans and the ones who did not."
—*St. Louis Post-Dispatch*

"An intriguing tale of Bohjalian complexity. . . . Plotted with an elegance worthy of an Etruscan. It pivots between creation and destruction, the past and the present, and the uneasy chimerical points where they collide." —*The Miami Herald*

"Masterfully crafted." —*The Washington Times*

"*The Light in the Ruins* elucidates, haunts and raises moral quandaries. . . . Riveting." —*USA Today*

"Bohjalian subtly and skillfully manipulates our suspicions. . . . Well-researched, historically interesting."
—*The Boston Globe*

"A spellbinding mix of history and mystery." —*Parade*

"Brilliant. . . . A page-turner that the reader will not soon forget." —*BookPage*

Chris Bohjalian

The Light in the Ruins

————————

Chris Bohjalian is the critically acclaimed author of seventeen books, including the *New York Times* bestsellers *The Sandcastle Girls*, *Skeletons at the Feast*, *The Double Bind*, and *Midwives*. His novel *Midwives* was a number one *New York Times* bestseller and a selection of Oprah's Book Club. His work has been translated into more than twenty-five languages, and three of his novels have become movies (*Secrets of Eden*, *Midwives*, and *Past the Bleachers*). He lives in Vermont with his wife and daughter.

www.chrisbohjalian.com

THE
Light
IN THE
Ruins

A NOVEL

Chris
Bohjalian

VINTAGE CONTEMPORARIES

Vintage Books

A Division of Random House LLC

New York

FIRST VINTAGE CONTEMPORARIES EDITION, APRIL 2014

All rights reserved. Published in the United States by Vintage Books,
a division of Random House LLC, New York, and in Canada by
Random House of Canada Limited, Toronto, Penguin Random House
companies. Originally published in hardcover in the United States by
Doubleday, a division of Random House LLC, New York, in 2013.

Vintage is a registered trademark and Vintage Contemporaries and
colophon are trademarks of Random House LLC.

The Library of Congress has cataloged the Doubleday edition as follows:
Bohjalian, Chris.
The light in the ruins : a novel / Chris Bohjalian.—First edition.
pages cm
1. Murderers—Fiction.
2. Nobility—Italy—Fiction. I. Title.
PS3552.O495L54 2013
813'.6—dc23   2012046269

Vintage Trade Paperback ISBN: 978-0-307-74392-3
eBook ISBN: 978-0-385-53482-6

Book design by Maria Carella

www.vintagebooks.com

Printed in the United States of America
10 9 8 7 6 5 4 3 2 1

*For Andy Bohjalian
and—once more—
for Victoria and Grace*

I dream of the hills around Siena, and of my love whom I shall never see again. I shall become one gaping wound—like the winds, nothing.

—From a note hidden in the seam of the shirt of an
anonymous civilian executed by the Gestapo in Rome, 1944

*Part
One*

A WOMAN IS sitting before an art nouveau vanity, brushing her hair in the mirror. It is, at least according to the police report, somewhere between midnight and three in the morning, on the first Tuesday of June 1955. For dinner she ate a small portion of an impossibly rich pasta—a fettuccini with pecorino cheese and great ladles of truffle oil—at a restaurant popular with wealthy American and British expatriates five blocks west of the Uffizi and a block north of the Arno. She was one of the few Italians there who weren't part of the kitchen or wait staff. She has since bathed, soaping off both her own perfume and the cologne that was worn by her dinner companion—the fellow who had come back here to the apartment, made love with her on the thin bed no more than three feet from the vanity, and then left. He was a suspect in the murder investigation, but only briefly. If he had had even the slightest inclination to spend the evening, there is every chance that I would have executed him that night, too.

At the moment she is wearing her nightgown (which is not especially revealing), though at some point very soon it will be cut off her. Yes, cut. Not even pulled over her head. Sliced from the opening at her collarbone down to the hem, which, when she stands, is mid-shin. By then, of course, she will be dead. Bleeding out. I will have sliced open her neck from one side of her jaw to the other.

Just so you know, that art nouveau vanity is not particularly valuable. The white paint is chipped, and two of the whiplike finials along the right side broke off years ago. Before the war. Moreover, her nightgown is cotton, and the material has started to pill. I mention this so you are not envisioning this room as more glamorous than it is. The woman is still beautiful, even *now, in middle age, and despite the horrific, seemingly unbearable losses she endured a decade ago, in the last year of the war. These days she lives in a neighborhood of Florence that is solidly working-class, a section the tourists visit only when they are impressively, almost hopelessly lost. A decade ago, she would not have known a neighborhood like this even existed.*

The apartment has neither a doorman nor a primitive intercom connecting the wrought iron and frosted glass street door with her modest unit. It is locked, but not all that difficult to open. (Really, it wasn't.) According to the police report, at some point in that roughly three-hour window in the early hours of that first Tuesday in June, I used a blunt object (the handle of my knife, as a matter of fact) to break a pane of the glass near the doorknob. Then I reached in, turned the lock, and opened the door. Remember, this is an unassuming little building. Then I moved silently up the stairway to the third floor, where she lived, and knocked on her door. She rose from the vanity, her brush still in her hand, and paused for a moment on her side of the wood.

"Yes?" she asked. "Who is it?"

And here I lied. I said I was her dinner companion, speaking into my gloved hand to muffle my voice.

So she opened the door and would be dead within moments.

And why did I slice open her nightgown? I didn't violate her. It was so I could cut out her heart. A woman with the lilting name of Francesca Rosati, who had once been a Tuscan marchese's daughter-in-law, was my first.

But, as you will see, not my last.

1943

THE PLANES FLEW in great flocks that May over the Crete Senesi, the lunarlike landscape that marked the Tuscan countryside southeast of Siena. By night the planes were British or American bombers and their destination was Bologna. By day they were German, long streams of Junkers, and their destination was either Sicily or Naples. After that they would attempt to reach Tunisia and reinforce the Axis troops there, but most—and Cristina Rosati knew this from the BBC, not from her own country's newspapers—would be shot down and crash into the Mediterranean Sea. The Italians and Germans in North Africa were finished, and there was absolutely no chance of evacuating them; the army might as well have been on the moon. Sometimes Cristina wished that her brothers were in Tunisia so they might be captured by the Allies and sent to England, where they could await the end of the war in the safety of a prisoner-of-war camp. Instead, Marco was in Sicily, preparing the beaches there for the anticipated Allied invasion. He was an engineer. Vittore, an archeologist, was safe in Florence, but there was bombastic talk on the radio and in the newspapers about the need for total war, and no one in her family would have been surprised if he were suddenly given a rifle and sent off to Sardinia or Greece or some battery along the coast. Both of her brothers were older than she was; barely eighteen, Cristina was the baby of the three Rosati children.

For a long moment she stood outside on the villa's southern terrace and watched the planes, the dark fuselage of each aircraft gleaming in the sun. She was holding four cloth dolls that belonged to her young niece, as well as the scraps of red and gold napkins from which she was crafting Renaissance dresses for the two princesses and tunics for the two men—neither of whom, according to the little girl, was a prince. Cristina had been playing with the child on the terrace when the girl's mother had informed them that it was nap time and herded the child and her brother—who at that moment had been running like a madman along the edge of the swimming pool, using a thin beech branch as a saber—upstairs to the nursery.

And so Cristina was alone when the planes droned southward, high above the Villa Chimera. She was fascinated by them, held almost spellbound. Someday, when the world once again was at peace, she would fly somewhere in an airplane. To Pisa, maybe. Or Naples. Or perhaps all the way to Paris. She couldn't imagine anything more glamorous.

Now a pair of small lizards raced past her, faster than snakes, darting just beyond her toes into the lilacs that grew along the edge of the loggia. Nearby she heard the bells on the sheep and, farther away, the low thrum of a distant tractor. She thought she heard one of the estate's horses whinny. Arabella, most likely.

Finally, when the planes had disappeared far to the south, she ventured inside. Her sister-in-law appeared almost at the same moment, tiptoeing down the stairs so she wouldn't disturb her children. She was shaking her head.

"The planes are starting to scare Massimo," Francesca said. Massimo was seven, old enough to understand the connection between the planes and the dangers his father might soon face in Sicily. He'd overheard the conversations of the more injudicious grown-ups about where the Allies would strike when they had finished with Africa. And then there was all the talk of the bombing in Genoa and Turin, and the possibility that their family might take in urban children whose homes had been destroyed by the Allied air attacks.

"And Alessia?" Cristina asked. Her niece was five and utterly fearless.

Francesca shrugged and poured herself a glass of iced tea. "Oblivious. The world is a game to that child. Fortunately." Then she sat down and stretched out her long legs before her. She, too, was barefoot, but somewhere she had found a bottle of polish and painted her toenails red. She was wearing one of the elegant floral skirts she had purchased when they had been in Florence just before Christmas. It was inappropriate here in the country in the middle of the afternoon, but it swayed like a ballerina's when she moved, and Francesca wasn't made for a world of scarcity or sacrifice. She was nine years older than Cristina, twenty-seven now, and had always seemed to her younger sister-in-law to embody the chic that Cristina had glimpsed in her visits to Rome or Milan or, more frequently, Florence. Francesca dyed her hair the color of honey and clearly had no intention of allowing herself to grow round while her husband was in Sicily and she was here alone with the children.

"I hate airplanes," she added after a moment. "No good has come from an airplane. Ever. You realize that, don't you?"

Cristina smiled. Francesca was fond of great, sweeping pronouncements. "You know that's not true."

"I know nothing of the sort," she said. "I saw you from the window. You were watching the planes. Someday you'll be looking up and they'll be bombing you. Us. The estate. You watch. Someday the bombs will be falling on our heads."

Outside, they heard a car winding its way up the gravel road that led to the villa, and Cristina wandered to the dining room window. The automobile was a long, black army staff car. No doubt people had been talking as the vehicle had wound its way through the narrow streets of the village, past the hulking medieval granary, and then up the hill to the estate. She watched as the young driver, a private, hopped out and opened the rear door for the two officers, one German and one Italian. She didn't recognize either

of them and felt a pang of anxiety. They couldn't possibly be bringing good news, she thought, but nevertheless she tried to reassure
herself. The closest her brother Vittore ever came to danger was
his arguments with the Germans when they wanted to steal some
treasure in Arezzo or Florence and take it to Germany—and those
disputes, he insisted, were civilized. The Germans would ask and
he would say no. They would grow more adamant and he would
explain why the painting or statue or vase could not be moved.
And then they would either ignore him completely and loot the
artifact anyway or—for reasons that were inexplicable to Vittore
but he guessed had everything to do with whether the Germans
had already promised the piece of art to a spouse or mistress or a
more senior officer—back down and choose a less valuable item
from the collection.

But if they were not here about Vittore, did that mean that
something horrific had happened to Marco? She tried to convince
herself that this wasn't likely either. Francesca's husband was in
Sicily, and there was no fighting there. Still, he was a soldier—a
captain—as well as an engineer, and the idea that he might be
wounded or dead caused her to feel a wave of nausea, and she
placed her palms flat on the stucco windowsill for balance. She told
herself that she was overreacting; this had to be something else.
Why would the army dispatch two officers to inform the family
that an engineer was dead on a Sicilian beach or an archeologist
had died at his post in a . . . a museum? Didn't they send telegrams?

She felt Francesca breathing behind her. "Do you know them?"
Cristina asked her sister-in-law.

Francesca shook her head. "Why would I know some thug and
his sorry little sidekick?"

The driver was standing beside his vehicle, but the officers
were approaching the villa. The German outranked the Italian but
looked a decade younger: mid-thirties, Cristina guessed. Maybe
thirty-five. The Italian had his dark hair pomaded almost flat on
his head and a thin mustache he had waxed into a pair of curls. His
cheekbones were sharp; he was a handsome man. The German

was two or three inches taller, his hair the washed-out color of the wheat fields in August. He was carrying a sidearm; the Italian was not.

"They're going to want something, you know," her sister-in-law added. "The barbarians are here to commandeer something. One of the cars, maybe. Or a truck. Maybe they're after the sheep."

"I hope that's all it is," Cristina murmured.

With one hand Francesca briefly rubbed her sister-in-law's back and shoulders and reassured her: "You don't need to worry about the boys. I am sure this is another annoyance. Not a new tragedy."

The front door was open to catch whatever breezes might come in from the west, but the officers hovered in the entryway, their caps in their hands. Francesca beckoned them into the foyer, a wide and airy room itself, with a long flat window and shelves of Etruscan vases, amphoras, and kraters—some replicas and some original, but so common that the museums hadn't a use for them. "My children are sleeping, so you'll have to speak softly," Francesca said, her way of greeting the two men.

The Italian nodded. "I am Major Lorenzetti. This is Colonel Decher." He glanced into the kitchen and the dining room and continued, "Your home is as lovely as I'd heard. I presume you two are the marchese's daughters."

"I am the marchese's daughter-in-law," Francesca corrected him, emphasizing her father-in-law's title in a fashion that conveyed how absurd she thought it was. Francesca believed that the very notion of dukes and princes and counts in the middle part of the twentieth century was ridiculous. She found it a source of unending wonder that her people were ruled by a dictator and a puppet king and her father-in-law owned a small fiefdom. Cristina knew that Francesca was fundamentally apolitical, but when pressed to claim an affiliation with any political structure or school of thought, the woman would express a vague predisposition toward the Hollywood star system in America, because studio heads and movie stars dressed well, made art, and left her alone. "This," she continued now, motioning toward Cristina, "is the marchese's only daughter. My father-in-law has two boys and this one lovely girl."

The Italian major bowed just the tiniest bit. "Of course. I spoke without thinking. You must be Francesca," he said. "And you must be Cristina. Is the marchese home?"

"He and his wife, the marchesa"—and here Francesca again briefly paused—"are down in the olive grove with the overseer."

"They'll be back soon?"

"That's likely."

"Then we can wait."

"If you wait quietly. Remember, my children just started to nap."

The Italian nodded, but the German shook his head and scowled. Cristina worried that her sister-in-law's insolence had gone far enough and jumped in. "Please, let's wait for my father on the veranda," she said. "It's shady there and you'll be more comfortable. I can bring you some iced tea."

It was clear, however, that she had already waited too long to try to mollify their guests. In an Italian that was heavily accented with German, Colonel Decher snapped, "We don't have time to wait, we're due back in Florence. I don't see why you can't show us what we need to see as well as your father could. I understand there was a dig on your property in 1938. That's why we're here. We want to see the necropolis, and given our time constraints, we want to see it now."

Cristina almost laughed. She had been shivering slightly, and now her whole body relaxed. This visit had nothing to do with either of her brothers. It had nothing to do with the needs of their armies' quartermasters. This pair wanted nothing, it seemed, but to see the underground tombs on the far side of the vineyard. The family had come across the burial site when they had expanded the vineyard in 1937 and broken ground for a new shed that would accommodate a larger press and additional barrels. The builders had understood quickly that they had unearthed, literally, a small Etruscan tomb. The first vestiges they discovered? Three columns.

Two were mere stumps, but one still towered seven feet high when they cleared away the cedars and the brush and the soil. Then they found a pair of funerary urns. At that point the family moved their plans for the new shed to the other side of the vineyard, and a few months after that the archeologists and historians arrived for the dig. The younger of Cristina's two older brothers, Vittore, had joined the group and found his calling.

"Yes, I can show it to you," Cristina said. "But I hope you won't be disappointed. It's not really a necropolis. That would imply it's much, much bigger than it is. And there's not a lot there now. The artifacts that had value—the urns and the sarcophagi and the larger vases—all went to the museum in Arezzo."

"Which means they're probably in Berlin by now," Francesca murmured, but she was staring out the window as she spoke and so Cristina did not believe that Decher had heard her.

"Fine," the colonel said. "Show us whatever remains. Do we drive or walk?"

"We can walk," Cristina told him. Then she said to her sister-in-law, "I'll get some candles and take the gentlemen there. That way, you can stay with the children. If Father returns, I'm sure he'll want to join us." She glanced out toward the automobile, where the young driver was studying a map. For the first time she really looked at the private. He was German and might have been as young as she was. "Would your driver like to wait inside while we're gone?" she asked Lorenzetti, but before he could respond, Decher said, "He'll remain at his post." And then the colonel pivoted smartly on his heels and started outside. Lorenzetti rolled his eyes and shrugged, a small apology of sorts, and motioned for Cristina to go first, as if they were entering a ballroom for a dance. Behind them, Cristina heard her sister-in-law snort.

⚜

They passed the statues beside the loggia and in the garden, Venus and the chimera, and then continued out toward the fields. The air was dry and the grass felt like twine as it brushed over

Cristina's toes, and she found herself gazing at the high black boots that the two officers were wearing. She had slipped into her sandals before they had left the villa, because eventually they would have to cross a thin path carved into rock to reach the tombs. The path was no more than sixty meters long—two millennia earlier, it had been far more extensive—but there were sharp points on the tufa stone and it wasn't smart to walk there in bare feet. Still, Cristina could not imagine wearing high leather riding boots in the heat of the afternoon the way soldiers were expected to. She had a pair a bit like them, but this time of year she wore them only at the very beginning or the very end of the day, when she was placing a saddle on her beloved Arabella and going for a ride.

Overhead they heard birds. They smelled jasmine and olean-der. Neither Decher nor Lorenzetti said a word as they walked, and she stifled her own need to speak, including her interest in why they wanted to see her estate's underground ruins. They passed the long rows of Sangiovese grape arbors and then descended a steep slope, and Cristina cut ahead of them because the brush was growing thicker and higher and they were approaching a path they would have to navigate single-file. In a moment they would reach the Y. If they turned right, they would continue through a copse of cedar and beech and reach the small Rosati family cemetery, including the modest Roman temple her grandfather had built. If they veered left, it would feel to them as if they were sinking into the earth: the path would narrow as the ground around them rose up to their hips, then shoulders, then heads. The walls would turn from sod to stone, and it would seem as if they were walking inside a crag in a cliff. The sky would be reduced to a thin swath of blue, broken in parts by the branches of the trees that grew above them along the sides of this ancient channel. The stretch reminded her of the photos she had seen of the trenches from the earlier world war, minus the wooden planks on which the soldiers stood. And at the end they would reach the Etruscan tomb.

Finally Lorenzetti broke the silence. "Have you heard from Marco lately?"

She turned back to the major, surprised. "I didn't know you knew my brother."

"I don't. Well, I don't know Marco. I know Vittore."

"How?"

"From Florence, of course. Sometimes we work together."

She considered this, aware that Francesca would probably have interrogated the pair if she had been present and Lorenzetti had just announced that he knew Vittore. "Why didn't you tell us this back at the villa?"

"I started to. But your sister-in-law didn't seem especially pleased by our visit."

"More the reason you should have."

He shrugged. "Neither Colonel Decher nor I has any need to curry her favor."

"Does Vittore know you're here?"

"No."

"Are you an archeologist? An art historian?"

"The latter," said Lorenzetti. "I could bore you to death with what I know about Donatello and bas-relief. These days I am merely a soldier—or, to be precise, the host for Colonel Decher. The colonel has joined us from Paris. He's come to the Uffizi because apparently there has been some discussion that select artistic treasures may have to be moved to Germany for safeguarding until the end of the war. Lately there seems to be a particular interest in Etruscan artifacts."

She understood that *safeguarding* was a euphemism for theft. According to Vittore, the Germans were much more likely to commandeer art from the museums and cathedrals in the occupied lands than they were from their ally here in the Mediterranean, but as it grew apparent that Italy would be invaded, the German presence, measured in both curators and tanks, was growing.

"Of course, I know very little about the Etruscans," Lorenzetti added. "I find their bucchero aesthetically interesting but understand next to nothing about the firing process—how some of their pottery wound up that remarkable black. But ask me about the old sacristy in San Lorenzo? My lectures could have you sleeping like a baby in minutes."

She turned to Decher. "Is your specialty Etruscan art?"

He dipped his chin and for the first time offered the tiniest hint of a smile. "Before the war I was an architect. Now I'm a soldier. All I know about the Etruscans comes from a single book I read in my quarters the other night."

"Well, they were a great mystery as a people. Vittore finds it intriguing how little we know about them." Then: "And you both work with Vittore at the museum? He's never mentioned you."

"I've known him since February," said Lorenzetti. "But the colonel has known him barely a week. He and his adjutant just arrived. We all happen to be billeted at the same hotel and are all, to varying degrees, a part of the same little museum . . . team."

"What do you do, Major Lorenzetti?"

"Just like your brother," the Italian officer said, his voice delighting in the irony, "I oversee and preserve our nation's rich artistic heritage."

For a long moment, Cristina watched as the two officers stared at the arched doorways cut into the stone. The German paused to decapitate a couple of mushrooms with the tip of his boot. She had taken guests here before—family friends, her father's business associates—and she had been present when Vittore had led his fellow students on tours. Initially everyone was unimpressed.

The thin path opened upon a small cul-de-sac, the earthen and rock walls composing it little more than three meters high. Field grass grew along the roof of the tombs, and the roots and longer strands dangled over the archways like bangs. Altogether, two rectangular windows had been unearthed, and four arched doorways. And then there were the remains of the columns: one seven feet high, and a pair that barely would reach the knees of a grown man. Once the columns had helped to support a great sloping roof that in all likelihood had spanned the cul-de-sac. Now the roof was gone and weeds climbed up between the stones. The artwork and ornamentation that long ago had graced this section had faded into nothingness over time, and it looked primitive—the home of cavemen, Cristina thought.

It was only when visitors ducked their heads and wandered underneath the archways, extending before them their flashlights or candles or lanterns, that they began to understand the magnificence of what had once been here. There were six tombs, the chambers cut deep into the hillside. Inside, the artwork was better protected from centuries of erosion and wasting and sun. Paintings of musicians and dancers, invariably in profile, ran along the walls and low ceilings, as did drawings of fruit trees and birds and, in a corner of one tomb, a young fisherman. From one entrance a visitor could walk smack into the short row of pedestals with saucerlike tops on which urns the size of thigh-high rosemary shrubs had once rested. From another entrance a person might discover the tomb with the long platforms on which the Rosatis had found the sarcophagi, two of them, both beautifully preserved, one with a sculpture of a young man atop the lid and the other with a man and a woman—a husband and a wife. And though the urns and the sarcophagi and the funeral artifacts had been exhumed and sent to the museum in Arezzo, the musicians and the dancers and the birds remained on the walls.

Cristina handed a candle to each of the officers and kept one for herself. She started to fumble with the matches, but the Italian major had a cigarette lighter and lit all three of the tapers in an instant. Then together they stooped and she led them through the middle archway, into the first of the rooms with the low ceilings where two and a half millennia earlier perhaps her very own ancestors had been laid to rest.

1955

IT FRUSTRATED SERAFINA BETTINI when the other detectives tried to spare her their stories from the worst of the crime scenes. She was the only woman in the small homicide unit in 1955, and despite her work with the partisans in 1943 and 1944—when, in fact, she was a teenager—the men still treated her with either ham-handed attempts at chivalry or outright condescension. Serafina honestly wasn't sure which she found more exasperating. Most of the men in the Florence *polizia* didn't even know that Paolo Ficino allowed her, against regulations, to stash a Beretta in her purse. They no longer asked her out, but that was largely because they had all come to the conclusion, much as it pained them, that she was probably going to marry that American banker with whom she was living. If only, the men sometimes said to her, feigning either wistfulness or disapproval, her mother and father were still alive. Still, no one ever commented on her right ear if a breeze blew aside her hair; no one mentioned her neck when she let down her guard and loosened the high collar of her blouse against the heat. For that she was grateful.

But she was a woman, and so, even though she was at her desk the afternoon that Francesca Rosati's body was found in her small apartment on the Via Zara, Paolo Ficino almost didn't take her with him. It was too grisly. The chief inspector put down the phone, thought back on what he himself had seen in the war—which was, in his opinion, blessedly limited, and mostly involved camouflaging firing platforms for arrogant, impressively cold-blooded Nazi sharpshooters—and wondered if he should assign a different pair to this new crime scene. Paolo viewed Serafina a bit as he did his own daughter, and he sure as hell wouldn't take his daughter to an apartment where someone had cut out the heart from a woman's chest and left it beside the vanity mirror. *Good Lord, how do you even cut out a human heart?* he thought. What sorts of tools or surgical instruments did this crazy person carry about with him? But he and Serafina had the lightest caseload, and the men in the unit were investigating Florence's more civilized, less gruesome murders or they were off for the day. Besides, she was his partner. That was the reality. She was his partner because he was the whole reason she had been allowed into the unit, and because no other man was going to work with a woman. So he grabbed his gun and his straw hat, and despite his reluctance told her to join him as he passed through the office.

"It won't be pretty," he said, looking up ever so slightly at Serafina as the two of them started down the sidewalk to his badly dinged little Fiat. Though he knew he was roughly Serafina's height, the younger detective rarely wore a shoe with anything less than a two-inch heel. She was not an especially tall woman, but Paolo was—and this was being generous with his self-image— of only moderate height for a man. Serafina's heels, he surmised rightly, were both a fashion statement and a reminder to the men in the unit that she was formidable, too.

"And it's a woman?" she asked him, ducking her head and squeezing into the sweltering car.

"It is. The officer said her throat was cut and . . ."

"And?"

"Someone cut out her heart."

Briefly, just as Paolo had, Serafina tried to imagine what kind of knife or bone saw someone was carrying around Florence. She guessed she would be offered an inkling in a few minutes. "And did someone take it?" she asked.

"No. He left it in the apartment."

"Do we have a name?"

He nodded as he pulled out into the street, barely missing a young man who roared past them on a red Vespa. "Francesca Rosati. Thirty-nine years old, lived alone. Worked at a dress shop near the train station."

"Children? A husband?"

"I don't know. But she has a sister-in-law. Cristina. It was Cristina who found her. So at least at one point she had a husband. The officer said Cristina was supposed to have lunch with the victim today."

Serafina lit a cigarette and gazed at the small flame for a long moment before blowing out the match. She thought of her own siblings. Two brothers. She recalled, as she always did when she first thought of them, where she had been when she learned that the Nazis had executed the pair. She was in the camp in the woods midway up Mount Amiata, waking up to the hunger that greeted all the partisans that winter; she hadn't eaten dinner the night before, and there would be nothing for breakfast that morning. "Did she go to work today—Francesca?"

"All I know right now," Paolo was saying, "is that this sister-in-law was supposed to meet her at the dress shop and Francesca wasn't there. So she had not come to work today, to answer your question. Cristina went to Francesca's apartment, and that's when she found her."

"So she was killed last night."

"Unless she didn't go to work yesterday either."

"Are the two women from Florence?"

He shrugged. "I meant it—you now know just about every single detail that I do."

"One more question."

"Go ahead. But don't expect a very satisfying answer."

"Where is the woman's heart? You said whoever killed her didn't take it."

Paolo glanced over at her and saw that she was staring straight ahead. She was, he had always assumed, responsible for a disconcerting number of the dead in the Tuscan hills to the south.

Granted, she had killed no one in a decade. Since the end of the war. But once she had been at least as proficient and hardhearted as those Germans he'd known whose job it was to put a bullet into the brain of any British or American with an officer's bar on his uniform.

"It's on her vanity," he answered, after he had turned his attention back to the street. "It's in an ashtray before the mirror. I told you, this isn't going to be pretty."

Whoever had opened Francesca Rosati's sternum and pulled apart the ribs had not been a surgeon. Or if he had, he had not been especially concerned with tidiness when he had sawed through the bone and sliced the arteries and veins that sprang from the heart like tree roots. Blood had puddled inside the body cavity and plenty more had been sponged up by the woman's nightgown, but two long streams, nearly black now that they had begun to congeal, ran along the otherwise imperceptible slope of the wooden floor, from just inside the front door back toward the small bedroom. More blood had splattered the living room side of the door, the beige raincoat that hung on the coat rack beside it, and the side of a very tired-looking blue couch. Meanwhile, the heart sat in a scallop-shaped ashtray in the apartment's bedroom, just as Paolo had told her.

Three people were waiting for them inside the apartment: the building's concierge, the dead woman's sister-in-law, and the uniformed officer the concierge had found on the street when Cristina had pounded on his door, hysterical, to tell him that someone had killed Francesca. Cristina was sitting in a chair by the living room's lone window, hunched over and staring down at the street, since it was the only view that wouldn't include either her sister-in-law or her sister-in-law's heart. Before Serafina went to talk to her— and the detective understood intuitively that the division of labor would involve Paolo questioning the concierge while she took the lead with the sister-in-law—she pulled the policeman aside. He was a fellow her age, with a pencil-thin mustache, whose name was Nino, and she could sense that he was the sort who would make a pass at her even before she and Paolo had left the apartment.

"Tell me," she said, "has the concierge said anything to you about the door to the building?"

"What about it?"

"There was a little glass window—rare in a front door. And the glass was gone in the pane by the lock. Did someone break it to get in? Or has the glass been missing for ages and people have been waltzing in and out of the building?"

"He found the glass broken this morning. He swept it up."

"Did he report it? Call the police?"

"He said he guessed if someone had broken in and stolen something, one of the tenants would have told him. He said he was going to ask around as he saw the tenants, but he wasn't alarmed."

"And the glass is in the garbage?"

"One would presume." The officer shrugged. "He figured it was just some kid. Or maybe a tenant who locked himself out."

She nodded. She was a little surprised there wasn't a crowd in the hallway, but she attributed this to the fact that it was early afternoon and most people were either at work or savoring their siesta. She would be sure to get a list of the tenants from the concierge, but she would also knock on some doors before leaving.

She turned back and saw Paolo squatting beside the corpse, staring at two flies that were resting on the dead woman's hip. He sensed she was watching him and looked up at her. "I called for a photographer and someone to dust for prints before we left the office," he said to her. "And the coroner." Then he stood. "Let's seal the room until they arrive."

Serafina led Cristina downstairs and down the block to a small café that had two dingy tables outside, one beneath an umbrella faded almost white by the sun. She suggested that the woman sit at the table with the shade. On the way there, Cristina explained to her that Francesca had been married to her brother Marco, who had died in the war.

There were no customers at the café, either inside or out, but Serafina spied an old woman at the glass counter, with a line of liquor bottles and an espresso machine behind her. There was a metal tray with a white linen napkin and half a dozen biscotti on the counter.

"Espresso?" she asked Cristina, and the woman nodded half-heartedly. "Cigarette?"

"I don't smoke," she said, her voice a little numb.

"Okay," Serafina said, and she went and ordered for the two of them, opening a fresh pack of Serraglios and lighting a cigarette for herself while the old woman made them their coffee.

"So, where are you from?" she asked when she rejoined Cristina, placing the two small cups and saucers on the table. When she took her seat, she was careful to sit so the rear of the chair didn't graze the right side of her back. "Florence?"

"No. I live in Rome. With my mother. But I grew up in Monte Volta. It's near Pienza."

"I know where Monte Volta is. I was nearby when the Nazis blew up that old granary when they were retreating."

Cristina smirked ever so slightly. "They only blew up half of it. It had two towers. Only one fell."

Serafina nodded but said nothing. She and the other partisans had witnessed it crumbling from a distance. She had been standing between Enrico Tarantola and his wife, Teresa, on a hill on the outskirts of the village.

"It was built in the fifteenth century," Cristina went on. "They modeled it after the tower in Siena. Maybe because it wasn't going to be as tall as Siena's, they decided to build two. Who knows? Anyway, the Nazis were using them as spotting towers, and claimed they had to blow them up so the Allies couldn't use them the same way. But really they were just trying to punish us. And they failed. Only knocking down one of the towers? Pathetic."

"Monte Volta is beautiful."

"My family used to have a villa there. Technically, we still do. You can see it from that old tower—from that granary. It was a farm. Not huge: we had no tenant farmers. But we had an olive grove, a small vineyard. We had sheep and cattle and a couple of horses. We called it the Villa Chimera."

"After the . . . creature?"

Cristina nodded. "We even had a statue of one in a garden. We had Venus and we had a fire-breathing monster."

Serafina tried to recall the three animals that made up a chimera. She knew a lion was one and perhaps a snake was another. But the third? No idea.

"Ours—the one my grandfather had sculpted—resembled the Chimera of Arezzo," Cristina was saying. "But our goat wasn't quite as fierce. And I never understood a goat anyway. Goats are cute. They're silly. They give us cheese."

"Why would your grandfather have named your estate after a monster?"

"I think it was more about magic. And my family had always suspected the Etruscans had once lived on our land." She sipped her coffee. "Of course, you can't live in the villa these days. Not that my family ever would. It would be too painful. And the animals are long gone."

"The war?"

"The Germans—and the partisans. But mostly the Germans."

Serafina had no recollection of commandeering food or supplies from a villa in Monte Volta. They tended to descend upon the properties closer to Mount Amiata. But there had been one farm near that village where some of her partisan band had hidden from the Nazis for a few days in 1944. And of course there had been the brutal firefight at that beautiful villa near Monte Volta, just hours after the granary fell, where she had been wounded. But hadn't that been in Trequanda? The Germans were moving north and Enrico had decided they should try to block their retreat. Stall them so the British or the Americans could catch them. But he had underestimated badly the fight left in the Germans, as well as the firepower they had with them. The partisans had fallen back to the villa. It was a wonder that everyone in their small group hadn't been killed; it was certainly a miracle, a physician said to her later, that she was still alive.

As she listened to Cristina, she couldn't help but speculate whether this woman's family had in fact been German sympathizers—supporters of Mussolini, even as late as 1944—and if that was why the partisans had raided their farm for provisions. Perhaps they were exacting a measure of revenge. She hoped the family had just been in the wrong place at the wrong time, because she wanted to like Cristina. It always made things easier if you liked the victim's family. The truth was, the last two years of the conflict had been a near civil war in Tuscany, with small bands of partisans sprouting like mushrooms. They supported the Allies—in some cases were supplied by the Allies—and did battle with both the Germans and the Italians who continued to champion the Fascist cause. They were peasants and aristocrats, communists and monarchists. Sometimes they were mere opportunists. All that most shared was a hatred for the way the Blackshirts and the Nazis had led their country into a ruinous war.

"The villa is rubble?" Serafina asked Cristina.

"Not all of it. But it's certainly not livable. Whole walls are gone. Big holes in the roof. It needs more work than my mother and I can afford to put into it, or Vittore would be willing to put into it."

"Vittore?"

"My other brother."

Serafina tasted her espresso. Then: "So you drove all the way up here for lunch? It must be a nine-hour round-trip from Rome."

"If I was tired, I would have napped at Francesca's. Either I'd nap during siesta or I'd spend the night and drive home tomorrow. I've done that before."

"Spent the night."

"Yes."

"Any idea who killed your sister-in-law?"

Cristina shook her head. She was a slender young woman, small and almost skinny, with eyes the gray of a moonstone. She was using her sunglasses like a headband, keeping a sleek mane of ash-brown hair off her face. She was pretty, and Serafina tried not to be jealous of the way the woman could wear earrings or simply pull her hair back behind her ears. "No," Cristina said. "I don't."

"Was she seeing someone? Did she have a new man in her life?"

"She always had men in her life after Marco died. But none were serious and she never introduced me to them."

"Can you give me some names?"

She shrugged. "Pick names from the phone book. I could give you eleven first names and they'd all be correct."

"What about her parents? Where are they?"

"Her father died years and years ago, when she was a little girl. Her mother died in 1941—no, 1942."

"Sisters? Brothers?"

"Francesca was an only child."

"I presume she doesn't have any children."

"She had two. A boy and a girl."

"With your brother Marco?"

"Yes."

Serafina analyzed Cristina's use of the past tense. She felt a twinge of apprehension when she asked her next question: "Where are they now?"

"In heaven," Cristina answered.

Serafina nodded. "I'm very sorry," she said. She thought of the dead children she had seen in the war and the dead twins she had seen on a case her second year here in Florence. Those boys had been killed by their father, after he had shot their mother. Then, with one final bullet, he had taken his own life. In her experience, dead children, unlike dead adults, always looked as if they were sleeping—though she understood that there was an element of wishful thinking whenever she had come across corpses that young.

"Well, at least now they have their mother again," Cristina

said, folding her arms across her chest and sitting back in her chair. "They have both their parents. And my sister-in-law is no longer alone."

"You're trying to find a silver lining in Francesca's murder?"

"No. But at least they're all together now."

"Tell me how they died—your niece, your nephew, and your brother," Serafina said.

"It was during the war. We knew the Germans had mined the roads. We didn't know they had mined parts of the estate. We thought the children would be safe near the tombs."

"The tombs?"

Overhead they heard an airplane, and Cristina brought her hand to her eyebrows like a visor and followed it for a moment. Then she turned her attention back to the detective and said, "Some people called it a necropolis—a city of the dead. But that's the wrong word. It wasn't nearly that large. But it was a burial vault for some powerful Etruscan family. We found it on our estate years after my grandfather died, and it's a testimony to his . . . instincts. He knew the property was Etruscan, and he was right." She paused. Then: "Who knows? Maybe he was on to something when he named the estate after a monster."

I HAD NO compulsion, no perversion, no need. I did not saw through the sternum because I had to.

I did it because it gave people a reason to suppose I am more disturbed and violent than in fact I am—than in fact I ever was. I wanted to be sure that everyone knew I was not merely another in a long line of secretly pathetic serial killers. (I have read that psychiatrists and "profilers" presume that most serial killers are impotent. They really do. In their opinion, the men are likely to be failures. Obsessed with their mothers. They are disappointments and malcontents and losers acting out.)

And so instead I cut out their hearts. Trust me, that's rare, even by the standards of the truly psychotic.

Besides, I was not randomly choosing my victims. I was not looking for whores in the shadows of Florence or noblewomen whose morals had fallen as far as their status. There was nothing arbitrary about what I was doing, and soon that would be clear. Even the Italian police—a group that gives life to clichés about Italian ineptitude, corruption, and sloth—would see the connections soon enough.

I considered leaving my first victim's heart at the scene and taking a bite out of it. Making sure that the shape of a human mouth was unmistakable. But I didn't. The gesture of consuming, cannibal-like, even a mouthful of human organ meat would have been animalistic and bizarre—beneath me.

I have standards.

And of course my first was Francesca. Her heart was, in my mind and in my experience, far more than mere organ meat.

Think of the Italian phrase "Il mio cuore e per voi."

In English? My heart is for you.

It's an expression of profound, limitless desire—not one diner offering to share his entrée with a companion.

So I lifted the heart from Francesca's chest and placed it totemically on her vanity. Then I left her tawdry little apartment and began to plan how I would kill her mother-in-law. Beatrice Rosati, the marchesa herself, would be next.

1943

AFTER THE TWO army officers had left the Villa Chimera, Cristina went upstairs and drew herself a bath. The children were awake by then, and her little niece sat on the tile floor by the side of the deep porcelain tub and chattered away as Cristina watched the dust from the tombs lift off her skin and float upon the surface of the water. Alessia was annoyed that the grown-ups had gone to the ruins without her. She viewed the site as her own private playground, even though she was not allowed to venture there without an adult to see to her safety—and to the safety of the ancient artwork on the ceilings and walls.

"When my father comes home, we are going to camp there," she was informing Cristina. "We are going to play hide-and-seek and have a picnic, and I am going to paint whatever I want on the walls. I am going to add pictures of me dancing. I can draw one of you, too, if you'd like."

"You're sweet. But you know that none of us are allowed to touch the walls. Besides, I'd rather have a drawing like that on paper, so I can hang it in my bedroom. You know how I love your pictures." Then she closed her eyes and stretched her legs so that her feet emerged from the water at the far end of the tub. She wondered what it was at the site that those two officers had wanted to see. They'd been evasive when she'd asked.

"But the walls in the caves are magic," Alessia was saying. "Drawings there last forever, you know."

"Nothing lasts forever," she corrected the child, but she opened her eyes and tilted her head toward the girl, smiling as she spoke.

"Next time you go, I want to come. Don't go when I'm napping. Please?"

"I'll take you tomorrow," Cristina said.

"I'll bring my dolls!"

Cristina wished there were a phone in the corridor of the hotel in Florence where her brother Vittore was billeted. She wanted to ask him how he knew this Major Giancarlo Lorenzetti. Vittore called every fourth or fifth day from the hotel lobby, and he had phoned the house yesterday, which meant that he wouldn't ring them again for at least another two days. And he never called them from the museum. She guessed she could phone him there, but what if Lorenzetti or one of the Germans was in the room? What if the Gestapo or the Italian Fascists were listening in on the line?

"And you know what else?" Alessia asked.

"Tell me," she murmured.

"At night, when no one's there, the dancers and the musicians on the walls come to life and there's a glamorous ball. Sometimes their lights are so bright I can see the glow from my bedroom."

Outside the open window, Cristina heard her mother and father speaking with Francesca on the terrace. Francesca was telling them about the visit from the two soldiers and Decher's unwillingness to wait for Father's return to inspect the ancient burial vault. Beside her, Alessia chirped happily that her grandfather and grandmother were back and raced downstairs. And so Cristina submerged her ears beneath the water and the world grew a little quieter; her hair fanned out atop the plane and she ran her fingers through it and was reminded of a goddess in a Renaissance painting. Her mind wandered far from the villa and the ruins and her unshakable sense that her world was about to change.

Beatrice Rosati, the marchesa, had not yet grown round with middle age. She was, like her daughter and both of her sons, willowy and tall. Statuesque. Still, she had often worried as her children were growing up that her boys appeared sickly and Cristina looked frail—and that her daughter was too slender to be pretty. Now in her two grandchildren, Marco and Francesca's little ones, Beatrice saw the same thing and had the same fears: They were tiny. Their legs were sticks, their arms were twigs. Moreover, Massimo was a scaredy-cat, no match for his younger sister. Their grandfather assumed they were small because their diet the last year had been spotty. Even at the Villa Chimera the family had not been spared the privations that came with a ration card, and so much of what they grew and their animals produced was confiscated by the government.

Nevertheless, there was also a part of her that rather enjoyed the idea that her grandson and granddaughter were so easily portable. Her husband, Antonio, could still lift one in each arm and carry them around the farm like two baskets of olives. When Marco was home on leave from Sicily, he spent long hours with them in and around the swimming pool, the children either using his shoulders as a diving platform as he stood in the shallow end or being pitched by him into the deep end as if they weighed little more than the firewood he might toss into the shed. Alessia could still disappear behind the statue of Venus off the loggia; Massimo could hide behind the columns atop the temple steps in the family cemetery. Neither looked a match for the chimera in the garden.

Now she and Antonio sat alone in the kitchen, each nursing a glass of red wine from last year's vintage. In the distance their remaining Chianina cattle were grazing, the animals' hides so white they glistened when the light was right. Once the estate's herd had rolled across the whole meadow, and from afar one might have supposed that the ground was blanketed by snow. Now all but a dozen had been confiscated, the herd winnowed three and four at a time by the government.

"Perhaps I should go to Florence," Antonio was saying. "Ask Vittore why he thinks those two officers were here today."

"I'll go with you. I want to see Vittore, too."

"I find it so typical of the army to just descend on us with no warning, not wait for me to return, and then disappear into the night like common criminals."

"From what Francesca said, when they returned from the tombs they were unimpressed. It sounds like they were not even especially civil."

Antonio shook his head and stared for a long moment at the translucent film the wine had left in his glass. "Nothing," he said finally, "is ever civil when the Nazis are involved."

The shade from a great statue of a horse fell upon the face of the archeologist like a beard. He leaned against the pedestal and watched the crowd mill about the piazza. A breeze blew across the square and the young man leaned into it. He had wandered outside to escape the Germans who had arrived earlier that week, half a dozen architects and amateur art historians who seemed to have nothing in common but the fact that none of them had more than a tourist's knowledge of the Renaissance or Italian history. Most were officious and condescending, especially Erhard Decher—not quite a decade his senior, but already a colonel—and Vittore Rosati knew this batch was going to pose far more serious problems than its predecessors. Those men had been more dabblers than bullies. Moreover, Italy then had viewed itself as a partner with Germany, and the Nazis had at least given lip service to that notion. No more. As it had become clear that it was only a matter of time before the Allies would invade Italy, and Germany would (once more) have to bail them out, the Nazis had grown more vexing. More annoying. More arrogant.

Now Vittore slid a Nazionali from his cigarette case and broke it in half so the pack would last longer. He lit the stub, inhaled deeply, and closed his eyes. He might not have opened them for a long moment had he not heard his name. He recognized the voice. It was Decher's adjutant, an overly eager young pup whose last name was Strekker. The fellow was twenty-three, just about three years Vittore's junior, and he seemed to have no interests other than the army. Vittore couldn't imagine how he had wound up in Florence instead of Russia or Africa or garrison duty in someplace meaningful. He was insufferable in a way that was different from the other Germans: it was his enthusiasm that was exhausting, not his disdain.

"I love how hot it is here," Strekker was saying. "You have no idea. Where I come from, sometimes we get snow in April. One year it snowed in May."

"And that is where?" Vittore asked. Out of necessity, he had learned German over the past three years, but he didn't especially like the sound of the language, and it seemed almost blasphemous to be speaking it here in the shadows of the Palazzo Vecchio.

"Oh, you've never heard of it. Kesselsdorf. Just outside of Dresden. My father works at the museum there."

"In Dresden."

"Yes. It's considered the Florence on the Elbe, you know."

"No, I did not know," Vittore said. He restrained himself from asking which part of the museum or what the man did there. But it didn't matter, because in a moment Strekker was telling him anyway.

"He's a curator," the German said. "His specialty is dinnerware. Silver. China. Stemware. You'd like him."

"I'm sure I would."

"You're being sarcastic. But you two have more in common than you realize."

Vittore sighed. He gazed at a pretty young woman in a black skirt and a white blouse, her dark hair a little flat in the heat. She turned and he noted how her lips were parted ever so slightly, but before he could even nod in her direction or smile, Strekker continued, "Like you, he is very protective of his art. He views all those eighteenth-century place settings as his responsibility. One time the Führer requisitioned a silver service that had belonged to Frederick the Great. My father sent him instead a service that looked like it but was really only fifty or sixty years old. It was a big risk—the Gestapo would have sent my father God knows where if anyone had discovered the substitution."

When Vittore glanced back to find the woman in the crowd, she was gone. He was feeling generous and offered Strekker one of his cigarettes.

"No, thanks," Strekker said. "They make me nauseous."

"How did your father know that Hitler wouldn't notice the difference?"

"He met him."

"Hitler?"

Strekker raised his eyebrows and pursed his lips. "You sound surprised."

"I am."

"He really doesn't know the Führer. But the Führer has come to Dresden twice, and my father was among the curators who guided him through the museum. The Führer views himself as quite knowledgeable when it comes to art. My father would disagree. He was less worried about the Führer discovering the substitution than someone in the Führer's inner circle."

"When was this?"

"A year ago. Apparently no one's noticed. My father still has his job."

"And you're safely in Florence."

"Not by choice."

Vittore didn't believe that for a moment, but he remained quiet. And, as he expected, Strekker instantly filled the silence.

"But I do love your country," he said. "I learned Italian in gymnasium. I was studying the Renaissance with Heydenreich—"

"Our Heydenreich?" Vittore asked. One of the Nazis in charge of the museum was Ludwig Heydenreich.

"Yes. He was one of my professors in Berlin when the war

started. Still, I wish I were serving my country—our alliance—in a more meaningful way."

"You'd rather be off getting shelled in the Ukraine, I suppose? Or trapped right now in Tunis? Waiting to be captured or killed?"

"I was in Russia."

"Really?"

Strekker had been leaning against the pedestal of the statue, too, and now he fell to one knee and rolled up the trouser leg that was perpendicular to the ground. It took a few seconds for Vittore to comprehend what he was seeing, but then he understood. Where there should have been an ankle and a shin, he saw instead leather straps, a silver buckle, and a bone-white shaft made of wood.

Alone in his quarters, the sky growing dark, Friedrich Strekker unbuckled the straps that held his prosthetic ankle and foot against the stump two-thirds of the way up his shin. There were buckles where there should have been the actual joint of his ankle and another pair three inches above his knee. He was oblivious to the ones at the ankle, but the clasps above his knee chafed his skin. When tape or gauze was available, he would place a strip between the buckles and his leg, and that helped. It was not, however, a perfect solution: the edges of the buckles might still leave bruises. Consequently he was always spinning the straps and rotating the metal clips, trying to spare any one part of his thigh too much pain. The army doctors told him that once the war was over, there would be much-improved prosthetics and he should be patient. In the meantime, when he went to bed at night he would find himself transfixed by the rococo-like contusions and marks on his skin.

Usually he felt no self-pity. There were times, such as when he forgot himself and tried to run or when he realized how slowly his compatriots climbed stairs when he was beside them, but they were infrequent. There were also moments of guilt that he had been spared so much fighting and been relegated these days to an academic world of amateur soldiers and middle-aged men. To quarters that were more cushy than a university student's bedroom. He actually had a room of his own, and though it was modest, it was within a block of the Arno River. The mattress on his bed was plump and the handles on his dresser were finished with ivory. He had an armoire for his uniforms that was taller than he was, the wood stained the color of bourbon. Until recently the room had been part of a clean but unexceptional hotel.

It was his father, the curator, who had gotten him this post, knowing of his interest in Italy. His father had been a Party member for well over a decade and had a surprising amount of clout. He was also friendly with Heydenreich, and when the time came had reminded the scholar that his son had been studying the Italian Renaissance with him in Berlin when the war started and thus had knowledge the army could use.

Now the soldier gazed at the way his right leg ended in the gently rounded point of a club. At the scar tissue, still too pink in his mind for real skin. Today had been a complete and utter waste. Colonel Decher had him assisting Vittore catalog bits of pottery that looked no more interesting than fragments of seashells, while the colonel and Major Lorenzetti had gone off without telling anyone where. They had taken a driver, a private, who had nothing to do with their group. Friedrich had overheard Lorenzetti remarking in a tone that was somewhere between amusement and disgust that the young fellow had never set foot inside the Uffizi or even heard of the Medici family. Friedrich could not help but wonder at the secrecy. Plunder, he decided finally. That was the answer. Probably they had been commandeering some painting or tapestry for Decher's wife or Lorenzetti's lover. He rested his head in his hands, a little appalled by the idea. He was not uncomfortable serving as Decher's adjutant, but he did not especially like the man, and this was a new experience for him. In combat, Friedrich had tended to honestly like his commanders. He'd respected most of them. But he didn't respect Decher. The colonel was out of his element here. But then, fighting probably wasn't his element either. Decher had never commanded soldiers in combat and—like many men who had never been shot at—claimed to long for the opportunity. He'd come here from Paris.

It was ironic, but it seemed to Friedrich that the more time he spent in Florence, the more he was becoming his father. Until recently he had always considered his father slightly absurd. Effete. A man too interested in the way an artist or artisan from another era might have fired a plate. No longer. Sometimes Friedrich even wondered how he would now handle the trials and hardships of a real soldier if, for some reason, he were thrown back into the breach. Once, he knew, he had been an excellent soldier. He had the decorations to remind himself, if he ever forgot. Even this post was a decoration of sorts, a station he had earned after he was crippled, a thank-you for his valor in France and Greece and the Ukraine. He had been a sergeant at twenty-one, and now, at twenty-three, he was a lieutenant—though he was a lieutenant with access to drivers and a car but no real soldiers at his command.

He unbuttoned his tunic and loosened the collar of his shirt, trying to clear his mind. Then he swung his legs onto the bed and lay down to rest. Decher had scheduled a staff meeting for eight o'clock at the museum and Friedrich wanted to be fresh.

1955

SERAFINA UNDERSTOOD THAT her living arrangements were scandalous and would probably have shocked her family. But because her family had all been dead since 1943, she really didn't care. She had one of the two bedrooms in an apartment on the south side of the Arno with a beautiful view of the river and the hordes of tourists that had begun to crowd the Ponte Vecchio in search of bargains in silver and gold jewelry. Her roommate was an American banker named Milton, who was nearing forty but still had a thick mop of magnificent red hair, cheekbones that most actors would have killed for, and a male lover closer to Serafina's age than to his, who was a purser on the transatlantic SS *Cristoforo Colombo*. Whenever the *Cristoforo Colombo* was docked in Italy and the purser came to Florence, Serafina would make herself scarce as a courtesy to the pair. Otherwise, however, she was content to serve as Milton's beard and live in a neighborhood and an apartment that were well beyond her means. Milton paid the lion's share of the rent, and most people, including the other detectives, presumed he was her lover. In reality, he was her best friend. Given the numbers of people he, too, had killed in the war—twice with a knife and once with only his hands—they shared a wistfulness and a rectitude and, when they really thought about it, a guilt that was rare in the cafés on that side of the river.

In truth, Serafina had no idea whether her family would have been disappointed in her because they believed she was sleeping with a man out of wedlock or disgusted at the idea that her clos-est friend was a homosexual. Her family had all been slaughtered before she was old enough to have a definitive sense of which was worse in their opinion, premarital sex or living with a gay man.

The night after she had seen Francesca Rosati's heart sitting black and still in an ashtray and then had espresso with Cristina, she got home well before Milton. She poured herself a glass of wine, got a pack of matches, and thought about the Rosati family—as well as her own. Their families were demographically identical. Or at least close to identical. Both she and Cristina came from families of five and they both had a pair of older brothers; in other words, the two of them had been the babies in their families, the youngest child and the only daughter. Cristina, of course, still had a mother and a brother; Serafina had no one and had had no one for nearly twelve years. Cristina, the two of them had determined, was nine months older than she was.

Now she sat in her high-collared blouse and skirt in an ornate wrought iron chair on her and Milton's terrace, her bare feet on the balustrade over the river, and watched the sky grow dark and the lights emerge across the river. She had most of her weight on her left side, as she did always when she reclined, careful to keep the back of the chair from pressing against the thick pink scars that spiraled like ornamental filigree from where her neck met her skull to her waist. It wasn't painful when anything pressed against them; instead she would experience a tingling around their edges and then a disconcerting numbness in their center—it was as if her back was hollow—which could all too quickly take her back to those long days of agony when she awoke and there was little that anyone could do for the burns. They'd told her they had thought she would die; among her first words in response, they said, was that she wished she had. Apparently she had begged them to shoot her. Today she hid both disfigurment and disability. Only Paolo knew that she was unable to raise her right arm over her head. But he wasn't worried; he'd told her one evening, shrugging, that he never expected her life would depend on her ability to shoot a bird from the sky.

Now she lit a match and let it burn for a moment before blowing it out. Then she pressed the still-smoking tip against the skin on the inside of her thigh. She did this three times, tossing the three burned matches into the ashtray, and felt a little better when she was done.

She recalled what Cristina had said as they were talking on the street outside that depressing little café near Francesca's apartment: *At least they're all together now.* Meaning Francesca and her husband and their two children. This wasn't a clue, in Serafina's opinion, because it was evident that whoever had killed Francesca hadn't been trying to effect a heavenly reconciliation. Rather, it spoke to how unkind life had been to the woman—and how far the Rosati family had fallen since they had lived in that villa in Monte Volta.

In the end Serafina had pressed Cristina for the names of any men Francesca had recently mentioned, and Cristina had come up with three: Giovanni, Aldo, and an American who was named either Richard or Russell. The American was married and lived in New York, but he worked in a museum there and came to Florence periodically on business. Cristina had no idea what either Giovanni or Aldo did for a living. Francesca hadn't brought up any of these men in the past six months. Perhaps longer. Cristina couldn't say whether her sister-in-law had a lover right now, but she guessed that she did because sex was how Francesca had smothered her sadness and grief since the war.

And while Serafina and Paolo could joke that whoever had ripped out Francesca's heart wasn't a surgeon because the crime scene had been such a cataclysmic mess, the reality was that whoever had killed the woman had indeed used a bone saw—or a tool very much like a bone saw. So it wasn't inconceivable that the murderer worked in a hospital or a morgue.

Behind her she heard the apartment's front door open and recognized the sound of Milton's keys falling upon the glass-topped table in the entryway, and then his footsteps as he strolled through the living room to the terrace. He leaned over and kissed her on the cheek, and she could smell a vestigial trace of the sandalwood lotion he had rubbed on his face after shaving that morning.

"So, any mayhem and madness today?" he asked in Italian. "Or were the Florentines too done in by this heat to kill one another?"

"I saw a human heart."

"Where?"

"In an ashtray."

"That's disgusting."

"The rest of the body was far worse."

He sat in the chair beside her, his elbows on his knees and his chin in his hands.

"Is that a new suit?" she asked. It was a summer-weight gray pinstripe, the lapels cut into deep, sharp triangles just below his collarbone.

"It is. Do you like it?"

"I do. Very much."

"Tell me all about your day," he said gently. "Clearly yours was far more grisly than mine."

⚜

Serafina was back at Francesca Rosati's apartment house the next morning by seven, knocking on doors. By nine she had spoken with everyone in the building she had missed yesterday, asking them to tell her all that they knew about the dead woman, her lovers and friends. Francesca, everyone agreed, kept to herself; when she didn't, when she ran into her neighbors in the stairway or along the thin corridor, she was acerbic or aloof. Either she would allow herself a sardonic passing remark on the walls' desperate need for a paint job or she barely would nod. No one knew much about her past, even though she had lived on the Via Zara almost a year and a half, but everyone assumed that once she had been rather spoiled and well off—no doubt, they surmised, because she had been some Blackshirt's mistress. A kept woman. The sort who'd never married. She had not, in her neighbors' opinions, grown accustomed to her diminished social standing and genteel poverty. They knew she had different men come to her apartment, but they knew also that she worked in a dress shop, and no one thought she was a prostitute.

The closest Serafina had come to a helpful lead was offered by an old woman who had one of the other two apartments on Francesca's floor. The woman was a widow who, like everyone else in the building, had no idea that Francesca had lost a husband and both of her children in the war. But she did tell Serafina this: about a month ago, Francesca had asked her for the name of a good locksmith in the neighborhood. She had come straight home to the apartment from the dress shop where she worked and was uncharacteristically agitated when they met on the front steps.

"She saw someone she recognized whom she didn't like—someone who frightened her. I didn't think that woman could be scared of anyone," the old widow had told Serafina. And while she had recommended a locksmith a few blocks to the west, as far as she knew, Francesca had never gotten around to contacting the fellow or putting a more substantial lock on her door.

The dress shop was called the Sunflower, and although it was near the train station, it had a largely local clientele, Florentine women who could not afford to shop at the tonier boutiques along the Via de' Tornabuoni or the Via dei Calzaiuoli. The owner was a gaunt woman in her sixties with a haughty face, thin lips, and a sheen of cold cream across her forehead. Her name was Isabella and she reminded Serafina of the grandmother of a fellow she'd dated a few years ago, a woman who always managed to look down her slender nose at whomever she was talking to.

"I'm so sad," Isabella was saying now to the detective, as they spoke in a small, windowless room with two sewing machines behind the shop, but she really didn't seem especially devastated. Serafina had the sense that the woman was more annoyed that she had lost a salesperson who also could sew than she was saddened by the fact that Francesca was dead.

"Did Francesca tell you where she was going after work the day before yesterday?" she asked Isabella.

"The day she died."

"That's right."

"No. But I knew she had a date. A new man."

"What was his name?"

She sighed, and for a second Serafina presumed the shopkeeper was trying to recall the name; then, however, she realized that Isabella was pausing because she was disgusted. "She saw too many men. This one was a lawyer. He worked in Bologna and was only coming to town to take her to dinner and then have his way with her."

"His name?"

"I never asked."

"Did she say what kind of law he practiced?"

"He was wealthy. At least Francesca believed he was."

"Did she believe he was going to marry her someday?"

"Maybe. But I'm not sure she cared about that."

"Getting married."

Isabella nodded and looked down at her fingernails. The polish was red and starting to chip.

"Did any of her boyfriends ever come to your store?"

"No. Francesca's private life? She would give us little clues, little tidbits, but really share nothing. She said she had once lived in a beautiful villa, but who knows if that's the truth. Maybe it was." She shrugged. "Maybe she was Mussolini's mistress. Maybe she slept with the Germans."

"You think she was a collaborator during the war?" Serafina asked. She found it interesting that she, too, had briefly wondered the same thing yesterday about Cristina—about the whole family. From what Cristina had told her, however, the shopkeeper was mistaken: Francesca, Cristina said, had detested both the Nazis and the Italian Fascists. She considered correcting the woman.

"I think she had done things in her past that she was ashamed of," Isabella said. "Otherwise she would have told us more. She would not have been so secretive."

"What about the other salesgirls? Maybe she told them something that might help us."

Isabella rolled her eyes and cackled. "My other salesgirls? There was Francesca and there is Sofia. Talk to Sofia when she gets here this afternoon. She won't know anything more about Francesca than I do. I promise."

"Did Francesca tell you where she and this lawyer from Bologna were having dinner?"

"Il Latini. Very elegant. Francesca made sure we knew that her lawyer friend was only taking her to the very best."

On her way out of the store, Serafina glanced at a red velvet sheath dress on a mannequin. She paused in front of it for a long moment, admiring the rhinestone flower at the bodice, and might have asked Isabella how much it cost. But then she saw how low-cut it was in the back and realized it wasn't for her.

⚜

A waiter at Il Latini recognized Francesca from a photograph and remembered her well. Apparently she had men take her there often. And while he couldn't recall her companion's name from her most recent visit, he described him as short but broad-shouldered and handsome. He had a thin mustache and a high forehead and was somewhere in his late thirties or early forties.

When she got back to the office, however, she found that the description was unnecessary. Mario Spagnoli had read about Francesca Rosati's death in the newspaper that morning and was coming to Florence that afternoon to share what he could with the police about the woman's last night on this earth.

⚜

"Can you imagine," the coroner was saying to Serafina and Paolo as they stood beside the corpse on the angled autopsy table, "surgeons are starting to operate on the heart. In America—in Minnesota. In Germany. It's . . . miraculous." Alberto Carli had been a coroner in Florence since before the war—since before Mussolini—and spoke with the slow, mannered cadences of a more elegant era. He was a regal grandfather to everyone in the homicide unit, more benign (and more supportive) than an actual relative because he was so serenely nonjudgmental. He was almost completely bald but for a cowl of gray hair cut short along the back of his head and the great tufts of white in his ears. His eyes were a little watery with age, and his spectacles were American; the frames were thick and black. He had the long, graceful fingers of a pianist.

"So," Paolo asked, "the killer might have been a surgeon after all?"

"No, the incisions were not that precise. They were rather ham-handed. Amateurish. But he had a surgeon's tools. He began with a scalpel. He made a vertical incision down the chest, fourteen inches long. He plunged the scalpel very, very hard into the victim at the center of her collarbone—right here—and dragged it down the length of the sternum toward her navel. He dug it deep into the subcutaneous tissue. Then—and look at these marks, if you can, I want you to see the distinction I am making—he used a manual bone saw—"

"A manual bone saw?" Serafina wondered.

"Versus an electric one. We now have electric bone saws. Very speedy. But the smell? Awful. They create so much friction as they cut that they actually burn the bone. And burning bone smells a tiny bit like burning hair, but a thousand times worse. In any case, whoever removed this woman's heart was using an old-fashioned one. He had to saw by hand down the sternum," Alberto said, moving his right arm back and forth, up and down, as if he were sawing a piece of wood. "And although the heart wasn't beating by then, our killer was going to have to work through an ungodly mess, an oozing chest wound. And then, of course, he had to spread the ribs—and it looks to me as if he had an actual rib spreader at his disposal. Let me show you."

He reached into one of the white cabinets behind him and pulled out a device that struck Serafina as the sort of thing an Inquisition torturer might have used in a stone dungeon hundreds of years ago. It looked barbaric. "As you can see, it's basically just a retractor with a hinge and a couple of C-shaped cups. Turn this crank and it mechanically widens the arms with the cups, spreading apart the ribs."

"And the killer had one?" Paolo asked.

"I think so," Alberto said. He put the spreader down on the table beside Francesca. "There are marks on the ribs that suggest precisely this sort of instrument. And he would have found the heart right behind the sternum. Right . . . here. To remove it, he would have used scissors or a scalpel. If it was scissors, they were very sharp. I honestly can't tell you which. But he severed the pulmonary artery here on the right and the aorta here on the left. At that moment, I suspect, there would have been an enormous release of blood. A torrent, most of which, it seems to me, wound up absorbed by her nightgown and puddling on the floor. Then he cut the superior vena cava at the top of the heart and the inferior vena cava at the bottom. And last but not least would be the four pulmonary veins at the rear of the organ."

"Eight cuts," Serafina murmured.

"That's it. And then, presto, into the ashtray."

"But she was definitely dead when the chest was being opened," Serafina said.

"Oh, definitely. He was very thorough when he cut her throat."

"Did he use that scalpel?"

"No, I think he used a knife with a serrated edge. A much thicker blade."

Paolo leaned against the wall and counted on his fingers. "So he had a knife. A scalpel. A bone saw. A rib spreader. And scissors." He needed every one of his fingers.

The coroner smiled. "Indeed. Whoever did this didn't travel light."

"And still you're sure the killer isn't a physician?" Paolo asked. "It seems to me, only a doctor would know how to cut all those arteries and veins."

"I know their names and what they do. I think it's likely the killer just kept cutting and cutting until he could pull out the heart."

"Could he be a medical student?"

"Maybe."

"A coroner?"

"Very funny," Alberto said.

"Are these sorts of tools hard to find?"

"No. But maybe you're on to something. While I don't believe the killer is a physician, it's possible that he works at a hospital. Maybe he . . . borrowed these instruments."

"I presume butchers use bone saws, too. Don't they?" Serafina asked.

"Yes, they do."

"So the killer could be a butcher."

"Could be?" the old coroner said. "It seems to me that regardless of what he does for a living, whoever did this most certainly was a butcher."

THE NEWSPAPERS WERE aghast, but they loved it. A woman found with her nightgown slashed down the front and her heart cut from her chest? Some suggested the killer was a spurned lover with a broken heart and—tragically for Francesca Rosati—a psychotic streak. Others wondered if this was indeed going to be the start of a killing spree and Florence had a lunatic in its midst along the lines of London's Jack the Ripper.

In 1955, Jack the Ripper was the gold standard for homicidal maniacs, a frame of reference that made the unimaginable real. Only a decade earlier, in the Second World War, Marcel Petiot had been injecting cyanide into his victims in Paris, telling them it was a required Argentine inoculation before they escaped from occupied France and set off in secret for South America. He killed dozens—literally dozens!—of people, but there was so much confusion around his story that he never entered our consciousness the way Jack the Ripper did. When he was guillotined in May 1946, there were people who believed his story that he had only executed collaborators and was actually a part of the Resistance.

But what interested many newspaper readers was the innuendo that surrounded Francesca Rosati's descent. Her fall from life in a villa in the Tuscan countryside that may not have rivaled a Medici palace in opulence, but might have in square footage. The seemingly unbearable tragedies that beset the Rosati family in 1944. The things she saw that no wife and mother—even, in their opinion, Francesca—should have been forced to endure. To witness.

I imagine her acquaintances in Florence were surprised by what they learned in the papers. I understand that she kept to herself. Even her lovers *knew little about her, other than her rather forward-thinking assumption that sex might keep her depression at bay.*

So, how long between the first and the second execution? Given the time the press spent on Francesca's past, once I had killed her mother-in-law, people would note the rather obvious connection. The police would see trails and tales worth pursuing.

And though Marco and the children died during the war and Antonio soon after, that still left Beatrice Rosati—who, as I have told you, would be next—Vittore and his family, and Cristina.

Cristina, like her mother, was all alone in the world. She would be last.

I was younger then, of course, and presumed that I had a long life before me. I could wait. These were . . . errands, and as some Italians like to ask with a smile, Why do today what can be postponed until tomorrow?

That all changed when Beatrice came to Florence. When I saw her, I realized that I had dramatically underestimated my zealousness and desire. I could not, in fact, wait—and I wouldn't.

1943

In all of the Villa Chimera—an imposing residence with seven bedrooms, four of which overlooked the swimming pool, as well as separate quarters for the maid and the cook—only Antonio and Beatrice's bed was bigger than Cristina's. As the marchese's daughter and the youngest child, Cristina was aware that she had always been treated as something of a princess. But she had never tried to hide her small privileges, and so tonight, as occurred on most evenings, her nephew and niece had swooped upon her room. She was reading aloud to them while Alessia played with her dolls beneath the bed's salmon-colored canopy and Massimo moved his toy soldiers across the floor. Tonight she was reading the tale of a queen who was bewitched by fairies and gave birth to a son who appeared to all the world to be a pig. The story was easily four hundred years old, but Cristina and Francesca found the paintings of the creature in the book to be eerily contemporary: their own king, Victor Emmanuel III, stood barely five feet, had squat, misshapen legs, and was certainly not—to use one of Francesca's favorite expressions—the sharpest knife in the cutting block. The Italian court, it seemed, had been as dogged by inbreeding as any other on the continent. The children, however, simply savored the way the fairy-tale pig would marry two women, both of whom would try to murder him in the night because he was a pig, and both of whom would wind up dead, speared in the smallest hours of the morning by his hooves. Eventually the pig would marry a woman who loved him as he was and returned his affections—and thus discovered that he was in fact a handsome prince.

When Cristina had finished reading, she placed the book beside her and watched Massimo. The boy had put a pillow on the floor and upon the mountain of down he had set a group of soldiers in a circle facing out. Around the pillow he had wrapped her shawl, the teal of the sea. Aware that his young aunt was surveying his work, he said, "This is Sicily. They're protecting Sicily."

And so he suspected, as they all did, that eventually the war was going to come to Italy. Tunis would fall and Sicily would be next. He understood that his father—her brother—would be one of those soldiers defending the island at the toe of the boot. Did he imagine him captured or killed? She doubted it. But she couldn't be sure. She wasn't precisely sure what even she envisioned would occur in the coming year. She thought of the newsreels she had seen in the cinema, especially the footage of the Italians who had been in Russia until the fiasco at Stalingrad, and as horrific as that was to watch, she suspected the reality was far worse than the sanitized footage that was shared with the people. She recalled the explosions and columns of smoke in the film, the skeletal frames of buildings that collapsed in the blasts.

It occurred to her now—and she found this recognition troubling because it suggested just how spoiled she was—that the principal deprivation she had endured so far was this: she was lonely. She had no suitors. No lovers. When Francesca had been her age and the world had not been at war, there had been dances and balls. No more, at least not here in the country. The people who danced now were Nazis and Blackshirts and their women in Rome. In Florence. In Milan. And then there was her schooling—or, to be precise, her lack of schooling. The Rosatis had always been educated, even the women. Her mother had graduated from the university in Pisa. But Cristina's education had ended abruptly last year because the teachers had been pressed into service. Even the professors in Pisa were fighting now. The dormitories were billeting soldiers.

"We should make her a blue dress," Alessia was murmuring, and she held up the princess doll with hair the color of poppies.

She smiled down at the girl. "Why blue?"

"I like blue. It's the color of the sky. And you like the sky. You're always looking up at the airplanes."

From his spot on the floor, her nephew glanced at them. "Our mother hates airplanes," he muttered.

Abruptly Alessia jumped from the bed, and, holding the doll as if it were an airplane, the princess's arms as its wings, she flew it over the soldiers guarding the Sicilian coast. She circled them once, twice. Then, with absolutely no warning, she had the plane swoop down upon the men, attacking them, trying to replicate the sound of a machine gun with her mouth. And Massimo, much to Cristina's surprise, played along: he added to the noise the sound of explosions, and then, with the back of his hand, he wiped his soldiers into the sea.

The streetlamps still burned in Florence because no one believed the Allies would dare bomb the city. There were rumors, however, that any night now the lights would be dimmed and there would be a curfew. Just in case. But events had not yet become that dire. And so from the conference room window in the museum, Vittore could see the mongrel dog and the little boy who was trying to convince it to drink some water. The child had a small bowl made of tin, but the dog, so thin and wobbly that Vittore was shocked it could stand, didn't seem interested. Still, it was easier for Vittore to watch the boy and the dog than to make eye contact with Lorenzetti. He was furious with the major and felt betrayed. It wasn't merely that Lorenzetti and Decher had gone to the Villa Chimera that afternoon, as disturbing as that notion was; it was the fact that they had gone without telling him. He didn't like the idea that a Blackshirt and a Nazi had been around his family, and he was frustrated that he hadn't been able to warn his parents that they were coming. Nor did he approve of the pair wandering through the Etruscan tombs on the property. Picking at the artwork. A man like Decher was oblivious to the fragility of the remains on the walls.

"What are the plans for those tombs after the war?" Decher was asking, and Vittore realized that the colonel was speaking to him. He turned away from the boy and the dog. It was after ten and the meeting had begun to wind down. There were seven of them at the table, three Germans—including that young pup with the prosthetic foot—and four Italians. He'd never noticed it before, but Decher looked a bit like his adjutant. He was twelve years older than Strekker, but still the two could pass for siblings.

"My family has already agreed to turn it over to the government," Vittore answered. "It needs to be cared for. Preserved. And people will want to see it."

Decher smiled glibly. "You're going to allow strangers to traipse across your land? Become an attraction for travelers? I can't imagine your sister-in-law would be especially accommodating. I don't suppose you would have been pleased today if you'd known ahead of time that Major Lorenzetti and I were going to drop by your estate."

"The access wouldn't have to interfere with my family's life or the business of the farm," he said calmly, essentially ignoring the tenor of the colonel's remarks.

"Besides, there won't ever be droves of tourists," said Lorenzetti. "It's a small site, and people don't flock to Monte Volta. Expect students and archeologists. And the Villa Chimera isn't exactly the most accessible of venues. I thought I was going to vomit on the road up to the estate."

"And the sarcophagi and vases are gone," Vittore added. "The alabastron, the amphora, the cups. The plates. The pieces of the deity's head. They're all at the museum."

"I know an amphora is a kind of pot," said Decher. "But what is an alabastron?"

"A sort of flask," Vittore answered. "They were used for oils and unguents and perfumes. Often, as you might expect, they were made of alabaster."

Decher seemed to think about this. "I want to see them—the artifacts."

Lorenzetti shrugged. "Why not? We can drive to Arezzo tomorrow. It's not like there's a war going on."

"Why aren't they at the archeological museum here in Florence?"

Patiently, as if speaking to a child, the major said, "I told you in the car this afternoon. Most of the artifacts from the site at the Villa Chimera went to Arezzo. We could have stopped there after Monte Volta."

Decher shook his head, annoyed either with himself or with Lorenzetti. "You told me when we were arriving at the villa. I wish you had reminded me later, when we were leaving." He folded his arms and glared at Vittore. "Tell me, why Arezzo? Why not Florence?"

Vittore shrugged. "No mystery—it was closer to our home. When we found the site, we called the museum there first. The curator took me under his wing."

"I assume you realize that Herbert Kappler has a profound interest in Etruscan art."

"Who's Kappler?" The question had come from a young Florentine named Emilio. Like Vittore, he was an archeologist first and a soldier second. The Germans at the table turned toward him, astonished that he didn't know and had the naïveté to ask. Vittore wondered how dismissive Decher would be in his response.

And the colonel did pause before answering, trying to decide just how caustic he should be. In the end, he setttled upon professional disdain. "Herbert Kappler was a great friend of Reinhard Heydrich before the vermin killed Heydrich last year in Prague. Now he is our SS liaison to Il Duce and a security consultant to the Fascist police in Rome. His specialty? He is very good at suppressing resistance. He is very good at rounding up Jews and partisans and other enemies of the state," Decher said, and then added the dagger: "Would you like to meet him? I could arrange an introduction."

And so, partly to rescue Emilio and partly because of his resentment at the idea that Decher had trespassed at the Villa Chimera, Vittore asked, "Colonel, may I inquire why you're so interested in the tombs?"

"It's neither complicated nor mysterious. Officers at the Ahnenerbe have seen the images on Kappler's pottery—particularly on a krater and on a plate—and want to learn more about the Etruscans. And, thus, so do I."

Vittore thought the Ahnenerbe was the part of the SS that obsessed about German ancestral heritage. But he wondered now if he was mistaken. Why would a group dedicated to the myth of Aryan supremacy give a damn about the Etruscans? He was about to press his luck and ask Decher what, specifically, the Ahnenerbe wanted to learn when Lorenzetti jumped in.

"There may be Nazis on vases, Vittore," he explained. His smirk was perceptible, but only barely.

"I've seen dancers and musicians on Etruscan work," said Emilio, "but, I must confess, never a Nazi."

"They would be hard to miss," Lorenzetti agreed.

"Well, I can assure you, there were none on the artifacts from my family's land," Vittore said. "But perhaps from the Tarquinia dig in '39. You know how warlike the Etruscans were in Tarquinia."

"You're all very funny," Decher told them. "But I have heard from reliable sources that this is a matter of interest to the Reichsführer himself."

"Himmler?" Vittore asked reflexively, unable to mask the incredulity in his voice. "I would think he has more pressing concerns," he continued, and he saw in his mind the troops trapped in a small corner of North Africa and the troops—including his brother, Marco—preparing to defend Sicily.

"Yes, the Reichsführer," Decher said. "It seems there were

Germanic tribes here. And the Reichsführer is interested in the origins of the race—why we are who we are."

"You are who you are because your country is too cold. Really, I couldn't live there," Lorenzetti said.

One of the other Germans, a lanky Bavarian with sad eyes that were all but lost to the dark bags beneath them, Jürgen Voss, sat forward in his chair and folded his hands before him on the table. "The Reichsführer has suggested that the first tribes may have come from either the highest mountains of Tibet or the Arctic, so it makes sense that we are comfortable in a climate that can be rather frosty." He was completely sincere, and Vittore didn't know what to make of this lunacy. The man had worked with Decher at the Louvre for two years before being transferred here.

"Of course, your Reichsführer also believes in Atlantis," Lorenzetti observed dryly.

"Just so you all know, spring and summer are lovely in Dresden," Strekker said, his voice typically exuberant and collegial. He didn't seem bothered in the slightest that the Italians were having fun at the expense of his precious Reichsführer. "Moreover, it seems to me that it snows in Italy, too—in the Alps and in the mountains not far from here. Mount Amiata, for instance."

"As a matter of fact, Vittore," Lorenzetti went on, feigning sincerity, "I recall an Etruscan plate with a dancer shaping his body into a swastika. Sixth-century B.C. Found in the dig at—"

"Enough, all of you!" Decher snapped. "I don't see the humor in wanting to understand our roots, and it's too late in the evening to debate the weather." Then he mapped out for them their day tomorrow and how he wanted to visit Arezzo. Vittore was relieved when, this time, Decher ordered him to accompany them. In the end, he might not be able to prevent the artifacts, including the ones from the tombs at the Villa Chimera, from being sent to Germany or to the Gestapo in Rome, but at least he would have the chance to speak in their defense.

Outside the window he heard the dog bark and he turned. Somewhere the boy had found a bone the size of a boot, a little meat still clinging to it. Abruptly the dog, despite its unsteady gait, took the gift in its mouth and started to run down the street beside the Arno. The boy smiled, his hands on his knees, and then stood and waved at the animal as it disappeared into the night.

Alessia tucked her chin against her collarbone and rolled head-first, her fine hair billowing out beside her as she tumbled. The sun was reflecting off the black chimera, turning it almost silver, and the lion's eyes looked a little wild as it watched the child. Alessia somersaulted three times along the grass beside the pergola for her mother and her aunt, a display triggered, the women presumed, because her brother, Massimo, had just swum all the way to the bottom of the deepest section of the pool for the very first time.

"A somersault is nothing new," Massimo reminded them all.

"No, but three in a row? Your little sister has never done that," Francesca told her son. "I'm proud of both of you." Then she brushed the dry grass from her daughter's shoulders and the back of her bathing suit. She pulled a strand of lavender from the girl's hair and replaced it with a rose from the nearby trellis. Meanwhile, Massimo decided he would drown his disgust: he pinched his nose shut with his thumb and forefinger and jumped back into the pool, trying to make as large and as annoying a splash as he could. In the distance they could see two farmhands tending to the grapes at the edge of the vineyard.

"I thought Vittore sounded good on the phone this morning," Cristina said to Francesca. He had grown testy when she'd pressed him about the officers' visit to the villa, because he was still piqued that they had gone there without him, but he was excited by the prospect of seeing his family today. Instead of Florence, however, they were going to meet in Arezzo, a smaller city than Florence but no more than thirty-five kilometers from Monte Volta. He was going to be there with the contingent from the Uffizi, show-ing the Germans the Etruscan art—including, he'd said, the relics from their estate. He didn't believe he would have time for a meal with his family, but he was confident that he would be able to steal away with them to a café for perhaps an hour in the middle of the afternoon.

"He sounded a little annoyed to me," said Francesca. "And he should be. Coming to his home without telling him? That's infuriating." When her daughter looked up at her, curious, her tone softened. "We should change out of our bathing suits. Your grandfather wants to leave for Arezzo by noon. You're going to see your uncle Vittore."

Cristina smiled at the child. Then, overhead, she heard engines. In a moment they all did, even Massimo as he slapped frantically at the water with the palms of his hands. Almost as one they glanced up at the cirriform sky: another flock of German planes was motoring its way to the south.

1955

LATE WEDNESDAY AFTERNOON, Paolo Ficino sat across from this aging marchesa from a village southeast of Siena in which he had not set foot once in the forty-eight years he had been on the planet, and tried to empathize with what she was experiencing. There was the grief that her son's wife was dead—not merely murdered, but eviscerated—and now there was the indignity of having to sit across from a homicide inspector in the police headquarters in Florence. She told him she was sixty-four years old, and certainly she had earned the deep lines around her eyes and her mouth. She had outlived her husband, one of her two sons, and a pair of grandchildren. And now Francesca. But Beatrice Rosati was still beautiful: courtly and elegant and serene. Her daughter, Cristina, was sitting beside her, and he could see the resemblance in the shape of their eyes and the austere chiseling that marked their cheeks.

"Are you sure you would not like some coffee?" he asked the two women now.

"No, I'm fine," Beatrice said, her hands folded demurely on the small red leather purse in her lap. "It's too late in the day for me to have coffee." She was dressed for mourning in a black skirt and blouse and a modest string of pearls. Her daughter was in a rather cheerful sleeveless summer dress; it was white with lavender flowers.

"If you change your mind . . ."

"Thank you."

"Serafina will be joining us. She is the detective who interviewed Cristina yesterday," he said, directing his remark to the marchesa. "She's on the phone with America."

The older woman nodded but remained quiet.

"So," Paolo began, "any idea of who did not particularly like your daughter-in-law?"

"I'm sure there were lots of people," Beatrice said. "My daughter-in-law had an acerbic tongue and she did not suffer fools or foolishness."

"Okay. Can you give me some names?"

"I could, but it would include almost everyone she ever met."

He thought about this. "Did you not like her?"

"No, I loved her. It's just . . ."

Cristina patted her mother on the knee and jumped in. "It's just that Francesca was always a little difficult. Opinionated. After my brother was killed and the children died, it got much worse. I think that's understandable. She was always angry and always judging. Everyone. Everything. Before, it had just been a dark sense of humor. But after the war? She was a different person. My mother hadn't seen her in years."

"How many years?"

"Four and one half," Beatrice answered. "I last saw Francesca over Christmas 1950."

"But you continued to see her," Paolo said to Cristina.

"Yes. When I came to Florence, sometimes we would have lunch or dinner. We'd get manicures and pedicures together—the way we did when I was a teenager and she was a young mother."

"Were you planning on visiting a salon this time? Did you have other business in Florence?"

"No, I didn't. We didn't. I was just coming to visit Francesca."

He reached into a folder, pulled out the photograph of Mario Spagnoli, and placed it at the edge of his desk so both women could see it. "This is the person Francesca had dinner with Monday night, a few hours before she was killed. He read about her death in the newspaper and immediately came forward."

"So this is the man who might have murdered her?" Beatrice asked, gazing almost in wonderment at the image.

"Maybe, but I don't think so. He's a lawyer, forty-four years old. Lives and works in Bologna. Never married. Knew Francesca because he once bought a dress for another woman from her shop. He says he took her to dinner at Il Latini and—" He stopped midsentence. Spagnoli had been upfront about the fact that he and Francesca had made love, but did the marchesa need to know that? Probably not. Apparently, however, the woman knew enough about her former daughter-in-law that she was able to finish the sentence for him.

"And then they went back to her apartment together," Beatrice said.

"Yes."

"That was her way. It wasn't, of course, her way when she was married to Marco. When she lived with us. But it was how she was at the end."

"But you said you hadn't seen her since 1950," Paolo said, not precisely sure why he was challenging her and defending the dead woman's honor. It was almost a reflex.

"I know what she had become," Beatrice said.

"So you were aware of her . . . habits."

"We all were," Cristina said. "It was how Francesca coped. That's all."

The marchesa glanced briefly at her daughter and then stared out the window behind him, her face absolutely impassive.

"Why don't you think this lawyer might have killed her?" Cristina continued.

"I've done this awhile, I can tell. He doesn't seem the sort to own or borrow bone saws. He doesn't seem the type to cut out a human heart. And it may be as simple as the fact that he came in well before we found him ourselves. He volunteered to give us fingerprints, which will of course be all over the apartment. And his alibi is good—though far from airtight."

"And that is?" Cristina asked.

"His alibi? He says he left your sister-in-law's apartment around eleven p.m. and drove back to Bologna. Got there about twelve-thirty."

"That's not an alibi at all. Serafina told me that my sister-in-law was killed sometime after midnight."

Paolo couldn't help but smile. The prosecutor in charge of the case had said the exact same thing. "And, of course, he lives alone with his dog," Paolo added. "So there isn't even anyone to confirm when he arrived in Bologna."

"Then he might have killed her."

"We asked to look at his car. It was clean."

"Do you mean there was no knife?" Cristina pressed him.

"I mean it was clean. There was no blood. And whoever killed Francesca would—forgive me—have been a mess. But clearly the car hadn't been . . . sanitized. It was absolutely covered with dog hair."

"Do you know for sure he drove that car that night? Maybe he took the train."

Paolo sighed. He was confident that the worst thing Mario Spagnoli might have done was corroborate Francesca Rosati's belief that men were after but one thing. But since clearly Francesca was after that one thing as well, he doubted that Mario had done even that.

"I assure you, we will look into it," he said.

Over the marchesa's shoulder he saw Serafina approaching and he stood. He introduced her to Beatrice and pushed his chair around to the side of the desk so she could sit, too, but she shook her head and leaned against the wall by the window. So he sat back down. He decided it didn't matter if the Rosatis were present while Serafina shared with him what she had learned from the Americans.

"I don't have much to report," she told the three of them. "The FBI is going to send us a list of museum executives or curators in New York whose first names are Richard or Russell. If one has been in Italy this week, we'll pursue that lead. I've started calling hospitals to see if any are missing a bone saw or scalpel, but I don't think we're going to learn much. They really don't inventory such items."

Paolo noticed that Beatrice was staring intently at Serafina and assumed it was because the marchesa had never before seen a female detective. Then, however, he noticed that the woman was focusing on the side of Serafina's head and her neck. After a moment Serafina sensed the attention. She met the marchesa's eyes briefly but then glanced down at her notes.

"Serafina," Beatrice said, not so much speaking to the young detective as rolling the name around on her tongue as if she were tasting a new wine. "That's a beautiful name."

"Thank you."

"I presume you know what it means."

"The burning one," Serafina answered.

"Interesting," Beatrice said. "I would have said the fiery one. I guess it's a small difference."

"But a meaningful one," Paolo said. He regretted the offhand remark instantly. Already Serafina was looking down at him, her eyes a little wide with anger.

"You can spend all the time you want on jilted lovers," Milton was saying to Serafina after dinner, leaning against the restaurant's brick wall at their corner table. Before them both were small blue glasses filled with limoncello. "A jilted lover doesn't cut out a human heart. That's just . . . depraved."

"But what about a jilted depraved lover?" she asked, only half kidding. "Think of what the heart means. It's a message."

"It's a message, all right. It's a message that you're dealing with a crazy person."

"So if it's not a lover, where would you look?"

He sipped the liqueur and smiled. "Seriously, if I am ever asked to transfer back to the United States, I'm quitting. I'm sorry, but you cannot find alcohol like this in Pelham or New Rochelle."

"You didn't answer my question," she said to him.

"Well, she knew whoever killed her. You said that she let him into her apartment."

"That's what we believe, yes."

"And nothing was stolen?"

"We don't know that for a fact, but it doesn't look like anything was. There was a jewelry box on the vanity, right beside the ashtray with the heart, and nothing appeared to have been taken."

"Appeared?"

"There was a pair of beautiful ruby earrings right there. Extremely valuable. Also a diamond ring she had worn when she was married to Marco Rosati. If this were a robbery, they would have been gone."

"Well, then, devil worship, perhaps? Satan? I'm kidding, but not by as much as you think."

"Wouldn't they have taken the heart if it were for a ritual?"

"Damned if I know."

She looked around at the other couples that remained in the restaurant. It was after eleven and the women and men who were still there all struck her as young and in love. She counted diners at four other tables, each with but two people. She tried to decide which couples were married and concluded, in the end, that none of them were. Two of the pairs were holding hands across the tablecloth.

"But it does seem to me," Milton was saying, "it's someone who clearly feels that Francesca wronged him—and who is not especially good at managing his temper."

"So you're positive the killer is a man."

"Yes, I think my gender can take responsibility for this one. Women don't cut out other women's hearts."

"We can."

He thought about this. Then: "Look, you and I both did things in the war that, in hindsight, we may not be especially proud of. I know that. But I would not view your personal history as emblematic."

"No, probably not. But you may be on to something."

"That the killer is a man with a bad temper? Somehow I don't think that's a particularly brilliant insight."

She shook her head. "Maybe this has something to do with the war. For someone to kill someone in such a . . . a dramatic fashion suggests a deep connection. A defining connection. And all the defining moments in Francesca Rosati's life seem to go back to the war."

He raised his glass in a toast. "You may be spot on," he said. "But then again, you could probably say that for all of us. For our whole generation." Then he swallowed the last of his limoncello and reached into his breast pocket for his wallet.

⚜

Cristina and her mother had a room that was barely big enough for its two slender beds in a modest hotel not far from the Uffizi. But they were going to clean out Francesca's apartment over the next two days and certainly couldn't commute back and forth from Rome. Florence was four and a half hours distant if Cristina was driving and a solid five hours if Beatrice was behind the wheel.

"I still believe Vittore will come help us, if we ask him," Beatrice said. She stood in her nightgown before the window, which looked out on a street barely wide enough for two Vespas to pass. Cristina was lying in bed. She noticed a print of a horse on the wall, and though the artwork was journeyman at best, the animal reminded her of Arabella.

"He knows she's dead. If he wanted to help, he would have volunteered," Cristina told her mother.

"There's so much to do."

"Not really—especially since we're giving her clothes and furniture to the church. Francesca didn't have much at the end."

"She still had the ring Marco gave her. And her rubies. The police said we might as well take them. They're not evidence."

"You have them?"

"Yes."

"Good."

"And Vittore really isn't coming?" her mother asked.

Cristina sighed and rolled away from the horse. The painting managed to prick her sadness. Watching it was like worrying a hangnail.

"No, Mother," she said finally. "He isn't coming." Her brother lived in Rome, too, but in a different neighborhood. He worked at the Vatican Museum. He and his wife and their two children had a lovely apartment on the Via Crescenzio, only blocks from Vatican City. Cristina knew he wanted to waste no energy burying their late brother's dead wife.

Beatrice turned away from the window and seemed to think about this. Then: "Did you look at the photographs?" she asked.

Cristina understood instantly what her mother meant: the photographs that had been taken of Francesca's corpse. What Serafina had referred to as the crime scene pictures. "I didn't have to," she answered. "I saw the real thing."

"I don't know how you are going to bear that."

Cristina had made sure that her mother had not viewed the pictures. She herself had endured a flood of bad dreams last night, and she feared that she would again this evening. Serafina had offered to get them some pills so she and her mother could sleep. Now, as she pressed her head deeper into the hotel pillow and curled her knees up toward her chest, she wished that she hadn't declined.

The truth was, however, that she hadn't noticed Francesca's heart until after the police had arrived. The principal image that was going to dog her forever was of her sister-in-law's ribs: four of them sticking up like scaffolding against the inside of Francesca's flesh—her sister-in-law, inside out. Whoever had ripped out the heart had pulled back the rib cage with such thoroughness that the ribs rose from the black marsh that had been her sister-in-law's chest like dead, branchless trees. Like the trees near the tombs at the estate. The Nazis had blown up the medieval granary in the village as part of their withdrawal, but then, realizing that the British were already behind them, they had retreated back inside the grounds of the Villa Chimera. There they had fought like cornered wolves. Eventually most surrendered; some clawed their way out. By the time the soldiers were gone, the olive trees had become creosote-colored matchsticks; the cypresses had been all but incinerated. And the villa was mere ruins.

No, Cristina thought now. She might forget the deep gash under Francesca's jaw; she might forget how unexpectedly beautiful the woman's hair had looked against the floor; she might even forget the sight of her vagina, exposed because of the way the nightgown had been ripped asunder; but she would never forget those ribs.

Before turning off the light in her bedroom on the other side of the river from the Rosatis, Serafina sat before her own small vanity. She thought of Francesca Rosati at hers, but she knew that she would have been thinking of the dead woman regardless of where she was sitting right now. Her own mirror was, by choice, much smaller than Francesca's; it was the size of a hand mirror and rested on a thin, unadorned mount. She used it for applying her lipstick and makeup, and it was the only mirror in her bedroom. She did not want a bigger one because of the risks that came with a large mirror—the chance that she might accidentally glimpse the dwarf piece of pink cartilage that was all that remained of her right ear or the scars that tattooed her neck and back.

She placed a new auto club map of Chianti and Siena on the narrow table. It showed the roads near Pienza, Montepulciano, and Monte Volta. She stared at it, recalling the hills in which she had lived in 1943 and 1944, the roads on which she had traveled at night. Her eyes kept circling back to Monte Volta, however, and the granary the Nazis had blown up. She tried to remember details of the firefight at the villa nearby, but the memories mostly were lost; the fact that it had occurred would be forever scored upon her flesh and in her recollection of her agony when she'd finally awoken—both the physical pain and the terror when she felt the scalp behind her right ear and discovered that most of her hair there was gone. Burned off in barely an instant. Certainly she knew of the firefight because the British Army doctors had told her about it at the hospital they had commandeered in Montepulciano. There was one physician who would shake his head as she lay on her side and he worked on her back, meticulously debriding the dead tissue, remarking that the only reason she was still alive was that she was young and strong. Infection alone would have killed most people, he said. He'd added that it wasn't the worst of her burns that were the most painful; in those areas, the nerves were far too badly damaged to inform the brain that they were hurting. Months later, they had grafted skin from her legs onto her shoulder and back, but the procedure had done little to beautify the whorling topographic map there. And by then the scar tissue had made it impossible to raise her arm much higher than parallel to the ground.

Still, her last memory that she knew was precise—not fabricated from things people told her after the fact, her imagination crafting for her stories to use in lieu of accurate recollection—was the explosion at the granary. She was close enough to the village that she had witnessed the medieval brick and stone pancake into the small piazza before it. A whole group of the partisans had stood there watching, including Enrico, his wife, Teresa, and Salvatore. There had been a flash of light along the base, the concussive blast, and then the tower had fallen.

But not its twin. Cristina had been correct. When Serafina thought back on that moment now, she did indeed see that the second tower had remained upright and standing. Nevertheless, Teresa had taken her hand, as if they were witnessing the end of the world. Even Enrico, usually stoic and self-possessed, was shaking his head slowly in disbelief, stunned, his eyes wide and his slender lips parted ever so slightly. In much the same way that Teresa had taken her hand, Enrico had rested his fingers on his brother Salvatore's shoulder, as if he needed help with his balance.

And then what? What happened next, as always, eluded her. It existed like fog, present but impossible to grasp. She would always have the hairless, nerveless scars on her back and her neck, the ruined right ear, but they were a reminder of nothing. Nothing at all.

On the other side of the apartment she heard Milton turn off his light. She tried to imagine where the Villa Chimera was in proximity to Monte Volta, but couldn't. She tried to find a reason that someone would wait eleven years to exact revenge on Francesca Rosati and couldn't explain that either.

And so she pulled up her nightgown to her waist, lit and blew out one last match for the day, inhaling the smell of the sulfur, and pressed the black tip hard against the inside of her thigh. She held it there a moment longer than usual. Then she rose from the vanity, switched off the lamp by her bed, and climbed beneath the sheets. She knew it was going to be a long while before she slept.

BEATRICE ROSATI, Francesca's mother-in-law, was not named for Dante's muse, the inspiration for La Vita Nuova, as well as, more famously, the poet's guide in the last book of La Divina Commedia. You might recall—and then again, you might not—that Beatrice relieves Virgil because Virgil was a pagan and thus never going to be allowed past the crowd control barriers that cordoned off Paradise. The Beatrice that obsessed Dante was a Florentine named Bice di Folco Portinari. Envision this moment (and, in all fairness, I am envisioning it the way Henry Holiday did in his exquisite nineteenth-century painting): Bice is walking beside the Arno River, dressed in white, the fabric clinging to her legs and outlining her slender thighs, and there is Dante. He meets her at the corner of one of the bridges that span the river. His left hand, at first glimpse, is moving casually toward his hip; it is only on a more careful study that one realizes his hand is actually going up to his heart. Meanwhile, his right hand is resting on the bridge's waist-high stone balustrade, as if Bico's beauty is such that he needs to steady himself when he beholds her.

Florence, too, is magnificent in the painting. It's the Florence I love, the buildings on the south side of the Arno built right up against the water but a pedestrian sidewalk separating the buildings on the north side from the river.

Beatrice Rosati was named for an aunt who lived in Pienza. Nothing magical, nothing poetic.

But how could I not think of Bice when I planned how I would kill Beatrice? How could I not think of Florence and the Arno, and how fitting it was that Dante was reaching for his heart when he saw her?

So here was my fantasy: after I had cut Beatrice's heart from her chest,

I would leave it atop the corner of the Florentine bridge precisely where Holiday had painted the poet's hand.

The problem was this: How could I be sure that an animal would not carry the heart away? Or, what would be even more frustrating, how could I be sure that some idiot human, not realizing what it was, didn't swipe it into the waters below? And that would mean labeling the item as if I were a biology professor. And the label, if I wasn't careful, would be evidence. (Likewise, if I wasn't clever, I would risk embarrassing myself.) And wasn't the extraction of a human heart a sufficiently memorable calling card? Good Lord, one would think so.

Consequently, I resolved to box up the heart when I left it along the balustrade. Eventually someone would open the box and take it to the police.

1943

CAPTAIN MARCO ROSATI, an engineer before he was mustered into the army, stood in the sun on a limestone hillock that overlooked a Sicilian beach beside Gela, staring out at the Mediterranean Sea through binoculars. The Allied ships were out there somewhere. Marco was sure of it, as confident as he was that centuries ago Aeschylus had sat on these very rocks, gazing at the waves and pondering murder in the Oresteia. These might not be the very ships that would lead the invasion of Sicily, but they were out there, splitting in half the sea waves.

There was a myth that Aeschylus had died here when a great bird dropped a turtle on his head, mistaking his bald skull for a rock. In Marco's opinion, this was unlikely but not inconceivable. The bearded vultures of Sicily were known for dropping turtles onto stones, hoping to crack open the shells. And it seemed that this island had at least as many vultures as soldiers. So, as odd as the story sounded, it was at least possible.

Unlike Aeschylus, Marco had a thick mass of curly black hair, making it improbable—so he told himself—that he would ever be felled by a falling turtle. Besides, there were far greater dangers here.

On the beach his men were laying mines. There were eight of them, local Sicilians, and they were working with their shirts off and bandannas tied around their heads. They were working carefully, laying the mines in jagged rows that began at the very edge of high tide, moving away from the water as if they were painting a floor. This was the fifth consecutive day that their assignment had been land mines, and they had the drill down to a well-rehearsed dance. Today they were laying antipersonnel mines; yesterday they had been planting the ones that could disable a tank.

Still, the task was endless. The beach was endless. How did you defend the whole shoreline of Sicily, much less Italy? Marco found the question unfathomable. When they had finished with the mines, they would have to unspool the barbed wire, massive coils that would stretch for kilometers. And then there were the wires that would trip the magnesium flares and turn the night into day. And the bunkers and firing pits to construct in the hills. And finally there was that pier. It was a thousand feet long, and when the time came they were going to blow the damn thing up.

It was a waste. What was the point of defending the island if the defenders themselves were going to destroy it? His son, Massimo, would love that pier. Alessia might, too. The local children had been diving off it before they had been evicted by the soldiers.

He sighed. More than anything, he missed his children. He missed them even more than he desired Francesca, and he desired her a lot. He had not been home to the Villa Chimera since a brief leave in February. He had, he feared, missed more of Alessia's childhood than he had seen.

Behind him, he heard someone running along the ridge, and he turned. It was the engineer named Moretti, a stout, meaty fellow with round eyes and a champagne cork for a nose. He had a red forehead and he always looked a little overwhelmed.

"It's over!" he was crying, a little breathless. "It's over!"

"What's over?" Marco asked, but he knew. They had surrendered in Africa.

"The battle in Tunis! The whole Italian First Army is gone!"

"Gone? Or in captivity?" For a brief moment, the word *gone* had him fearful that the Germans—psychotic, all of them—had convinced the Italians to fight to the last bullet. That was, it seemed to Marco, the sum of Nazi military strategy these days. In his mind he saw Italian corpses piled in the desert like dunes.

"Surrendered," Moretti said, and he bent over, his hands on his knees, his broad back rising and falling from running.

"You need to take better care of yourself," Marco told him. "You look like you're dying."

Moretti lifted his head and scowled, but his eyes were so doe-like that even when he was angry he appeared only startled. "It means we're next, you know."

"We always were next."

"Unless the Allies bypass us. I would, wouldn't you? Why waste your time on Sicily? Or, for that matter, on Italy? I would go straight into France. I think there's a chance of that, don't you?"

Marco shook his head. The Americans and the British were methodical, and this was for them a war of territorial liberation. Soon there would be Allied battleships pummeling them and Allied aircraft bombing them and Allied paratroopers falling amid them. And waves and waves of Allied soldiers storming this very beach. He presumed they would be younger than he—closer to Cristina's age than to his. And it wouldn't matter how many hundreds or thousands were maimed and killed by the land mines that were buried in the beach like turtle eggs, ten times that many more would survive and take Sicily. And perhaps maim or kill him. And Moretti. And those eight peasants carefully placing the metal disks in the sand.

"Marco?"

He looked back at Moretti and shrugged. He stared up into the sun and tried to imagine what was occurring that moment at the estate in Monte Volta. Whether his children were napping. "There's always a chance they'll go elsewhere," he said finally. "But I wouldn't count on it."

※

The group from the Uffizi left in two large staff cars, but they hadn't segregated the Italians in one vehicle and the Germans in another. They did that sometimes, Friedrich Strekker had noticed. He attributed their decision not to today to a combination of the prosaic and the profound. The prosaic? Colonel Decher wanted to ask Vittore about the relics from the burial vault at the Villa Chimera. The profound? After the fall of Africa, they were all being slightly more gentle with one another, more brotherly. They were all a little scared. After Tunisia, Italy was next. Suddenly the war was looking as bleak in the west as it was in the east.

And so Friedrich had wound up in the front seat beside an Italian driver while Vittore sat in the back between Colonel Decher and Major Lorenzetti. The colonel had been peppering Vittore with questions. He wanted to know which pieces they were going to see at the museum, the images that were painted or carved onto them, and what Vittore knew about the Etruscans who had lived in this corner of Tuscany so many centuries ago. Only when they were approaching the outskirts of the city and were trapped in a long column of cars and trucks and donkey carts that had come to a complete halt did Decher finally pause. He stared out the window, his arms folded across his chest, his pale skin looking a little rosy in the heat. But he said nothing about Italian incompetence, as he might have another day, especially since the traffic jam was not the result of Italian backwardness: too many donkey carts or a road that was badly maintained. Last night the Allies had bombed the rail yards and a munitions factory in Arezzo, and the work crews were still trying to clear the debris from the road. Here there was no sign of the attack; there was only the long line of cypress trees on one side of the road, the edges of an estate owned by some Fascist confidant of Mussolini, and on the other the first decrepit, low-slung buildings that would grow taller and closer together as they approached Arezzo. A few kilometers ahead of them, however, Friedrich envisioned great mounds of rubble and chewed-up stucco and cement, and railroad cars that had been tossed around like small toys and mangled. He'd seen such things before.

"There will be nothing left of this country when the war is over," Vittore mumbled, and he wiped the sweat off his forehead with the cuff of his shirt.

"We're all making sacrifices," Decher reminded him. "We have all lost something."

"A foot, for example," Friedrich said, surprising himself. It was a reflex, born of the fact that no one in the car had lost what he had, and they were all hot and uncomfortable and anxious to get to Arezzo. The black car was like an oven.

"Indeed, Lieutenant, you have certainly made a sacrifice," Decher agreed, his voice uncharacteristically avuncular.

"Well, I'm not going to bake inside here any longer," Lorenzetti announced, opening his door and exiting the vehicle. "Anyone care to join me for a cigarette?"

Though Decher didn't smoke, he followed the major. Jürgen Voss emerged from the car behind them and sidled up to the pair, too. Friedrich was contemplating whether he would be more comfortable outside as well when Vittore asked him from the back seat, "Was it a land mine?"

"My foot? No."

"My brother, Marco, spends his life mining the beaches in Sicily." He sighed. "So if it wasn't a mine, what was it?"

"A shell . . . more or less. A building collapsed. In Voronezh. It was almost a year ago now."

"I'm sorry."

"It's not all bad. If I hadn't lost my foot, I would have continued on to Stalingrad. And no good would have come from that."

"Stalingrad. Tunis. We seem to be losing whole armies this year."

"I know."

"What happened?"

"In Voronezh?"

"Yes."

How much to tell? Usually Friedrich didn't like to talk about his foot; he wished he had kept his annoyance to himself and not brought it up. Besides, the injury had happened so quickly. One minute he was with his unit inside a butcher's shop, abandoned now, like everything else in that section of the city. The hooks and the refrigerator cases were empty. He was watching through the broken window as a Russian tank smoldered across the street and a pair of crows picked at the body of the gunner who had managed to climb from the burning hulk's turret before expiring. And the next minute? The sound of screaming cats, the shrill, whining noise that signaled the imminent arrival of shells from a Katyusha rocket launcher. Immediately he fell below the windowsill and curled himself against the wall. Unfortunately, the wall collapsed.

"Katyusha rocket," he said to Vittore. "The Russians decided the best way to slow us was to bring down half the city."

"And some of the city landed on your foot."

"A butcher's shop wall, yes. Crushed it."

"Lovely."

"So you have a brother," he said to Vittore, hoping to change the subject from his foot. "How many sisters?"

"Just one. Cristina."

"And she's coming to Arezzo for a visit this afternoon?"

He nodded. "Along with my parents and my sister-in-law and the children. The whole crowd."

"Was it Cristina whom Colonel Decher met yesterday?"

"Francesca, too. But Cristina's the baby of the family. She's only eighteen. She spends her days, as far as I can tell, with my seven-year-old nephew and my five-year-old niece. Or with her horse. She's a very good rider."

"You're older than Marco?"

The Italian said nothing for a moment, then smiled. "Do I look old? I must. No, Marco is older than I am. He's thirty."

"And he's a captain."

"And an engineer." Vittore seemed about to say something more when, much to their surprise, they heard the drivers in the vehicles ahead of them starting their engines and Decher, Lorenzetti, and Voss climbed back into the cars. Apparently that single lane was just about to be cleared.

☙

By the time Cristina and her family got to see Vittore, the shock of what they had witnessed on the outskirts of Arezzo was starting to lessen. The museum was in a section of the city that had been spared, and this added a veneer of normalcy to their visit. Still, Cristina was left with a feeling that was somewhere between unease and actual fear. It struck her as odd—horrific and odd—that some parts of the city were completely untouched while others had been destroyed in a fashion that made her think first of Pompeii and then of the newsreel footage she'd seen in the cinema of the Allied air raids on Genoa and Turin. They had driven slowly past the dollhouse cutaways of stone and brick buildings, some of the rubble still sending dry mists of pollenlike dust into the air, as well as the charred husks of the wooden structures, the stout vertical timbers and chimneys blackened and smoking like candlewicks.

Nevertheless, the image that kept coming back to Cristina was the field of corpses along the rail yard, an almost perfect rectangle. Because of the traffic jam, she had been able to count forty-eight bodies. Most were flat on their backs, but a few were on their sides with their legs curled against their chests, as if they had died while trying to hide from the bombs and rigor mortis had set in well before the bodies had been recovered. The stench was not yet overpowering, but it would be by the time the sun had set and the corpses had had a full day to bake. Most of the dead were adults, but at the farthest edge of the field there were three small bodies, the children as young as her nephew and niece. She had done all that she could to prevent Massimo and Alessia from seeing the corpses, but their car had spent so much time stalled that the siblings had started to fidget and climbed over Francesca and her mother and spied the remains from the windows. Since then they had been absolutely silent.

Finally they all heard footsteps, the sound of heavy boots echoing on marble down the hallway. They were standing in the vast, windowless corridor outside the room where the relics from the Villa Chimera were kept. When Cristina looked up, she saw a group of soldiers approaching, Germans as well as Italians. She saw Lorenzetti and Decher, the pair who had first come to see the tombs, before she saw her brother, because he was a few paces behind them. But then he was standing in front of her, grinning a little darkly, as Lorenzetti and Decher and four other men disappeared down a perpendicular corridor before reaching them. He embraced his parents and next wrapped his arms around Francesca and her two children. Only then did he turn his attention toward Cristina.

"You are as bad as those two," he said to her, pointing at his nephew and niece. "I leave you alone in Monte Volta for a few months and look how you grow up!" She smiled, but before she could respond he was saying to their father, "That must have been some drive you had today. I'm so sorry."

"Frustrating, disturbing, yes."

"I fear it's just a taste of what's coming."

Behind her brother Cristina saw another soldier approaching, a German. He was walking with a slight limp. He was about to veer off down the corridor where the other soldiers had gone when he noticed her and her family and paused for the briefest of seconds. Then he started toward them.

"So this is your family," he said to Vittore. He was tall and slim, and his eyes were a blue so vivid she was reminded of the hyacinths that grew along the winding road up to the villa. He was smiling, his lips full and a little feminine. He removed his cap and wiped his bangs off his forehead. His hair was the color of mustard flowers. "I'm Lieutenant Strekker," he began, extending his hand to her father. "I have the pleasure of working with Vittore."

Her father took the young man's hand awkwardly, surprised that the soldier had reached out to him. Cristina thought he was accepting it largely because it would have been unheard of for a man in her father's position not to shake a hand that was offered.

"I just saw the artifacts from your villa," the lieutenant said. "Wonderful. The chimera on that pot, it's—"

"It's not a pot. It's a hydria," Vittore said patiently. "It was used for carrying water."

"Still, the beast is beautiful. Terrifying, but beautiful. And the detail on the flames? Remarkable. I was sure it could breathe fire. I felt the heat on my skin. And then there were those dancers on that plate. I know Colonel Decher was very interested."

Vittore looked away, unable to suppress a small, wry smirk. "His colonel thinks he saw the roots of fascism in a piece of plate and a pot," he said. "Or perhaps a way to curry favor with the Gestapo in Rome."

"So your colonel is Decher," her father observed. "He was one of the officers who came to my house yesterday."

"That's right," Strekker said.

The marchese nodded, but he looked a little exasperated. He introduced the rest of the family to the lieutenant. When he reached his daughter, Strekker bowed his head in her direction. "I love the name Cristina. It was my mother's name, though I'm sure you spell yours differently. My mother's version has a *z*. She was half Hungarian."

"What happened to her?" she asked reflexively, and just as the words were escaping her mouth she worried that the question was far too personal.

"She died—but it was a long time ago."

Before he could say more, Francesca was beside the two of them, telling the German in a whispered voice that nevertheless had a hint of venom, "Your uniform is frightening enough to my children. They've just seen a field of corpses. Please don't make it worse by talking about how your mother died."

"I understand completely," he told Francesca, seemingly unperturbed by her anger. When Cristina glanced down at Massimo and Alessia, they were staring up at the lieutenant as if there were no other adults in the corridor.

"I only have a little while," Vittore was telling their father. "There's a café a block from here. We should go."

"Would you like to join us?" Cristina asked the young soldier. "After all, you work with my brother." She had proffered the invitation spontaneously, aware only after she had spoken how forward she must have sounded.

"It's been a pleasure to work with Vittore—a gift to have an expert such as your brother show me Florence firsthand."

Vittore looked at him quizzically. Then he remarked, "That's me. I'm not an archeologist. I'm a tour guide for visiting Germans."

"And every day you find something exquisite to share," he said, his eyes on Cristina.

She wondered if she was blushing. "So you will come to the restaurant, Lieutenant—" She paused, trying to recall his name.

"It's Strekker," he said. "But please, you must call me Friedrich. And I would be honored to join you."

Francesca was rolling her eyes in annoyance, but Cristina knew that her parents would never be so rude as to disinvite the lieutenant, even if he was a German. When they started from the museum, she was a little glad he walked with a limp; it meant that she could fall behind her family and get to know him a bit on her own.

1955

MIDMORNING, BEATRICE GAZED at the dresses and skirts in the armoire in her daughter-in-law's bedroom in Florence. She did not recognize a stitch of clothing, but that didn't surprise her. She hadn't seen the woman in four and a half years. Still, she folded each piece carefully before placing it in one of the boxes for the church.

She had resolved to remain here in the bedroom while Cristina was once again at the police station, because she grew nauseated whenever she ventured into the living room and saw the chaotic splotches of cranberry on the walls near the front door and the way a great swath of the wood on the floor was stained reddish-brown. It was no longer a crime scene, but it was still horrifying.

Serafina had come by the hotel that morning and asked her and her daughter to tell her about what they had experienced in the war and whether the motive for Francesca's death might have gone back that far. Once again Beatrice found herself gazing at the detective, at her sickle-moon eyebrows, so carefully plucked, above those dark, dark eyes. Her nose was dainty, her chin was small. Her hair fell in drapes. Beatrice had seen her somewhere before, she was quite sure of it. For that reason alone, she almost joined her daughter at the police station. But the truth was, she didn't feel up to that conversation, and so Cristina and Serafina had ventured to the station without her.

Which meant that she had wound up alone at Francesca's apartment on the Via Zara. The windows were open and she could hear the occasional car or motorcycle roaring down the street, but the building itself was quiet. She would have turned on a radio, but it seemed that Francesca didn't own one.

Finally, after almost an hour of work, she sat down on the bed and surveyed the room. The vanity. The mirror. The headboard beside her. How had it come to this? A dingy apartment—and it was dingy, with its walls the color of dirty bathwater, too few outlets for too few lights, and furniture that was inelegant and shoddy.

She sighed. She had loved Francesca, but she had never liked her. Her husband had. So had Cristina and Vittore. And, of course, Marco had adored her. But when Beatrice was honest with herself, she had never really liked the woman, even though she and her children had moved into the Villa Chimera as soon as Marco had left for the army. Francesca was simply too angry for Beatrice's tastes— and, yes, too comfortable with her newfound status and wealth. Beatrice didn't mind that her son had married beneath him, but she had always been a little annoyed at the way her daughter-in-law had grown accustomed so quickly to the small extravagances that came with her status—and then how she would complain when, over time, the war made those luxuries unobtainable.

Nevertheless, she had agreed in a heartbeat to have the body sent back to Monte Volta. There was no question in her mind; she was already anticipating that Francesca would be buried there even before Cristina had suggested that they make arrangements to have the woman returned (and that had been Cristina's verb) to the Villa Chimera. Francesca should, and would, be interred beside her husband and children in the family plot Beatrice's father-in-law had designed at the estate. Once it had been beautiful, with a small Roman temple overlooking the monuments and the flower beds and the great square slabs of marble that formed the courtyard. Now? Like everything else at the Villa Chimera, it was sad and dark and succumbing to ruin.

She wondered what Cristina would tell the detective about what the war had been like. She herself couldn't imagine who from that era might have murdered Francesca. The woman was never popular in Monte Volta, but what could she possibly have done that would drive someone to cut her throat and rip out her heart? Hadn't she suffered enough? She had lost her husband and both of her children; she had been reduced to living in this shabby apartment and spending her nights with men who were never going to marry her.

She looked up when she thought she heard a noise in the apartment corridor. Or perhaps in the living room. A footstep. A floorboard groaning beneath the weight. She had left the front door ajar because there was an open window at the near end of the hallway and she wanted to get as much fresh air into the apartment as possible before the midday heat would force her to close the shutters. She guessed she heard Cristina, returning now from the police station, and she was glad. It was not merely depressing to be alone here in Francesca's apartment, it was disturbing. She felt almost the way she had those few times she had wandered alone to the Etruscan tombs at the villa. The dead were too . . . present.

"Cristina?" she called out, more of a stage whisper than an actual shout. When no one answered, she called again, rising slowly from her spot on the bed. She peered into the living room, quite sure that she saw a shadow in the corridor outside the front door, and paused.

"Hello?" she asked, her voice unexpectedly small.

And while she told herself that her heart was racing because she was in the apartment of a woman who had been brutally murdered earlier that week, she could not deny the fact that suddenly she was scared. She was too old and she had seen too much to feel this way, but she did. She stepped back into the bedroom, two quick, silent steps, and closed the door. There she stared at the handle, wishing there were a lock. There wasn't. Her eyes went to the window, and she realized that she was prepared to go to it and scream as if her life depended upon it—because perhaps it might.

She mouthed her daughter's name one more time, both a prayer and a plea. *Cristina,* the *s* sibilant and long, the last syllable more expiration than exhalation. Now she was positive that someone was on the other side of the wood, and for a long, long moment she stared at the doorknob, waiting perfectly still, aware of the way her heart seemed somehow to be beating between her ears. Whoever had mutilated her daughter-in-law had returned for a reason she couldn't begin to fathom, but there he was, only a meter from her, breathing in the very same air.

She couldn't have said for sure how long she had been standing there when she heard them. Two minutes? Three? She heard a pair of somber voices, Cristina's and that female detective's. Serafina's.

She threw open the door and there they were, strolling into the apartment living room. They both looked a little flushed from the heat and the walk up the stairs.

"Mother?" Cristina began, taking her hands in hers. "Are you all right?"

She nodded.

"You look scared."

"Was there someone in the hallway?" she asked her daughter.

"No," Cristina said. "There was no one anywhere."

"Did you see something?" Serafina asked in response. "Was there a reason you had the bedroom door closed?"

"A minute ago I thought someone was out there," Beatrice said, and she watched, fascinated, as the detective pulled from inside her jacket a square pistol.

"Stay with your mother," Serafina said to Cristina, and then she kicked off her heels and sprang into the hallway like a cat, leaving the two of them in Francesca's apartment.

"Maybe it was just you and Serafina opening the front door to the building," Beatrice said, but her daughter brought a finger to her mouth—actually pressing it lightly against her lips—and they stood there in absolute silence, listening, as the detective checked the corners and corridors on five floors of the building.

When she finally returned, Serafina said, "I didn't see anyone, but that doesn't mean you didn't hear something. I didn't knock on every apartment door. I may now. But there was no one else in the hallways or the stairwells. So tell me, what exactly did you hear?"

And Beatrice replied, her voice that of an old, old woman in her mind, "Nothing, really. I thought I heard footsteps. The floor-boards. I thought I saw a shadow. But it must have been nothing. Nothing but my imagination."

&

That afternoon Serafina emerged from the hospital through the side entrance, the one nearest the wing with the operating rooms, and walked down the long, shaded alley the ambulances used. When she finally emerged into the piazza, she was struck by the sunlight and the crowds. Over the past few summers she had noticed a marked increase in the number of tourists, as well as how likely she was now to hear French and English—the latter spoken with both British and American accents. The visit to the hospital had really been a waste, she decided, only corroborating what she had learned yesterday on the phone. Anyone could have taken the tools necessary to extract a human heart and anyone could have returned them. No one itemized bone saws and scalpels.

She slipped her sunglasses on as she crossed the cobblestones, the right earpiece balanced awkwardly on the deformed stub of cartilage, and thought about what Cristina had told her about the end of the war. She worked her way through the crowds and the pigeons and the great statues, most of them replicas, on her way back to the police station. The Nazi retreat, it was clear, had been an absolute cataclysm for the Rosati family. Cristina had a memory for dates, that was obvious, but it probably wasn't difficult for most people to recall the precise moment when they watched their older brother being tortured by Nazis or when their nephew stepped on a land mine.

Certainly Serafina knew the dates when her own mother and father and, later, her brothers had been killed. Likewise, she knew the date in between when she met the band of partisans in the woods and resolved to fight and die with them. She had been seventeen then, a cauldron of rage.

But there was a limit, it seemed, to what the mind could—or

would—absorb. She could recall so much from the week when she had seen the old granary in Monte Volta fall, but so little from the precise day. She knew the granary had been blown up the morning before the firefight at the villa. But everything that occurred on the afternoon when she was forever scarred? The brief, violent battle itself? The details of her fight for survival? Nary a clue until she woke up in the hospital bed and realized the physician looking down at her was a British soldier.

She told herself that when she got to the office, she would go over with Paolo the notes she had taken while with Cristina that morning. Perhaps he would see something she'd overlooked; perhaps she herself would find a connection that hadn't struck her as she had listened to Cristina because she'd been writing it all down—or at least writing down all that she could. She feared that she'd missed something, because there were so many parallels with her own story, and she could not help but see in her head the small memories her mind would offer as tantalizing, but—in the end—unsatisfying, glimpses of what may have occurred.

She guessed that tomorrow she would go to Rome to interview Cristina's surviving brother, Vittore. She might even take two days and visit the Rosati villa in Monte Volta. Maybe she would learn something from its ghosts.

Paolo leaned back in his chair behind his desk and blew a smoke ring out the open window beside him. "So, 1944. How long had the Germans been using the estate?" he asked his partner, Serafina.

"Almost since the Allies had reclaimed Rome. The Allies marched into the city on June 4. Cristina says within days the Germans had commandeered the villa. The officers were in the main house, and at least five or six dozen soldiers were billeted in tents on the grounds."

"Infantry?"

"No. Artillery. Big howitzers. Four of them. The Germans set them up on the hills facing south."

"And the family? Let me guess—they were ordered to sleep in the cattle barn."

"Not that bad," Serafina said. "But I guess they could have taken some bedding and gone there. The soldiers had butchered the last of the cattle, so there was plenty of room."

"Then where?"

"They were given the children's bedroom, the big nursery that Francesca's two children shared. All of them had to sleep there, including Antonio and Beatrice. They were squeezed like olives into the room."

"I am sure the marchese and marchesa loved that. Sleeping on the floor. I am sure Cristina was thrilled." Now he sat forward and took a pencil from a coffee cup and started writing down names. "Who was living in the villa at the time?"

"Well, the marchese and the marchesa, of course. Cristina. Francesca and her two children. So there were six of them, which isn't a lot of people, unless you are living with Nazis and have to share a single bedroom."

"Where were the brothers?"

"Vittore was still with the Germans here in Florence. At the Uffizi. And Marco, Francesca's husband, was with a lot of the Italian officers who had failed to hold Sicily the previous summer. He was more or less slave labor. He was building fortifications for the Germans and filling the holes in the roads from the Allied bombs."

"And the peasants who worked the estate?"

"First of all, there had never been a lot. At its largest, according to Beatrice, the estate had needed only a dozen farmhands, and they all lived in the village. Whoever was working on any given day would appear in a big truck or oxcart in the morning and leave at night. There were no tenant farms or tenant farmers."

"It wasn't like La Foce."

"No. It was nowhere near that large. And by the summer of 1944, all of the farmhands were gone. Either the Germans had pressed them into service or they stopped coming when the Nazi soldiers started pitching their tents. Besides, the animals had been slaughtered, and it was painfully clear there wasn't going to be a grape or olive harvest that year."

"And where were you?" Paolo smiled when he asked the question, but his eyes were dark and he stared at Serafina.

"In June, I was in the woods of Mount Amiata. But before the Germans occupied the estate, it sounds like other partisans went there and demanded food."

"But not Enrico's little band?"

"No."

"Were the Rosatis . . . supportive?"

"It doesn't sound like they were. They gave the groups food, but they probably didn't have a choice. The problem for the Rosatis was the problem for lots of landowners once the Germans controlled Italy: if the Nazis believed they were feeding the partisans, they might have killed them; but if the landowners didn't feed us, we might have killed them. You know that. It was chaos after Mussolini fell . . . and then it was anarchy once the Germans brought him back and propped him up."

"As I recall, some of you were actual anarchists," Paolo said, chuckling.

"Not my group."

"No. Not your group. Tell me, when was the battle for Monte Volta? I'm guessing the middle of July."

"It wasn't much of a battle, at least in the town. Mostly it was just a withdrawal. The Nazis blew up the granary, packed up their big cannons, and tried to head north. But the British were already behind them, and so some of them retreated back inside the Rosati estate, outside the village. Right about then, Marco reappeared."

"Deserted his work crew?"

"I guess that would be the term."

"So now there were the seven of them."

"Yes."

"And where were you in the middle of July?"

"And this matters . . . why?"

"Because you don't have a father or a mother to ask you these questions. You only have me."

She folded her arms across her chest. She thought of her dead brothers as well as her dead father and mother. The Nazis had executed her parents because her father had been Dino Grandi's assistant, and Grandi had led the coup against Mussolini in July 1943. Grandi had fled to Spain, however, the moment the Nazis had swooped in, and when they couldn't kill him, they had murdered her father and mother instead. Called them both traitors. And so she and her brothers had fled north from Rome, hoping to find safety with her aunt and uncle near Chianciano. Instead they had linked up with a small group of partisans led by a friend of a friend. The assemblage was mostly communists and miners, and the siblings hadn't planned on revealing that their father had once worked for Mussolini's minister of justice, a man who on occasion had been a fierce opponent of the political left. But one of her brothers had slipped and the truth had come out. Instead of killing them, however, Enrico had welcomed them. Deduced right away that they weren't Fascist spies. They were merely three young adults trying to stay alive, and generously he took them in. Was, in fact, grateful to have them. Besides, even if their father had not been innocent of Blackshirt crimes, he, like his boss, Dino Grandi, had grown disenchanted with Il Duce early in the war. He had always hated the Nazis, and now he had paid with his life.

Originally she and her brothers had stayed together among the partisans; her brothers hadn't wanted her out of their sight. Five months after they had joined the band, however, the Germans surrounded the group in a combing operation along Mount Amiata, and the women and men had scattered in all directions. And she had lost sight of them both. For three days she and two men had hidden in the shed of a tenant farmer on the farthest outskirts of La Foce, the estate owned by a marchese and his expatriate British wife. She had hoped—had, in fact, believed—that her brothers were still alive. On the fourth day, Enrico had found them and they had returned to their camp on the mountain. The day after that she had awoken, hungry and cold, to the news that her brothers were dead.

"So," Paolo asked her again. "July 1944."

She rolled her eyes and she answered, but only because he was her boss and she might as well humor him. "There was another villa, not the Villa Chimera, where we had been hiding for a few days that month. But it was not the Rosatis'. The villa we were using was near Trequanda."

"And you're positive you were not involved in the firefight?"

"I *was* involved in a firefight. You know that. Just not the one at the Villa Chimera."

"And your conversation with Cristina brought back nothing."

"Nothing," she repeated.

He snuffed out his cigarette in a marble ashtray that looked like a turtle. The shell was hinged so that he could open it when he was smoking but then shut it tight when he was done, concealing the cigarette butts. It was by far the most opulent object on his desk.

"Did Cristina recall the names of any of the Germans who occupied the villa?" he asked.

"Yes. She gave me the name of the captain. Muller."

"Any others?"

"A lieutenant named Bayer."

"Do we know what happened to Captain Muller or Lieutenant Bayer?"

"Cristina thinks they might have died in the fighting at the estate. But she doesn't know that for a fact. She never saw their bodies. Most of the Germans were killed or surrendered, but she's pretty sure that at least some of the soldiers fought their way out."

She saw that he had written down the names Muller and Bayer in a separate column from the Rosatis'. "Let's come back to Francesca. And motive. Did she do anything to anyone in that period that might have . . . angered someone?"

"She hated the Germans."

"A start. Maybe. Did Cristina mention anyone in particular—and anyone who might in return have hated Francesca?"

She nodded. "There were some men who worked with Vittore in the museum, and Francesca absolutely despised them."

"Go on."

"Two Germans and one Italian," Serafina said, glancing down at her own notes. "There was a colonel named Erhard Decher. He was an architect. There was an Italian major named Giancarlo Lorenzetti. He was an art historian."

"And the third?"

"Cristina said she didn't recall his name."

"But you doubt that, I can tell. You think she does."

"Maybe. I think she regretted saying there were three instead of two."

"And they worked together here in Florence."

"Yes. But they had been coming to the Villa Chimera since 1943—for a year, in other words."

"Because of Vittore?"

"And because of the ancient tombs on the property."

"Etruscan?"

"Yes."

"Did Francesca ever do anything to this Erhard Decher or this Giancarlo Lorenzetti?"

"Nothing, according to Cristina, that would have led them to cut out her heart eleven years later."

He had written down the names of the German colonel and the Italian major on his notepad, and he gazed at the columns before him. "That's the thing that makes Contucci question why this woman's murder could have anything to do with the war," he said, referring to Sergio Contucci, the prosecutor in charge of the case. "Me, too. I don't want to be dismissive of your idea, but why would the killer wait eleven years? If Francesca did something so horrible in 1944, why would the killer wait until 1955 to slash her throat?"

"Maybe he couldn't get to her sooner."

"Because he was incapacitated? Because he was in jail?"

"That's interesting—I didn't think of jail."

Paolo shrugged.

"But," she went on, "you see the possibility. Maybe he simply was elsewhere. Maybe he didn't know where Francesca was. Maybe he saw her in Florence or ran into her on the street and . . ."

"And decided to cut out her heart."

"Perhaps. Remember what the old woman on Francesca's floor said. Francesca had seen someone and wanted a more substantial lock."

"Well, I'm glad you're going to talk to Vittore. That will be helpful."

"But you think it's a waste of time to go to Monte Volta."

He sat forward. "I don't think it will be fruitful for this investigation. But I think you personally will find it very interesting. Will this be your first time back?"

"Yes."

"Well, then. Be careful."

"You're worried about my safety? No one's going to hurt me in Monte Volta."

"No, of course not. But your memories? Those could be daggers."

"I have no memories," she reminded him.

He flipped shut the shell on the turtle ashtray on his desk and stood. "Not yet," he said. "But you will."

ALL I NEEDED *was twenty minutes. But I heard the marchesa's daughter opening the building's front door three stories below me, and so I did not kill Beatrice Rosati that morning when she was alone at Francesca's apartment. I would have to wait to place her heart on the balustrade of a bridge along the Arno.*

But I am nothing if not patient. I had waited a long time for Francesca. I could wait another day for Beatrice.

So later that day I went to the Uffizi. I sat contentedly before Caravaggio's The Sacrifice of Isaac *and gazed at the way Abraham uses his left hand to hold his son's head down, pinning him. Abraham's hand is grasping the boy's neck from the rear, his thumb pressed into the child's cheek. In Abraham's right hand is the knife. And while there is a very great deal to be appreciated in the painting—how Isaac's skin is so much paler than his father's, the dark of the copse in which Abraham is about to slaughter the boy—what I love best is the utter terror on Isaac's face. His mouth is wide open and his eyes are dark and scared.*

And if I could not find Beatrice alone later that week in Florence?

I could wait.

Or I could go to Rome.

Or I could see if she was going to return at some point to Monte Volta—perhaps to bury her daughter-in-law. There would certainly be a moral rightness—an ethical bookending, if you will—to slaughtering a Rosati in Monte Volta. After all, that little village will always be the innermost ring of my own private inferno.

But I was invigorated by the idea of killing Beatrice now, while she was still here in Florence—of leaving her moldering heart on the bridge.

So, I said a small prayer before the Caravaggio. I prayed that I would have the opportunity to butcher the marchesa in this beautiful city, perhaps within blocks of where I had killed her dead son's loving wife.

1943

CRISTINA WAS JUST emerging from the swimming pool, fixing the skirt on her swimsuit where it had bunched up beneath the ribbon in the back, when she heard the car coasting to a stop in front of the villa. She tilted her head over the tile, took her hair in her hands as if it were a column of rope, and wrung the water from it. It puddled at her feet in the shape of a flower.

"Who is torturing us now?" she heard Francesca murmuring as her sister-in-law sat forward on the chaise. She was wearing a straw hat, movie-star sunglasses, and a pair of red slacks that were far too tight to be matronly. Massimo and Alessia were playing in the dry grass near the chimera, using both his lead soldiers and her cloth dolls. They had apparently concocted a game in which scale and historical authenticity were irrelevant: the dolls were at least three times the size of the soldiers.

"Is Father expecting someone?" Cristina asked. She was feeling a pang of nervousness, and the apprehension grew worse when she heard the sound of heavy boots crunching along the white stone path from the front of the house.

But her breath caught in her throat and she found herself reaching for a towel on one of the wrought iron chairs when she saw who it was. And then—emboldened in the same strange way she had been at the museum, first inviting Friedrich to join them in Arezzo and then sitting beside him at the café—she resisted that urge and stood perfectly still in her wet bathing suit, leaving the towel on the headpiece of the chair, as the German lieutenant limped with care along the uneven stones toward the pool. She had wondered in the bath just last night when she would see him again. She had heard his voice in her head when she had slipped beneath the water, and felt acutely the weightless tingling she had experienced when his left leg inadvertently had brushed against hers under the table. She was at once impressed with what she imagined was the bravery that had cost him his foot and the intellectual rigor that had led to a posting at the Uffizi. She had not dreamed of him—at least that she could recall—but she had thought of him in bed before falling asleep and immediately upon waking. She had thought of him as she had ridden Arabella that morning. And now here he was.

"I hope I'm not interrupting anything," he said, and he stopped walking only when he had reached her. Abruptly Francesca rose to her feet and strode over to them. She grabbed the towel Cristina had left on the chair and foisted it upon her young sister-in-law. Pushed it with unexpected urgency into her hands. A little defeated, Cristina wrapped it modestly around her waist; she knew if she didn't Francesca was likely to embarrass her.

"I was retrieving some paperwork and a painting in Siena," Friedrich continued, "and I realized how close I was to Vittore's home. And so I had my driver make a short detour. I thought perhaps I could see the Etruscan tombs that so dazzled Colonel Decher and Major Lorenzetti."

A sentence formed in Cristina's mind: *No,* she thought, *you have come to see me.* But because Francesca was beside them, radiating anger and protectiveness like a hot oven, she kept the words to herself.

"You're a resourceful soldier," she said instead, a quiver of nervousness in her voice that she hadn't expected.

"And a good student. I want to learn," he told her. His hands were clasped behind his back and his heels were together. His posture was so erect that she almost wanted to laugh, especially since his eyes were so incongruously playful. She decided that his officer's belt, wide and black and sinister on some men, looked more like part of a pretend uniform or costume on Friedrich.

"So you were ransacking a painting from Siena. You must be so proud," Francesca said to him, her voice acid. "Which picture?"

"One of Martini's. A minor work."

"There is no such thing as a minor work by Simone Martini. Did you pillage it from the Duomo?"

"It came from the gallery," he answered, offering her a small smile. "And it will be returned. It needs some restoration work, that's all."

"You must be parched after your drive," Cristina said to him. "What can we get you?"

"Water will be fine, thanks."

She recalled that he had preferred sparkling water when they were in Arezzo. "We don't have sparkling water here. Do you mind?"

"No, not at all," he said, laughing. "Really, I don't want to be an imposition."

"You're not," Cristina said. "I'd be happy to show you the tombs."

"Thank you. That's very gracious of you."

"But we will need candles," she went on, the giddiness in her voice surprising her. Given the reality that he had but one foot, she considered suggesting that he wait here by the pool while she retrieved the candles up at the house, but that would also mean leaving him at Francesca's mercy. And so she continued, "Come with me to the villa. I think you'll appreciate the view of Monte Volta. The granary towers, especially against the sort of sky we have today, look like something by Perugino."

"I don't know Perugino," Friedrich said, and he offered Cristina his arm. Despite Francesca's glare, she accepted it.

"You work at the Uffizi and you don't know Perugino?" her sister-in-law grumbled, shaking her head in disgust. "So this is what it has come to—we have Germans who don't know Perugino or Martini deciding what's art. What a brilliant use of resources. No wonder we're losing the war."

✠

At first they walked in absolute silence, and once they could no longer hear Massimo and Alessia splashing in the pool, the only sound Cristina was aware of was their feet—especially his odd tramp—as they walked along the olive grove. On the opposite hill she saw the teenage boy Ilario moving the sheep onto the western slope, and she waved. Ilario was one of the younger farmhands. He saw her, she knew that, but he pretended to ignore her and didn't wave back.

Initially she moved a little more slowly than usual to accommodate Friedrich's disability, but he seemed to walk at a spirited gait, as he had in Arezzo when they had gone to the café. He really had no trouble keeping up. The sun warmed her skin and she could not imagine the soldier was comfortable in that gray-green uniform with the cap and boots. She had donned a white linen blouse when they had gone to the villa for candles, and even that felt to her a bit like a quilt in this heat. Occasionally the cypress trees were bent ever so slightly by a breeze, and in those moments the jasmine became more pronounced and she inhaled the scent deeply.

Only as they were nearing the stone crevice that led to the vault did he break the silence. He told her that he did not believe how fortunate he was to have been transferred to Italy. As handsome as he found the landscape in his corner of Germany, nothing could compare to the countryside here. He said—and for a second she wasn't sure she heard him correctly—that he hoped peace came to Italy before the invading armies did. Before there was real damage. It was a comment that hinted at defeatism, something she never expected from a German officer.

And so she said, "But there already is real damage. I've seen Arezzo firsthand." She recalled the perfectly rectangular field of cadavers.

"I don't want to see your country endure what Russia has. Or Poland. I don't want it to become another battlefield."

"And you think it might?"

"If people don't come to their senses? I do. My mother used to get so frustrated with my father. He was a veteran from the earlier war. She used to tell him that if there was a peaceful way to an end or a violent one, people, especially Germans, would always choose the violent route. And that was years before this war began. Years!"

"You loved your mother very much, didn't you?"

"I did. But what makes you say that?"

"You've mentioned her twice in the two times we've been together."

"It's probably because you have the same name."

"And I look like her?"

He chuckled. "Not in the slightest," he said, and she was relieved. Francesca had once joked that weak men always tried to marry their mothers. Vittore had been present and had murmured in response, "Well, that means my brother must be very strong." It had been a small dig, but Francesca had let it go.

"What did she look like?" Cristina asked now.

"A bit like a wild boar," he said, his voice completely earnest. "A very pinched face, a long nose. A snout, really. And I hate to admit this, but I think she could have grown very thick whiskers if she had wanted."

"You're horrible!"

"Perhaps."

"And I know you're exaggerating."

"I am—ever so slightly. But yes, I loved her. Even if she was as homely as a fairy-tale creature. She might have resembled a boar, but she certainly didn't have a boar's temperament. She was sweet and loving and very, very smart. And I remember that she had a voice like an angel when she would read to me as a little boy."

"Is your father . . ."

"Homely?"

She nodded, laughed once.

"Odd-looking. A little feminine. But some women find him attractive. The older women and the younger widows who live near the museum all think he'd be quite a catch."

She focused on the word *widows*. "Are there that many?"

"Widows? Absolutely. I'm sure this village has seen its share of death."

She thought about this. Monte Volta had been fortunate. It was a town of perhaps eight hundred people, and she knew of only three families who had lost a husband or a son. Her mother had spent time with the grieving families because she felt a distinct noblesse oblige as the marchesa. But Cristina herself had been spared even this responsibility so far.

"The wounded and the maimed were everywhere when I was last home on leave. As common as children," he went on. Then, trying to lighten the mood, he added quickly, "I fit right in!"

She peeked down at his feet. The glance had been an impulse and she wished that she had been able to restrain herself, because he had noticed. He brought his fingers underneath her chin and gently lifted her face toward his. "It was a joke, because it doesn't bother me," he told her. "And I don't want it to bother you either. I mean that."

"All right," she said, her voice softer than she would have expected. Then she watched him close his eyes and lean into her, and so—much to her surprise—she found herself closing her eyes, too, and parting her lips for his.

The next day Friedrich ambled along the cobblestones beside the Arno and watched the crowd before him on the Ponte Vecchio. Though any moment now the Allies were likely to invade Sicily or the mainland itself, there was little panic in Florence. Food was growing scarce, but it had been all year. Fruit was getting hard to find, despite the season. So were most vegetables. A chicken demanded hundreds of lire, and a black market ham might go for a sterling silver place setting. But the wealthy and the Blackshirts and the Germans were still shopping (he, in fact, was shopping), and they were drinking their ersatz espresso in the cafés. They were sunning themselves in the city's great piazzas.

Nevertheless, despite the apparent normalcy he saw all around him in Florence, it took only a few moments of conversation to get a sense of the unease that flowed just below the surface here. Everyone was a little anxious, a little wary. A little hungry. Things could not continue as they were.

Now he stared into the window of the jewelry store on the bridge and wondered what sort of necklace would look best on Cristina. Against that spot on her collarbone where her slender neck started to slide into her chest. He gazed at the gold and silver, at the diamonds that he could not afford, and at the amethyst that he could. He saw a pair of delicate gold earrings that were shaped like bunches of grapes. In the midst of each was a green stone the size of a peppercorn. An emerald or a peridot. The earrings were small, and so, unlike a necklace, he might be able to afford them. A lot would depend on the jeweler and his feelings toward the Germans. He might loathe Friedrich on sight or he might see him as an ally. Or—perhaps his best hope if he wanted to leave the store with the jewelry—the owner might be frightened of him. Friedrich would prefer that he did not have to intimidate the fellow, but he was prepared to narrow his gaze and stand a little taller if he had to. He wanted those earrings.

It was interesting that Vittore thought he was such a child, when Vittore had never killed a man. Friedrich, of course, had. He had killed men and he had commanded men. He . . .

Quickly he cleared his mind of Vittore, literally shaking his head. The fellow had no interest in being his friend; that was fine. There was no reason to be angry right now.

Arguably, this whole errand was insane. He was buying a piece of jewelry for a woman he'd seen twice in his life and spent four hours with, total. But three of those hours were yesterday, when they had wandered alone around her family's estate and held candles up to the ancient paintings on the walls of a tomb. As, afterward, they had kissed for the first time, and then sat holding hands in the shade of a beech tree at the edge of the vineyard.

He ventured inside the store, the bell on the door tinkling like a wind chime, and he saw an old couple hunched over the counter with, Friedrich assumed, the owner. Friedrich guessed the jeweler was somewhere between his age and theirs. He was forty-five or fifty, a slight man with dark skin, wide ears, and thinning hair that was just starting to turn from black to white. All three of the Italians turned toward him when they heard the bell, and he knew instantly that he was going to be satisfied with whatever he took away with him when he left the shop. The jeweler and his customers seemed to think a hungry lion had just crossed the threshold, and they all shrank a little in stature at the mere sight of his German uniform. Still, he smiled at them, unblinking, and asked if he was interrupting. They seemed so intent on their transaction. As he shambled over to the counter, he understood why. The elderly couple was not buying something this morning; rather, they were trying to sell jewelry they owned. Their clothing—her floral print dress and shoes, his blazer and trousers—was tired and shabby. There were small tears in the seams of his jacket, and the hem on her dress was starting to sag. They were thin and gaunt and their skin had grown sallow. They needed food.

On a piece of felt on the counter he saw a string of pearls, a pair of diamond earrings, and a collection of silver bracelets that reminded him of the ones his mother had worn. She had been wearing them when she had left for the hospital for the last time, though not when she had come home. She had survived that final cancer surgery, but just barely, and then his father had brought her home to die. Most of the time she was either sleeping, thanks to the morphine, or in excruciating pain. Her last words to him? *Go. Just . . . go.* She was not quite conscious, and he was a boy on the cusp of adolescence. Her skin had grown pale as paper and looked to him a little like candle wax. Her bracelets were sitting on the nightstand like coasters.

"Can I help you?" It was the jeweler speaking to him. Already the fellow had whisked the old couple's jewelry off to the side of the counter.

Friedrich said he was interested in the earrings with the green stones in the window. He said he hoped they were peridots.

"Emeralds," the jeweler answered.

"That's a shame," Friedrich murmured, trying to affect a tone balanced perfectly between disappointment and subtle pressure. "I can't afford emeralds."

"But you want something green?" the old woman asked.

"I hadn't thought about it that specifically. I just liked the earrings."

She reached into a fraying velvet bag and pulled from it a slender gold necklace. At the center was a lustrous green stone. It was shaped like a rectangle, the corners tiered as if it were a miniature picture frame, and it must have been the size of the nail on his pinkie. The edges had a beveling that reminded him of the shapes on the pedestals he had seen in the tombs on the Rosati land, and of the bands of geometric shapes—specifically, two rows of *L*'s—that had bordered one of the images that remained on the tufa stone wall. It was even a little reminiscent of a necklace that had been painted onto one of the dancers he had glimpsed by candlelight in the ancient vault.

"It's an emerald, too," she said, as her husband looked away.

Instantly Friedrich could envision it around Cristina's neck, the stone against the skin on her chest. He could imagine the way it would accent her lovely gray eyes. But he also knew he couldn't afford it. There was a lot of gold and a lot of rock there. And so he said to the woman that it was beautiful, but it was even further beyond his means than those earrings.

She looked at him, studying him with her rheumy eyes. "How old are you?"

"Twenty-three."

"I would have guessed that. We have a grandson who is

twenty-two and a granddaughter who is twenty-four. They left Florence when they were teenagers—when our two sons moved to America."

"Are they in America now?"

The woman nodded. "They are all in New York City. Thank God. They left Italy in 1936."

Friedrich put his hand gently but firmly on her arm. He knew well that people—not only Vittore—often mistook his outward implacability for naïveté. He had used that perception to his advantage in the past, and he thought he might here. "Certainly they'll be safer there," he said, trying to smile sincerely. He thought again of the unsettling power of his uniform. "Your grandchildren, too." He took his fingers off the woman's arm and offered her husband his hand. "My name is Friedrich. Friedrich Strekker."

The old man hesitated ever so slightly, but then he accepted it. "Stefano," he said. "And this is my wife, Nicoletta."

The woman picked up the necklace, and Friedrich worried that she was going to place it back in the small bag. Instead, however, she held it out to him. "It's for your wife home in Germany, yes?" she asked him.

"No, it's not. It's for—" He broke off, unsure how he wanted to describe Cristina. And so he summarized their relationship as simply as he could. "I have an Italian associate at the Uffizi. And he has a younger sister. I was looking for something for her."

"You want to marry her?"

He laughed. "I barely know her."

"But she is pretty?"

"Oh, she is. She is very pretty."

"And you work at the museum?"

"I do."

"Tell me something."

"Go on."

"Have you ever done something you were ashamed of? Something you would be sure someday you would never, ever tell your daughter?"

"That's an odd question," he said, stalling, as he tried to guess at her agenda.

"But it's not a difficult one to answer, is it?" She raised her eyebrows.

"No," he said, and then he understood the hidden portent behind the inquiry. "I can tell you honestly, I've done my duty as a soldier in France and Greece and Russia. I have no regrets and no secrets."

She nodded, and then suggested a price for the necklace. Friedrich found himself shocked at how little she wanted. He wondered whether it was hunger that was driving the number or whether this woman was merely a romantic he had charmed. He decided it was probably a little of both and the proper response was to ask if she was serious.

Nicoletta said that she was and repeated the figure. "I may never be able to give it to my granddaughter. I may never be able to give it to my grandson to give to whatever girl he falls in love with. But if I sell it to you? I'll know at least that it helped to fire a romance."

And so Friedrich agreed to buy the piece on the spot. But he had a thought. "I imagine your ration cards aren't as helpful now as they were a few months ago," he began. "I, on the other hand, seem to have access to meat and potatoes and sometimes even real coffee. The problem? I don't have a kitchen where I'm billeted. And even if I had one, I really can't cook. But let me send something special your way."

"You don't need to do that."

"I want to. Give me your address. I want to thank you."

Stefano and the jeweler looked at each other as if this young German had lost his mind, but Nicoletta volunteered the name of the street where they lived, and Friedrich scribbled the address on a scrap of paper he found in his wallet.

"I am a man of my word," he told them. "I never forget a kindness—or a slight. I keep my promises. Keep your eyes out for a package."

He was about to place the necklace unceremoniously in his

tunic pocket when the jeweler motioned him over. The fellow reached into a drawer in the tall wooden cabinet behind him and pulled out a felt-covered box with a snap at the front. When he handed it to Friedrich, he said, "This is a fitting presentation for a necklace so lovely."

"Thank you."

"Take good care of that Italian girl," the jeweler said.

"I will."

"May your love survive many years," he added, a benediction of sorts.

Stefano glanced over at the jeweler and corrected him. "May it survive a single year," he advised. Then he shrugged. "May we all survive a single year. My wife is an optimist. She doesn't believe me when I tell her what's coming."

Just before dawn, Cristina tiptoed into the room the family still called the nursery, even though Massimo and Alessia were no longer toddlers. The children were both sound asleep in their beds, and Cristina knelt on the floor beside Alessia and kissed the girl on the cheek. The child's skin smelled of lavender soap. When she opened her eyes and saw in the dim light that her aunt was already in her riding clothes, she started to speak, but Cristina shushed her, smiling, and led her downstairs. The night before, Cristina had laid out an outfit for Alessia, and now she helped the sleepy girl climb into her jodhpurs and, it seemed to Cristina, impossibly small boots. Then together they walked down the hill through the damp grass to the barn where the estate's two remaining horses lived with the remnants of the Rosatis' herd of Chianina cattle. Ilario and one of the other farmhands had already walked the cattle out to the hillside above the estate's small pond for the day, so the barn was empty but for the horses: Arabella and her mother, Oriana.

As Cristina brushed the animal's back, Alessia said, "When the war's over, my papa is going to get me a pony."

"That's right," Cristina told her niece.

"And she is going to be all black. And her mane is going to be like silk."

Arabella was a light chestnut with long patches of white on her forehead and chest. Her mane was mostly cinnamon, but when the sun was right it seemed to have streaks of red. When she would first see Cristina for the day, her dark eyes would follow the young woman wherever she went in the barn. The marchese once joked that the horse was the sister Cristina never had. Arabella had been born on the estate when Cristina was ten, and the animal had been Cristina's since birth. Now she was tall and muscular, her back strong and smooth from withers to croup.

"She'll be as beautiful as Arabella," Alessia went on. "But she'll be even faster."

Cristina draped a blanket over the horse and then gently lowered the saddle onto the tall animal. "Arabella's very fast," she reminded her niece.

"I know," Alessia said, and then she reached down and handed Cristina the girth. "So we'll race. You and me and our horses."

"I accept your challenge."

Alessia leaned back against the side of the stall. Oriana stretched toward the girl, nuzzling her blouse to see if she had a piece of an apple or a sweet hidden in a pocket there. The child giggled and then kissed the horse on the nose. "Mama says you have a new friend," she said. "A German."

"I do."

"Is he handsome?"

"I think so."

"Mama doesn't like him."

Cristina rolled her eyes to herself. "Did your mother say why she doesn't like him?"

"No. But you know what else?"

"What?"

"When I get big, I will have a fast horse and a boyfriend. Just like you."

"Your mother says my new friend is a boyfriend?"

"Yes."

Cristina liked this idea and rolled the notion around in her mind. She and Friedrich had kissed, but did that make him her boyfriend? She wondered what impression they radiated to others when they were together.

Once Arabella was saddled, the horse turned toward Cristina and raised her long nose, flaring her nostrils ever so slightly, and snorted. The animal was indeed in the mood to run today, but the horse would have to wait. This was Alessia's morning first, and Cristina had no plans of letting go of the lead line. "Ready?" she asked her niece.

Alessia nodded, and Cristina hoisted her off the ground and into the saddle. Then she took the leather strap and slowly led the horse and the girl from the barn and out into the dawn. Maybe in an hour, when Alessia was tired of walking and the sun was higher, she would send the girl back to the villa and she and her horse could run a little wild. She thought again of what her sister-in-law had said about Friedrich and smiled.

Suddenly more groups of officers from both the Italian and the German armies were visiting the Villa Chimera to see the Etruscan tombs there, and the artifacts that had been removed from the site years ago and sent to Arezzo, where they had been gathering dust for half a decade, once more seemed to matter. The Germans wanted some of the relics in Berlin and some in Rome; the Italians wanted them to remain here in Tuscany. Though the particulars of the discussion were lost on Massimo and Alessia, even they understood that a veneer of glamour now coated the ancient crypt on the Rosati estate. It was Massimo who had suggested to his mother that today they have their picnic on the grass atop the site. Across the small ravine, amid the cypress, they could see the Rosati cemetery: the modest temple and the stone cross, the half circle of headstones around the marble walkway.

As he sat on the blanket between his mother and his aunt, the sun high overhead, Massimo scowled at his younger sister. She was wandering nearby, picking wildflowers for a bouquet. The family didn't have the largesse for a picnic they would have had even in the spring, but they had the very last strawberries of the season (which Beatrice had hidden from the army quartermaster when he came to requisition fruit), as well as a carafe of goat's milk they had not turned into cheese. Even this small feast, however, had made Cristina uncomfortable. When she had been in Monte Volta that morning, she had seen the village women standing in lines that stretched beyond the granary, hoping to get a cup of milk to divide among their children. The peasants had ration cards, but they were essentially useless.

"You look worried."

Cristina glanced up at Francesca. She hadn't realized that her anxiety was so obvious on her face.

"I was thinking of the milk lines in the village this morning."

"Milk lines are the least of your problems."

Massimo looked at his mother. She brushed a lock of hair off his forehead and away from his eyes. He brushed it right back, stood up, and wandered to the hill that banked away from the tombs. His sister put down her bouquet in the grass and went to join him. It looked like the children were inspecting the view.

"You were probably thinking of that German," Francesca continued.

"If I had been, I would have been smiling."

"See? That's why you should be worried."

"The other day you told Alessia he was my boyfriend."

"I was being polite. I could have chosen a different word. I could have chosen very different words for you both."

Abruptly the children threw themselves onto the ground and started rolling like spindles down the slope. Their laughter carried up and over the small hill.

"I think he's handsome—and sweet," Cristina said.

"He's trouble. He's a Nazi. Nothing more."

"I haven't discussed politics with him."

"You should. You'll see he has the same ridiculous opinions as the rest of the Germans. You'll see he hates Jews and Russians and—"

"I doubt that," she said. "He's not like that." Then, trying to change the subject, she asked, "Do you ever think it's ghoulish that we picnic beside a tomb?"

Francesca nodded. "All the time. When Alessia tells me her stories of the dancers on the walls coming to life in the night, I shudder."

In a moment they saw the children reappear, giggling. Alessia was moving unsteadily on her feet, still dizzy from her roll down the hill. Nevertheless, once again she fell into the grass beside Massimo and started spinning her way back to the bottom.

"I'm serious," Francesca warned her sister-in-law now. "Steer clear of that soldier."

Cristina shook her head, a little exasperated. "I doubt anything will ever come of it," she said, but she didn't mean it. She hoped very much that something would come of their flirtation. She thought of what it had been like to be inside the burial chambers beside him, whispering, the shadows from the candle flickering against those strong cheekbones and beautiful eyes. At one point they had stood side by side and stared at a pair of nudes on the wall—dancers, a male and a female—and almost as one they had brought their candles near the image. Never before had she thought the painting was in the slightest way erotic, but that changed when she gazed upon it with Friedrich. She had been planning to highlight for him the necklace the female was wearing, but their fingers and candles had touched and a little hot wax had dripped onto her wrist. She had gasped, but the sensation had been filled with as much pleasure as pain.

"He will return, you know," Francesca said.

Cristina rose to her feet and brushed the grass off her thighs. She could abide Francesca's wariness no longer. "I hope he does," she replied, a small purr rippling through her voice. Then she went to watch her nephew and niece play on the hill.

FROM THEIR HOTEL *room window, the marchesa watches her daughter sling her purse over her shoulder and then adjust her sunglasses against the morning sun. From across the street, I can see them both. Lucky me. Framed by the open window, she follows Cristina with her eyes until the young woman is around the corner and—forgive my conjecture—she is wishing she were younger. Less done in by the last decade and change—by her daughter-in-law's death now. I imagine Beatrice had wanted to accompany Cristina when she met with the nuns who were going to distribute Francesca's earthly belongings to the poor. But even getting dressed this morning had been a chore. Exhausting. She needs to rest before she and Cristina finish emptying out Francesca's apartment on the Via Zara in the afternoon. The two of them are planning to leave Florence tomorrow.*

So envision what I am about to tell you. (I do. I recall it often.)

Once more Beatrice is wearing a black skirt she deems suitable for mourning, but she is still in her stocking feet. Perhaps she had thought that she might lie down and read a book until her daughter returned. (She is not going to read the newspaper, I assure you—not with an article somewhere inside it on the fiend who ripped out Francesca Rosati's heart and left it resting in an ashtray.) But first she decides she will venture down the corridor to the water closet.

Which brought her to me.

I am alone in the hallway when she emerges from the bathroom, my valise by my feet on the black-and-gold carpet. She almost walks right past me. Oh, she sees me, but don't forget, this is a marchesa. Not quite a princess, but well above a countess. She presumes she is meeting only another guest of the hotel, and why would she deign to acknowledge some stranger in the hallway of a hotel that is, in her opinion, beneath her station? But then the veil rises from her eyes and she remembers. She remembers it all, she remembers me. At least she thinks she does. After all, it has been a long time. So I allow her a moment of recognition: long enough for the taste of the madeleines to return to her mouth, but not long enough for her to cry out.

Honestly, I am not even sure that she saw the jagged edge of the blade as more than a blur. I yanked back her head by her hair, exposing her still-slender, still-regal neck, and ran the knife hard and fast from one hinge of her jaw to the other. Then I dragged her back into her hotel room, left her to finish bleeding out on the floor by the bed while I retrieved my bag with my tools.

I had brought with me a wooden box for the heart, the sort in which a man might stash a wristwatch and a pen and some change, but when I was removing the bone saw I noticed that the mother and daughter had retrieved from Francesca's apartment the whore's red velvet jewelry box. Once I had removed the top shelf for earrings, the heart would rest nicely, snugly, inside it.

And how perfect: later that day some tourists would spy the box on the balustrade of the bridge by the Uffizi, open it up, and discover Beatrice Rosati's heart.

Though of course they would not know at the time that the heart belonged to the first victim's mother-in-law. They might not even be sure it was human. They would simply take the box with the heart to the police. And the police would know now that this was a vendetta against the Rosati family. This was not about Francesca Rosati's present, sordid and squalid as that was; it was about her—and her family's—past. And so they would warn Cristina and Vittore, they would protect them.

Fine. They would not be able to protect them forever.

Or even, I suspected, for very long.

1955

ON HER WAY to Rome, Serafina detoured first to Monte Volta. It was about a third of the way to the city, an hour and a half south of Florence, and her plan was to spend today there and then tonight drive the rest of the way into Rome. Tomorrow morning she would talk to Vittore. She recalled Paolo's gentle admonition that this return might undermine the psychological dam she had built between before and after, and cause whatever memories she was living comfortably without to flood back. Milton had offered a similar caution. Paolo said he had even considered going to southern Tuscany and then Rome himself, so she wouldn't have to. But she had insisted that she would be fine, and Paolo had to admit, Serafina had never in her life been uncomfortable with violence and trauma and, this week, a killer whose idiosyncrasies tended toward gruesome.

And so now here she was in Monte Volta.

In another life, she thought.

In another life . . . what?

She had parked Milton's BMW on the eastern side of the village and immediately walked the length of the small town. Since she was going to see no one today from Homicide, she was wearing flats, and she was glad. Tomorrow, in Rome, she would wear less sensible shoes. The walk took barely ten minutes. The village was largely unchanged from the place she remembered: one long street, barely wide enough for two cars to pass side by side, and a series of

even narrower ones winding their way up to the oldest neighborhood. The granary sat at the southwestern edge, its one remaining
tower rearing up today against a cerulean-blue sky. A black kite
was nesting along the chess piece–like masonry at the top, and for
a moment she watched the bird circle, gliding on the high currents
of wind, before abruptly plunging at its prey in the field beside
the massive obelisk. Because the village had neither a duomo nor
a museum, tourists from America and northern Europe had yet
to discover Monte Volta the way they had some of the larger vil-
lages in southern Tuscany. Places like Pienza and Montepulciano.
The main street had a police station, a butcher shop, a bakery, and
two small cafés at one end and an unassuming school at the other.
There was a pharmacy, a barbershop, and a small grocery smack
in the middle. The main church existed up a slender street that
wound its way to the highest point in the village.

Although she had called ahead, she checked in at the police
station. The officer on duty couldn't have been more than twenty-
two or twenty-three; he was slender, and his uniform hung badly
off his shoulders. The poor kid was still fighting a losing battle
with acne along his cheeks and neck. He was from Pienza and
knew virtually nothing about the Rosatis. One time that spring
he had wandered among the ruins of their estate, but it was only
because it was a sunny day and he had had nothing else to do. He'd
never met any of the family.

Outside, Serafina saw an old woman sweeping the front steps
to her home and asked her what she recalled of the war, and the
woman immediately told the story of how the Nazis had tried and
failed to blow up the remaining granary tower.

"Did you know the Rosatis?" Serafina asked her. "The marchese and marchesa?"

"No. But I knew people who worked their land. My nephew
was one of their farmhands," she answered. Then she told Serafina
about the overseer of the olive grove, now dead, and the fellow
who had managed their vineyard, now employed by wine growers
in Montalcino. She put her hands atop the handle of the broom,

not precisely leaning upon it but resting, and said, "My nephew works at the terra-cotta factory."

"In Petroio? I passed it on the way here."

"That's the one. You should talk to him."

"He knows something?"

"He might. He's married now, of course. But as a boy, he had such a crush on that girl."

"That girl? Francesca? Cristina?"

She nodded ruefully. "The younger one. The pretty one. Cristina—the one who slept with the Germans."

⚜

Before leaving the village, Serafina spoke with a pair of old men sipping espresso in one of the cafés, as well as the pharmacist, the butcher, and a young mother pushing her baby in a stroller. None of them could add anything to what the first woman had told her of Cristina—or, to be precise, what that woman had alleged of Cristina—but the butcher admitted that some people had certainly been jealous of the Rosatis' wealth. One of the old men she interviewed said there was a necropolis on the property but all of the artifacts had been confiscated by the Nazis; then his friend corrected him, insisting that the relics were given by the family to the museum in Arezzo long before the war, and there were far too few tombs to call it a necropolis anyway. They bickered until Serafina thanked them and moved on.

Finally there was the pharmacist. He sucked in deeply on his cigarette and said that he most certainly remembered Francesca: she had a fierce, wonderful tongue, he recalled. He wasn't surprised that a marchese's son had fallen in love with her; he said he thought she was the most interesting woman ever to walk the grounds of the estate. She actually belonged in a villa named after a beast that breathed fire.

"You liked her?"

"I did," he said ruefully. "I really did."

"Can you think of a reason why someone might have killed

her?" she pressed him. "Can you think of anyone who hated her enough to murder her?"

"No," he said, shaking his head. "Especially after what people say she went through. They say her husband died right in front of her eyes—in her arms. Marco, right?"

"Right."

"And of course Francesca outlived her children. Was it three?"

"Two. A boy and a girl."

He nodded. "They say she was at the villa when the children were killed in the fighting."

"It was after the fighting," she corrected him. "A land mine the Nazis had left behind."

"That's awful."

"It was," she agreed. "Did you know Marco?"

"I would have recognized him on the street. But he wouldn't have known me."

"So you can't think of any reason why someone would have wanted to kill her."

"No. Her family, maybe. But not her."

"What do you mean, 'her family'?"

"Well, the Blackshirts and the Nazis looked favorably upon the Rosatis. Obviously, that didn't sit well with some people."

"As I understand it, the Nazis commandeered the estate," Serafina said.

He shrugged. "Commandeered it? Or were they welcomed? When a lot of people were hungry in the war, the Rosatis seemed to want for nothing."

"Were they that close to the Fascists?"

"There were plenty of stories. And there were Nazis at the villa all the time in 1943 and 1944. The staff cars were always coming and going."

She thought about what the old woman had alleged of Cristina. "What do you remember about the youngest of the marchese's children? Cristina?"

He smiled a little wistfully. "She was such a young beauty."

"She still is. How well did you know her?"

"I knew her better than Marco, because she would come into the shop as a little girl and then as a teenager. She was always with her mother or the cook or, later on, with Francesca."

"What else?"

"There is no what else."

"And Vittore? The middle child?"

"A bookish boy. A bookish man. A scholar of some sort."

"An archeologist."

"Where are they now? Vittore and Cristina?"

"In Rome."

He sighed. "It's a shame to see the villa in such disrepair. If they can't afford to live there, they should sell it. Someone should fix it up. Maybe those Americans who are always coming to see Pienza. The tourists."

"I gather repairing it would be an expensive proposition."

"It would be," he said.

The bell on the door behind them tinkled as a customer strolled in: another young mother, a little boy in shorts holding her hand. The pharmacist snuffed out his cigarette and turned to the woman, and so Serafina thanked him and left. She thought she would head up to the Villa Chimera; she wanted to wander around the grounds of the estate and still have time to interview the fellow at the terracotta factory before it closed for siesta.

Milton's BMW groaned as it bounced its way up the twisting gravel driveway to the villa, and Serafina parked at a pull-off fifty meters from the main house and walked the rest of the way. The weeds were rampant and rose through the white rocks like wheat. Likewise, the lavender along the walkway to the villa was so overgrown that a person could barely see the stones. A tortoiseshell cat, rangy and feral, leapt through a broken window along the first floor of the once proud estate and raced down the hill toward the Tarantine marble hole that had been the swimming pool.

The front door was long gone and so she walked right in. Immediately the two pigeons that had been perched on a high shelf in the foyer dove through the entryway, nearly hitting her head on their way past, and flew up into the blue sky. They could, however, have escaped from the house even more easily through the enormous hole in the roof. She found the smell of cat urine almost overwhelming; clearly that tortoiseshell did not live here alone. She wondered how the birds and the cats cohabited in this shell of a house, and presumed the birds took the high ground and that was that. There was bird shit, some of it calcified, along the kitchen counter beneath a rafter and on the stone windowsills.

As Cristina had told her, most of the furniture was gone. Anything left inside the villa was broken and worthless. Still, she found a massive two-legged dining room table at roughly a forty-five-degree angle and a great pile of brown rags in the shadows. After a moment, she realized that once they had been white linen napkins and a tablecloth. There were colorful pieces of broken glass all along the floor in the kitchen and the pantry. Murano glass, she suspected. Wine goblets, based on what looked like a pair of stems. Two sconces dangled by their electrical wiring along one wall, and on the wall opposite them she saw two holes where another pair had been ripped out.

She walked around the corner into what she expected would be a living room or conservatory and was instantly bathed in sunlight: the exterior wall, all the way to the second floor ceiling, was gone. The fissure was easily eighteen to twenty feet high and perhaps a dozen feet wide. The sides were charred black. There was a small pile of rubble she navigated carefully, and once outdoors, she saw a much larger mound of debris shoveled to the side.

From here she could observe the olive grove, which was the same riot of growth as all the gardens and grass on the estate, and what she guessed were the rolling hills on which the sheep and the cattle had once grazed. Where Cristina had ridden her horse. In the far distance, she noted Mount Amiata. Much closer, no more than three kilometers distant, she could see the village of Monte

Volta and that hulking, iconic granary tower. The town was separated from the Villa Chimera by a deep valley. She walked farther into the grass and sat down, breathing in the aroma of the wildflowers and yellow broom. She stretched out her legs, and her mind moved back and forth between the stories Cristina had told her of Francesca's children at play in that swimming pool and what she herself had experienced somewhere near here. Based on the vista and the angle of the granary, she guessed the villa where they had fought and where she had nearly been killed was a few kilometers to the west.

It couldn't possibly have been here, she tried to assure herself. The views of the granary and the village were all wrong.

She sighed. She tried to recall what her mother and father had sounded like and she couldn't. She tried to recall either of her brothers' voices and those were gone, too.

Instead she heard in her head the imagined laughter of Francesca's little boy and little girl as they amused themselves in that swimming pool. Massimo. Alessia. Cristina had told her that she used to make doll clothing for Alessia and they played together with the dolls on the tile and the chaise longues beside the water. But that vision wouldn't linger either. Her mind kept roaming back to the sounds of the British rifle she had used throughout the summer of 1944; she felt once again the bruising, painful thud against her shoulder each time she fired it. It was either pathetic or grotesque, but while Cristina was playing dolls with her niece by that swimming pool, she was shooting German engineers at railheads or taking an ax to railroad ties. Her first assignment, in the late autumn of 1943, had been to slice the tires of Wehrmacht staff cars parked at an estate outside Pienza and cut the phone lines she found extending from the villa. A month after that she had helped ambush a trio of particularly despicable SS officers and their three guards when they were dining at a restaurant in Radicofani. In response the Germans had rounded up and executed thirty-six men, women, and children from the village—six Italians for each German who had been killed. They had lined them up against the eastern wall of the church and emptied half a dozen machine guns into them. It was more or less what Enrico and Salvatore had hoped would occur: the SS officers would be dead and the Nazis would respond in a brutal, draconian fashion. Then, the two brothers expected, the area villagers would rise up against their occupiers. Instead, however, the Tuscans had remained sheep after the slaughter; their partisan band had actually lost volunteers. Five members defected, no longer trusting Enrico's judgment, and went home. She, of course, had stayed. She had no home to return to. Besides, Enrico and Teresa and Salvatore were her family now. The Tarantolas. The miners and winemakers and a couple of renegades from the Italian army. A few girlfriends. A sister. A wife. At the group's largest, there were forty of them. By the time she was nearly killed, they had scattered into detachments of five and six.

Now she stared up into the cloudless sky, wishing she had brought her cola here from the car, and licked her lips against her thirst.

Mostly she had killed Germans in the war. But not entirely. Though she had never executed a collaborator, she had shot other Italians in one violent battle with a group of Blackshirts as the Fascists had retreated north with the Nazis in the summer of 1944. That would have been eleven years ago now.

And then there had been the brief, vicious skirmish not far from this very villa. It was an incendiary grenade that had almost killed her.

She closed her eyes and tried desperately to swim through the mist that enveloped her memories. She was near here and then she wasn't. She was whole and then she was wounded. Forever scarred. And in between? Unknowable, it seemed. Absolutely unknowable.

A few years ago she had had a lover who was a physician, and he had examined the ruin that was the flesh on her back and neck and the side of her head and wondered how she had endured the pain when she had first been burned. He had guessed a lot of morphine. He'd told her it was possible the phosphorous had continued to smolder hours afterward. *Imagine,* he'd remarked, almost talking to himself, *white smoke wafting into the air from your shoulder and side like a campfire the next morning.* He'd made a bad joke that he would have begged someone to shoot him. He had no idea that she had. Once, when they were making love, he had noticed the small, recent burn marks dotting the insides of her thighs. Each was the size of a match head. She had tried to convince him they were bug bites. He had begged her to stop.

In 1952 she had made an attempt to find Enrico, hoping he would tell her precisely what had happened. Aside from her, Enrico and Salvatore were the only members of their small brigade who hadn't bothered with fake names. Even Enrico's wife had made one up. They did this so that if they were ever captured, they couldn't give the Germans real names and thus endanger real families. Neither she nor Enrico and his brother had any family, so it didn't matter. And so it would not be until after that last firefight, when she woke up from whatever stupor had engulfed her—protected her, really—that she would change her name. Serafina. The burning one. Her new identity. It was and would be forever who she was. What she was.

She never did find Enrico. Even with the resources of the police at her disposal, she was unable to track him down. In all likelihood he had died in 1944 or 1945. Or perhaps he and Teresa had survived and moved to America. He'd sometimes fantasized about moving to New York City. Actually talked about the Statue of Liberty, which, like many Tuscans, he considered to have been inspired by Pio Fedi's memorial for Giovanni Battista Niccolini in Santa Croce. Thought Fedi should have gotten more credit. Either way, dead or alive, Enrico and Teresa were gone.

She opened her eyes and focused on the granary tower. Its collapse, she feared, was forever going to be the last thing she would recall from that day.

🜍

Before leaving the estate, she went down the hill to try to find the tombs, following the directions Cristina had given her. She walked gingerly along the prickly tufa. She passed the remnants of the grape arbors and then, as Cristina had instructed, turned to the left and felt as if she were descending into the earth. She worried briefly that she had made a mistake, especially when the ground had risen up around her on both sides and the crevice grew narrow. But then she arrived, almost suddenly, at the cul-de-sac. She counted four arched doorways and randomly selected one. She passed the remnants of the three columns, ducked her head, and went inside.

And swore. Her purse was back in Milton's car, and that meant she had no matches to really see the burial chambers—or whatever was left of the chambers. The paintings on the walls of the dancers and musicians she'd been told about. The images of the fruit trees. Inside, it was not quite as cold as a cave, but the air was markedly cooler than it had been a dozen feet behind her. Here was a small world never to be warmed by the sun.

She felt before her as she moved in the dark because Cristina had warned her that the pedestals for the funerary urns in the first rooms were still present, as were the platforms for the sarcophagi, and she didn't want to trip over them in the dark or crack her shins against them. In a moment she found one of the pedestals, touching it first with the toe of her shoe and then with her fingers, and sat down, staring back through the blackness at the window of daylight. If she breathed in deeply through her nose, she could smell faint vestiges of the ground above her—field grass and wildflowers—but mostly she smelled mold and dampness and something vaguely fetid. She thought of the corpses she had seen at the morgue and the odor of the polluted wounds from the war. The smell of her own back and skull as subcutaneous flesh fought infection and tried desperately to heal in that summer of 1944.

This odor was reminiscent of that, but also of something else. Something distantly familiar but nevertheless, like so much else in her life, unreachable.

One of the older partisans, a fellow who might have been forty (which, when she had been seventeen and eighteen years old, had seemed downright geriatric; no more), had managed a vineyard and talked often about the flavors of wine. Wines, in his vocabulary, could have hints of blackcurrant or burned toast, of green olive or aged oak. Of spices and fruit trees and resins. Everything had an association.

Finally she rose and started back to the villa, frustrated with herself for having left her purse in the car.

The old woman's nephew was named Ilario, and he was muscular and short and his black mustache was thick. He sat beside her in one of the wooden chairs the factory workers had placed in a copse of chestnut and fir trees. He explained that when they didn't go home for siesta, some of the men would come to these chairs and sit and smoke in the shade. He said he was married, which she already knew, but he volunteered proudly that he was going to become a father for the first time that autumn. Serafina had guessed he was twenty-eight, and she was close. He said he had just turned twenty-seven.

"So why has a detective come all the way from Florence to talk to me? Should I be scared?" he asked, the otherwise casual remark made toxic by the flippancy of his tone.

"Unless you've done something wrong, I doubt it."

He smirked a little lecherously and looked down at her legs. "You haven't had a baby yet," he said. "A man can tell."

"Have you heard about Francesca Rosati?" she asked, ignoring him.

"I heard just this morning. People were talking about it when I got to work. No baby?"

"No baby. How well did you know Francesca?"

He was wearing a sleeveless T-shirt and pretended to rub at his biceps. In fact he was flexing it, showing it off. "I knew her. Not well. I didn't have time for the likes of her. I had a job to do at the Villa Chimera. Many jobs, in fact. But mostly I helped manage their sheep and their cattle. Me and an idiot Sardinian twice my age. I was only a teenager, you know. But still, I had real responsibility."

"What do you mean by 'the likes of her'?"

He looked Serafina in the eyes and said, "They said someone cut her throat and then cut out her heart. At least that was what people said was in the newspaper. Is that true?"

"It is."

"Well, then, it was only a matter of time. She was . . . Oh, you're a lady. A lady with a gun, maybe. But look at your dress, your shoes. I can tell you don't use the word I would use to describe Francesca."

"Try me."

He shook his head. "I will say only this—she saw people as toys. Especially men. She thought she was better than all of us."

"She wasn't a good wife?"

He smiled and spread out his arms, palms up. "You misunderstand me. I presume she was a fine wife. What other man would have touched her? She was—forgive me—a bitch." He said the word almost innocently. "Whoever killed her did it because she deserved it."

"She deserved to be killed? You honestly believe that?"

"Okay, not killed. I give you that. But she was a bully. She bullied her family, she bullied men, she bullied me."

"How?"

"She treated us all like donkeys. We were the brutes who did the heavy lifting and the farming and the milking and the pruning and the cutting. Never said a kind word. Never treated us like men. We were all donkeys to her, that's all."

"Did the other farmhands dislike her as much as you?"

"I think so. We all made fun of her."

"Anyone hate her enough to kill her?"

"I'm sure someone did. Frankly, I was not especially fond of the marchese or the marchesa either. I worked for that family because I had to. But I didn't really like any of them."

Serafina thought of what Ilario's aunt had told her about him.

"What about Cristina? The marchese's only daughter? Did you hate her, too?"

He raised his eyebrows and then looked into the trees. "She was a traitor. And before that she was a—" He stopped midsentence.

"Your aunt said you had a crush on her."

"My aunt said that?"

"Yes."

He smirked. "Well, I did. I was stupid. Cristina Rosati was nice to me, but she was really just a . . . a tease. I am using that word because you're a lady. But she was much worse than a tease."

"She led you on?"

"She led us all on. Prancing about in a bathing suit with Francesca's daughter like she was just an innocent five- or six-year-old, too. Wearing dresses that always caught the wind just right to show off her legs. Riding around in tight pants on that horse. She would sometimes bring us carafes of lemonade. How could I not have a crush on her? I was young and, yes, stupid. But she showed us her true colors. She showed us all her true colors. She started sleeping with a German. And not just any German. One of those spineless thieves who stole from the museums."

"Do you recall his name?"

He sat back and took a breath. "Friedrich Strekker. He was a lieutenant. And a cripple."

"What do you mean, he was a cripple?"

"The fellow was missing a foot."

"And you know he was her lover."

"I do."

"How?"

"A man can tell."

She stared at him, meeting his eyes. "Do I have a lover?"

"No," he answered. "But you want people to think you do."

Behind them, she heard the wide garage door opening, the signal that siesta was beginning and the other workers were about to descend upon them.

"Seriously, can you think of someone who might have had

such a deep grudge against Francesca that he was willing to kill her?"

"She dishonored men. She and Cristina both. If I'm surprised by anything, it's that whoever killed the woman waited so long to cut her throat."

"Okay, then, Ilario. Tell me one more thing. Where were you on Monday night?"

"Is that the night Francesca died?"

She watched a squirrel scramble up the trunk of one of the chestnut trees. "Technically, it was the early hours of Tuesday morning."

He nodded. "I was home in Monte Volta with my beautiful wife, Detective. You can ask her. I promise you, as much as I hated that woman, it wasn't worth the cost of a train ticket to Florence to kill her."

Serafina used the telephone in a small restaurant on the outskirts of Orvieto to check in with Paolo in Florence. It was between lunch and dinner and so the restaurant was closed, but she showed the chef her badge and he let her inside and allowed her to call from the owner's small office.

She really wasn't quite sure whether she had learned anything of value in Monte Volta, but a notion was starting to form in her mind. If Francesca's murder did have something to do with the end of the war, then perhaps Cristina was in danger now. It was, however, just a vague concept, founded on the misogyny of one terra-cotta factory hand and the possibility that the Rosatis may have been more allied with the Germans than Cristina or Beatrice had told them.

She was just starting to outline for Paolo what she had learned when he cut her off. "It's not a wild idea at all that Francesca was murdered because of something that occurred a decade ago. It is, in fact, a very logical assumption," he said.

She could tell from his measured tone that something had happened. "Go on," she said.

He cleared his throat. Then: "About ten-thirty this morning, Cristina found the marchesa dead in their hotel room. And about an hour ago, some American found a human heart in a jewelry box on the Ponte Vecchio."

"God . . . ," she said, her own heart sinking.

"I know."

"How is Cristina?"

"Not as hysterical as you might expect from a woman who has found two dead relatives in a couple of days with their hearts cut from their chests. Mostly she's in shock. Morose."

"Scared?"

She heard him lighting a cigarette, sucking in deeply on the first draw. "I don't believe she fully comprehends that she might be next."

"Or Vittore," she said.

"That's right. Or Vittore."

"Remind me—how did their father die?"

He paused. "Are you thinking that perhaps it wasn't of natural causes?"

"I think we have to wonder about that now."

"I'll find out."

"I assume Vittore's on his way to Florence."

"He is. No need for you to continue on to Rome. You should just come back here yourself."

"Okay. I'll be back by six or six-thirty tonight, unless I'm behind a slow-moving tractor. I'll meet you at the station."

"Good. I want to hear all about Monte Volta."

After she hung up, she put her head into the kitchen to see if the chef was there so she could thank him. He was slicing chanterelle mushrooms when she walked in, and she paused. The aroma was taking her back to the Etruscan tombs. That was precisely what she had been breathing back there in the dark. Mushrooms.

And she hated mushrooms. Hadn't been able to abide them since the war. Since the time she had nearly been killed. When she was healing, someone had tried to feed her some and she had recoiled at the stench. Almost vomited. Now, as she inhaled their smell in the kitchen, it was once again 1944.

She realized she was going to be late for her meeting with Paolo. She was going to return to the Villa Chimera on her way back to Florence.

SO, CRISTINA. VITTORE.

And Vittore's family. He had a lovely wife: Giulia. They had a pair of adorable girls, one who was four and one who was not quite two—a toddler.

My work was more complicated now that even the feebleminded knew that a Rosati was next. But as I said, how long could the police protect them? A week? A month? Not years.

In my mind, this would not be five separate executions. It would be two or three moments of operatic grandeur. First I would exact my revenge on Vittore's family, but not on Vittore. In one evening I would still—and extract—three beating hearts: Giulia's and the two children's. Was three at a time gluttonous? Unseemly? Arguably. It did suggest binge butchering. But it also had a logic to it, because then, separately, I would kill Vittore and, finally, Cristina. The last of the Monte Volta Rosatis.

But I did fantasize one other possibility: a single bacchanal on the grounds of the villa when the clan's survivors buried Francesca and the marchesa. My instincts, however, told me it was unlikely I would have that opportunity.

Besides, that funeral was only days distant. And when I was done? After I had finished my work?

After that, nothing. At least nothing of consequence. I would have completed my labors, handled my business with integrity, been—and I was thinking this way—an avenging, albeit evenhanded, angel. Character is fortune, and their characters had started this bloodbath. I was only the instrument of retribution, and a rather blunt one at that. Think bone saw.

And so completion meant also that I would have absolutely nothing to look forward to, nothing to . . . anticipate. (And make no mistake: I had relished murdering Francesca and Beatrice and spreading wide their ribs.)

I would, alas, merely grow old and bored, waiting to die myself.

1943

SHORTLY BEFORE MIDNIGHT, Colonel Erhard Decher stood in his T-shirt and underwear in the hotel room where he was billeted, staring aimlessly at the pile of Italian books on his dresser, which he could barely read, and wishing that he were anywhere but here. His responsibilities were somewhere between ludicrous and degrading. While the armies of the Reich were fighting for their lives in Russia or preparing to defend themselves against numerous assaults in the west, he was supposed to track down Etruscan art and send what he found to Berlin or Rome. Satisfy the artistic eccentricities of the Gestapo in the Eternal City. It was appalling. He understood well that he should view himself as fortunate; all he had to do was watch Friedrich limp to know how lucky he was. But he still felt unmanned. He had never been a soldier and certainly hadn't expected a soldier's posting when he had been recruited. He was, he was told, needed because he was an architect and had valuable knowledge of architectural history. Yes, he did. And so how he had wound up in the Uffizi and what he was doing in a world of Etruscan pottery was beyond him.

And he hated the climate here. He found the heat oppressive and the stench from the Arno unbearable. Had there ever been a river that smelled this rank? He'd overheard another German remarking that some afternoons it reminded him of an enormous slit trench that an army had used one day too long. Often he found himself wondering, *What is the Ahnenerbe thinking? We couldn't possibly be descended from people like this.* In his armoire he had a pair of the new tropical-weight uniforms the Wehrmacht now offered soldiers in southern Europe—they were made of cotton and had an open collar—and he decided that one of these days he was going to have to break down and wear them. So far he had resisted, however, because the uniform might signal to other soldiers just how new he was to the army.

Now he took one of the books from the dresser and thumbed through the illustrations of pottery. He studied the profiles of strange doglike animals and nude dancers in block silhouette. There were serpents. There were lions. There were swastikas. According to eyes more learned than his when it came to this sort of thing, the lettering and orientalizing resembled the artwork on relics left behind two millennia ago by the tribes to the north. He'd been given reams of paper to read by the Ahnenerbe about the ancient peoples of India and Scandinavia, the differing theories about the earliest true Aryans. But Italians? Please. He realized he hated Italians. They were almost as bad as the Slavs and the Jews.

Outside his window he heard a clap of thunder in the distance. At least he hoped it was thunder. Conceivably, it was the start of an air raid. Or partisan sabotage in the northern section of the city. If it was the latter, those idiots would have to know what they were in for. The reprisals, as always, would be ghastly. A moment later there was another rumble and he realized it was only an approaching storm. He was relieved, but partly because a storm meant this sauna of a city might actually be cooled. One could hope.

He tossed the book aside and thought of the tombs at the Villa Chimera. He thought of Cristina and his young assistant's infatuation with the Italian girl. It was an inappropriate romance. Completely inappropriate. Hitler had misjudged the Italians. They'd shown their true stripes the moment the real war had begun. They'd lost wherever they'd fought. Friedrich shouldn't be wasting his time with the marchese's daughter. It was like horses and zebras. There was no possibility of a future. The moment the Americans or the British put their boots on Italian soil, Mussolini would be gone.

And where would that leave the lieutenant and Cristina?

Besides, she and that sister-in-law, Francesca, were just like Vittore. Detested the Germans—their supposed allies. Still, he had been impressed with the family estate. The villa. The first time he had stood in the entryway, he'd seen not a single Madonna or martyr hanging anywhere on the walls. Thank God.

Nevertheless, he decided he would have another talk with the young officer in the morning. The lieutenant needed to be reminded of the impropriety of a relationship with a girl who had no interest in the Axis cause or—worse, because this could not be cured with counsel or remediation—blood that was unsuitable for a man of his lineage. And, he had to admit, Vittore and Francesca and the girl's parents probably felt the same way about her relationship with Lieutenant Strekker.

He wiped his forehead with a handkerchief and felt how moist the cotton had become. The word *tainted* came to mind. He was not as rabid a purist as some of the officers of the Ahnenerbe who worried constantly about the contamination of Aryan blood, but the fact remained: these Italians were of a race that was profoundly inferior to the Germans, and it was only a matter of time before Berlin figured that out.

⚜

There was just the hint of a breeze rolling up from the olive groves at the Villa Chimera, and Friedrich paused before the front door to the house. It was wide open. He knocked and called inside, but there was no response. His driver, a nineteen-year-old private, was sitting on the stone wall beside the end of the driveway, his cap in his hands, licking melted chocolate off his fingers. Earlier that morning the two of them had delivered a big box with bread and chicken and coffee to that old couple who had sold him the necklace. They were shocked. They admitted that they had never expected to see him again.

Finally Friedrich turned away from the villa entrance, disappointed, and started back to the car. All the way from Florence he'd imagined standing behind Cristina here in Monte Volta—perhaps at the pool where she had greeted him in her swimsuit, like one of Diana's nymphs—and draping the necklace around her. Gently pulling aside her hair so he could snap shut the small, delicate clasp.

"Onward to Pienza?" the private asked him. There they were supposed to retrieve a gold crucifix from the cathedral altar.

He nodded, hoping his exasperation wasn't evident. He had detoured here to Monte Volta for nothing. All that would come of this side trip was more grief from Colonel Decher—another ridiculous lecture about horses and zebras and why Vittore's sister wasn't worthy of him—because certainly Decher would ask him why they had returned to Florence so late in the day.

As he was climbing into the passenger seat of the vehicle, however, he heard her voice. Cristina's voice. She was calling out to him from a stretch of the road below them, her arms so full of wildflowers that he could barely see her face. She was wearing a white linen dress that was tapered at the waist and the large, round sunglasses that her sister-in-law had been wearing when he had been here the other day. And so he motioned for the driver to relax and started down the road with the pebbles as white as Cristina's dress, his vexation evaporating instantly in the Crete Senesi sun.

"What are you doing here?" she asked, smiling, and pushed her sunglasses up and over her forehead until they had pulled her hair completely away from her face.

"I have an . . . errand . . . in Pienza. So I came here first. Where is your family?"

She shrugged. "Out and about. My father is with an army quartermaster, my mother is meeting with Father Mancini. We may be taking in some refugees whose homes were bombed in Bologna. I don't know. And Francesca and the children are in the village."

"Why didn't you join them?"

"I wanted to be alone. I wanted some quiet."

He paused. "I hope I'm not intruding."

"No, not at all! I was actually getting bored." She took a yellow flower he didn't recognize, each of its petals shaped like a pinecone and spotted like a leopard, and placed it behind the pin that held the Iron Cross to his tunic. "There. Now you have some color," she said. Then she shook her head and added, "You must be roasting inside that uniform."

"I am."

"I promise, you won't be court-martialed if you take off your jacket. I won't tell a soul."

"What about the flower?"

She plucked it from behind the medal and placed it behind his ear. "Better?"

And with that, he unbuttoned his tunic and slung it over his shoulder. He felt the box with the necklace in his jacket's hip pocket bounce against the very middle of his back.

She was vaguely aware of the necklace as she kissed him on the terrace beside the swimming pool, but mostly she was savoring the same dizzying rush she had experienced when they had stood alone together in the tombs. Now, as she felt his tongue against hers and his fingers upon the sides of her face, she was conscious of the way that seemingly every nerve in her body was tingling. She stood on her toes in her sandals and could feel her legs shaking. Her whole body was trembling. Certainly she had kissed other men—boys, actually. Other boys. She had felt boys' hands on her breasts; she had been aware of the desperate urgency they felt—she, too, sometimes. Never, however, had she felt quite this same voraciousness. This hunger. And so for the briefest of moments she wondered what it was about this kiss that was different, and she recalled a painting by a Milanese Romantic from the previous century: a man in a hat and a young woman in a mauve dress that fell to the floor. Her face was in his hands, too. But the image lasted in her mind only as long as a breeze, because then she was relishing the feel of his lips against hers and the way their whole mouths and tongues seemed to be merging. She wrapped her arms around the small of his back and pulled his body against hers, and suddenly they had moved in such a way that his thigh was between her legs—Had she done this? Had he? No matter, no matter at all—and the pressure against her groin was causing her heart to race. She was quivering between her legs, and the sensation became electric when his hands slid down her body, down her neck and her ribs and her hips, and suddenly they were caressing her rear, just the merest wisps of cotton clothing separating her skin from his. She allowed her own hands to drift down from his back and across his hips, reaching for the bulge at the front of his uniform pants, all the while rubbing and grinding herself against the hard muscle of his thigh.

That small part of her that had momentarily analyzed their kiss—that had seen in her mind a painting by (and the name flashed in and out of her head) Francesco Hayez—had now been subsumed by desire. All she was aware of was his tongue and his hands and his thigh, the fact that they were all alone, and how beautifully their bodies fit together.

⚜

Francesca sat on the terrace and watched the late afternoon sky growing black in the distance, and how the cypress trees at the edge of the village, across the ravine and near the granary, were starting to bow in the breeze. The storm would be here in minutes. She sipped her wine and listened to her children giggling as they played a card game on the rug in the library behind her, on the other side of the open doors. The German lieutenant had returned to the villa three times in the two weeks since he had given Cristina that necklace, and this worried Francesca. She neither liked this Strekker nor trusted him, in large measure because he was a Nazi, but also because he was a part of that whole crowd at the Uffizi that her brother-in-law loathed. Idiots and philistines and racists, the whole lot of them, Vittore had said. And yesterday when the lieutenant had been here, he had hinted that even more of his associates would be coming in a few days to see the Etruscan tombs and the estate. Not just the usual crowd—that Decher and Lorenzetti and Voss. A swarm of others. And this time, the lieutenant said, he wanted to show them all of the villa and the gardens and the cemetery, because, he insisted, the Villa Chimera itself was a work of art.

She wished her in-laws would draw a line in the sand and stop this lunacy. Tell their daughter to steer clear of that Nazi lieutenant. She wished Antonio would forbid the Germans from setting a single foot on his land. Wasn't he (and even in her mind she said the words with disdain) a marchese? She was confident that if Marco were here he would intervene. He would talk to his sister. He would talk to his father. He would end this madness.

When she looked up, she saw Cristina in the doorway. Her sister-in-law was leaning against the frame and smiling. "I love it when the air is this charged," she said.

In the distance they could both hear the tinkle of the bells on the sheep as they were herded into their barn.

"Right now you love everything," Francesca scoffed.

"It's true. I think I feel like you must have felt when you and Marco were first dating."

"I rather doubt that. The man I fell in love with didn't walk around in a German uniform and pillage our country's sculptures and paintings."

"I know who he really is. I know what's beneath that uniform."

"Do you? Well, that is nothing to be proud of."

"You know what I mean."

Francesca stood up and sighed. She threw the last of her wine into the grass beside the terrace. "Come," she said. "We should close the shutters before the storm arrives."

Vittore paused for a long moment on the thin curb on the Via Ghibellina outside the Bargello, honestly not sure where he was going. Then he decided. He started walking east, away from the city center, toward the cramped apartment where a woman his age named Giulia slept with him for a variety of reasons, not the least of which was that he brought her food. Her husband had died

fighting in Greece, and her father had been dead for years. Her
mother now lived in Fiesole, and sometimes he walked there with
the young woman—she wasn't precisely his girlfriend—especially
when he had brought food for her mother as well. Giulia had a
face as round as a cheese wheel, the gloriously plump cheeks of a
toddler, and eyes that were at odds with the reality of the world:
they always were filled with mirth, even when she was tired from
her job as a typist at the radio station. She was not heavy—it was
impossible to be heavy these days—but Vittore presumed that ten
or fifteen years from now, when this war was merely a series of
horrific and degrading memories, she might be. Sometimes he fantasized that they would be married then. He imagined that she
would be a wonderful mother. In his mind, they were living in
Rome. He had always wanted to live in Rome. Her hair was the
brown of a clove, and it framed her face like a wimple.

He found a vendor in the piazza near Santa Croce who sold
him two eggs, a couple of stale rolls, and a slice of moldering ham
at a price that was exorbitant, but not nearly as high as it would
have been if he weren't wearing a uniform and armed with a pistol.
Then he continued on his way to Giulia's.

Giulia wrapped herself inside Vittore's shirt because it was
the first article of clothing she found on the floor by her bed, but
she only buttoned the bottom third. As she stood, he pulled at the
tail from his spot on the mattress, less because he desired one last
glimpse of her round derriere (*Is there any part of her that is not spheri-*
cal? he wondered briefly) than because he knew it would make her
feel desired. She swatted at his hand good-naturedly and continued on to the apartment's only other room, a square with a single
window the size of a serving tray that was part kitchen, part dining
room, and part den. There she boiled the eggs and put the rolls
beside the pot of water so the heat from the top of the stove would
soften them. She wasn't quite sure what to do with the ham.

"Fry it," Vittore suggested. He had pulled on his pants and followed her. "Won't that kill whatever's on it?"

"Maybe. Maybe not."

"It is a very scary piece of meat," he agreed.

"And you were assured it was ham when you bought it?"

"I was. The fellow swore on his life."

"I think it's from a rat."

He held up the meat between his thumb and forefinger. "Too big. Have you ever seen a rat this big?"

"You've never been to the basement of this building. The rats are bigger than dogs."

"I say you fry it in oil."

"I say we fry it in kerosene."

"Then we can't eat it."

"I know. But I also won't have to fear that whatever creatures are on it will hatch and crawl into my bed tonight."

He dropped the meat onto the wooden block on the counter and pulled her to him. He ran his hands under the shirt—his shirt—and massaged her back. "Only I'll crawl into your bed tonight."

"And shouldn't I fear you?"

"No one fears me," he said.

She dipped her head and rested it against his chest. Her hair felt as soft as velvet and shone in the ray of light that came in through the window. "Maybe I fear you'll stop coming," she murmured.

He lifted her head and spied the long crevice between her breasts. "Why would I stop coming?" he asked. He resisted the urge to push the fabric aside and take one of her nipples between his lips.

"Because you'll get yourself killed. It's what you men seem to do. And then we women starve. Or we sleep with archeologists and we still starve." Her words were playful, but her voice, he realized, was completely earnest. She meant every word that she said.

"I don't expect I'll get killed."

"No one expects to get killed."

"I may die of aggravation. But I won't get killed."

She pushed against his chest and he released her. She put some water in a cast-iron skillet—she hadn't any olive oil—and tossed in the slice of rotting meat.

"I don't imagine you have to eat like this when you are at your villa," she said. "In my mind, I see honey and goat cheese and wine."

He shrugged. "I'm never there. Strekker is, it seems. But not me."

"Is that the German who has designs on your sister?"

"Yes. He has no foot, but he has a driver. He has no knowledge of Italian art, but Decher is always sending him off to Pienza or Siena to bring some back. Me? I am in the museum protecting the collection from our vaunted ally. But here's the damnedest thing—I actually think Strekker's interest in my sister is growing . . . serious."

"A marchese's daughter? He'd better be serious. It's not as if your sister is some slatternly Florentine secretary. You know the type—will give herself to the first nobleman in a uniform who comes calling with a couple of eggs and a piece of rat meat."

"You're selling yourself short."

"I've just sold myself for rat meat," she said, and she turned from him and lit the stove.

While much of the estate was resting or asleep during siesta, Beatrice and Antonio braved the high summer sun and walked along the edge of the vineyard and surveyed the Sangiovese grape arbors.

"The Germans are taking some of the relics we gave to the museum in Arezzo. One of the amphoras and the hydria," Antonio said when they came to a stop. He stood with his hands on the wooden fence, and Beatrice noted how he was gazing out at the long field as he spoke. He wouldn't—or couldn't—meet her eyes. "That Major Lorenzetti told me."

"Where are they taking them?" she asked. "Berlin?"

"No. Rome. Colonel Decher is giving them to some Gestapo liaison there. He wants him to see the triangles and what he insists are swastikas along the lip of the urn. He wants him to see the profiles of the revelers, the shape of their skulls. It's a . . . a gift."

Beatrice frowned. "I really don't like that man."

"Decher? He's not the worst. He's actually starting to grow on me. I found him rather clever the last time he was here. He was an architect before the war."

"He likes our wine and our cheese. He likes the view from the terrace. That doesn't make him clever."

"He's Vittore's boss," Antonio said. "Don't forget that."

"He's a Nazi. Don't you forget *that*."

"I don't."

"So they are stealing Etruscan pottery from the museum and giving it away like hostess gifts," she said, her tone vacillating between resignation and disgust. "What next? They'll pinch a Botticelli for some field marshal in France?"

"At least the pottery is remaining in Italy."

Somewhere in the brush at the edge of the vineyard they heard a wild boar snort. Beatrice thought the ground looked a little dry, even for this time of the year, but the leaves on the grapevines seemed healthy enough. "It won't for long," she said.

"Perhaps not," Antonio agreed.

She looked at him. "There's something more."

"There is."

"Go on."

He resumed his stroll and so she did, too. "Decher and Lorenzetti want to bring that Gestapo fellow here—the one from Rome—so he can see the tombs for himself. It seems he is interested in Etruscan art."

"We can't allow that," she said. "We can't have Gestapo here."

"I don't think we really have much of a choice. Besides . . ."

She waited, but she feared she knew what he was going to say. "Besides," he continued, "I think we need to be good citizens.

Loyal. We have to for Vittore's sake and we have to for Marco's sake. And let's face it," and here he paused and waved his hand over the vineyard and then in the direction of the olive grove and the fields where once there had been herds of cattle and flocks of sheep, "we have to if we want to hang on to all this."

"They just keep coming," she said, aware of how plaintive and desperate her tone suddenly sounded. "First it was the Nazis from Florence and then it was the Nazis from Arezzo. And now it's these Nazis from Rome."

"And then there is Cristina's . . . friend. The lieutenant."

"They're losing the war, Antonio."

"They're? *We're* losing the war, my dear. *We're* losing the war."

"And yet we seem to be getting in ever deeper with the Nazis."

Overhead they heard the planes that so interested their daughter, and reflexively they both looked up. "I know," her husband said. "I really do. But I don't know what else to do."

1955

SERAFINA KNELT CAREFULLY before the mushrooms, hoping to conjure a memory from 1944. She tried to focus, allowing her fears to trickle out, and held lit matches over the caps—a few the size of her fist—and the stems. Already she had examined the pedestals and the paintings in the tombs, concentrating on the Etruscan men with their angular Vandyke beards, some of whom were eerily reminiscent of the partisans with whom she had lived and fought. Now, even though the smell almost made her sick, she breathed in and out, hoping to resurrect a moment, any moment at all, from that awful summer.

Finally, angry at the way memory was failing her once again, she stood up and lit a cigarette. She walked once more through the different chambers, using matches to gaze at the paintings on the walls. And then she paused. Looked up. She climbed onto the pedestal so she was nearer the ceiling and brought the small flame close to the image there. There were birds. Seven, eight . . . nine of them. They were darting amid nearly black clouds, though there was also a portion of golden sun peering out from behind one of the thunderheads. And suddenly she knew that if she followed the sun's rays across the vault's ceiling, she would see that they were illuminating a boy in a boat, a young fisherman, who despite his age was manfully managing the small vessel against waves taller than he was.

She jumped off the pedestal and climbed onto the one beside it, following the sunlight. Sure enough, there was the boy and there was his boat. And there were more birds.

She'd seen this ceiling before, and it was clear that it could have been at only one time in her life: when she was in the hallucinogenic agonies, in and out of consciousness, after she had nearly been burned to death in the firefight. Someone was holding her hand, telling her to be brave. Be brave. They were getting her help. She recalled a man's voice. And a woman's. She remembered them forcing her to drink whenever she awoke, the water tasting fetid and stale, but the burns had left her so dehydrated they were constantly trying to get fluids into her. And was it possible that they had a small fire at the edge of the chamber and were boiling water? They were draping wet rags on her wounds. Somewhere nearby was machine-gun fire. And explosions that she thought were grenades but might have been small artillery.

And, kept always on her side because of the way her back was an undulating swamp of seared flesh, by the light of a torch she had seen the birds and the boy and that sun whenever she had awoken and looked up.

It may have been hours and it may have been days, but at some point before the British had secured Monte Volta, the partisans had taken her away from the battle and out of the sun and hidden her here in an Etruscan home for the dead.

⚜

"Where is Vittore staying?" Serafina asked Paolo after she arrived at the police station Friday night and settled in with a cola on the other side of his desk.

"The Boccaccio. I moved Cristina there, too. I couldn't let her stay in the hotel where her mother was killed. We have a man on the corridor of their floor and a man watching the lobby."

"And his family in Rome?"

"There is a wife, Giulia, and a couple of little girls. They have a guard, too."

"But we can't watch them forever."

He shrugged. "We'll see. For all we know, they're in no danger at all. Maybe whoever killed the marchesa just wants Vittore and Cristina."

"He killed Francesca."

"Point noted."

"What about other relatives? Cousins, uncles, aunts?"

"The war and old age seem to have already taken many of them," Paolo said.

"But not all."

He reached for his notes and his eyeglasses and looked at the papers. "Let's see. Beatrice had a brother and a sister. Her brother died in a car accident in 1928 in Bologna. No children. Her sister is a widow. She married in 1919 and her husband died of cancer last year. Her name is Elena and she lives in Naples. She and her husband had three children, two boys and a girl. The boys were killed in Greece in 1941 and Egypt in 1942. The daughter married a British soldier after the war and they now live in London. Her name is Bianca. They have a child who's five. Antonio—the marchese—had a brother who died when they were boys. A hiking accident of some sort."

"So there is Elena and Elena's daughter's family in London."

"That's right. At the moment, Elena has protection. Her daughter in London—that whole little family—does not."

"Any progress on those names Cristina gave us?"

"Francesca's lovers or those soldiers from the war?"

"I was thinking of the war, but I guess that's just my bias right now."

"Let's start with Francesca's lovers. We have come across no American museum curators or executives visiting Italy this week on business or pleasure. We have found two Aldos living in Florence who have criminal records, but I don't see either as the sort whom Francesca would have dated—or, to be specific, the sort to have taken her to restaurants like Il Latini."

"Any Giovannis?"

"With a criminal record? One. He is seventy-seven."

"Not Francesca's type."

Paolo nodded and passed her his notebook so she could read in detail about the two felons named Aldo. One, she saw, was a young thief who lived with his mother and worked at a gas station at the edge of the city; the other was an accountant who once stole from his company. Now he worked for the municipal utility and lived with his wife and two children. Neither had ever done anything violent.

"What about the Italian major and the German colonel?" she asked. "I don't see anything about them here."

"Giancarlo Lorenzetti now teaches at the University of Milan."

"And?"

"And it is the summer. He is at his wife's family home in the hills outside Messina."

"In Sicily."

"Yes."

"And we know he was there the night Francesca was killed?"

"That's what he and his wife say."

"And the German colonel?"

"Dead," Paolo answered, and here he paused. "But it is interesting how he died—or rather, what he did in the days before he died. And maybe *interesting* is the wrong word. Perhaps I should say interesting and horrifying. In the middle of June 1944, Erhard Decher, like many of the Germans who had mostly been looting art, was pressed into real service. On July 14, days before the Germans withdrew north from Arezzo, he was among a group of Nazis who went to a village just south of the city and massacred twenty-three villagers, including the parish priest. It was a reprisal for a partisan attack. They took them to an olive grove and made them shovel a single very large grave. There they bayoneted them one by one, and then placed explosive charges among the bodies. When the British arrived, there were bits of bloody clothes—still damp, apparently—and human limbs dangling like fruit from the trees."

"I remember hearing about that massacre in the autumn. When they started telling me what I had missed. The massacre wasn't all that far from Monte Volta and Trequanda."

"As you know as well as anyone, it wasn't uncommon for the Germans to execute innocent villagers in response to your . . . activities."

"And Decher was there?"

"He was. He did not order the executions, but he was in charge of carrying them out."

"Where did he die?"

"A little south of Arezzo. The Allies got him only hours after he had all of those villagers butchered. But like so many Nazis whom we now see for the war criminals they were, his cause of death should, in hindsight, be considered mysterious."

"No body?"

"No, there was a body. But it was unrecognizable and not wearing a dog tag. Presumed to be Decher by the kit beside it and the pay book found in a tunic pocket." He reached for another piece of yellow paper on his desk and glanced at it. "It seems that a sizable portion of the body was blown apart or"—and here he paused before continuing—"burned away."

"So Decher could still be alive," she said, careful not to react to Paolo's discomfort.

"Apparently," he agreed.

"What of the Germans who fought at the villa? Muller and Bayer?"

"As Cristina presumed, they both died in the battles around Monte Volta."

"Their bodies accounted for?"

"Muller's, yes. Bayer's, no."

She nodded. Then: "I believe I have the name of that third visitor who was going to the villa in 1943 and 1944—and going there often. That German whose name Cristina claimed she forgot."

"Go on."

"He was a lieutenant named Friedrich Strekker. He was missing a foot and part of his leg."

"I can tell you have a theory why Cristina pretended she'd forgotten his name."

"I believe they were lovers."

He pulled off his glasses and rubbed at his eyes. "You know," he said, "we should not lose sight of the fact that there could be reasons someone doesn't like the Rosatis that have nothing to do with the war."

"I agree. It's possible."

"But you think it's unlikely."

"I do."

"Well, then," he said after a long, quiet moment. "Tell me about Monte Volta. What was it like for you?"

꙳

Vittore was tall and thin and a little gaunt. But Serafina instantly saw a resemblance to Cristina: he had the same almond-shaped gray eyes, and his hair, though receding high on his forehead, was still dark brown on the sides, with faint waves of cinnamon. He might at first glance have been mistaken for an American, because his face was clean-shaven. She and Paolo sat with him and his sister in a small anteroom off the hotel's lobby. The room was dusky and windowless, but it was private, and somewhere Paolo had found two more chairs, bringing the total they could place around the side table with the lamp to four. No one was smoking, but Vittore had dragged the young officer guarding him to the bar across the street and brought back a tall, vermouth-heavy Negroni to sip. They had been talking for fifteen minutes now and the glass was almost empty. Vittore, like his sister, insisted that he could think of no one who hated the family so much that he would murder first Francesca and then Beatrice. Twice he had asked for assurance that an officer in Rome was keeping watch over his wife and his children. The second time he had even wondered whether a single officer was enough, observing that whoever had killed and mutilated his sister-in-law and his mother was both insidious and violent.

"This just makes no sense," he was saying. "And you really haven't any clues at all?"

"Not good ones," Paolo answered. "There were no fingerprints in your sister-in-law's apartment from any criminal in our files. And while there are fingerprints all over the corridor upstairs—I'm honestly not sure it has been dusted since the war—it will take us a long time to make any sense of them."

Serafina thought about her boss's use of the word *war*. She hadn't been sure whether now would be a good time to bring up the German lieutenant who was missing a foot. Should she wait to ask Cristina alone? At the moment the woman was sitting hunched over, her head bowed, her hands in her lap. She had, according to Paolo, stopped crying early that afternoon, and although he had considered calling a physician over lunch and getting her one of those French tranquilizers that were becoming the rage, in the end he hadn't bothered. Finally Serafina decided to probe a different lead.

"A woman on Francesca's floor said your sister-in-law had wanted to know the name of a good locksmith," Serafina began. "This was a month ago. She never did change her locks, but this woman said Francesca had seen someone that day who'd frightened her. And whoever killed her had not broken the door to the apartment or the lock, so most likely Francesca knew him. Any idea of someone who might have scared her?"

"I lost touch with my sister-in-law years ago," Vittore said, his tone a little sad. "These days, all I ever knew of Francesca was what Cristina told me about her."

"Why?"

"Why did we lose touch? Because the Rosati name once meant something. And Rosati men do not associate with . . . with the sort of woman Francesca had become. After the war she started pulling away from us. From my mother and my father. From our family. Maybe that makes sense after what she went through. But, my God, my family experienced it, too. So we wanted to help. We wanted to rebuild our lives together. But she didn't want our help. She didn't want to see us," he said. He glanced at Cristina and then added, "Most of us, that is."

"Did you know any of her lovers?" Serafina asked him.

"No."

"The other day Cristina told us that you worked with Erhard Decher and Giancarlo Lorenzetti at the Uffizi and the two of them used to come visit the Villa Chimera."

"What could that possibly have to do with my sister-in-law's and my mother's deaths?" Vittore responded.

"Maybe nothing."

"Both men were animals. Decher was a snake. Lorenzetti was a weasel."

She thought about this. Then she addressed her next question to both Rosatis. "Decher massacred twenty-three villagers just south of Arezzo in July 1944. Did either of you know that?"

Cristina came a little more alive. "He was there?" she asked, looking up at Serafina.

"He was in charge."

"Frankly, I'm not surprised," Vittore said. "I told you, the man was a snake. Cold-blooded and vicious."

She recalled how Cristina had said the other day that the last time she thought Decher or Lorenzetti had gone to Monte Volta had been April 1944, but she decided to ask Vittore the same question now.

"Late April," he answered after a moment. "Maybe early May."

"Was it just the two of them?"

"I wasn't with them," Vittore said.

"It was just Decher that last time," Cristina said. "And some of his staff." She looked up and reached for Vittore's glass. Briefly the siblings' eyes met and then she swallowed the last of his drink.

⚜

Cristina and Vittore were both given accommodations on the sixth and highest floor of the Boccaccio, with an officer in the lobby and another in the hallway outside their doors. Now Serafina nodded at the guard, a fellow younger than she who she knew was from Siena, and walked Cristina back to her room.

"Good night," Cristina said, a small tremor still marking her voice. "Thank you."

Serafina nodded. "Don't thank me yet. Can I come in? I want to talk to you about something. I didn't want to bring it up in front of your brother."

Cristina pressed the key into the lock, opened the door, and motioned the detective inside. Then the woman turned on the light, tossed her purse onto the bed, and pulled wide the shutters to the single window facing the street. Outside, Serafina heard the plates and glasses and the laughter from the bar in the small piazza. She watched Cristina stand against the wall beside the window and close her eyes. She was exhausted and beaten. "Go ahead," she said.

"When you were first telling me about Decher and Lorenzetti, it felt to me that you were about to give me a third name. Another soldier."

Cristina's face didn't change; her eyes remained shut.

"Am I right?" Serafina pressed.

After a moment Cristina opened her eyes, but she seemed to be gazing at the wall behind the detective. Serafina saw that, as red as those eyes already were, despite all that she had cried that day, once more they were starting to grow moist. "His name was Friedrich Strekker," she answered. "We used to . . ."

"Go on."

"He was billeted at a hotel a few blocks from here. I would come to Florence so we could be together. So we could be alone."

"And he worked for Decher?"

"He was his adjutant. But I assure you, he had nothing to do with the massacre near Arezzo. And I can promise you this, too—he would never have killed either Francesca or my mother."

"And you are sure of that . . . why?"

A single tear started to slide down one of her cheeks, and she brushed it aside with two of her fingers. "Because he loved me," she said simply, standing up a little straighter. "And because I loved him."

Serafina leaned gingerly against the hotel brick wall that faced the piazza and watched as Paolo reached over and lit her cigarette for her. She shared with him what Cristina had told her when they had been upstairs just now in the woman's room.

"If she and this Lieutenant Strekker loved each other so much, why did they never marry?" he asked when she was through.

She found herself staring at a young couple walking past her, the two of them holding hands and the woman—eighteen or nineteen, Serafina guessed—pressed against her boyfriend in the dark. "She assumes he died. She never heard from him after the Germans retreated north."

"When was the last time she saw him?"

"July 1944. At the villa."

"You know, if he reported to Decher, there is every reason to believe he was with Decher at the massacre."

"But he had only one foot. Just because Decher was reassigned doesn't mean Strekker was."

Paolo shrugged. "You don't need two feet to bayonet unarmed peasants in an olive grove. But we'll see what we can find. We'll see if we can find out where—if—he died."

"She says she really didn't expect to hear from him during the last months of the war. After all, he was now the enemy. But all summer long in 1945, after the Germans surrendered, she waited. Then in the autumn, when she hadn't heard from him, she wrote letters to the museum in Dresden where his father had worked. She wrote in the winter, too, and then again throughout 1946. But she never heard anything back. Not a word. She has no idea if the letters even got there. She says she even tried to find him through the Red Cross, but Dresden and Kesselsdorf were in the Soviet zone—"

"And Dresden was rubble," he remarked.

"Yes. In any case, she never heard anything from the Red Cross either."

Paolo stamped out his cigarette with the sole of his shoe and sighed. "I talked to Mario Spagnoli again today," he said after a moment, referring to the fellow Francesca had dined with on the last night of her life.

"Oh?"

"I wanted to know if Francesca mentioned this Decher or Lorenzetti. I wanted to know if she had said anything about being frightened by someone she might have seen on the street here in Florence."

"That would have made for an interesting first date if she had."

"She didn't," he grumbled.

"Did she say anything at all about the war?"

"Only what you'd expect on a first date. She talked a little about the marchese and the marchesa—their pretensions and affectations. She told him her children had died in the wake of the fighting at the villa. But no details."

"No mention of any Germans."

He shook his head. "No. No mention of any Germans."

"Tomorrow I'm going to see if there is anyone left at the Uffizi who might have known them—Decher or Lorenzetti or this Friedrich Strekker."

He looked up through the buildings at the starless sky and then adjusted his straw hat. "We should get some sleep," he said. "Your boyfriend will not be happy with me if I never let you go home."

Serafina woke early Saturday morning and went to the Uffizi, arriving there hours before it was open to the public and entering through the office doors opposite the main entrance. There, in a windowless conference room, she met with an assistant director and an exhibits manager, both of whom had worked at the museum during what Florentines now referred to—a little disingenuously, in some cases—as the German occupation. For most Italians throughout most of the war, it was an alliance, not an occupation. In any case, neither fellow had seen Decher since July 1944, and they guessed, since the colonel had wanted so badly to be in combat, that he was probably dead. Strekker, too. They told her that Lorenzetti was thriving at the University of Milan, which she already knew, and that Ludwig Heydenreich and Jürgen Voss were both somewhere in Germany. The two of them had been part of the German Military Art Protection Front in Florence, the Nazi group responsible for crating up whatever paintings and sculptures it could and sending them north to be hidden in the salt mines near Heilbronn or displayed in some minister's estate outside Berlin. In point of fact, the assistant director said, Heydenreich had undermined his superiors wherever possible and prevented the worst of the pillaging, even protecting Bernard Berenson's collection in the Villa I Tatti from Hermann Göring. When Heydenreich had heard that German soldiers had mined the bridges across the Arno, like a madman he had photographed them all so there would be a record of Florence before the destruction.

"You know who you should really talk to?" the exhibits manager said finally. "Roberto Piredda. He works at the museum in Arezzo. He used to be here once or twice a month, or we used to see him in Arezzo."

"He didn't like the Rosatis?" she asked.

"Oh, I'm sure he liked them just fine. He was the one who went to that estate of theirs in Monte Volta before the war, when the family discovered the Etruscan tombs. He supervised the excavation. Over time he became a mentor for Vittore—Vittore really looked up to him. They may still be friends, or they may have lost touch. I couldn't say for sure, because Vittore and I haven't seen each other in years. But Piredda might be able to tell you more about"—and here he glanced quickly at his associate, smiling at what was clearly an inside joke—"the old gang."

🜚

"I knew I was going to make my life here eleven years ago. It was June 4, 1944," Milton was saying on Saturday night to the group of American and Italian bankers and their girlfriends and wives gathered at the private room in the back of the restaurant. There were sixteen people, eight women and eight bankers, including the bank president from New York City. Serafina had heard Milton tell this story before—the liberation of Rome by the Americans and the wondrous, welcoming response of the Italians—but tonight he was using it because the American and Italian banks together were financing the massive Kariba hydroelectric dam in Africa. And the tale, she knew, allowed him both to praise his European host nation and to celebrate the friendship that now existed between the two countries. He was standing at the head of the table, holding a glass of prosecco.

"The irony, of course, is that two days after we entered Rome, my compatriots—as well as a great many Brits and Canadians—landed in Normandy, and so the liberation of the Eternal City very soon was eclipsed and relegated to the inside pages of most newspapers," he said. "But, my God, was it exciting for us—and for me personally. Rome is one of the most beautiful cities in the world. And while I didn't get to spend long there that June, I spent enough time for my fondness for your country—and, of course, for your wine—to grow even deeper. So it is with that small introduction that tonight I will, as I have hundreds of times this past decade, raise a glass to our friendship. To the United States, and to Italy!"

They toasted, and as Milton sat down, the fellow on Serafina's right, an Italian named Vincenzo with an impressive mop of barely groomed silver hair, an equally hoary mustache, and weathered, deeply brown Sicilian skin, said, "Milton tells me you're a detective."

"That's right."

"Not easy work for a beautiful young lady."

"Or, I would imagine, a handsome young man."

"Excellent—well put." He chuckled. "I must admit, I have never met a female detective."

"I'm the only one."

He nodded, digesting this information. Then: "How long have you and Milton been dating?"

"Two and a half years."

A pair of waiters began placing on the settings before each of them a small plate with delicately fried squash blossoms filled with goat cheese.

"What does he think of your . . . work?"

"He doesn't mind."

"And why are two such delightful young adults not married? You should be."

"Someday."

"I probably sound like your father. Forgive me," he said, and he cut into the first of his squash blossoms.

"No forgiveness is necessary."

"We like Milton very much. That's all."

"I do, too."

"What kind of detective are you?"

"A very good one."

Again he laughed. She glanced at Milton's end of the table and saw that he was charming the women to both sides of him.

"Seriously," the banker went on, "what do you investigate? I have a feeling you do more than find stray kittens and bring home lost babies."

"Murder."

His face went grave. "You're joking."

"I'm not."

"We have female detectives and they're investigating murders? Right here in Florence?"

"We do. Me."

"Do you . . ."

"Go on."

"Do you carry a gun?"

"Yes."

He shook his head. "How did this happen? How did you wind up carrying a gun and looking for killers?"

"I asked."

"Really?"

"In the war, I picked up special . . . skills. It would have been a shame not to put them to use. And so I went to Paolo Ficino and asked for a job."

"The chief inspector?"

"That's right."

"It was just that simple?"

"No," she said. "Nothing is ever that simple."

"But that's all you're going to tell me."

"Inspector Ficino is a very good man. He knew I needed to work and he took me under his wing. He took a risk."

"I would not want my daughter doing what you do. But I have a feeling you are quite capable."

"Thank you."

"Do you know anything about that poor woman—excuse me, those poor women who had their hearts cut from their chests?"

"A little." She smiled wryly, flirting really, and asked, "Do you?"

He put down his fork and raised his hands. "Innocent, I promise you."

"That's what I thought."

"But you can't talk about it."

"No, I can't. I'm sorry."

"I never met the marchese," he said, "but I knew people who knew Antonio."

"Oh?"

"Don't get your hopes up. I have no—what is that American expression?—smoking gun."

"What did people say about him?"

"He was a good man and deserved his title. He looked out for his commune and the peasants who worked his land. But then came the war, and like everyone else, he made compromises."

"Such as?"

"Well, he sold out to Germans. But then, didn't we all?"

"No. We all didn't."

He grinned as if he were a proud grandfather and said, "Okay, I may have no smoking gun, but you—and I think this is how the Americans use this word for a sharp woman—are a pistol." Then he raised his glass with the last of the prosecco and clinked it against hers.

"What do you mean, he sold out to the Germans?"

"I shouldn't have said anything. Really, all I have is rumor and innuendo."

She reached over and for a long second placed two of her fingers on the back of his hand and gazed at him. "You must tell me. Please. For all you know, what you have heard may help me save a life." She feared briefly after she had spoken that she had taken the flirtation too far, but when he looked back at her, she knew he was going to open up like a cooked mussel.

"Well," he said, his voice a little ruminative, "we surrendered in North Africa in May 1943. The Allies invaded Sicily two months later. Early July. They bombed Rome for the first time a week or two after that. And it was clear by then that it was over. It really was. Everyone knew it but the Germans. So we arrested Mussolini. You remember. By the end of the month we had even kicked out the Blackshirts. And we all know how well that worked out."

She nodded. She thought of her mother and father. Their execution. The new Badoglio government initially pledged its loyalty to Berlin but by early September had surrendered to the Allies. Within days the Germans had occupied Rome, rescued Mussolini from the ski resort in the Apennine Mountains where he was being held prisoner, and reestablished a puppet Fascist government with Il Duce as the figurehead. And she and her brothers were on the run.

"It was like a civil war in the midst of the world war," he was saying. "And Antonio Rosati, people said, made the mistake of siding too long and too often with the Nazis and their Blackshirt lapdogs. Either he couldn't see the future or he wouldn't."

"What did he do? Specifically?"

"While the rest of us were starving, people said his estate never lacked for honey and beef. Never. His grandchildren always had milk. And throughout the second half of 1943 and 1944, while Italian patriots were fighting the Germans in the woods behind their lines, Antonio was matchmaking, trying to arrange marriages between his daughters and Nazi officers. He held a Christmas ball in December 1943 for the Germans at the Villa Chimera—his estate."

She thought of the rooms she had seen there that now were rubble. "He had only one daughter," she said, not so much because she wanted to defend Antonio as because she wanted to see if this clarification might jog Vincenzo's memory. "He had two sons, one of whom was married to Francesca."

A waiter cleared away the plates that had held the squash blossoms and brought them bowls of thick ribollita, the tomatoes and carrots in the soup conspiring to give it a beautiful, orange terracotta hue.

The banker sat back and seemed to be surveying the next course. Then: "That's right. But the one girl. Cristina, right?"

"Right."

"She was a friend of many Germans, they say. And one of the brothers was, too. Didn't he help the Nazis loot Florence?"

"Or, arguably, he tried to prevent them from looting the city."

He tasted his soup. "You barely touched the squash blossoms. This is delicious. I think you'll like it." He took another spoonful and then went on. "I know this—Antonio and Beatrice Rosati entertained Nazis and Blackshirts throughout 1943 and 1944. They billeted German officers in their home after Rome fell. I'm sure Antonio was not happy about the fact that his friends from the north decided to make their last stand at the Villa Chimera, but he had no one to blame but himself."

She glanced toward Milton, and he winked at her. She smiled at him and then turned back to the Italian banker beside her. "And what did you do during the war?" she asked him.

He shook his head. "Not enough," he said, his tone a little rueful. "Not nearly enough."

THE MURDERS OF *the Rosati women gave the tourists who descended on Tuscany something to think about other than wine and cheese and taste-less little trinkets of Michelangelo's* David. *The elegant Boboli Gardens at the Pitti Palace look very different if you are imagining satanic rituals in the woods behind the amphitheater and a murderer cutting the hearts from his victims. The Via de' Tornabuoni becomes more than a mere tony shopping street. You glance casually up at the apartments above the lingerie and dress stores, the shops that sell chocolate and leather, and you imagine . . .*

Well, you know what you imagine. I don't.

Even a magnificent city such as Florence becomes more intriguing if there is a demon at work in the alleys. It's as if the Uffizi is no longer enough. The Duomo and the tower and the Baptistery doors (they are rep-licas, you know; the real ones are kept safe from the elements in the Museo dell'Opera del Duomo) are less enticing than the notion that there's a fiend in the shadows.

But of course you are in danger only if you are related to a Rosati. So you can enjoy the thrill ride with no fear of falling yourself.

I have always found it interesting that two women were executed for murder that summer, one just before I started my work and another very soon after. On June 3, the Americans sent Barbara Graham to the gas cham-ber in California. On July 13, the British hanged Ruth Ellis in London. And yet, curiously, no one in the Italian media conjectured that I might be female.

Other news that summer of 1955? You'll recall that the pope excom-municated Juan Perón in June. Eighty-three spectators died in a Le Mans race-car cataclysm. Antonio Segni formed a new government in Rome. In America, Walt Disney opened an amusement park.

And in Florence, someone was savaging the remnants of a Tuscan nobleman's family. It made for a great story . . . and, I must confess, I did succumb to a giddy little narcissistic rush as I devoured the articles.

Clearly the police would be watching Giulia Rosati and her girls, and so I considered taking a breather. I could travel to their little home on the outskirts of Vatican City in a week or a month or a year. As I have told you, there was no rush. I was feeling no insatiable compulsion.

But then I read a quote from police detective Paolo Ficino in the newspaper: "Nothing will happen to either Cristina or Vittore Rosati—or to Vittore's family. We will be there for them."

Can you imagine? He was challenging me, goading me on.

Well, I have never backed down from a challenge. I packed my valise and drove south to Rome.

1943

CRISTINA STOOD IN the window in the hotel in Florence and wished either that Friedrich's room were on a higher floor or that the building across the street were shorter so it wouldn't obstruct her scrutiny of the moon as it began its descent. She presumed that Vittore's room, which was two stories above her, might have a view, but Friedrich's didn't. Briefly she imagined her older brother standing by his window frame, too, his hands on the sill, scanning the sky. In all likelihood, however, he was sound asleep . . . somewhere else. It was not yet four a.m. and Vittore was doubtless unconscious—no one slept more deeply than he did—wherever it was that he had chosen to lay his head. But that bed wasn't in this hotel. At first she had been so afraid that her brother would discover she was here with this German that she had been reluctant to come. But Friedrich had been right: it wasn't simply that Vittore hadn't set foot on this floor ever, as far as Friedrich could tell; he spent as many nights as he could away from the hotel. Although he had never spoken directly to Friedrich about where he went, it was common knowledge among that small cadre of officers at the Uffizi that Vittore was seeing a secretary named Giulia who worked at a radio station, and he was either with her or with her and her mother in Fiesole. Still, Cristina had made it clear to Friedrich that they had to be gone from the hotel before breakfast. Her mother and father and Vittore believed she was spending the weekend with a family friend named Donata, a woman Francesca's age who always put romance before responsibility and—as Cristina had expected—had been happy to cover for her once she had been introduced to the German lieutenant. Donata was the mistress of one of Mussolini's generals and had a floor of his spectacular townhouse here in Florence to herself.

In the bed behind her she heard Friedrich stir, and she turned. His eyes were still shut, but his long arm had fallen onto the side of the mattress from which she had just risen. She watched him stretch his fingers and roll them aimlessly along the sheets and the edge of the pillow as he slowly woke up.

"What time is it?" he asked. He rubbed his fists against his eyes in a manner so boyish that she was reminded of her nephew back in Monte Volta.

"Four."

"Come back to bed then."

"I couldn't sleep."

"The hotel mattress?" he asked, his voice light. "Having to share a bed with a snoring German soldier?"

She smiled. "You weren't snoring."

"I'm relieved. I've been told that I do."

"Not by other women, I hope."

"No. Only by other German soldiers who really do snore." He sat up, kicking his legs over the side of the bed, and motioned for her to come sit beside him. She did, and he pulled her toward him, against him, resting his hands on the small of her back. "So why couldn't you sleep?" he asked.

She realized he was worried about her. He was afraid she had regrets, either because they had made love for the first time or because she had lied to her family. Or perhaps because she was in a man's room in the small hours of the morning. But in fact she had no regrets at all. She felt suddenly like a grown woman. She was excited. This was the sort of romance and exhilaration that thus far the war had denied her. Yes, she had missed the sorts of galas and balls that Francesca had enjoyed when she had been eighteen and nineteen, but Cristina had something she decided now was much,

much better: she had a lover. She had beside her in this bed a man with whom she knew she was falling in love.

"Tell me," Friedrich asked her again. "Please."

She kissed him. "Because I like it here," she murmured softly.

"In Florence?"

"With you. In your room. I guess I don't want to sleep through the night."

"I would take you dancing, but obviously nothing is open right now."

As he spoke, she found herself starting to flinch, expecting the sentence to end differently: *I would take you dancing, but obviously I can't dance.* She was aware right now of the way his shin ended in a club: his left foot was flat on the foor, while his right shin was hovering well above it. This was why he had beckoned her to him rather than rising and coming to her in the window. Earlier in the night, when they were making love and discovering the idiosyncrasies and imperfections that marked each other's bodies, she had explored his legs and his disfigurement. She had caressed him and kissed him, determinedly overcoming her own squeamishness to run her fingertips over the stump—the skin hairless and glassy—where even now he said he felt only the odd tingle.

"You dance?" she asked, teasing him. Her forearms were draped on his shoulders, and she began to massage the back of his neck.

"I do. I am not as elegant on the dance floor as I once was. But I can still manage the occasional very precise gavotte."

"Precision. That does matter to you Germans, doesn't it?"

He smiled. "And I'm not even Prussian."

"Someday you'll show me how well you dance. Maybe even this weekend."

"That would be wonderful, yes."

Outside Friedrich's room, along the hotel corridor, they heard doors opening and the sound of men running with great urgency. There was a sliver of light now beneath their door because someone had turned on the hall sconces. And then there was the sound of someone knocking, pounding really, for Friedrich to wake up and join Colonel Decher downstairs. It was Jürgen Voss. Apparently the Allies had begun to invade Sicily.

⚜

Captain Marco Rosati's first thought was that an animal carcass was rotating on a spit: he heard what he presumed was a crackling fire and the air was filled with the aroma of cooked meat. But as he opened his eyes, he understood that he was in that foggy moat between sleeping and waking, and his dream of a cooked pig or boar was quickly erased by the fact that his new adjutant was shaking him awake by his shoulder, the young man's eyes wide with panic. He had been, it seemed, asleep in the chair by his desk in this modest second-story apartment in Gela, where he was billeted. He recalled ruefully that he had been writing another letter to Francesca.

Now he forced himself fully awake and stood and listened as this absolutely terrified fellow, whom everyone called Lungo, told him of enemy paratroopers between them and the airfield behind them, and the waves and waves of enemy landing craft that had been spotted off the Sicilian beach and were working their way through the waves. He was just reaching for his holster and pistol when there was a series of colossal explosions—behind him, beside them, before them; it was almost like dominoes—and he was hurled against the coatrack next to the writing table and then onto the floor. The lone light went out and the room was lit only by the moon. Marco felt plaster dust raining gently upon him when the shaking stopped. He saw that Lungo was trying to tell him something, but Marco's ears were ringing and he couldn't hear a single word. Then the fellow closed his eyes and rolled onto his back, and Marco saw that the adjutant's shirt had been shredded by shrapnel, his abdomen all but scooped out, and his intestines were protruding like a nest of baby snakes. Marco leaned over him, stifling his gag reflex and wishing that he had the slightest idea how to help him. But the engineer's fear and sense of absolute helplessness lasted but a moment, because Lungo's chest abruptly stopped heaving as the body stopped straining for air and the fellow expired. So Marco found where he had dropped his pistol and moved as quickly as he could through the debris and clutter that now marked the way from his room to the stairs. He bumped into furniture that had been upended and felt his way along walls that suddenly were pockmarked with holes. He was aware that his hearing was already starting to return, because now he could hear women and soldiers screaming alike, and the sound of machine-gun fire nearby. From the beach he heard the thunder of artillery fire, and he imagined the massive American and British battleships sitting safely at sea and pummeling his desperately frightened men in their wholly inadequate bunkers. Initially he had assumed it was a bomb that had ripped into his quarters and killed his adjutant, but it dawned on him now that it had probably been a shell hurled from those behemoths floating out in the waves, well beyond the range of the Italian guns on the beach. Still, this revelation passed almost instantly through his mind, whisked from consciousness because he heard the shrill whistle of another missile approaching. He was at the top of the building's stairs and so he raced down them, leaping the last few steps as if he were jumping into the pool at the Villa Chimera, and though he landed awkwardly and twisted his ankle, he continued outside into the chaos of the piazza—into the stream of horrified women pulling their thin-legged children by their hands and the frightened men with their carbines trying to muster in the street for their officers—just as another building along the corniche seemed to evaporate in a deafening roar of smoke and hot ash.

Beatrice Rosati heard about the Allied invasion of Sicily from her husband, Antonio, who had heard the news from their overseer. Nunzio had learned of the attack from a villager who had been listening surreptitiously to the BBC while eating breakfast and understood perhaps a third of the words on the airwaves. Immediately Nunzio had raced back up the hill to the villa to tell Antonio that there was a battle of some sort in Gela. The marchese, in turn, had switched on the radio the family kept hidden behind a shelf of old leather books in the library, and now he and Beatrice and Nunzio were crowded around the mahogany box with the gold fabric across the speaker, listening as that impeccably proper British voice droned on about the waves of Brits and Americans who had already captured the Sicilian port city. Antonio translated what he was hearing for the overseer while Beatrice gazed out the window at the blue sky and the clouds whiter than goat cheese. Her heart hurt. Her chest hurt. Somewhere in the midst of that news, in the midst of all those bullets and bombs, was her older son. Marco. Any moment now Francesca would return from the walk she had taken with the children, and Beatrice knew that she would have to tell her that the invasion had started, and it had come to the very city on the very island where her husband was stationed. It had come, in fact, to the very beach.

She found herself shivering, despite the July morning sun, and wrapped her arms around her sides. In her mind, she prayed for her son. She prayed that he would survive the day and come home safely to Monte Volta. Behind her, she listened to the sound of the men's voices—the British one through the static of the radio, which she could understand all too well from her years at the university in Pisa, and her husband's, which in her opinion made the English sound pedestrian—and saw in her mind the newsreel footage of battles in Africa and Russia that had been shown in the cinema. But those, of course, were only the sanitized versions the Fascists were willing to share. Handsome young men sitting atop tanks, sometimes with their shirts off, eating their rations with unbelievable ardor; the recoil of artillery pieces with cannons pitched higher than olive trees, the men with their hands pressed against their ears; the occasional image of a bombed city block in Italy or Germany, the purpose of which was to convey how demonic the Allies really were—though the footage never showed anything like the field of corpses she had seen with her own eyes back in May in Arezzo. The films never showed the lifeless bodies that were pulled from beneath hillocks of fallen stone, whole pockets of flesh gnawed away by rats.

Nunzio murmured to her that Marco was smart and he was quite sure that he would be fine; she shouldn't worry. Then he discreetly left her and Antonio alone.

"Nunzio is right, you know," Antonio told her, and his voice indeed sounded unencumbered by trouble. Still, the lines around his eyes looked a little deeper in this light, and for the first time she noticed that his cheeks, once so patrician and firm, had become a little jowly with age.

"Nunzio is a fool," she said.

"You don't mean that."

"No, of course I don't. But he was just spewing forth platitudes. Yes, Marco is smart. But there is no reason in the world to believe he will be fine. I don't think bombs distinguish between the smart and the dull."

"But it helps to be smart. Marco won't take unnecessary risks. Not with two children and a wife waiting for him here. And he's not about to sacrifice his life for Blackshirts and Nazis."

"No."

At the base of the hill, near the parapet for one of the lower gardens, she saw her grandson, Massimo, running with a stick for a saber. Francesca and Alessia couldn't be far behind. And so she stood a little straighter and prepared to tell her daughter-in-law that the invasion had begun, and that it had begun on the very beach where Marco was assigned. The news might result in a thunderstorm of anguish and rage, but Francesca also might grow melancholic and quiet; you could never tell with her. The woman had always been moody, but she had grown even more caustic and mercurial since Marco had left for the war. Perhaps with her children nearby, Francesca might behave properly—behave like Antonio Rosati's daughter-in-law and accept the news with stoicism and grace. Beatrice couldn't decide. Just in case, she rehearsed in her head precisely what she would say and how she would remind her daughter-in-law that no matter what, this was the beginning of the end.

⚜

Cristina spied her brother before Friedrich did, and the idea crossed her mind that this wouldn't be happening if the Americans and the British had waited just one more day before invading. Vittore wouldn't have been summoned back here if the fighting hadn't begun last night in Sicily. But here he was, across the lobby of the hotel where he and Friedrich were billeted, carving his way through the throngs of officers and their women—did no officers sleep alone here? she wondered—using his hands and his elbows to part the crowd. The sun was brightening the curtains in the long windows and streaming in through the glass doors, but the lights—rows of globes that were reminiscent of streetlamps in the corners and above the concierge's desk—were still lit. Initially she wasn't sure what to say, but she could see by the way her brother's brow was furrowed with anger and his eyes were wild with disbelief that the first thing she had to do was warn Friedrich. The lieutenant hadn't yet noticed her brother. And so she squeezed his elbow and murmured, "Look, Vittore's coming," but almost instantly he was upon them, and then, without a word of preamble, he slammed his fist into the side of Friedrich's face, separating her lover from her and sending him sprawling onto the lobby's thick carpet. Vittore dropped to his knees to lift the dazed German up by the lapels of his tunic, and she heard herself shrieking for Vittore to stop, to let him go, when Friedrich, stupefied as he was, lashed back, grabbing her brother by his shoulders and wrestling him down to the floor. There they scuffled like hungry dogs on the street.

"Get off him!" she was yelling at Vittore, but already Friedrich had regained his equilibrium and was wrestling from a position equal to Vittore's. "Stop it!" she screamed at them both while grabbing uselessly at someone's arm—her brother's or Friedrich's, she honestly wasn't sure—as it jackhammered back and forth in the air. It was like trying to catch a seagull: each time it slipped away. Eventually the two men tumbled together into an end table, overturning it and shattering the art deco lamp, a porcelain black panther, that had been resting upon it. And while Cristina was game to try once more to separate the two men, a pair of burly Italian officers appeared and disentangled them, laughing as they pulled at tunics and arms and legs. One of the Italians was actually hauling her brother away by his ankles, tugging him in the direction of the bar. A whole group of officers and their girlfriends were surrounding them now, mostly chortling, though one, a German captain, looked a little dismissive of the brawlers.

Finally she knelt on the floor beside Friedrich, absolutely furious with her brother. He wiped at the blood that was streaming from his nose and a cut on his lip with the back of his hand and then smiled a little darkly. "That must have been lovely to watch," he observed. "Just lovely."

"It wasn't your fault," she reminded him, and she found a handkerchief in her purse that she could use to blot the blood on his face.

"I should have a little talk with Vittore," he told her. "Just the two of us. Alone."

"No, I should talk to him. Then he should apologize to you."

Over her shoulder the men were laughing, and a German with a severe mustache and a complexion as translucent as olive skin patted Friedrich on the back and said—clearly unaware of the fact that Friedrich had already lost a foot—"I don't think they award much for a bloody lip. You'll have to lose much more to get an Iron Cross." Another lieutenant leered at Friedrich and said, "You're supposed to pillage Sabine women, not Vittore's sister, for God's sake."

Cristina looked up at the fellow. Once that sort of remark would have made her feel dirty. Now? Strangely, not at all. She understood how these men were viewing her: Friedrich's whore. But she felt a bit as she had hours earlier, as she had stood in the window in his room, when she had watched the night sky and searched for the moon. She was merely one woman among many here, certainly younger than most (though not all), and while the men might say dismissive things about the girls on their arms, they desired them. And even now, as she pressed a handkerchief with a delicately embroidered lilac against her lover's lip, she felt a distinct glamour. Nothing like this would ever happen in Monte Volta.

Friedrich rested one of his hands on her fingers and pulled the cloth away from his mouth. "Fine. We'll go talk to him together," he said, and motioned with a small nod of his head toward her brother. "But he should know, I will not always be quite this forgiving."

"Of course not," she agreed. "He ambushed you!"

Vittore was staring at them from a plush sunken chair near the bellman's station, as two Italian soldiers stood behind him like bodyguards, their hands pressing down firmly on his shoulders. They were both, it appeared, struggling mightily to keep a straight face. Slowly Friedrich climbed to his feet, a little wobbly from the fight and because he had a prosthetic foot, and together they marched across the lobby to her brother.

⚜

Francesca gently patted her little boy on the small of his back and watched as he raced up the villa's front stairway to his bedroom. Her daughter was on the terrace, just outside the window, apparently in the midst of a staring contest with a lizard: Alessia was on her tummy on the sun-warmed slate, facing the creature, and neither was moving.

Francesca's eye caught a framed photograph on the side table, of Marco and her on their wedding day. She and her mother had wanted them to be married in the Duomo in Pisa, where her family was from, but there was no way a Rosati would be wed anywhere but the church in Monte Volta. And so that was where they were, on the steps just outside the north portal, when that photograph was taken. There was Marco in his black suit, and there she was in a dress more the color of bone than white. It fell an inch below her knees, and it was as elegant as it was simple. The neck scooped low on her chest, but her mother thought there was just enough lace in just the right places for her to defend her daughter's decision. There had been some discussion between her mother and Beatrice over whether she should wear a more formal wedding gown—one that swept the floor as she entered the church—but Francesca had seen what American actresses were wearing in Hollywood, and she desired a dress that was reminiscent of the pictures she had clipped from the magazines.

She shuddered ever so slightly when she tried to imagine what her husband was enduring right now in Sicily. She thought of the beach near Gela and the great coils of barbed wire he had described to her. In her mind, she saw battleships with guns the size of Corinthian columns.

Behind her, she heard her mother-in-law approaching. "No matter what," Beatrice was saying once again, "this is the beginning of the end."

"Have we learned anything more?" she asked. Her father-in-law had been trying to get more information on the radio from the BBC, fiddling with the dial, but a few moments ago, when she had been in the kitchen, the government had begun jamming the signal.

"No. All we're getting now is the Saturday morning opera and the Fascist news station."

"What are they saying?"

"The Fascists? There was a story about the way some unpatriotic women were trying to commandeer extra rations of bread in the cities by pretending they were pregnant."

Francesca nodded. She was a little nauseous with worry. She had known an invasion was coming, but she had hoped desperately it would come anywhere but Sicily.

"Before we know it, the war will be over," her mother-in-law continued. "No one wants us to be fighting in Naples and Rome. No one wants to experience again on our soil what we endured in Caporetto. No one would allow it."

"So we will just surrender?" she snapped, aware as she spoke of how angry she sounded. She took a breath to calm herself. Then, more quietly, she said, "Even a fat man like Il Duce won't roll over just like that. And even if he wanted to, Hitler wouldn't let him."

"I don't know, Francesca. But it makes no sense to continue. Someone will see reason and we will negotiate a treaty. Isn't that what's done in war?"

"Blackshirts and Nazis don't negotiate."

"I said I don't know. But—"

"But this will get worse before it gets better. And right now there are people shooting at my husband—"

"And my son," Beatrice reminded her.

For a long moment the two women stared at each other. Francesca wished that her father-in-law would just give up on the radio. She didn't know which she found more annoying, the static, the Fascists, or the opera. It was the marchesa who looked away first, turning her attention to the wedding photo on the side table. She picked up the frame and said, speaking more toward the image of her son and her daughter-in-law than to Francesca herself, "I am telling you, no matter what happens, this is the beginning of the end."

⚜

Vittore's gaze was not precisely forbidding, but he was scowling. He was exasperated, his patience gone. His skin, flushed from the fight, looked sunburned and raw, and his hair had fallen over his forehead.

"What are you doing?" Cristina asked him. "Have you completely lost your mind?"

"Look at him," he said, referring to Friedrich. "Look at you. You're . . ."

"Yes?"

Vittore glanced up at the soldiers on either side of him in the hotel lobby and put his hands out before him, palms up, in a gesture of capitulation. "Are you finished?" one of the men asked him, grinning, and Vittore nodded that he was. The pair smiled at each other and took their hands off his shoulders, allowing him to rise from the chair in which they had confined him. It seemed to Cristina that Friedrich was about to say something to her brother—she didn't like the way his eyes were still smoldering—and so she asked Friedrich to wait where he was.

"Is that really what you want?" he demanded, glaring at Vittore.

"Yes. That's really what I want," she said. "I want to talk to my brother alone." Then she drew Vittore to a corner of the lobby where they could speak without every soldier and guest in the hotel reception area eavesdropping. Already crowds had begun milling about in search of news of the invasion, trying to separate the rumors, such as the notion that Allied paratroopers were already in Rome, from reality.

"I'm serious. Have you gone crazy?" Cristina inquired once more. "Why in the name of heaven would you attack a German lieutenant in the middle of Florence?"

He paused, and she could see that he was grinding his teeth, the sockets at the edge of his jaw ballooning the sides of his face. "Why in the name of heaven would you sleep with one?"

"It's not like that."

"No?"

"No. What we do is—"

"I just found my sister in a hotel with a Nazi," he hissed, cutting her off. "I think my reaction was perfectly sane."

She considered this, restraining the urge to slap him hard on the face because her family had already made a scene. And so instead she turned brusquely on her heels and started toward Friedrich, but Vittore caught her by the elbow and spun her back around so she was facing him.

"Cristina, don't you see what the Germans are? They are even worse than our Fascists!" he said, his voice low but intense. "They are taking over the country, they're stealing our art. They hate us—they hate everyone who isn't one of them! Who knows what they're really doing to the Jews, who knows what—"

"Friedrich isn't responsible for any of that. He—"

"They are loathsome. There is a reason the world is against them—and against us for losing our minds and siding with them. And now, you of all people—"

"You work with them! How dare you criticize me?"

"I work with them because I haven't a choice. I work with them because I have a gun to my head."

"You don't. While our brother is right now fighting for his life in Sicily, you're here in Florence dusting off pottery chips." She spoke without thinking, and only when she had finished did she realize how deeply the remark might have hurt him. But he didn't seem wounded. He lowered his eyes for just a moment and smirked, shaking his head.

"You are such a child," he said, his voice softening with bemusement. "First of all, Marco is as much under the Germans' thumb as I am. And he is every bit as disgusted by that reality, if not more. Why? Precisely because he is fighting for his life right now. But he hadn't a choice either. Second, you have no idea what I do. None. I spend my life trying to prevent your boyfriend and his fellow Nazis from sending all of Florence or Arezzo to Berlin, or to some swaggering Prussian's estate on the Baltic. Or even to the Gestapo in Rome. But fine. Fine. Really, why should I care if my little sister has become a Nazi's whore?"

This time she didn't worry that people were watching: she took her right hand and swung it, palm open, as hard as she could into her older brother's cheek.

1955

On Sunday, Giulia Rosati kissed her children good night in the bedroom the siblings shared. The family's home was on the second floor of an apartment building in the shadow of Rome's Castel Sant'Angelo. Then she turned off the lamp and left the door open just enough to allow a sliver of light from the hallway to help them feel safe. She still had not told them that their grandmother was dead and that was why their father had suddenly rushed off to Florence. Nearly a week ago now, when she and Vittore had first learned that Francesca had been murdered, they'd both presumed that her death had resulted directly from her lifestyle. Giulia wasn't as judgmental as Vittore, but she agreed that most likely it had been an angry or jealous lover who had killed the woman.

The death of Beatrice, however, seemed to suggest this was something very different.

When Giulia returned to the living room, the uniformed police officer was reading the newspaper. She gazed for a long moment at his holstered gun. He sensed she was watching him, bent down the top of the newspaper, and shrugged. He had a long face and a seemingly lipless mouth. She guessed he was, like her, in his late thirties.

"The babies asleep?" he asked.

"I think my four-year-old would not be happy to be called a baby," Giulia told him lightly.

"She is headstrong then. Like my daughter."

"Yes," she agreed. "She is a bit headstrong."

He put the newspaper down on the side table. "You'll be fine," he said after a moment. "Nothing is going to happen to you or your children. Not here in Rome."

"Not anywhere."

"That's right," he said. "Not anywhere."

Giulia's mother still lived just outside Florence, in Fiesole. She had told her daughter on the phone that all anyone in the city was talking about was the killer with the vendetta against the remnants of a Tuscan marchese's family. She'd added that some people, it seemed, had gone from worrying about their own safety after Francesca had been killed—who was this madman who had cut the heart from a woman?—to viewing it more as an unbelievably interesting spectacle that didn't concern them. After all, if you weren't among the last of the Rosatis, you weren't in danger.

"Would you like more coffee?" she asked the officer.

He nodded and handed her his cup and saucer. "Thank you," he said. "You want me awake tonight."

She passed the mirror that hung on the wall between the living room and the kitchen, but didn't notice herself in the glass as much as she did the carvings of Venus and Mars at the base of the gilt wood frame. The mirror was just under five hundred years old, and according to Rosati family myth, it had once belonged to Piero de' Medici. It had survived the shelling and then the looting at the Villa Chimera, when Beatrice herself had dug a hole in the high grass beyond the swimming pool and buried it.

Giulia had never seen the estate before it was charred trees and rubble. She had never seen the chimera. But she had seen pictures of the villa before the war had come to Monte Volta.

In the kitchen, she packed as much coffee as she possibly could into the espresso machine filter. She did indeed want to be sure that this policeman was awake until morning. She presumed she would be, too.

Chief Inspector Paolo Ficino tossed his own newspaper into the trash can on the sidewalk before climbing the stairs to his apartment. He knew his wife had already seen the latest articles Sunday afternoon about the butcher who was cutting the hearts from a Tuscan family in Florence, but there was no point in bringing those sorts of lurid headlines into their home for their sixteen-year-old daughter to read.

The reporters hadn't yet made the leap that whoever had murdered the two Rosatis might have done so because of the war, and neither he nor the prosecutor had volunteered that theory when they had been interviewed. Maybe they never would. Because maybe there really was no connection. After all, Paolo kept asking himself, if this did go back to the war, why had the killer waited a decade to start his work? And it had been a decade. Paolo had looked into Antonio Rosati's death, and the fellow had died of a heart attack on a sunny summer afternoon, walking through the Villa Borghese in Rome. There were witnesses galore. Paolo knew he was taking the idea that this vendetta had something to do with the war seriously only because of Serafina. Clearly the prosecutor, Sergio Contucci, gave very little credence to the notion.

When Serafina had returned from Monte Volta, she told him that she believed she had been to the Villa Chimera before. After the firefight in the summer of 1944, when the partisans had retreated from the hills outside Trequanda, they must have taken her to the Rosati estate. She had been hidden there, shielded inside the Etruscan tombs from the sun and the Nazis. But, Paolo wondered, did this have any bearing on the investigation? Again, he couldn't imagine how. He hoped she was telling him everything, but he honestly wasn't sure. So much of her life was a mystery to him and, he guessed, even to her. He recalled the intense, wounded sparrow who had come to him in 1947, wanting to be a detective. He would have dismissed the idea right away if he hadn't noticed her neck and her ear; her disfigurements had been more obvious then. He knew, as young as she was, this wasn't play-acting. He knew she had a history and it was a history that might make her a worthy apprentice. A worthy pioneer. He discovered quickly how smart she was. And, at her insistence, what a good shot she was. He gave her a gun, suggested she not advertise that she had it. For years, almost nobody knew. Now those who did looked the other way.

Paolo considered whether he should be more worried about Beatrice's sister in Naples or her niece's little family in London, but his instinct told him that these murders had nothing to do with them. Still . . .

He stood for a moment and breathed in the night air, grateful that it was a little cooler, a little less humid than he had expected. Then he started up the narrow stairway to his wife and teenage daughter.

☙

"Vittore and Cristina are planning to bury their mother and Francesca with the rest of the family at the estate in Monte Volta," Serafina told Milton as their paths crossed in the kitchen in their apartment Monday morning. For breakfast Milton would have either coffee and a cigarette or a day-old chocolate pastry, if he happened to find a leftover one on the counter. It was pretty much how she started the day, too.

He seemed to think about this. He was holding a pair of neckties in his hands, and she pointed at the blue-and-gold one.

"Really? I'm wearing a gray suit today. I was leaning toward the red one."

"The blue always looks good against your eyes," she reminded him.

"Can't argue with that," he said. Then: "Will you be there?"

"At the funeral?"

"Uh-huh." He draped the red necktie over a chair and started tying the blue one around his neck. He was using the chrome side of the toaster as a mirror. She'd bought him the toaster for Christmas last year, thinking he would want to heat bread in the morning because he was an American, but he used it rarely and only, she presumed, because he loved her and wanted her to feel that he appreciated the gift.

"Yes. I think Paolo and I will both go."

"When is it?"

"Soon. Wednesday, I believe."

"Family only?"

"What's left of it. But Cristina says some villagers will probably come out of respect for the marchesa. And maybe some of the peasants who once worked on the farm."

"Such as that delightful young man you told me about who's now employed at the terra-cotta factory?"

"Ilario? Perhaps. We'll see."

He had finished with his necktie now and he took a puff from her cigarette. When he had replaced it in the ashtray, he wrapped his hands around her upper arms and asked, his voice firm, "And how are you? You've told me about some of the people you interviewed when you went to Monte Volta, but almost nothing about what it was like for you to be back there."

"Maybe later."

"Maybe later because it's a long story or maybe later because it's a wrenching one?"

"Just long."

"You're lying."

She took his right hand off her arm and kissed it. "Yes, I am," she said. Then she licked her fingers and wiped her lipstick off his skin. "But it's a long story, too. And we both have to get to work."

When Serafina arrived at the police station, she had a cable waiting from West Berlin. Friedrich Strekker was listed as missing and presumed dead. In October 1944 he had been promoted from lieutenant to captain and transferred to a newly formed Panzer-grenadier combat division. The division had been almost entirely wiped out in the battle for Budapest in the early months of 1945. No more than two or three hundred men escaped the city on February 13, and a one-legged captain was not among them.

"Serafina?"

She looked up and saw Paolo.

"The Rosatis are here," he said.

"Thank you." She put the wire into a folder. She wondered how she would tell Cristina.

Serafina and Paolo sat on one side of the table in the drab interview room down the hall from the detectives' desks, and Vittore and Cristina sat on the other. Serafina hoped the Rosatis had each gotten a good night's sleep, but based on the bags under their eyes, she doubted it.

"Have you given any more thought this weekend to who doesn't like you?" Paolo asked. Then he focused his attention on Vittore. "The sooner you can give us any direction, the sooner we can apprehend this lunatic and your wife and children will be safe. Your aunt in Naples will be safe."

Vittore sat back in the wooden chair, his hands in his lap. "Obviously people were jealous of us. But by 1944 they should have pitied us. Really, who lost as much as we did?"

Paolo shrugged. "But since the war? Did you offend someone at the Vatican? Did your mother—"

"Even if I did offend someone at the Vatican Museum," he said, emphasizing the word *museum*, "why would he kill Francesca? Why not kill me? Besides, I spend my life examining and cataloging five-hundred-year-old pieces of sculpture. I design exhibits for tourists. I'm not sure it's possible for me to offend someone."

"Why did you lose interest in the Etruscans?"

"I didn't. I lost interest in Arezzo and Florence and Tuscany. Giulia and I wanted to live in Rome. I work with Renaissance sculptures because I was able to get a job at the Vatican Museum. It's not complicated."

The older detective turned to Cristina. "And why did you and your parents move to Rome instead of remaining in Monte Volta?"

"After what our family endured there? That would be too painful. None of us could ever live there. Someday, perhaps, we'll try to sell it. Besides, if you saw the villa . . . ," she said, her voice trailing off. She turned to Serafina and continued. "Remind him what you saw when you went there the other day."

Paolo held up both hands. "I know your estate is in very bad shape. But why not take a place in the nearby village, where you had roots? If money is tight, I would think it would be much less expensive to live in Monte Volta than in Rome."

"Our father was a marchese and our mother a marchesa," Vittore answered. "Given their station, it would have been beneath them to live among the villagers."

Cristina shook her head and smiled a little wanly. "Honestly, Vittore, you make them out to be such snobs. They weren't. Especially Mother. My parents and I lived in Rome to be near Vittore and Giulia. Then, after Father died, my mother and I stayed there because Mother wanted to be near her grandchildren. It's just that simple. She wanted to be near you and Giulia and the kids, especially after the loss of Massimo and Alessia." Then she said to the two detectives, "We didn't lose everything in the war. Obviously. We can afford our apartment in Rome."

Serafina leaned forward, her elbows on the table. "A wire came in early this morning. From Germany." She watched both siblings grow alert. "Your lieutenant, Cristina—Friedrich—died in the battle for Budapest. I don't know if it matters, but he died a captain."

Cristina nodded ever so slightly and breathed in deeply through her nose. Then she sighed. "Where is he buried?" she asked after a moment.

"We'll never know. The body was never recovered. Let's face it, Budapest was in ruins. A city of rubble by the time the Nazis and the Soviets were finished with it."

"Maybe he was taken prisoner," Cristina argued, but it was halfhearted.

"A captain? By then the Russians weren't taking captains prisoner," Vittore said, and although Serafina knew he was right, she wished he hadn't been so blunt.

"I'm sorry," she told Cristina. "I really am."

"It is what I assumed all these years. Obviously."

"It's probably a relief to know, isn't it?" Paolo added.

Instead of agreeing, however, Cristina looked directly at Serafina and said, a small hesitation in her voice, "My mother told me something interesting after she met you."

Serafina waited. She had a sense of what was coming, and while Cristina probably wasn't sharing it consciously as a quid pro quo—*This is what you get for confirming that my Friedrich is dead*—Serafina understood that on some level it was.

"She thought she knew you," Cristina said. "She thought she had seen you before."

"Serafina?" Paolo asked. "Your mother thought she knew Serafina?"

"Yes."

"How?" he asked. "Where?"

Serafina sat unmoving, a hum in her ears. Inside her head. She thought of the birds amid the black clouds on the ceiling of the tomb and an Etruscan boy steering his small boat against maelstromlike seas. She saw them now from the stone floor where the partisans had placed her nearly ruined body. She recalled the agony of the burns and how she had noticed the painting—and yes, the sun behind the thunderclouds—first through her tears. She had had to blink them away to be sure that what she was seeing was not a hallucination. In her mind, she smelled the mushrooms.

"She said she thought you were the burned girl," Cristina was saying. "The partisan burned girl. She thought you had died in the tombs."

Serafina felt everyone at the table staring at her. "Did she tell you anything else?" she asked.

"About you?"

"Yes. About . . . me."

"At first, on Wednesday, she honestly wasn't sure where she had seen you before. But then on Thursday, when she saw you run out of Francesca's apartment, she noticed your ear. And then she knew."

"Go on."

"My mother said she brought you the very last of our olive oil. She gave it to the men who carried you to the tombs. She even gave them the last of Francesca's face cream. They took it, but mostly they wanted soap and rags they could boil. They wanted water. They really didn't want my mother's help. They were going to nurse you themselves."

"Especially the woman," Serafina said. She was thinking of Teresa, Enrico's wife. Teresa was as capable of shooting a German officer as she was, but Teresa was eight years older. She was no longer a teenager and thus mothered their small band. She could be tender; she *was* tender. The men adored her and Serafina revered her. So much of what they did as a group was simply waiting—waiting for orders, waiting for food, waiting for dark—but Teresa seemed always to be moving. She cooked. She scouted. She wrote notes for the men who couldn't read. Like her husband, she felt acutely every death and every defection. Now Serafina could imagine how hard she and Enrico must have worked to keep her alive.

"The woman," Cristina agreed. "But the men, too."

"And then the British arrived," Serafina said. It was a statement, but she really wasn't sure.

"Yes," Vittore said. "Then the British arrived."

"So you were in Monte Volta, too?" Serafina asked him.

"No, I was here—in Florence."

"And where were you, Cristina?" Paolo asked. "Did you see Serafina when the partisans brought her to your estate?"

"I never saw your face. I only saw your . . . back," she said, almost swallowing the last word as if it were an obscenity. As if seeing the wound had been a violation of sorts. "You were lying on the floor in the kitchen," she continued after a moment.

"This wasn't in the tombs?" Serafina asked.

"Not at first," Cristina said. "The Germans had blown up the granary that morning before leaving and there was fighting in Trequanda, the next village over. I remember the ground literally shook from the granary blast, even at the Villa Chimera. That night the partisans came and you were brought to the house. But then the Germans returned. The British were already behind them and so the Nazis were going to make a last stand at the estate—they liked the high ground." Then she looked right at Serafina. "And so my mother and father had me take you all to the underground tombs to hide. I think they expected you to leave in the middle of the night. Just disappear. At least that's what they hoped."

"But we wouldn't leave," Serafina said. "Because they were afraid to move me again." She watched as Vittore draped his hand on his sister's and squeezed it. Outside, a delivery van honked and someone yelled for a double-parked automobile to move off the street. She heard a motorcycle race through the congestion. And down the corridor, in the room with the detectives' desks, she heard laughter and a typewriter. In her mind, she still couldn't see Beatrice in 1944, she couldn't recall the marchesa bringing them water and oil and lotion, but somewhere very far away she heard a man's voice and she had a sense it was Antonio's. He and Enrico were arguing, and they were arguing about her. The small band of partisans had refused to leave the estate, retreating only as far as the Etruscan tombs. It was in all likelihood the reason that she was alive today.

⚜

As the two of them left the police station for a bite to eat, Paolo surprised Serafina by offering her his elbow. She took it, but she was puzzled.

"So you think Captain Friedrich Strekker died in the battle for Budapest," he said casually.

"I don't think it. I know it. I have the cable from Berlin."

"A one-legged man who has been out of combat more than two years is promoted to captain in a Panzergrenadier division.

That's what you believe." He motioned with his free hand at a lavender dress in a shop window. "I should buy that for my wife. The only thing stopping me? Many thousands of lire."

"The Nazis were desperate for manpower by the end of the war," she reminded him. "They were commandeering fifteen-year-old boys and fifty-five-year-old men. Think of the Volkssturm."

"This wasn't Volkssturm. This was a Panzergrenadier division. This was the battle for Budapest."

"What are you suggesting?"

"Honestly? I don't know. I'm puzzled. Cristina Rosati's Romeo—her desperate first love—might very well be dead. In fact, he probably is dead."

"But . . ."

"But I don't believe he was ever in Budapest in 1945."

1943

CRISTINA REACHED THE barn on the estate and dismounted. She rubbed Arabella's long nose, savoring the aroma of the field grasses that clung like perfume to the animal, and then walked the horse into the shade. It was early September. She stretched her back and gazed toward the fields, where she saw Ilario and another, much older field hand repairing one of the irrigation channels in the distance. They were working with their shirts off. Ilario looked up and saw that she had noticed them, and so she smiled and waved. Then she bent over to unstrap the saddle. As she was lifting it off, she saw that Ilario was jogging toward her.

"You don't need to stop what you're doing," she said when he reached her, assuming he wanted to help her hoist the saddle onto its shoulder-high prongs in the barn and sponge down Arabella. "I can do this."

He paused and looked a little confused. Apparently this wasn't why he had come over at all. "No, I . . ."

"Go on."

"I didn't know if you'd heard. I just learned myself."

"What?"

"The British have landed! Americans, too, I think. They're in Salerno. Right this minute, they're fighting in Salerno. Maybe tomorrow they'll be in Naples."

She tried to focus. Everything was happening so fast. "And you know this for a fact? It's not rumor?"

"No rumor. The BBC."

She said nothing, wondering where Marco was. He had been among the soldiers who had been ferried across the Strait of Messina to the toe of the boot in mid-August, an evacuation of over one hundred thousand Germans and Italians, but they hadn't heard another word from him or about him in the three weeks since.

"I thought you'd be happy," Ilario said, his tone rippling between disappointment and disgust.

She had recurring visions of what it must have been like for Marco when the battleships had started shelling the island, based on the little—very little, actually—Friedrich had told her of his experiences in France and Russia.

"But you're not happy," Ilario was saying. "You're thinking of that Nazi you're in love with, aren't you?"

She looked at him. Why in the world had she ever thought there was something attractive about him? "No," she answered, correcting the farmhand. "I was thinking about my brother. But of course now I am thinking of Friedrich, too."

"Soon the Allies will be here, and he'll be gone."

She didn't understand why he would say that—why he would be so cruel. So hurtful. She couldn't see why he wanted to make her suffer. Her instinct was to lash out, perhaps remind him caustically that yes, Friedrich might soon be gone, but Ilario would be here forever, caring for sheep and propping up the sides of irrigation channels. But she kept her composure, telling herself that she was a marchese's daughter and there was no need to lodge a dagger in this . . . boy's heart.

"I need to cool down and brush Arabella," she said evenly. "The Allies may be in Salerno, but that doesn't mean all work here has to stop."

Vittore was kneeling before a statue of Giovanni dalle Bande Nere in a badly lit storage room in the Uffizi basement, trying to read the inscription that had been carved four hundred years earlier into the base. He was grateful to be working down here in the cool dampness this morning. The outside air was heavy, and he had found himself sweating as he had walked along the Arno on his way to the museum. When he heard someone running down the stairs and then racing along the corridor, he sat back on his heels. In a second he heard Lorenzetti's voice behind him and turned around.

"We've made peace with the Allies!" Lorenzetti told him breathlessly.

Slowly Vittore stood and brushed the dust from the floor off his pants.

"Aren't you listening to me?" Lorenzetti asked, his eyes giddy. "The war's over!"

"No, it's not."

"It is! We've surrendered!"

The Allies had taken Sicily and were fighting south of Naples. Clearly they had no plans to leave Italy. But, Vittore knew, neither did the Germans. "All that means is we're going to have to fight a different war," he said, rubbing at his temples. He wondered what this meant for Marco, and worried.

"What in God's name are you talking about?" Lorenzetti asked.

"The Germans."

"The Allies will be here any moment. We wouldn't have surrendered if there weren't a . . . a deal."

"What kind of deal? The Hermann Göring Division is going to part for the British and the Americans like the Red Sea? The Germans have been streaming south for months. All we are now is an occupied nation."

Lorenzetti leaned back against the cold wall. "You're wrong. You have to be," he said.

Vittore felt the pockets of his uniform pants, wishing he had even a stub of a cigarette. He didn't. "Have you seen Decher this morning?" he asked.

"No. Should we go find him?"

"He'll find us."

"If you're right, Vittore—and I'm not saying you are—where do you think that leaves us?"

He honestly didn't know, and so he said nothing. He tried to outline his options in his mind and didn't really like any of them.

Erhard Decher felt an exhilarating rush of adrenaline when he read the order. This wasn't combat, but at least it was confrontational. It was work that actually mattered. He was being sent a dozen men from the Florence garrison to round up and disarm the Italians in his group. Then they would have a choice: they could either pledge an oath to the new Italian government the Germans were propping up or become—and Decher rather liked this term, because it meant the Italians were not prisoners of war, precisely, and thus lacked protection under the Geneva Convention—military internees. Decher speculated that a gutless recreant like Giancarlo Lorenzetti would vow allegiance even to Hitler if it meant he'd be spared, but Vittore Rosati? He was less sure what Vittore would do—and he was less sure what he wanted Vittore to do. If the fellow knuckled under, he'd lose respect for him, and the truth was, Vittore was among the few Italians for whom he had any admiration. It would also mean that his adjutant would continue to sleep with the fellow's slatternly younger sister, and no good was ever going to come from that relationship. On the other hand, if Vittore showed a little spine, he would have to arrest him, and that, in turn, might result in Decher's having to forgo the pleasures of the Villa Chimera. And the colonel was fast growing accustomed to the charm of Antonio Rosati's estate. Besides, he liked taking people there; he knew it helped his career.

He looked out his office window and gathered himself. Then he barked out his door for Strekker to join him. When he didn't hear the lieutenant slide his chair back from his desk or the fellow's annoying limp, he shouted for him again. Irritated, he strode to the doorway to demand the young man's attention and was surprised to see that he wasn't at his desk. He shook his head, trying to recall what errand he or Voss must have sent the lad on.

♣

But the Allies were stalled at Salerno. Penned in for weeks.

Every day that September, Francesca studied an antique map of Italy that hung behind glass in the villa library, waiting for news of Marco or news that Naples had fallen or news that the British and the Americans were on the road to Rome. She waited, unlike Cristina, for news that the Germans were leaving Italy.

But that news never came that autumn. Naples was officially liberated on October 1, but it was clear that the Nazis were going to stand firm along the river Sangro, well south of Rome. The western edge of their defense would be particularly formidable: a chain of mountains anchored by a place Francesca was told was called Monte Cassino. Erhard Decher did not know or would not share all the details, but one night when he was dining in Monte Volta, she overheard him and an SS colonel—SS, she thought, galled, in the dining room of the Villa Chimera—boasting that the Germans had fifteen divisions along the line.

Meanwhile, Cristina continued to see Friedrich in Florence and here in the country, basking in the idea that she had a lover and in the particulars of the young man who had placed an emerald along the small of her neck. The children continued to romp in the swimming pool until it grew too cold, and then they took their dolls and toy soldiers to the quiescent grass along the hillsides above the Etruscan tombs. And Antonio and Beatrice watched the estate shrink—the harvests were smaller to begin with, and the Germans quickly absconded with whatever was grown or butchered—but still they entertained what was now an occupying army whenever the Nazis in Florence wanted a night in the country.

And while the Allied planes flew overhead with increasing impunity, no one took seriously the talk that the Germans were going to bring an antiaircraft battery to Monte Volta and set up the guns atop the medieval granary towers.

Now, the November air damp and the twilight falling early, Francesca once more turned from the map in the library and pulled tight a shawl around her shoulders. This was, she realized, neither heaven nor hell, and she recalled a canto from Dante. *My family,* she thought with disgust, *is commingling with the cowardly angels. We will pay. We will all pay.* It was only a matter of time.

Part
Two

I PRESUMED I WOULD first execute the police officer. The guard.

But I rather hoped I wouldn't have to. I took chloroform with me on the off chance that I could merely incapacitate him. Since I had not killed Francesca's lover the night when I pulled her heart from her chest, it had become an odd point of honor for me. No one should die, if I could help it, other than the survivors of Antonio and Beatrice's ugly little brood. This was not a hard-and-fast rule, mind you, and I was fully prepared to slaughter the guard if necessary. But in the interest of a certain moral tidiness, I was going to strive to spare him.

In any case, I packed my tools into my valise and drove south to Rome. I presumed I would need two nights, the first to study the Rosatis' apartment and see where the guard had positioned himself and the second to exact my revenge.

When I arrived, it was midday, and the sun was searing the city as I stood on a bridge overlooking the Tiber River. An American family saw me alone, smoking a cigarette, and asked me to photograph them as they posed with the Castel Sant'Angelo in the background. There were six of them: a father, a mother, and four teenaged children. A pair of boys and a pair of girls. I guessed the oldest child might have been attending university. They were all very blond, and it was the father who asked me in heavily accented but enthusiastic Italian to please "capture" their picture. The camera was German and I knew the factory where it had been manufactured.

I put my cigarette down on the railing, snapped two pictures, and then returned the camera. The American thanked me as I retrieved my cigarette. He pointed at my valise.

"Are you a tourist, too?" he asked.

"I am," I said.

He motioned toward the Via della Conciliazione, the wide concourse that links the Castel Sant'Angelo with the Piazza San Pietro and the Vatican. *"Any idea how many more blocks to St. Peter's? We've been on our feet since breakfast."*

"Once you're a block from the bridge," I answered, *"look to your left. You'll be able to see it."*

"So it's close?"

"It is."

"Tell me, if you don't mind, what are you here to see? I always like to be sure I've done my homework."

I spread wide my arms in agreement. *"Me, too!"*

"Okay, then: What's most important? Obviously the Pantheon and the Colosseum and the Vatican. What else?"

"I am after the heart of this city," I said, entertaining myself instead of really answering his question. I pointed in the general direction of Vittore Rosati's apartment. *"And I think I will find it just a few blocks from here."*

"So for you it's St. Peter's?"

I shrugged, smiled, and sent them on their way. Already in my mind I saw myself subduing the guard protecting Giulia Rosati and her two little girls and then mining their still-warm hearts.

1944

VITTORE'S KNEES WERE sore and his back ached. For five hours he had been kneeling on a wooden platform before a wall of five-hundred-year-old frescoes behind the altar of a Florentine church, swaddling the images in tinfoil and glass wool—protection from the bombing and fires that loomed. He had been at it since dawn and he had barely made a dent in the stories. He was still protecting the Old Testament prophets. John the Baptist and Mary and Jesus remained a long, long way away. He was working by the light of an Italian army flashlight and already he had run through half a dozen batteries. He didn't know how many he had left, but not enough to finish this project. If the sun would come out, there might be enough light for him to turn the flashlight off for a while, but it was an overcast summer day, the sky an endless sheet of pale gray.

When Vittore paused, craning his neck and stretching his back, he noticed Lorenzetti standing in the shadow of the scaffolding ten feet below him.

"Be sure to leave space between the painting and your covering. You don't want there to be any mold," he said to Vittore.

Frescoes were Lorenzetti's specialty, and so Vittore was able to restrain his urge to snap at him. "I'm trying," he said simply.

"After it rains, it can be very damp in here," Lorenzetti went on. Then he added, "And be careful not to mar the patina."

"I know."

In another section of the church, Emilio was swaddling a mosaic in burlap to keep the small pieces in place. Outside, Moretti was piling sandbags around a Pazzi sculpture in the courtyard. The Allies were moving north quickly now that the Nazis had given them Rome. The Germans were fighting a rearguard action as they retreated up the Italian boot, and no one could say for sure when the fighting would reach Florence. But everyone did know this: the Nazis were going to make their last stand at what they were calling the Gothic Line, a string of entrenchments and defenses along the peaks of the Apennines a good twenty to twenty-five kilometers north of the city.

"They're outside mining the bridges right now," Lorenzetti said, referring to the Germans, his voice tired and disgusted. "I couldn't watch anymore. Here we are trying to save as much as we can, and they're planning to blow up the bridges across the Arno. Even the Bridge of Santa Trinità. Nearly four hundred years old. Francavilla's magnificent statue of spring. And those philistines are going to dynamite it."

Vittore swung his legs over the platform and sat there. That morning Decher had told him that he didn't expect the British or Americans to reach Monte Volta for at least a week, and he didn't believe the Germans would make much of a stand there. He presumed Oskar Muller, the captain in charge of the artillery unit billeted at the Villa Chimera, would pull up stakes and retreat toward Arezzo. There, he expected, they might make a brief fight. But Monte Volta? Not likely, Decher said. He had laughed cryptically and told Vittore that soon his family would have their little place back.

"And you?" Vittore had asked him. "Do you think you'll miss Florence?" Decher had gotten what he wanted: he had been pressed into real service. Tomorrow he was leaving the Uffizi and a world of art historians and academics and going to join the fight. He had been ordered to Arezzo that evening and he was taking Friedrich with him, despite the fact that the lieutenant was crippled. Apparently Friedrich had demanded that he be allowed to accompany the colonel.

"I doubt it," Decher had answered. "I really won't miss this city. I'm sorry to admit that, but that's how it is. But you know something, Vittore? I will miss Monte Volta. You people are not meant for this sort of war or even this sort of world, but sometimes you build something special. And your family's estate? It's special." Then Decher had turned and left. It wasn't good-bye—not quite yet—but somehow it felt like it. Vittore had even expected him to extend his hand, and he honestly wasn't sure if he would have accepted it; he didn't like Decher, and he didn't approve of the way his father had opened up the estate to the Germans over the past year and allowed Cristina to spend so much time with Friedrich. He presumed his father regretted that hospitality now; he had been thanked for his kindness and generosity by having a Wehrmacht company take over the villa and grounds and force the entire family to live in the nursery. And Cristina, the marchese Antonio Rosati's only daughter? The whole world knew what she was doing with the Nazi lieutenant. No good could come from that once the Germans had retreated north of Florence. Still, at least the fellow would be out of his sister's life now. Friedrich would no longer be dancing in the villa and sunbathing beside the swimming pool. No doubt sleeping with Cristina when they were ostensibly picnicking in the high grass near the tombs.

Below him Vittore heard Lorenzetti saying something, and so he looked down at the major. "Did you hear me?" Lorenzetti was asking him. "Those bastards are going to blow up the bridges! This is not going to be like Rome. They're not just going to sneak away in the night with their tails between their legs."

"But at least they're going to leave," Vittore said.

"Not without a fight. And mark my words, any minute now they are going to take away your glass wool and tinfoil and give you a rifle. Me, too. You and I are about to be forced into becoming honest-to-God soldiers."

The grounds of the Villa Chimera had long been chewed up by the soldiers' jackboots and tent pegs and the deep ruts from the wheels on their lorries and jeeps, and now the estate was awash in dust and grime as the Germans packed up their gear and the four massive howitzers and prepared to retreat toward Arezzo. Some of the drivers were trying to camouflage their vehicles, using rope and twine to attach scrub from the vineyard to truck roofs and half-tracks, since they were going to have to travel by daylight, but even Cristina knew that the Allied planes would spot them when the convoy tried to blend in by the side of the road. After all, she'd been watching the airplanes for years.

She had been waiting for days for Friedrich to return, and now he had come and the timing couldn't have been worse. It was chaos, the soldiers barking orders back and forth and racing about like whirling dervishes. She knew that many of them were also pocketing whatever silver her mother hadn't buried—which, after all the humiliations they had endured the last month, should have been the least of her concerns, but she found the petty theft the final indignity. These soldiers, even the officers, were nothing like Friedrich.

She turned her attention from the gardens along the front walkway, which had been trampled into a riot of weeds soon after the Nazis arrived, to her lieutenant. She decided she would take him to the meadow above the tombs, one of the few corners of the estate where even during the past month she and Friedrich had found a measure of privacy. When he reached her, he took her in his arms and held her for a long quiet moment.

"You are like a statue in the midst of a sandstorm," he whispered into her ear, trying to make a small joke. She didn't smile. Instead she burrowed deeper against him, as if she could hide in his jacket from the sounds of the men yelling and running and the occasional roar as another motorcycle or lorry growled to life. Once she thought she heard Arabella whinny in the distance, but her horse would have to wait. Arabella and Oriana were the only animals remaining at the Villa Chimera. The last of the sheep and the cattle had been slaughtered the moment the Germans had encamped on the estate. The soldiers had burned many of the trees in the olive grove for cooking and bonfires soon after they'd arrived. When her mother heard the sound of the chopping, she had wept on the blankets where she was curled up on the floor of the nursery.

"You don't need to worry," he said. "The Americans and the British will treat you well. They are not like the Russians. They're a civilized people."

She considered telling him that she was relieved the other Germans were leaving and she wasn't frightened in the slightest of the approaching armies. Now she felt the sort of rage toward his countrymen that Francesca had lived with daily for years.

"How long can you stay?" she asked finally.

"Not long."

"Hours?"

He rubbed her back slowly. "Maybe one," he answered after a moment.

"Then come with me," she murmured, and she stood up straight, took him by the hand, and led him through the throngs of loud young men to the hillside above the tombs.

Antonio and Beatrice stood on the terrace and gazed over the soldiers at the village of Monte Volta across the valley. Francesca and their grandchildren were upstairs, trying to stay out of the way, but Massimo had been hypnotized all month by the four big cannons and was angry that his mother had not allowed him to watch the soldiers prepare to tow them away.

For a moment Beatrice stared at the twin towers of the granary. There was a rumor that the Germans were going to blow them up, but she didn't believe that. It would be a waste, and for what? The Germans were scurrying north like frightened lizards. The Allies would have no need of the granary as a spotting or reconnaissance tower. She felt her husband's fingers on her arm and looked at him. He gestured ever so slightly with his chin. She followed his eyes and saw Cristina and Friedrich walking hand in hand past the fields where as recently as last year there had been seemingly endless rows of grape arbors. No more. This year it was nothing but tall grass and weeds, the wild plants tangling the wooden stanchions where every other year there had been the robust Sangiovese vines.

"I say good riddance to him, too," Antonio said quietly.

"She'll miss him," Beatrice said.

He shook his head sadly. "Tell me," he sighed after a moment. "What have I done?"

She knew what he was referring to, because he had asked the question often that summer. It was a deep, visceral current of self-loathing. He had let this one soldier into his daughter's life. Then he had allied himself with the men his second son worked with in Florence. And suddenly he had found himself giving a personal tour of the Etruscan tombs to the Gestapo chief in Rome. Kappler, the man's name was. Herbert Kappler. He had come to Monte Volta with an entourage that filled three staff cars. He'd spent the night in the guest room overlooking the swimming pool. Dined with the marchese's family on the small plenty that remained at the Villa Chimera, while SS troopers stood guard outside the villa— and lined the roads switchbacking up to the estate—against partisans.

And somehow they had to feed those very same partisans when they came and demanded food, too.

Then Rome had fallen and the villa had been commandeered by the Nazis. Like his wife, Antonio had presumed there would be peace well before the fighting ever came to Tuscany. They were mistaken. Beatrice wondered where Kappler was now.

And so even though Antonio had been asking this same rhetorical question all month—*What have I done?*—once more she answered him. "Cristina fell in love with Friedrich before you did anything," she said. "He's not the reason the barbarians took over our home. He's not the reason the whole house smells like a stable."

"I wish it smelled that good."

"Fine. It smells like a toilet. But it's not Friedrich's fault—and neither is it yours."

Antonio sat down on the small balustrade, moving a little gingerly. "No? We make compromises. We look the other way. Then, when it's over, we can't look at ourselves in the mirror."

Once more she was struck by how fast he was aging. Today he looked especially tired and frail. Was it the latest degradation, sleeping on the nursery floor? Or was it the . . . betrayal? As recently as April he had hosted a weekend ball for the Germans and Italians who worked at the Uffizi with Vittore, and it had been a glorious spring escape for them all—except, ironically, for Vittore, who at the last moment had dug in his heels and expressed his disapproval by refusing to come. There had not been much food, but Antonio had brought in musicians from Arezzo. The weather had been perfect and the dancing had lasted well into the night. He and Decher and Lorenzetti had polished off the remaining bottles of last year's Brunello between two and three in morning.

But then Monte Cassino had surrendered and suddenly Rome was gone, too. And then Captain Oskar Muller had come to Monte Volta and taken over the estate.

"The war was going to come here no matter what you did," she added. "You couldn't stop it."

"They made us prisoners in our own home."

She nodded. "But soon we will have our home back. And in a few days Massimo and Alessia will be playing once again by the pool. We'll clean it, you'll see. And next year we will replant and we will start again. The important thing is that Marco and Vittore have survived the fighting. Cristina and Francesca are safe. And our grandchildren have been spared."

"We don't know that Marco has survived the fighting," he said, aware that he was speaking the unspeakable for one reason only: he was afraid that Beatrice had jinxed their son. They had not heard from him since the middle of May.

"No," she admitted. But eight weeks ago he had been repairing roads between Spoleto and Orvieto. Well north of Rome. Almost halfway between the capital and their estate. She was confident that the Germans weren't going to bother to bring their labor north. Instead they would press other Italians into their work gangs as they needed them. "But I have faith," she added. "He'll be home by the end of the summer."

He wrapped his arm around her shoulder. They could no longer see Cristina and Friedrich. "Thank you," he said.

She shrugged. "This war has taken a lot. But it hasn't taken the things that really matter. Our family is fine. And soon we will all be together again."

They lay in the grass like spoons, his body draped around hers. Occasionally Cristina opened her eyes and gazed up at the clouds, but mostly she kept them shut and felt Friedrich's breath on her neck. In the far distance, she heard the mechanical cacophony of the army preparing to retreat.

"You would like Dresden," he said softly, his elbow upon her hip and his hand on her stomach. "When I was first getting to know your brother, I told him we called it Florence on the Elbe. He scoffed. He really did. We were in the piazza just outside the museum. But Dresden is old and beautiful and one big gallery, just like your Florence."

She wound her fingers through his and shivered when his pinkie grazed her navel.

"You are always so ticklish there," he said.

She nodded. She was fighting back tears and was afraid she would cry if she spoke. High overhead, behind the overcast sky, flew the planes, Allied aircraft that roared through the air with impunity now. Closer to earth were the birds. She followed the grass with her eyes until she saw wildflowers.

"Someday you will see the city. And my father will see why I have fallen in love with you," he went on.

It may have been the implicit domesticity in his remark, the image of this aging Dresden curator, a widower, appreciating his son's choice of a . . . a bride. But suddenly her body was racked with sobs and she allowed the tears to run freely down her cheeks and into the ground. He felt her body trembling against him and held her tighter; he started to tell her that this would all be fine in the end, they would be together after the war, but she shook her head and pushed him away. Then she grabbed her dress from the grass and stood.

"It's all coming apart," she told him, her voice weak and choked. "I'll never see Dresden. You'll never come back. You know that."

He rolled over and reached for his shirt. "Cristina," he said, as he started to force his arms through the sleeves, "I don't know that and neither do you. I love you. I—"

"None of that matters to Hitler or Mussolini or your Colonel Decher," she said, cutting him off. "None of it!"

"If I could make you a promise, I would."

It seemed to her that he wanted to say something more. But he didn't, and after a moment he shook his head ruefully and buttoned his shirt. She watched him adjust the buckles that held his prosthetic foot against the stump of his leg, his long fingers lost for a moment in the even longer grass.

From the stable they heard the sound of the horses: loud, unhappy whinnies from both Arabella and Oriana. "Come," she said to him, wiping her eyes. "Get dressed. Something is upsetting Arabella. Besides . . ."

"Yes?"

"You should say good-bye to her, too."

They were still a hundred meters distant when they came over the top of the ridge and saw the German lieutenant named Bayer and a pair of privates trying to lead the two horses away from the barn. Oriana was merely straining her long face against the lead line, trying to pull free of the young soldier. But Arabella was rearing up on her hind legs, her eyes wild and her nostrils flaring.

Both horses were neighing and snorting angrily. Finally the soldier trying to commandeer Arabella dropped the leather cord and, his hands before his face and head, darted a dozen feet away.

And so Cristina sprinted down the hill as fast as she could toward her animals, uncaring that she was leaving Friedrich behind to catch up.

"She's a demon," the soldier said to no one in particular, and cursed the horse despite Cristina's presence. A little blood was trickling from a cut on the side of his face.

"She's not," Cristina said, scolding him, and she started calmly stroking Arabella's nose. She recognized the private, but she didn't know his name. The horse was still eyeing the fellow warily, and she pawed at the ground before her, but with Cristina present, she was settling down quickly.

"Captain Muller has ordered us to take the horses," Bayer said to her. "We need them to help with transport."

"No! That's ridiculous!" she told the lieutenant. "You can't!" Although she had tried to avoid the soldiers that month, it was impossible not to cross paths with the artillery unit's officers, since they were staying in the villa. Bayer was sleeping in Marco's bedroom. She had found him gruff but not unreasonable. She guessed he was in his early thirties, though his hair was already turning white. He had a family, but she knew this only because he had once remarked that they spent most of their time living in an air raid shelter or their basement in Cologne.

"We can and we will," he said. "Since Private Schreiner here can't manage her, you will. Bring her to the front of the villa right now."

"I'm not one of your soldiers," she reminded him. "You can't—"

"Now!" he yelled, cutting her off. "Now!"

Arabella tried to pull away from Bayer's angry barking, but Cristina held the leather firmly with her right hand while caressing the horse with her left. Over Bayer's shoulder she saw Friedrich approaching. She whispered into the horse's ear that she was safe, nothing would happen to her, she wasn't ever leaving these hills. Meanwhile, Friedrich tried to reason with Bayer.

"You don't need these two horses," he said to the other lieutenant. "Over the last few years our armies have taken just about everything else from this family. Why don't you leave them these last two animals?"

"Who are you?" Bayer asked him.

"Friedrich Strekker." He extended his hand, but Bayer ignored the gesture.

"Oh, I've heard about you," he said instead, rolling his eyes and then leering at Cristina and Friedrich. "You're the museum fellow. You cart paintings back and forth," he added dismissively.

But Friedrich ignored the slight. "Give up on the horses. They can't be of real use to you. They're not even draft horses."

Bayer shook his head. "Captain Muller has ordered me to retrieve them. Move away."

"There's no point," Friedrich said. "I've seen your transport. You have plenty of trucks—"

"I don't have time for this!" Bayer shouted, pointing off to his left. "There are British tanks right now on the road to Petroio!" Then he motioned for the trooper holding Oriana to start up the hill, and the soldier and the older animal began moving away. But Cristina leapt after them, trying to wrestle away the lead line. Schreiner, the other private, quickly grabbed her and yanked her off the ground, swinging her away from Oriana and holding her firmly. She screamed for him to let her go, to leave her alone— to leave her horses alone. But he wrapped his arms around her waist and his grip was unyielding, and what happened next she saw through a mist, her fury and her tears conspiring to blur her vision. Angrily Friedrich had taken hold of one of Schreiner's shoulders and was turning him around when Arabella once again reared up on her hind legs. Schreiner released Cristina and tried to spin away from the animal, but he and Friedrich together spilled onto the ground. One of Arabella's front hooves fell hard on Schreiner's arm, and despite the animal's angry neighing, they all heard the sound of his bone cracking beneath her foot. It snapped like a dry olive tree branch. Again Arabella stood up on her hind legs, and Friedrich tried desperately to tug the cursing soldier out of the way. Before the animal could lash out once more, however, Bayer had drawn his sidearm and fired. The shot hit Arabella in the muzzle, shattering her teeth and sending a great spray of blood across Cristina's chest and neck and only enraging the horse further. Her feet landed on Schreiner's abdomen, knocking the wind from him, but this time the soldier's pitiable grunt was lost completely to the sound of Cristina's wails and Bayer's second shot, this one penetrating squarely Arabella's forehead. The animal's legs buckled at once. She looked around for the briefest of seconds at Cristina and Oriana and the uniformed men, her eyes wide and scared and confused, and then rolled dead onto the grass beside Schreiner and Friedrich.

Cristina threw herself at Bayer and was pounding feverishly at his chest, the smell of the gunshots a fog around both of them, when there was a colossal explosion and the ground around them began shaking. Everyone turned toward the village of Monte Volta, the direction of the blast, just in time to see one of the two medieval granary towers pancaking into the earth.

1955

SERAFINA STOOD BESIDE a fountain outside the museum in Arezzo, smoking and daydreaming and watching her shadow on the light stone of the piazza. Silhouetted, her arms looked like matchsticks. Her skirt was shaped like moth wings. She inhaled the aroma of the water from the fountain, its scent at once musky and cool. Finally she snuffed out her cigarette with the sharp toe of her shoe, a little bored with waiting. She reached into her purse for her matches and lit one, bringing the flame as close to her eyes as she could. She stared at it until the fire burned down to her fingers, held it for a full second longer, and then finally dropped it onto the stone. She looked at the two black marks on her fingertips. Neither would blister, but the one on her thumb would grow a little red and it would smart.

Once, over dinner perhaps a year and a half ago, Milton had asked her if she ever had flashbacks. *No,* she had answered, *I wish that I did.* She wondered now if that was going to change. Paolo and Milton had been correct: returning to Monte Volta was triggering something, beginning with those mushrooms and then continuing with the ceiling inside the Villa Chimera tombs. Perhaps viewing the artifacts the Rosatis had donated to the museum would amplify her memories further. She tended to doubt it, because the vases and the pottery and the sarcophagi had been removed by the time her brutalized body was laid inside the burial chamber. But then, this wasn't precisely why she had come to Arezzo today.

At the café at the edge of the piazza, she watched a young

man in a blazer with a crest on the breast pocket dip a biscotto the length of a quill into his coffee and then feed it to a blond woman across the small table. Serafina guessed they were Brits or Americans, and she envied how much they were in love. She saw them adjourning into a small hotel during siesta, louvering shut the blinds, and then . . .

But maybe they were Germans. The war had ended a decade ago now, and even some Germans these days were finding the money to travel. The pair was roughly her age. She speculated what they might have been doing eleven or twelve years ago if indeed they were German, and she didn't like the images that passed through her mind. She told herself once and for all that they were from the United States.

A thought came to her: Had Enrico and Teresa seen the irony that they were sheltering her from the Nazis in a tomb? They must have hoped she would live but believed she would die. Had the British arrived even a day later—perhaps hours, according to that British doctor—they most certainly would have found but a corpse.

She looked at her watch. It was finally time to go in. She started across the piazza toward the museum.

⚜

Giulia Rosati looked at the calendar, the telephone pressed against her ear, and found herself wrapping the cord anxiously around her fingers. "So," she said to her husband, "the funerals will be in two days."

"Yes. But I'll be home tomorrow," Vittore said. "Cristina and I are both hoping to leave for Rome in the morning. Our mother's body—and Francesca's—will be sent straight to Monte Volta."

"What do you think we should do about the children?" Tatiana was two and had only a toddler's connection with her grandmother. But Elisabetta was four and adored Beatrice. Neither child had even the vaguest notion that a woman named Francesca Rosati had ever existed and had been, technically, their aunt. Still, Giulia would soon have to tell Elisabetta about her grandmother, and she dreaded that. Beatrice had always been far more of a warm and enveloping *nonna* than a dignified marchesa around her granddaughter. Giulia resolved that when the children awoke from their naps, she would try to explain to her daughter that Nonna was in heaven with Mary and Jesus and the angels.

"I'm not sure. Obviously they understand nothing of death," Vittore answered. Then he added, "Who would have thought I would ever have said something like that about a Rosati? For a while there, from Marco's death to my father's, it seemed we had more than our share."

In the hallway she heard the officer flipping through the newspaper. Matteo was one of three police officers who were rotating in and out of her and Vittore's apartment.

"I want to bring them," she said after a moment. "Even if they don't understand the significance of what's occurring, I don't want them out of my sight."

"That's fine," he agreed.

"And it will be interesting for Elisabetta to see the crowd at the church in Monte Volta and the number of people who come to the Villa Chimera for your mother."

"It will be a lot smaller than you expect."

She recalled her father-in-law's funeral. He had died blocks from where she was standing right now, while strolling one Sunday afternoon through the Villa Borghese. The war was still fresh in everyone's memory and so the family had decided to have a graveside service only. The priest from the village had come to the estate, but otherwise no one but the family had been in attendance. Afterward, Beatrice had felt that they had made an egregious mistake and shamed her husband's memory: he had done nothing, in her opinion, to be buried in a manner more befitting a criminal than a marchese. Vittore and Cristina never forgot their mother's despair and vowed that her funeral would begin at the church in Monte Volta. At the time, however, they hadn't imagined that the funeral would occur when their mother was a mere sixty-four. They had supposed it was still years and years in the distance.

"Don't you think people have forgiven your parents by now?" Giulia asked. "The war was over and done ten years ago. And remember, until the middle of 1943, we were all on the same side as the Germans. Besides, your mother was a marchesa."

"A silly title."

"Maybe. But think of how many people once depended on your parents."

"Or, arguably, how many people they exploited."

"And don't forget what a magical place the Villa Chimera once was. Really, Vittore—people forgive."

He sighed. "Apparently, my love, not everyone does. Not everyone . . ."

🜨

Roberto Piredda, the director of the museum in Arezzo and for years the curator in charge of the collection's Etruscan artifacts, was a giant of a man. Serafina wouldn't have been surprised if he measured six and a half feet tall and tipped the scales at three hundred pounds. His shoulders looked as if they wanted to split his sand-colored suit at the seams. She guessed he was in his late sixties now, his hair completely white, but he was still vibrant and vital and he struck her as a rather energetic patrician. His size made him seem a little intimidating, but she hoped he might in reality be a rather gentle giant.

"I was devastated when I read about the marchesa's death," he said to her as together they lumbered down the long corridor to his office. "I must have missed the detail in the first stories that Francesca was Antonio and Beatrice's daughter-in-law."

"It's tragic. The whole family is tragic," she said. Her heels echoed along the tile. She recalled what he had said to her when she had called him to set up this interview: he would never forget the sound of the jackboots in the hallways whenever the Germans from the Uffizi would come calling.

"I know just what you mean," he agreed, nodding. "How is Vittore? Of all the Rosatis, of course I knew him best. After the war, my wife and I were both saddened when he chose the Vatican Museum over us. But we understood his decision. Still, my wife thought the world of him. We both did."

"I think Vittore is fine," she answered. "But honestly? I think he's angry. He's always going to be disappointed in his family. He's always going to be a little ashamed of the . . . the concessions they made in the war. Himself, too. The way they allowed the Nazis into their lives. He hasn't forgiven them and he hasn't forgiven himself. As a result, he's a pretty hard-edged customer."

"Well, he wasn't always angry. And I'm sure he's not precisely himself these days."

"No."

Piredda's office had three large windows, but they were shuttered against either the heat or the sunlight or both. His desk was drowning in papers, and a large worktable was awash in pottery chips, many black and red, on a white cloth. There were shallow metal tubs on each side, as well as a variety of tweezers and small brushes. On the shelves along one inside wall were four rows of broken vases and cracked pots—she recognized amphoras and alabastrons and kraters—each with a handwritten label with the name of the site where it had been unearthed taped beside it. And on the lowest shelf, beside a knapsack, were the tools she supposed he took with him on digs: Trowels and root cutters. A sieve. A utility saw. A dustpan just starting to rust.

Piredda lifted one of the two wooden chairs beside the worktable and spun it around so it faced the desk. Then he sat in his own leather chair, turned on the fan behind him, and aimed the air at her.

"I'm fine," she said, carefully settling herself in the seat so the ladderback didn't press against her scars.

"So how can I help you?" he said. "What do you need to know about the tombs that were found at the Villa Chimera?"

She was actually interested in the Germans and Italians who had been a part of Vittore's world during the war, but she had told Piredda on the phone that the Rosati dig was her reason for coming. And so now she asked a cursory question about Etruscan burial practices and listened patiently as he discussed cremation versus inhumation, urns versus sarcophagi. He told her that he found the tombs at the Villa Chimera intriguing, even though it was a small site.

"We thought at first it was going to be a necropolis," he told her, steepling his fingers together. "When the Rosatis showed us what they had discovered, I assumed this was but the tip of an iceberg. I expected another Cerveteri. The next Tarquinia."

"But it's not."

"Far from it. Still, for its size it's noteworthy. The artwork inside the chambers is brilliant. The artifacts we found there are extraordinary. And it has evidence of both cremation and inhumation—and at roughly the same time."

She nodded and thought of the images she had studied by matchlight on the ceiling and along the walls of the tombs. As if he were reading her mind, he asked, "Have you been there? To the Villa Chimera?"

"I have, yes."

He smiled. "This is a very thorough investigation."

"I was actually there during the war, too."

"No!"

"Yes."

"What a small world! Did you know the Rosatis then?"

She thought about how she should answer, because this really wasn't about her. She glanced around the room once more, and her eyes rested on the utility saw. On the serrated edge and the beveled point. The blade was about eight inches long. "I met the marchesa briefly," she said, turning back to him. Then: "You were exclusively in Arezzo during the war, correct?"

"I was. I had to go to Florence sometimes. Siena, too. And sometimes they came to me."

"The Germans."

"The Germans, the Italians. Everyone who was interested in either looting or protecting our artistic heritage."

"Did Vittore have enemies?"

He seemed to think about this. "Vittore's still alive. It's his mother and his sister-in-law who are dead. I think the better question is whether those two had enemies, don't you?"

"I guess I mean the family. Did the Rosatis have enemies?"

"Who knows? Those were very messy years. We all made friends and we all made enemies. Most of us did whatever it took to stay alive. By 1944, if the Germans weren't lining you up against a wall and shooting you for protecting the partisans, the partisans were lining you up against a wall and shooting you for collaborating with the Germans."

"And you?"

"Me? I just tried to keep my head down." He gazed for a long moment at the high collar of her blouse. At her neck. At the side of her face. "I have a sense, my dear, that you were not quite so fortunate."

Reflexively she touched her head and discovered that the breeze from the fan had blown back her hair, exposing her ruined ear and the scars on her neck. Quickly she pulled her hair forward, pivoting in her seat so it wouldn't happen again. "A birth defect," she mumbled.

"No. Burned flesh," he corrected her. "I'm sorry."

She shrugged and composed herself. Brought their conversation back to his war, not hers. "But you did allow the Germans to send some artifacts from the museum to the Gestapo chief in Rome," she said. "True?"

He sat back. "I hate to play semantics, but I did not *allow* them. That would suggest I had a choice. I had none. And *allowing* a few Etruscan vases and pots to be sent to some fellow in Rome to help keep the peace? Let that be the worst of my crimes."

"Have you been at a dig lately?" she asked him. "Off in the field?"

"Ah, I wish. There is a dig occurring right now near Volterra. But no, I am chained to my museum these days." Then he motioned toward the shards on his worktable. "I insist that the students and the professors at the site bring me back the occasional scraps. It's a tease, but a welcome one."

She considered pointing at his knapsack and tools but thought better of the idea. Other than the dustpan with its Rorschach of rust, everything, including that saw, was spotless.

Which, she decided, might mean everything . . . or nothing at all.

Giulia Rosati awoke in the night with a start. She was aware that the moon was low and guessed even before feeling for the clock on the nightstand and peering carefully at the numerals that it was two or three in the morning. It was, she saw once her eyes had adjusted, a few minutes past three. Beside her in her bed were both children. Elisabetta had been devastated by the idea that she would never see her *nonna* again, even if it meant that her grandmother was smiling at her from heaven with the angels. The four-year-old had howled when Giulia had told her, which, in turn, had set little Tatiana to wailing. The only way Giulia had been able to settle them down was to bring them into her and Vittore's bedroom, which was, in fact, where they had slept the past two nights and where she had presumed they would sleep until Vittore returned. She had not wanted her girls out of her sight.

Nevertheless, last night she hadn't expected that they would all have retreated to the bedroom quite so early.

Which, Giulia told herself, was why she had woken up now. She had already been in bed a long while.

She saw that both children were sleeping peacefully, Tatiana on her back with one small arm draped across her tummy and Elisabetta curled on her side, her face buried deeply in the pillow. They were all on top of the sheets. Giulia sighed, relieved that everyone was safe, and for a moment listened to the sound of their breathing. A floor below them, outside on the street, she heard a car—a cab, she presumed, at this hour of the night.

Only then did it dawn on her: the light in the hallway was off;

the lights in the living room were off. They were all supposed to be on. That idiot guard must have fallen asleep.

Furious, she climbed gingerly over Tatiana, careful not to wake her, and started across the bedroom toward the hallway. And then, in the doorway, she stopped dead in her tracks. The guard might have dozed off, but why would he have shut off the lights? It didn't make sense.

She stood there, thinking, and then she felt it. The small, barely perceptible breeze. She and Vittore had lived in the apartment since before Elisabetta was born. She knew the drafts, the way the eddies of wind might cool their home during the night, and the way the heat from the kitchen when she was cooking might settle for hours in the living room; she could sense when a window was open or closed, which doors were ajar. And even before she had peered anxiously down the corridor, she knew that the front door was open. Wide open. She knew it—and all that anger turned instantly into terror.

1944

THE COUNTRY WAS not broken, and he was relieved. At least not all of it was. At least not yet. The sheer speed of the German retreat, Marco Rosati decided, was going to spare his beloved Crete Senesi, this land of vineyards and olive groves and endless fields of sunflowers south of Siena. Although the sun had been rising for easily forty-five minutes now, he continued to walk. In the night he had struggled up the long hill from San Quirico d'Orcia to Pienza, allowing himself in the smallest hours to actually traipse along the side of the road, where the travel was far easier than through the brush. One small convoy of German trucks had passed, but their arrival had been heralded by the sound of the engines struggling to make headway up the steep switchbacks, and Marco had had plenty of time to crawl into the broom and hide amid the yellow flowers.

About four in the morning, when he had reached the parapets on the outskirts of Pienza, he had murmured a small prayer of gratitude as he gazed up at the silhouette of the Duomo. Then he had detoured slightly to the west of the town, picking up the road to Monte Volta a kilometer beyond the arch that led to the piazza and the Corso il Rossellino. He had been walking for three nights, hiding and resting during the day, since he had managed to run away from the work crew somewhere to the southwest of Mount Amiata. He had been more or less slave labor for the past five months, repairing the roads and railway tracks the Allies had bombed or building fortifications it was clear the Nazis were never going to use. Instead they were going to make their stand, everyone understood, much farther north, along the mountains that crossed the boot beyond Florence. And that, perhaps, was how he had been able to escape. The Germans were so fixated on staying ahead of the Allies that the guards had grown lax; self-preservation mattered more than ensuring that none of the Italian help slunk away in the night. He was one of three former Italian army officers who understood where they were and how they might be able to walk to their homes within days or weeks, and who had decided it was time to disappear into the countryside. They had slipped into the woods and then separated, and Marco had thought less and less about those other two soldiers, especially as he drew nearer to Francesca and Massimo and Alessia. He had not been able to communicate with his family since May. A German captain—like Marco, an engineer—was going to spend a few hours taking in the hot springs in Bagno Vignoni on a brief leave and took mercy on him. He agreed to drop by the Villa Chimera and reassure the Rosatis that Marco was alive and well—or, in any case, as well as any of the laborers could be, all of them working long hours in the summer sun with a daily bread ration that wouldn't have filled the stomach of a toddler. When Marco told the captain that his younger sister was involved with a German lieutenant, the fellow had grown especially obliging.

Now Marco wiped his brow with the sleeve of his shirt. Before him loomed no more than a dozen kilometers, though two of them were almost straight up. The last hill was the steep climb to Castelmuzio. Then he would pass the fountain with the statue of a wingless angel beside a toothless lion. This wasn't war damage; the sculptures had been that way since well before he was born. From the summit on the far side of Castelmuzio, he would be able to see his beloved Villa Chimera and the cedars that marked the entrance and dotted the hillsides. He sighed and inhaled deeply. The morning air was still cool. Ahead of him was a small farm he recognized from his childhood. He didn't know the peasants who lived there, but they would know him, or at least they would know his name. Marco, the marchese's older son. He decided he would rest there.

He would knock on their door and sleep on whatever bed or straw they could offer. Then, after dark, he would go home. When his children awoke in the morning, he would be waiting.

⚘

Cristina sat on the ground and stared at the columns of black smoke and white dust as they curlicued together into the sky, her horse's head on her knees. She was stroking the dead animal's mane, but her eyes were on what was left of the medieval granary. A single tower. A moment ago there had been two.

Friedrich and Bayer stood perfectly still and watched the spiraling ash, too, suddenly oblivious to her and the fact that Bayer had just shot a healthy, beloved horse and one of his soldiers was down. But Schreiner, the private with at the very least a broken arm, managed to sit up. The other private looked at him and then went to stand beside the two lieutenants.

It was Bayer who spoke first. "How the hell is the one still standing?" he asked. It was as if, in the numbness that seemed to envelop them all after the blast, he had forgotten that he and Friedrich had been fighting.

"I gather the plan was to bring them both down?" Friedrich asked.

Bayer nodded. "Do you have any field glasses?"

"No."

"It's the damnedest thing," Bayer said after a moment.

"What is?"

"These days," Bayer said, "the Italians can't do a damn thing right. But seven or eight hundred years ago? They could build a fucking granary we still can't blow up."

Friedrich turned away and knelt beside Cristina. Schreiner was looking down at the way his arm was hanging limply by his side.

"I'm sorry," Friedrich said to her, his anger subsumed by his grief. He was aware of how small and impotent his words sounded.

She realized she was shaking. Her whole body was trembling

and she couldn't stop crying. But she continued to gaze across the narrow valley that separated the estate from the village because she was afraid to look down into the eyes of her horse. The animal's head was dead weight in her lap. She thought of the uncountable hours she had spent riding and brushing her. As the marchese's daughter, Cristina had grown up in a rarefied and profoundly insular cocoon. She had not been friendless, precisely, but her world would have been far more lonely had it not been for Arabella. Likewise, the horse, Cristina knew, had trusted her. The horse had trusted her absolutely. And now? Now it had come to this. She felt Friedrich's hand massaging the back of her neck where it met her shoulders, and she turned her attention from the smoldering remains of the granary to Bayer. Then she looked down and noticed Friedrich's holstered pistol. A wisp of a thought came to her, vague but hungry, and she leaned against him, ducking beneath both his arms, and in one single, swift motion unsnapped the holster and pulled free the Walther pistol. He tried to grab her hands and stop her, but she was too fast. She rolled away from him and stood, aiming the gun at Bayer.

"You killed my horse!" she shrieked at him. "Your people took my house and you killed my horse! I hate you! I hate you all!"

Friedrich rose to his feet as quickly as he could, but it still took him a moment. By the time he was standing, already Cristina had switched off the safety and retreated two steps away from him. "Cristina," he began, extending his arm toward her, his palm open. "Don't do this."

Bayer glanced back and forth between Friedrich and Cristina, and Friedrich thought he looked nervous—but not nervous enough. Cristina was hysterical, covered in horse blood and at the moment capable of anything. "Rein in your girl, Strekker," he said, and there was just the tinest hitch in his voice.

Friedrich didn't give a damn if Bayer was shot dead; some people deserved to die. He didn't care if the two privates were killed, too. But he didn't want Cristina to shoulder that responsibility if she lived. And so, calculating how his tone needed to straddle a plea and a command, he murmured, "Cristina, give me the gun. Don't make this worse."

"Worse? Damn you! Damn you all! This can't get any worse! Look what you've done!" she yelled. "Look!" she ordered them, and she waved the gun for the briefest second between the smoke in the village and Arabella.

"I know," Friedrich agreed, and he hoped his voice didn't sound like he was only trying to mollify her. But he feared that it did. From the corner of his eye, he saw Schreiner watching intently from the ground, but the second private might be able to inch his way behind Cristina. He wished he could will the idea into the fellow's head. "But it can get worse. I know this as well as anyone. Things can always get worse. There is . . ."

"What!" she screamed back at him, sobbing. "What!"

The other private was going to be no help: Cristina had spotted him and moved farther back, so now she had all four of the men in front of her. But Friedrich also had the sense that the longer she didn't shoot, the less likely it was that she would. So he decided just to keep talking. "There is always going to be bad luck," he said. "There is always going to be war and destruction and buildings that collapse on our feet. There is always going to be someone who panics and shoots our horses. But what you're doing right now is just lashing out, and I'm telling you, you'll only make things worse. Save your anger and revenge for—" And then he stopped, because her eyes had moved off Bayer and him and on to something behind them. He turned and saw that Oriana had walked over to the dead horse on the ground. With her nose she was nuzzling the animal, trying to lift Arabella's head off the grass. To awaken her. But of course she couldn't.

When Friedrich glanced back at Cristina, their eyes met for just a second. Then she lowered her arm and marched past him, slamming the grip of the pistol into his palm. When she reached the two horses, she collapsed onto the ground and pressed her forehead against Arabella's and cried into the animal's long face.

Bayer exhaled audibly. "Schreiner," he said to the private, "can you walk?"

"Yes, sir. I think I can."

"Good." He ordered his two men to follow him away from the stable and back to the villa. "The British will be here any minute," he said, grabbing Oriana's lead line roughly and pulling her away from Arabella and Cristina. "Let's get the hell out of here."

The Germans were gone by the middle of the afternoon, and Francesca stood on the terrace overlooking the swimming pool, her hands on the balustrade. The pool, half empty, was a swamp now. A cesspool, the water the color of rust. The soldiers had used it first as a bath and then, once they knew they were leaving, to clean their kits. They used it to fill the radiators of their vehicles. The last thing three soldiers did before piling into the back of a lorry was to stand on the tile along the east side and urinate into the already fetid water.

"I'll clean it," Massimo said. She looked down. She hadn't realized that her son had joined her.

"Grandfather and I will clean it," he went on. Then he put his pinkie into his mouth and silently sucked on the finger. She guessed he did this because he knew he was far too old to suck his thumb, and when she and Beatrice had confronted him, he had said he was merely biting a nail. As if that were really so much better. The boy had started sucking his pinkie when the Germans had arrived. She hoped, now that they had left, he would stop.

She ruffled his hair. "Where is your sister?" she asked him.

"With Nonna."

"What?" Francesca asked, unable to hide the concern in her voice. She thought that her mother-in-law was down at the stable. She thought that both Beatrice and Antonio were there. They were with Cristina. Her in-laws actually believed they could bury Arabella. A marchese and his wife, both well into middle age, digging a grave big enough for a horse. Pathetic. Pathetic and ridiculous and sad. She didn't want her little girl either to see the dead horse or to witness the spectacle of her family struggling against the dry, rocky soil with shovels. "She's at the stable?"

"No. Only Grandfather and Cristina are there. Nonna is trying to find some sheets to make the beds. She and Alessia are upstairs."

Francesca turned and yelled up toward the row of windows that marked the second floor of the villa. "Alessia!" she called out. "Alessia!"

A moment later she saw her mother-in-law and Alessia both peer out of one of the two nursery windows. "What do you need?" Beatrice asked.

Francesca shook her head. "I just . . ."

Beatrice looked anxious. "Yes?"

"I just wanted to know where you were."

"We're right here," she said, and then she and Alessia retreated back inside the room.

"See?" Massimo asked.

She smiled down at him. The ruins of the granary had stopped smoldering. They had not heard the thunder of artillery in more than two hours now. She presumed the fighting was over. She and her in-laws were still holding their breath, wondering if they would be occupied next by the British. But she was holding out hope that for their family, the war was now finished. The tide had rolled over them, brutalizing them, but they had survived. She had her son by her side, and her daughter was upstairs helping her grandmother try to make the villa habitable once again. The battles would now be to the north. Her husband would return, and just as her mother-in-law insisted, they would start the long process of rebuilding their lives.

Somehow she knew this. She had never been more positive of anything in her life.

⚜

They couldn't bury the horse, Cristina feared, her heart sinking along with the sun. She and her father were physically incapable of breaking the earth—weeds and thistles and roots—and carving a deep enough grave. And even if somehow they did manage to excavate sufficient soil and rock, the idea of her father and her dragging Arabella by her legs into the hole made her a little nauseous. But she feared that her father was not going to stop digging until he was dead. They'd been at it with shovels and picks for nearly two hours. Every few minutes she was able to convince him to rest with her, and she saw that his shirt was as wet as her dress. Dirt and dust were epoxied by sweat to the fabric of their clothes, but when she looked down, she was relieved: Arabella's blood was lost to the stains from the brown Tuscan soil.

Now the two of them were leaning on their shovels, the spades wedged into the ground, and she saw that the flies once again were feasting on the deep black bullet wounds on Arabella's face. Cristina left her shovel and, as she had all afternoon, knelt before her horse and shooed the insects away. When she looked up, she saw her mother approaching.

"I couldn't find enough sheets for all the beds," she said. "Where did they go? Did the Germans steal them, too?"

Her father smiled grimly. "You should have buried the sheets instead of the silver. Instead of that old mirror."

"I'm serious. Why would the soldiers steal our sheets?"

"The medics took them," he explained. "They'll use them for bandages."

Beatrice nodded and then surveyed the insubstantial dent her husband and daughter had made in the ground, seeming to contemplate the sheer impossibility of what the two of them were doing. "You both should come back to the villa," she said finally. "Finish the job tomorrow. Maybe we can find something to eat."

"Really?" Antonio asked. "The Germans took the sheets but they left us some food? How very kind of them."

"I'm sure I can find us something," Beatrice said defensively.

Cristina stood and joined her mother. "Mother's right," she said. "We should rest. Tomorrow we'll be stronger."

"No, it can't wait until tomorrow," her father told her.

"Why?" Cristina asked.

"It just can't," he said stubbornly, his eyes darting briefly toward the thick brush on the far side of the barn, and Cristina understood. She understood instantly. If they left Arabella unburied tonight, tomorrow they would find a brutalized, half-eaten carcass. The wild boars would devour much, if not all, of the animal. And so with a renewed, fierce determination, she returned to the spot where she had been working and started to dig.

"Do we have more shovels in the barn?" Beatrice asked.

"Yes, of course," Antonio said.

Her mother glanced once again at the horse, and then, without saying another word, she marched into the barn to find a shovel so she could dig, too.

⚜

Antonio and Beatrice sat down in the grass, the last of the sun a fading thin ribbon of red to the west, the sky to the east almost plum. Cristina patted the hillock of dirt with the back of her shovel. The grave was shallow, but somehow they had buried the horse. Cristina thought that her back was more sore than it had ever been in her life, and the palms of her hands were awash in blisters that already had split open. They burned. The soles of her feet had deep cuts the shape of the shovel's footrest from her efforts, hours earlier, to break through the earth. She could only imagine her parents' agony. Yet her father had not allowed her horse to become food for the boars.

On the path to the villa, Cristina saw her nephew running toward them, but in the dusk she was unable to distinguish the features on his face. She presumed he was coming here because he was bored with his sister. Or perhaps Francesca was tired of waiting for all of them and of watching her children on her own and had sent the boy to retrieve them.

When Massimo arrived, he went straight to his grandfather. Antonio made no attempt to stand but instead pulled the child down onto the ground beside him.

"My boy," he said, his voice unexpectedly light, "I see your timing is perfect. We have just finished."

But Massimo neither laughed nor took offense. "Mama told me to get you," he said, panting. "You need to come back right now."

"Right now," Antonio repeated, smiling a little bit. "What's the big news? What could possibly have your mother so excited?"

"Partisans!" he said.

Antonio's voice instantly turned grave. "What about them?" he asked.

"They've come to the house! There must be five or six of them!"

Antonio pushed himself to his feet and then extended his hand to Beatrice, helping her to stand, too. Cristina limped over to them.

"Where are your mother and Alessia?" he asked the boy.

"They're in the kitchen. The leader is demanding food and medicine."

"Good luck finding either," Cristina said.

"Medicine," Antonio repeated. "Are some of them hurt?"

The boy nodded. "One. A girl. She's dying, for sure."

Beatrice looked Massimo in the eye. "A girl? Your age?"

"No, I mean Aunt Cristina's age. She's a partisan, too."

"Has she been shot?" Cristina asked.

The boy shrugged. "I don't know."

"How do you know she's dying?"

"They have her lying on her side and I saw her back," he answered. "It was horrible. Alessia cried when she saw it." Then he took his grandfather's hand in both of his and started pulling him toward the path. Grimly, Cristina and Beatrice followed.

1955

Giulia retreated back into the bedroom and pushed the door shut. Frantically she grabbed the wooden chair that sat before her vanity and angled it against the doorknob. Then she gazed at the dark room, at the shapes of her sleeping children. She tried to recall what there might be here that could serve as a weapon. In the kitchen there were knives, but she wasn't in the kitchen. In the living room there was a wrought iron poker beside the fireplace, but likewise, she wasn't in the living room. Some evenings she and Vittore had brought candles into the bedroom, but tonight the candlesticks were still on the dining room table. And the phone? It was on the other side of the apartment; it might just as well have been in another country.

She guessed that she could jump from the second-story window with Tatiana in her arms, but she was sure to break or sprain her ankle. And Elisabetta? She was four. Who knew how badly she might hurt herself in the leap to the cobblestone sidewalk? Besides, then what? She and the girls couldn't possibly elude whoever had—and she told herself she was panicking as the vision lodged itself in her mind—cut the heart from the police officer who was supposed to be protecting her and her family.

But she could cry for help out the window. She could scream—and to protect her children, she was prepared to scream loud and long.

She pressed her ear against the door, the wood unexpectedly cool, listening. But there was nothing, only the rapid thrum of her heart in her head. She breathed in through her nose, trying to calm herself, and she thought she detected a new aroma in the apartment. Lemons. Was it possible? She thought she might have had a lemon in the kitchen, but why would that scent come to her? Or was it her imagination? It must have been, she told herself, because if she smelled anything now, it wasn't citrus; it was a gas, a rotten gas. Something putrid, perhaps wafting up from the street.

"Mama?"

She turned and saw the silhouette of Elisabetta sitting up in bed. Giulia opened her mouth, but nothing came out. She realized she was afraid to move away from the door.

☙

"You should be sleeping."

Serafina turned and pressed the tip of her cigarette into the ashtray. She was sitting before the glass doors to the terrace, just inside their apartment. She saw Milton leaning against the wall in his pajamas. She hadn't heard him emerge from his bedroom. "I hope I didn't wake you," she said to him softly.

"No, not at all."

"You're lying," she said. She had been sitting in the dark and watching three apartments across the Arno that still had their lights on. She assumed that the people who lived in each had fallen asleep with a lamp or two on, because she had seen no movement in any of them. "Do you think there are people awake across the river?" she asked.

He ignored her question and flipped on the sconce on the far wall. It wouldn't be so bright that it would blind them, but it would allow him to see what he wanted. He pulled a chair around the table so he was sitting beside her. "So," he said, pointing at the ashtray. "You've smoked two cigarettes."

"I guess."

"But—let's see—there are seven matches in there."

Serafina sighed but said nothing. She knew where this was going, and there was nothing to say. She watched him lean over into her lap and very gently pull up the hem of her nightgown. Resigned, she put her hands on the sides of the seat for purchase and raised her hips ever so slightly, enabling him to settle her nightgown at her waist and expose her legs completely. She stared across the river at the three lights as he parted her thighs and then listened to him as he slowly counted to five. She didn't have to look down to know what the burn marks looked like, especially once he brushed away the ash.

"Serafina," he said tenderly, after he had sat up. He massaged her left shoulder, the corner of her back where she could tolerate being touched.

Without meeting his eyes she said, "Some people bite their fingernails. I do this."

Across the river there was absolutely no sign of life. She nuzzled her face into Milton's neck and wondered if she had ever in her life not been lonely.

In the morning Paolo had a long and entirely unsatisfying phone conversation with his counterpart in the police department in Rome, a tall fellow Paolo had met before with the oddly appropriate last name Torregrossa: tall tower. Paolo recalled Torregrossa as a rail with thinning brown hair and ears that seemed glued flat to the sides of his head.

"So the fellow has been fired?" Paolo asked him.

"He will be," Torregrossa said. "At the moment he has merely been suspended while we investigate. The important thing is that the family is fine—that nothing happened to them."

Paolo thought of the commedia dell'arte and the daggered, comic, and wholly ineffective Il Capitano. He and his wife had seen a performance two weeks ago not far from here. Five blocks, maybe. Last night must have been terrifying for Giulia Rosati and her little family, but in the light of day the big problem was that their guard was a stock character from a hyperbolic strain of Renaissance theater.

"Just how drunk was he when he was found?" Paolo asked. "Passed out, I assume."

"No, actually. Only hung over. And he wasn't found. He returned to the Rosatis' apartment just before daybreak. By then everyone was gone."

"Where are Giulia and the children now?"

"We took them to some family friends who live on the other side of the Vatican."

Paolo tried to re-create the critical moments in his head: Giulia Rosati lowering her four-year-old to the ground in a bedsheet in the middle of the night and then climbing down that bedsheet herself with a toddler cradled against her chest. "Do you know what time the guard left the apartment?" he asked.

"It was early. Still light out. He says he didn't leave the front door open. Insists a breeze must have opened it. He thought he was just going to run downstairs to a little place where he could buy a soda."

"And instead he bought a grappa."

Torregrossa chuckled. "He ran into friends. One thing led to another. The next thing he knew, he woke up, it was almost morning, and he was in the park by the castle."

"Those are fine friends."

"I know. I'm sorry."

"The family has another guard now—at their friends' apartment?"

"Yes. And this one will know not to excuse himself for a soda."

"Or a grappa."

"Indeed," said Torregrossa. "Or a grappa."

"When was the last time you saw Roberto Piredda?" Serafina asked Vittore that morning in his hotel's small dining room. Vittore was visibly agitated about the ordeal his wife had endured last night, and Serafina found it difficult to keep him focused. He kept circling back to the ineptitude of the Rome police and his desire to get on the road and drive home. He was not precisely chain-smoking, because he wasn't finishing his cigarettes. But he was continually lighting them, one American Lucky Strike after another, taking a single deep puff, and then forgetting them until they had almost burned out. Then he would light another.

"I don't know," he told her. "It's been years."

"That's what Piredda said. He didn't think he had seen you in at least five years—and the last time was at a lecture at the University of Milan, where he just happened to run into you. I think he was a little hurt that he's never met your children."

"Please. People change. Times change."

"But once he was like a mentor to you."

"Yes."

"Why did you cut ties with him?"

"Why do you think it was me? Maybe he cut the ties. Maybe neither of us did. Maybe life just intervened and we grew apart."

"Was he correct about when you two saw each other last?"

"At the university? It's possible. I don't recall seeing him since. I barely recall seeing him at that lecture."

"Did you two have a quarrel?"

"At the lecture?"

"Or before," she said.

He reached for the smoldering cigarette, took a puff, and then extinguished it. "Look, we grew apart during the war. Before the war he was merely an archeologist. He understood the tombs on our property. I viewed him as a scholar. But during the war—during the occupation—he became something else." He brought a fresh Lucky Strike to his lips, and Serafina watched the flame on his lighter when he raised it toward his face. After he had lit the cigarette, he continued, "He became a bootlicker. It was pathetic. Pathetic and sad. He gave away two-thousand-year-old artifacts to philistine Nazis. He encouraged this Ahnenerbe nonsense that there was some connection between Etruscans and Aryans. He was the worst of the toadies. But there was no explosion between us. I just felt dirty being around him."

"Did you feel that way around your father?" Instantly, the moment the words had escaped her lips, she regretted them. She wondered if there was a way to retract them, to take them back. But they were out there between them now, and of course she couldn't.

"My father and I had an agreement the last years of his life," he said, his voice leaden. "Giulia made sure of that."

"And that was?"

"I would abide his presence. I would be cognizant of the reality that he had lost almost everything—including, worst of all, his oldest son and his grandchildren."

"But you didn't forgive him."

Vittore remained silent. He glanced at his watch.

"And your sister. Have you forgiven her?"

"Yes."

"Why?"

"She was eighteen. Eighteen-year-olds make mistakes. Besides, a man expects more from his father than he does from his younger sister. In the war, she was still such a . . . a child."

"I was the same age as she was."

"So? What in the world has that got to do with anything?"

Serafina tried to gather herself. This was the second stupid thing she had said in the last minute. What she had been doing during the war was irrelevant.

"Let's go back to Piredda," she said. "You were mad at him."

"I was disappointed in him. There's a difference."

"Did he feel any anger toward you? Did he have any sort of grudge?"

"No. Not toward me and not toward my family."

"You see where I was going."

He reached for his cigarette, gazed at its blue smoke, but didn't take a drag. "Piredda killed no one. Really, he hasn't any reason." And with that, Vittore stood, taking the Lucky Strike with him.

"You're sure of that?"

"I'm sure of that. Now, forgive me, Detective, but I should be leaving. I have a long drive ahead of me and I want to get back to my family."

"Are you still burying your mother and sister-in-law tomorrow?"

"We are. I'm going to see you there, aren't I?"

"I am coming, yes. But I promise to be unobtrusive."

He closed his eyes and rubbed the bridge of his nose. Then he looked up and said, "I'm not worried about spectacle. I'm worried about my family. I want you and Inspector Ficino and anyone else you bring to be as obtrusive as you want."

Cristina sat in the passenger seat of her own little Fiat, wishing for the first time in her life that she smoked. A cigarette might mask the menthol stench from the aftershave of the police officer who, at the insistence of Paolo Ficino, was driving her all the way back to Rome. His name was Armando and she guessed he was a few years younger than she was. He drove like a madman and viewed his ability to terrify the periodic hay wagons—the farmers and their horses alike—he passed as they raced south through Chianti as a barometer of his masculinity. She'd been so shocked when he'd had the audacity to ask if she had a man in her life that she had failed to lie. She had just looked at him, a little aghast, and shook her head no. Then she had mumbled, "My mother is going to be buried tomorrow," hoping he would see the spectacular inappropriateness of asking her out now. He hadn't. He'd expressed his sympathy instead. Told her that he couldn't imagine why someone was cutting the hearts from her family. Then he added that, although he had been to Rome only a few times in his life, an older friend had told him of a very romantic restaurant on the Via Margutta, mere blocks from the base of the Spanish Steps. He offered to take her there that night.

She ignored him, her mind's eye transfixed by images of her mother's bedroom in the Rome apartment they shared. She saw the bed, which her father had had built after the war, incorporating the piece of a headboard he had salvaged from the ruins of the Villa Chimera, the family crest carved into the center of the wood. There was the long closet with her mother's two tiers of dresses and blouses and skirts. It was a big closet by the standards of the city but tiny compared to the small dressing room off the bedroom where the marchesa's clothing had been stored at the villa. On the bureau was an Etruscan psykter, which Beatrice had used like a vase, placing a fresh bouquet of flowers there every second or third day. She and her mother had a woman who came in twice a week to clean the apartment, but it had never been a demanding job; Cristina wondered whether she would retain her now. The woman needed the work; wasn't that reason enough? Meanwhile, she herself was going to need Vittore to help her understand better her assets—their assets. She felt infantilized by all that she didn't know.

And as she gazed out the window at the countryside, she tried to decide whether she was more sad or scared.

In the end it was her memories of Friedrich that tipped the scales. For a decade she had believed he was dead while allowing herself to hope he was alive. She had told herself that he was a prisoner somewhere in Siberia and eventually even the communists would let him go. Send him home. Technically, nothing Serafina had shared with her in Florence should have changed that. After all, there was still no body. But in fact there was now a concreteness to her fears. To his end. Budapest. The Eastern Front. As her brother had reminded her, by 1945 the Soviets weren't likely to take a German captain prisoner.

She wondered where Friedrich had gone after he had left the villa for the last time. She wondered when he had left Italy. Once, when Vittore had grown frustrated with the way she was pining for the lieutenant, he had tried to turn her against him by insisting that Friedrich was likely to have been with Decher when the villagers and their priest had been massacred just south of Arezzo. She had told him that wasn't possible. Friedrich wasn't capable of that sort of violence or brutality. He wasn't. It was just that simple.

"We'll be in Rome by the middle of the afternoon," Armando

was saying, one hand on the wheel, the other arm dangling outside the window. "It will still be light out. We'll park your car and lock you safely inside your apartment. Like a princess—which they tell me you are."

"Someone told you I'm a princess?"

"Someone did," he said.

"No," she corrected him. "Whoever told you that was mistaken."

He took a turn on a switchback so quickly that she fell against him. He smiled, pleased with even that small, inadvertent contact. She looked past him out the window at the sheep on the hillside and settled back on her side of the vehicle.

"I hear the drivers are maniacs in Rome," he told her. "But I'm an excellent driver. I can keep up with the best of them. I should race cars."

For a few seconds she was able to hear the tinkling of the sheep's bells through the open windows. It reminded her of her summers as a child.

"Maybe before we park your car, we should drive down the Via Margutta. Find that restaurant," he went on. "I bet I'd recognize the name if I saw it."

When she had been a teenager, from a distance some afternoons she would watch Ilario tend to the sheep. Clearly he loved the animals. It was a testimony either to how handsome he was or to how lonely and bored she was, but sometimes when she had taken him lemonade or almonds the cook had fried in olive oil and salt, she had daydreamed that together they would find romance. Not many years after that, her niece would create similar fantasies with her dolls: princesses falling in love with blacksmiths and stable hands. Unsuitable men for the princesses, which made it all the more romantic. And now? Now even Alessia was dead. All that remained of the anointed who had once walked the loggia at the Villa Chimera and managed the vineyards and olive groves—a family that, before the war, had seemed to glide effortlessly through the gardens and sunlight and rarefied air of the hilltop villa—was her brother and herself. It was as if the estate had become a necropolis, the contours of the fields but a ghostline, and the ruins of the main house a monument to the Rosati dead.

"My shift ends at ten," Armando told her, tapping the horn twice to scare an old woman with a walking stick who was strolling slowly along the side of the road. "But you have to eat, right? Me, too. So I'll find us that restaurant. Really, you'll like it—it's very romantic."

Cristina looked at him. She had absolutely no idea what to say.

IT WAS A missed opportunity. I would learn only later that Giulia and her children had been alone at the apartment, the police officer guarding them drunk on grappa a block away.

But that also gave me resolve. I would not make such a mistake again.

The Rosatis would be together in Monte Volta to bury the marchesa and her daughter-in-law. All of them—at least all of the ones who mattered to me. Now, I would not finish them all off at once; that would demand the sort of atomic option that was inimical to the surgical precision that I wanted to mark my little project.

But I would get one of them at the Villa Chimera. I would entice one of them away from the police and the crowd (though I was honestly unsure whether there would be a sizable number of mourners) and I would extract one more heart.

The day before the funeral, a little before dusk, I went to the estate. I saw that workers had already prepared the two plots and left. I inspected their work. And then I walked the grounds, surveying the melancholy rubble of the villa and the dreary remains of the outbuildings. It had all gone to hell— which perhaps was fitting. In a decade the vineyards had been lost entirely to creep and weed, and the olive grove had more dead trees than live ones. It was bleak. There were feral cats and rats and birds living inside the villa, while the roof of the cattle barn had collapsed and two of the walls had crumbled.

I was, of course, not displeased by the ruin and gloom.

That night I slept in my car, and I slept well, dreamless and long. I awoke with the sun, drove into Pienza, and drank my espresso beneath an unexpectedly welcoming touch: a bright red Campari umbrella.

1944

IT WAS DARK now and the power was out at the villa, but the kitchen was awash in candlelight. The candelabra from the dining room and the loggia had been brought here, as had a pair of oil lamps Francesca had found. Still, Cristina could not see the wounded girl's face because she was rolled on her side, her knees pulled up toward her chest. She lay on a pile of blankets on the kitchen floor. But Cristina knew that her mother could see the partisan's face: Beatrice was squatting on the tile before the girl, patting her forehead gently with a rag of cold water. Cristina could not help but wonder if her face was as badly burned as her back. From her spot near the stove, she could see the young woman's skull and her right shoulder, and she was riveted. Instead of skin, she saw a roiling landscape of festering black tissue and red hillocks, some oozing an almost hueless butter. The flickering candlelight made it look vaguely like lava, undulating and alive. She wanted to help, but she couldn't imagine how. Still, she asked her mother if there was anything at all she could get her, anything at all she could do.

"No," her mother said, and then she put the rag in the pot of cold water and took the girl's wrist in her hands, feeling the pulse with her fingertips.

The partisan was lying on a white sheet, but it had small blue and gold flowers embroidered along one of the edges and Cristina didn't believe it belonged to her family. Besides, it was filthy, browned by dust and grime from the road. Cristina speculated that the girl had already been wrapped in the sheet when the group had turned up at the villa. Her bare feet were exposed, and Cristina saw the cuff of what she guessed was a pair of men's gray work trousers. The feet, so dirty and small, were childlike. Somehow they managed to make the girl's back, charred and blistered and maimed, seem even worse. It was as if this had happened to Alessia.

Finally her mother stood and said to the couple who had been watching over her as she examined the girl, "What did you say your names were?"

"We didn't. But I'm Enrico. And this is my wife, Teresa."

"Well, Enrico. Teresa. This girl needs a hospital."

Enrico rubbed his forehead and then wiped his eyes. He was in his mid-twenties, his hair the ash blond of a northern Italian. His sleeves were rolled up not quite to his elbows. Teresa gazed down at the girl on the floor and then knelt beside her. Her hair was a shade darker than Enrico's, but it may just have looked that way because it hadn't been washed in days. It fell to her shoulders. "We know she needs a hospital," Enrico said, his tone somewhere between exhaustion and exasperation. "The villagers thought you might have a car. We want to get her to the hospital in Montepulciano. Or, if the Germans are still there, take her to one farther south."

Three more partisans were outside on the terrace, two men and another woman, and one of the men was wounded as well—though not nearly as badly as this girl. He had burns, too, but they were only on his left hand and arm.

"I'm sorry," Beatrice told him. "When the Germans left, they took our car."

He glanced down at the girl. "I gave her the last of the morphine," he said, sighing. "When she wakes up . . ."

"She might not wake up," Beatrice told him.

In the distance they heard the murmur of artillery, and on any other summer night Cristina would have assumed it was merely an evening thunderstorm arriving from the west. "Is she your sister?" she asked Enrico. Then she looked down at Teresa. "Or yours?"

Enrico stared at her for a long moment. It was as if he were noticing her for the first time. "No," he said at last. "She's not my sister. Nor is she my sister-in-law. But she's like a sister. She's like a sister to both of us."

"What happened?" Cristina asked him.

Instead of answering her, however, he said, "Tell me your name."

"Cristina."

"You're the marchese's daughter?"

She nodded.

"We were fighting in Trequanda and there were more of them than we expected. And they had incendiary grenades." He motioned with his eyes at the girl on the floor. "Her clothes caught on fire. Her head, her hair. The whole room was on fire. When we pulled off her clothes, we made it worse."

"Was anyone killed?"

"Three of us, including my cousin."

"I'm sorry."

"Me, too. What happened to your hands?" he asked.

She hadn't realized he'd noticed the blisters. "We had to bury a horse."

Teresa looked up from the floor. "Today?" she asked.

"Yes. Today."

Cristina spied Massimo in the doorway and wondered how long he had been watching. Enrico saw the boy and gave him a small salute with two fingers. The child ducked behind the frame and then raced across the front hallway and up the stairs to the nursery, where his mother and his sister were trying to stay out of the way.

"Is he your brother?" Teresa asked her.

"He's my nephew," she answered.

From the other side of the kitchen she saw her father approaching, shambling from exhaustion and loss. Enrico turned toward him. They had seen each other a few moments ago, when Antonio had returned to the villa with Beatrice and Cristina, but the two men hadn't spoken. Beatrice had instantly gone to the wounded girl.

"So you're the marchese," Enrico said. He stood a little taller, extending his hand, and Antonio shook it. But then Enrico didn't release his grip. "The villagers tell me you were a . . . a very good host to Captain Muller."

Antonio shook his head. "The Germans . . ."

"The Germans what?"

"They took what they wanted. They came and they took."

"And before Muller? The villagers also told me you entertained the Gestapo. You had parties."

"I had no choice. And the last few weeks? My family have been prisoners here."

Finally Enrico let go of Antonio's hand. "So you're not going to miss your Nazi friends." His voice was quiet, almost sultry, but still tinged with irritation.

"I was no Blackshirt," Antonio said, defending himself.

"No. Of course not. No one was." He collapsed back against the wall by the pantry and coughed once. "God, I'm tired," he muttered. Leaning beside him was his rifle, and almost sleepily he rested his fingers on the muzzle. When he saw Cristina watching him, he said, "It's a sniper rifle. British. All our weapons are British."

Somewhere Cristina heard the rumble of trucks. She thought they might be on the switchback hill that led up to the estate, and so she grew alert.

"My daughter-in-law might have a little face cream the Nazis didn't bother to steal," Beatrice said. "I might, too. And there might still be a little olive oil. But this girl needs a hospital, Enrico."

"We want her to live," Teresa said, standing. "She's the last of her family. She's all that's left."

"Of course you want her to live. But I don't see how she will without doctors."

Enrico grew watchful, his eyes darting to the side. Now he

had heard the groan of the trucks, too. They were getting nearer. Suddenly one of the other partisans ran into the kitchen from the terrace. "They're coming back," the young man said, a little breathless.

"Germans?"

"Yes."

"You're sure?"

"I'm positive. Definitely not British. There are six, maybe seven trucks. They're bringing back the howitzers, too. I saw them starting up the hill in the moonlight."

"Okay, let's go," Enrico said, and he knelt down to lift the girl off the tile, but Beatrice put her hand on his shoulder and stopped him.

"You can't take her with you," Beatrice told him. "How can you move her again?"

"Well, we can't leave her here," Enrico said, brushing her fingers off him as if they were flies. Then he lifted the girl in the sheet over his shoulder, hoisting her as if she were a burlap sack because he didn't dare try to carry her under her back and knees, as if she were a bride. "Where can we hide?" he asked. "Tell me."

"No, you can't hide here," Antonio said. "I forbid it."

"You forbid it? Think again, old man. We can and we will hide here. Because if you don't find a place to hide us, we're all dead—you, too."

"But there is no place!" Antonio barked. "There's nowhere to go!"

"Oh, I'm sure there is. Think. Now!"

Before her father could answer, however, Cristina spoke up. "The tombs," she suggested. "You can hide there. I can show you where they are." Then, even though the soles of her feet ached from the shovel, she started through the doors to the terrace and out into the night air. She paused by the balustrade and glimpsed the peaceful summer moon, so at odds with the way her heart was racing. When she heard the growl of the German trucks as they struggled up the hill, however, she continued on into the grass. She walked quickly but carefully, glancing behind her as she entered the path along which the lavender once flourished. She wanted to be sure that the partisans were following her. They were.

☙

Marco wanted only to hug his children, swing them one at a time in the air, and then hold on tight to his wife and feel her fingers kneading the back of his neck. He saw himself leaning against her, his head pressing against her brow. Instead, however, he was crouching in the dark in the high grass beside the tortuous gravel road that climbed up the hill to his family's estate, watching nervously as the last German truck rumbled past him on its way to the villa. He was no more than two hundred and fifty meters from the house. When he had first heard the vehicles, he had hoped they were British. He had assumed they were British. Weren't the Germans retreating north? Weren't they streaming away from the Val d'Orcia and the Val di Chiana? In the afternoon he had heard the fighting—he had seen the billowing black smoke from the artillery—and it was up toward Arezzo.

When the last of the German trucks had come to a stop at the summit and shut off its engine, he could hear the officers yelling their orders. And it all began to make sense. These soldiers were cut off. The British were already behind them and so they were going to create a perimeter and make a stand here.

He glanced down at the broom, its yellow flowers almost colorless in the moonlight. He hoped his family—Francesca and the children, his parents, Cristina—had fled. Here he had escaped the Germans and trekked all this way, constantly fantasizing about the reunion at the estate and the war's end for the Rosati family, and now he was praying that no one was home. He had seen firsthand what happened in battle, how mortars and missiles killed indiscriminately, the way shrapnel ripped apart flesh.

He considered retreating himself. Walking back toward the village and finding refuge there. Surely someone in the town would shelter him.

But what if Francesca and the children were at the house? Before he did anything, he had to know. He wondered how close he could get to the villa.

⚜

Since the German officers had taken the family's last remaining candles, Francesca could not even read to her children that night. And so she told them fairy tales to try to calm them—and, she understood, to try to calm herself. The reality was that Massimo and Alessia had seen these German soldiers tromping across the estate for a month now. Certainly Alessia was more annoyed than frightened; she didn't understand that a fight loomed when the British came to dislodge the soldiers. Mostly she was exasperated by the idea that once again tonight she would have to share her bedroom with the rest of the family. It was one thing to climb into bed with Francesca and Marco on those rare and wondrous occasions when her father had been home; it was quite another to be jammed together like jarred olives with her mother and brother and grandparents and aunt.

Meanwhile, Francesca worried that one of her children might accidentally mention the partisans who were hiding in the tombs. Massimo, who had been the first to see them and who had watched his grandmother examine the dying girl, clearly felt he had a sacred, secret knowledge, which, like any little boy, he was liable to blurt out at any moment.

"I'm hungry," Alessia whined suddenly.

"Shhhhh," Francesca said. She had expected that she and her mother-in-law would try to find something to feed the children as soon as Antonio and Beatrice returned from burying Cristina's horse. Instead, however, the partisans had arrived, and then the Nazis. As a result, her children hadn't eaten anything since lunchtime, when a young German private had given them the hard crackers and canned meat from his ration kit before climbing into the back of a truck and speeding off. Francesca knew the private thought she was pretty, which she guessed was the only reason that he had been so generous to her children. But you never knew. Maybe he had siblings Massimo's or Alessia's age.

"I won't be quiet," Alessia whimpered angrily, and she curled up on her side on the bed and made her hands into fists. She punched the wall once. "I'm hungry!"

"I am, too," Massimo told his sister from his spot on the floor. He was sitting with his back to the bed. "But there's no food left. So grow up."

Francesca stroked her daughter's forehead. Outside the window the men were shouting and grunting as they unhitched the big cannons and dug trenches and firing pits. She wondered if she could find that young private. She wished she had thought to ask him his name. "Maybe when they're finished working, I can get you both some more crackers and sausage."

"That wasn't sausage," Massimo said.

"You know what I mean," she said softly. She heard jackboots pounding up the stairs to the second floor and saw a light moving along the hallway. She braced herself.

⚜

Cristina was just emerging from the path near the swimming pool, moving carefully in the dark, when a soldier grabbed her by the arm and threw her onto the ground. She screamed and tried to roll away, but he took his rifle off his shoulder and pointed it at her.

"Who are you?" he yelled in heavily accented Italian.

"Cristina Rosati."

"What are you doing here?" His face was black with dirt and his eyes were a little manic. But he was not much older than she was, and he was angry and scared. He wasn't about to rape her.

"I live here," she told him, gathering herself.

He seemed to think about this. Then he said, "You live here."

It was a statement, not a question, but nevertheless she nodded. She realized he suspected she was a partisan and so she added quickly, "I'm the marchese's daughter."

"What are you doing outside right now?"

She paused, her mind strangely frozen as she tried desperately to find any explanation that was better than the real one.

"Now! Tell me!" he ordered.

"I was looking for mushrooms," she lied, stammering. "I was looking for anything we could eat."

"In the dark?"

"When I started, it was light out."

He shook his head in annoyance and slung his rifle back over his shoulder. For a brief second she thought he was going to help her up, but instead he continued on his way, running to the other side of the pool and up the stairs to the terrace.

There were two soldiers, and the first one nearly stepped on Massimo in the dark. The soldier screamed at the boy in German to get out, to move, and then, after noticing Alessia and Francesca on the bed, he yelled at them, too. Though blinded by the soldier's flashlight, Francesca scurried to the edge of the mattress and lifted Alessia into her arms. She had started to say something—in her mind, she was going to ask them to be careful, to please leave her children alone—when the first German took the butt of his rifle and smashed it through the half-open window, sending a spray of glass onto the tiles below. Alessia screamed and she felt Massimo grasping her leg through her skirt, his small fingernails seeming to dig their way through the linen and into the flesh on her thigh. She retreated to the doorway, her daughter's face buried against her neck, the child's tears running down her collarbone and between her breasts, and watched as the soldiers ripped the drapes from their mounts and tore the louvered shutters from their hinges. It took no more than half a minute. Then, as they caught their breath, one of them noticed that she and her children were still there, watching in mute horror as they destroyed the bedroom.

Again the first soldier screamed at her in German. He took his hands, including the one with the rifle, and motioned for her to shoo, to leave them alone. Then, his eyes wide in the moonlight that was streaming in through the window, he said, *"Il britannico!"* and pretended to fire his rifle out toward the courtyard. *"Il britannico!"* he repeated.

She nodded. Her children's bedroom was now the high ground for riflemen. She held Alessia against her with one arm and reached down for Massimo's hand. Then she raced across the hall and down the stairs, yelling for Antonio and Beatrice and Cristina. They had to find a place to take cover.

1955

SERAFINA STOOD BESIDE Paolo at the edge of the terrace at the Villa Chimera in a suitably high-collared black dress and gazed up into the late morning sun. She closed her eyes and savored the warmth on her face. At breakfast Milton had given her a gold brooch to pin to the dress: an eagle with colored beads for the eyes and the tips of the wings. It was, he told her, based on an Etruscan design and so he thought it would be fitting for the day. He'd seen it at a jewelry store and immediately thought of her.

"This place must have been gorgeous twenty years ago," Paolo was saying.

"I'm sure it was even eleven or twelve years ago," she corrected him. The two of them had made such good time driving to Monte Volta that she had suggested they stop at the Rosatis' crumbling estate before continuing on into the village for the church service.

"Indeed," he murmured. He was looking back at the side of the villa that had collapsed and the small mesa of rubble where once there had been a wall. He was wearing a dark suit today for the funeral, and a gray homburg instead of his usual straw boater. "Can you show me the tombs and the paintings you saw there?"

"Do you want to see them because you suddenly have an interest in Etruscan art or because you think it will be helpful to the investigation?" she asked.

"Neither, really." He smiled at her, his hands clasped behind his back. "Maybe it will help me understand you."

She watched a lizard race across the hot tile. "I don't understand me."

He ignored the remark and asked, "The tombs are near where the marchesa and her daughter-in-law will be buried, right?"

"The family plot is on a hill across from the entrance to them. Maybe thirty-five or forty meters away. No more than that."

"Interesting."

"The proximity?"

He nodded.

"It's just a coincidence," she told him. "The marchese's family has been buried there since the early part of the century—decades before the family discovered the vaults."

He glanced at his watch and then motioned at the village. "I don't imagine the Rosatis or their escort have arrived yet," he said, referring to the two police officers from Rome who were driving Cristina, Vittore, and his family to Monte Volta. In addition, Paolo was bringing a third officer from Florence, Luciano Cassini, although Cassini was going straight to the villa. His primary task would be to inspect the area near the Rosati cemetery for spots where assassins might hide. "But I wouldn't be surprised if there are already a few reporters at the church."

"I agree."

"So what do you think? Will there be more reporters or more of us?"

"I give the edge to the press," said Serafina. "After all, there will only be five of us, including the two fellows from Rome. There could be easily twice that many reporters."

"And the size of the crowd?"

"Do you mean the mourners?" she asked.

"Yes."

She recalled her day in the village and what people had said about the Rosatis. She thought about the pharmacist and the old men and Ilario. "It will be small. I have a sense that by the end of the war, the marchese and his family were not especially popular. And why should they be? They had cast their lot with the Nazis."

"From what you've told me, it was more complicated than that. The girl was only—"

"The girl was the same age I was. And I wasn't dating Nazi lieutenants. Besides . . ."

"Go on."

"I wasn't even thinking about Cristina. Really, I wasn't. I like her. I was thinking about her father, the marchese. The way Antonio entertained the Germans. The way he used this place for parties," she said, waving her arm behind her.

"I'm sure a lot of the village cast their lot with the Nazis. As I recall, they were our allies."

"A lot of us never viewed them that way."

"Actually, a lot of us did—most of us, as a matter of fact. Including, for a time, your own father. Now, you and your friends had the moral high ground. I grant you that. But you were among the few. Remember, 'Mussolini is always right,'" he said, reciting one of the classic Blackshirt maxims.

She smiled at him a little grimly and replied with another, equally popular Fascist motto: *"Me ne frego,"* she said. *I don't give a damn.*

⚜

As they were about to climb into Paolo's car and leave the villa, Luciano Cassini arrived. He was a small, heavy man with salt-and-pepper hair, a sunburned complexion, and clothes that always looked uncomfortably tight. Serafina knew that he had never approved of her. He was one of the older officers who thought Paolo had lost his mind allowing a woman to join the *polizia*. But he was calm and competent and knew what he was doing. The first thing he did was ask to see the Rosati cemetery.

"I think we have time," Serafina said to the two men. "The service doesn't begin for another forty-five minutes. But we should be quick."

"Is it far?" Cassini asked.

"Not really," she said as they started away from the villa. "It's actually rather modest. When I was here the other day, I counted thirteen small headstones around a stone cross. Some small pots for flowers. There are rows of cypress on three sides. It's pretty."

"Let me guess," Paolo said. "At least some of those small pots are not your typical terra-cotta, are they?"

"I don't know," she told him.

"What are you getting at?" Cassini asked Paolo.

"Don't be surprised if the pots are rather valuable—Etruscan."

"They're using museum artifacts as flowerpots?"

"We'll see," Paolo said. "From what Cristina told us, when they unearthed the tombs, the pots were like seashells at the beach. The valuable ones they gave to the museum in Arezzo. The others? The marchesa decorated with them."

"It must have been nice to have been the marchesa," said Cassini.

"Not at the end," Paolo corrected him.

"No," Cassini agreed. "Not at the end."

By noon a small crowd had assembled inside the church in Monte Volta. The church sat halfway up a hill, nestled between ancient brick homes on one of the narrow, winding cobblestone roads that rose up from the village center. Cristina and Vittore and his family had still not arrived from Rome, however, and so Serafina excused herself from the rear pew and went outside for a cigarette. As she had expected, the funeral was small; no more than thirty people were inside the church.

She stared for a moment at the matching pair of long black Lancia Aurelias with gold trim in the windows that dominated the street. Inside each had been a casket, the hearts restored to the cadavers. Now the coffins were at the front of the church. The other cars, including Paolo's Fiat, were parked down the hill, in a lot at the edge of the village. She guessed that most of those vehicles were from Florence or Rome, or in one case Arezzo. The

Arezzo exception? Inside the church, she had spied the museum director, Roberto Piredda.

She was not convinced the killer was here, either among the mourners or lurking somewhere back at the Villa Chimera with a rifle with a scope. But she was still glad that Cassini was with them, as well as the two officers who were coming from Rome. Cassini was not the sort who would leave them for a grappa, and she had to believe that the pair from Rome would be just as conscientious.

Now she leaned against the brick wall of the building beside the church and lit a Serraglio, restraining the urge to run the matchstick flame under her thumb, and inhaled the smoke deeply.

"Good morning."

When she turned, she saw that Piredda had sidled up beside her. "I saw you wander outside," he said. "I thought I'd join you."

"Oh?"

He shrugged. "That's a beautiful dress."

"Thank you."

"Of course, fashion is a rather brutal taskmistress. You are expected to wear a black dress to the funeral, despite the heat. Me? I'm a man. I can get away with light gray. You must be sweltering."

"I'm fine."

"And, alas, you need—or at least believe that you need—an especially high collar."

"I hadn't realized you thought so much about fashion."

He raised a single finger professorially. "I think about beauty. I imagine you once had a swan's neck before something happened to you in the war."

She shook her head and watched the smoke from the tip of her cigarette. "Nope. You would have been disappointed."

He smiled down at her but changed the subject. "I'm going to visit the tombs after the burial. I'm looking forward to that. It's such a fascinating site. I expect it will bring back for me very fond memories of the excavation."

"Are you looking forward to seeing Vittore?"

"I am, I am—though, obviously, I wish it were under different circumstances."

"Let's talk later today, after you've visited the site."

"Why?"

"Perhaps the tombs will trigger memories that will help me."

"Help you?"

She rubbed her eyes at the bridge of her nose. "I phrased that badly," she said. "Perhaps seeing the tombs again will make you recall something that might help with the investigation. Maybe you'll think of someone we should talk to."

"You—you and your inspector and your prosecutor—have absolutely no idea who killed the Rosatis, do you?" he asked, and there was an edge to the question that she hadn't heard from him before. Not quite disgust. More like condescension. Incredulity. He was squinting into the sun.

"No," she admitted, curious to see where he would lead the conversation if she was passive.

"Don't you people always go back to the basics when you're stumped?"

"Go on."

"You know—motivation? You sat across from me in my office just the other day and asked me this: Who hated the Rosatis enough to kill them?"

"And . . ."

"You seem to think it all has something to do with the Second World War. You wanted to know about the people Vittore and I knew a decade ago. Maybe your story goes back to the war, but I'm not sure this one does. It seems to me, if any of them—if any of us—wanted to kill them, we would have had ample opportunities in the midst of the battles that raged between Rome and Florence. We would have had plenty of chances in the first months after the Germans retreated north. It was chaos, absolute chaos."

She snuffed out her cigarette on the balustrade and then wiped the ashes over the side. "Meaning?"

"Maybe the Rosatis did something last month. The marchesa or Vittore or that first girl who was killed."

"Francesca."

"Yes, her."

"What could they have done?"

"As I've told you, I've not seen them in years. I have no idea." He walked to the center of the empty street and gazed in the direction of the villa. "Why, you ask, do people hate them? Maybe it has nothing to do with the Villa Chimera. Maybe it has everything to do with Rome."

"Rome," she repeated.

"It is where they all live, isn't it?"

"Not Francesca. And she hadn't had anything to do with the Rosatis in years."

"Well, you're the detective," he said, and suddenly he took two quick steps back toward the wall and leaned into her. He stared at her brooch so intently that for a moment she thought he was going to touch it. "A replica, of course," he said, "but lovely. Inspired by work from the third century B.C. Intelligent use of filigree and enameling. An eagle. Very well done." He looked up from it and added, "A brooch is perfect for you, Serafina. It draws a man's eyes precisely where you want them." Then he did touch her. With the gentleness of a parent he pressed his fingertips against the side of her head and added, "Skin grafting has come so far since the war. You know that, don't you? It's too bad they didn't know then what they know now." Then he parted her hair to stroke the ruin that had once been her ear.

Father Silvio Mancini had been the priest in Monte Volta since 1928 and once had known the Rosatis well. He had performed Francesca and Marco's marriage. Serafina guessed he was in his fifties, but he was completely bald and might have been considerably older. Still, his face was weathered, not geriatric, and he moved and spoke with great energy. Serafina had been outside the church with Piredda when the Rosati family cars had arrived, and she had watched the priest greet Cristina and Vittore and then Vittore's wife and children. There was an older woman among them, too, and Cristina guessed this was Elena, Beatrice's sister from Naples. The priest escorted the family into a narrow alley beside the church, no doubt planning to take them inside through a side door so they could discuss any last-minute details in an anteroom prior to entering the sanctuary. She noted that one of the two uniformed officers from Rome accompanied the Rosatis while the other went straight inside the church. She knew that Paolo was supposed to take charge of them before the service began. She nodded good-bye to Piredda and then returned to her pew in the rear of the sanctuary beside Paolo.

"I was beginning to think you weren't coming back," Paolo whispered, rising to convene with the police officers. "I was beginning to think you'd gotten bored and gone exploring."

She shook her head no and gazed at the lit candles at the front of the church, losing herself for a moment in the rows of small, beautiful, featherlike flames. She touched her ear where Piredda's fingers had been.

After the service, once the caskets with Beatrice and Francesca Rosati's bodies had been loaded back into the two hearses, Serafina watched the mourners start together down the hill to their cars. Ilario, his pregnant wife on his arm, nodded politely at her, and she thought the pair was a rather handsome couple. His wife was pretty. Ilario wasn't wearing a jacket, but his white shirt and necktie were as crisp as anything Milton ever wore.

She waited outside the church because she wanted to be sure that she saw the officers from Rome escort the family into their own vehicles. She wasn't precisely sure why; after all, this wasn't her job and she didn't believe the killer was in fact present. But here she was.

"Coming?" asked Paolo.

"You go on," she said. "I'll just be a minute."

"You want to see the Rosatis get into their cars."

"I do."

He smiled, adjusted his homburg, and stood beside her. A moment later a young man wearing a tan suit and carrying a notepad approached them. A reporter, but probably not from Florence, because neither she nor her boss recognized him. He introduced himself, and indeed, he was from Rome. She listened as Paolo talked to the fellow, answering some questions honestly and being charmingly evasive on others. Soon she saw the Rosatis emerge. She watched as Cristina and her aunt Elena climbed into one vehicle and Vittore and his wife and children climbed into the other. A police officer took the wheel behind each, and they started the long, slow process of turning the automobiles around in the thin cobblestone street. And then they gave up: someone had arrived late and parked beside the wide hearses, effectively penning the two family cars in. And so the vehicles started up the hill instead, farther into the labyrinthine warren of cobblestone roads atop Monte Volta. Quickly Serafina turned back to the reporter and Paolo, raising a finger to interrupt.

"What do you think about that?" she asked.

Paolo shrugged. "The family cars couldn't get around that new vehicle and the two hearses."

"I know. Should we follow them?"

"The cars with the Rosatis? I don't think so. Remember, this is their village. I say that metaphorically, but once upon a time, it practically was. I'm sure Cristina and Vittore can tell the drivers exactly how to return to the center. Besides, how many roads can really be up there?"

"You're not worried?"

He seemed to think about this. In a moment, however, it didn't matter. The automobiles were out of sight.

"Come on," he said to her. "We should head up to the villa, too." Then he shook the reporter's hand and they all started down the hill to their cars.

The two black hearses pulled into the weedy white gravel park-
ing square just outside the villa, and so did the automobile with
Cristina, her aunt, and Father Mancini. A moment later Serafina
and Paolo arrived, climbing from the Fiat and joining the mourners who had left before them. Serafina watched the police officer
emerge from the first family car and open the back door for the
Rosatis and the priest. Then the young fellow glanced down the
winding road that led to the estate. Like everyone else, he assumed
the second car was somewhere behind him. It would appear any
minute. It had to. And so they all waited and wondered as Cristina whispered something to her aunt and as Father Mancini said
something to the guard. Finally Serafina turned to Paolo. He was
staring down at his watch, but she could see he was worried.

"I presume Luciano is down at the cemetery," she said.

Paolo nodded. Then he motioned for her to follow him as he
ventured over to the officer. "The best thing you can do right now
is stay here with Miss Rosati and her aunt," he said to him. "Okay?
I'll have Serafina go get our man down at the cemetery while I
backtrack to the church. It's probably nothing, but let's be sure."

The young man said he would wait and, along with Cristina,
peered anxiously at the road behind him. Then Paolo walked
briskly toward his Fiat while Serafina started down the hill to the
Rosati family plot. Behind her a reporter called out to Paolo, but
she recognized the sound of his engine as he started his car. She
told herself, as she had over and over that morning, that the killer
wasn't here, he couldn't be.

But the truth was, she no longer believed it.

IT WAS A land where men ground rocks to make pigments and transformed tree sap and egg yolks into binders. The sky from a stone: lapis lazuli. They studied the way the world changed at morning and dusk and imagined how the sun might fall on the skin of a goddess. They painted their deities onto canvases and wooden slabs, onto their walls and ceilings and domes. The Son of Man and his virgin mother, the saints and martyrs and popes.

And before the monotheists, there were the polytheists with their temples and sculptures. Their Pantheon.

The church in Monte Volta, where the marchesa and her daughter-in-law were eulogized, had frescoes dating back five hundred years. There, fading but still impressive, was a mural along one plaster wall depicting the life and death of John the Baptist. Along the other was the story of the Annunciation. There were doves on one side, a decapitation on the other.

The cemetery at the Villa Chimera, where they were to be buried, had a temple modeled after the Minerva facade in Assisi and an angel that was, in my opinion, amateurishly derivative of the winged guardians along the Ponte Sant'Angelo in Rome. You could see the angel from the entrance to the Etruscan chambers; you could see the temple from the hillside above that opening in the earth.

Now, make no mistake, the battle for Italy was horrible. But it was nothing like the Eastern Front. That was an innermost ring far worse than anything even Dante conceived.

Still, for two days in the summer of 1944, the Villa Chimera was hell. It was—of this you can be sure. It's a wonder anyone survived.

During the war, I promised the dead I would never forget them. I stared at them, barely able to move myself. Pretended I was one of them. To this day I can recall the light in the ruins.

Eleven years later I watched the family and the mourners and the police file into the church across the valley from the villa. Then, of course, I was pretending only that I was civilized.

By the time they filed out, I was ready. The sky that day, if anyone had happened to paint it, was lapis lazuli.

1944

THE FIRST SHELLS fell in the pool, sending up oddly mischievous sprays of water—Massimo cannonballing into the deep end—along with the killing shards of marble. The wooden and wicker pergola beside the water erupted in flame, illuminating that side of the terrace, and the small statue of Venus in the raised garden near the loggia was decapitated. And then it was gone, obliterated in an instant. The chimera was butchered, the conjoined triplets—a lion, a snake, a goat—separated, gutted, and then blasted to pebbles. The remnants of the olive grove caught fire and the olive press started to burn.

And the Germans fired back, the great howitzers shaking the hillside, and Marco winced reflexively each time the ground around him heaved or a part of his childhood was destroyed. He was terrified. He was more scared now than he had ever been in the past year, more frightened even than when the Allies had first invaded Sicily or, months later, when he had thought the Germans were going to execute him rather than merely force him at gunpoint into a work crew. This was worse, much worse, because he was afraid that somewhere here on the grounds of the estate was his family. He told himself it wasn't possible, they had to be gone, long gone. But what if they were here, trapped amid the bricks and mortar that seemed sure to come down in the battle?

He knew enough not to move, at least at the moment, to stay crouched behind the tufa boulder. He recalled the rock from his childhood, because as a boy he'd pretended it was an asteroid.

When a shell would explode and briefly the night would become day, he would see tendrils of tobacco-brown smoke wafting up from the cratered gardens and lawn. He might have remained hidden there until the shelling subsided, curled in a ball as his home was destroyed, but amid the furious din of the artillery and the sounds of the Germans barking their orders, he heard a woman's voice screaming out his wife's name.

"Francesca! Father! Francesca!" He peered over the stone and there she was, his little sister. Cristina was running, hunched over, between the remnants of the gardens on the far side of the pool, trying either to get through the shelling to the villa or—perhaps—to escape from the house. He couldn't decide, because she was making no progress as she ran back and forth between the explosions, hysterical, calling out for their father and his wife. And so he emerged from his hiding spot and raced after her, grabbing her by her arms when he reached her and pulling her down to the ground. Then he rolled her against the marble blocks that marked the side of one of the raised flower beds and fell on top of her, shielding her from the shrapnel as best he could. He told her that yes, yes, it was him, he was home and alive. He could feel her body trembling, and her face was wet with tears and sweat. But she didn't seem to be wounded. He was about to ask her where everyone else was—their parents, his wife and children, whether Vittore was here, too, because clearly the family had not escaped—when a shell crashed into the hillside nearby and the ground beneath them rolled like an ocean wave and briefly they were lifted up. Then they were showered with small rocks and dirt, the stones bruising them as they fell hard upon their arms and legs. He realized they couldn't stay here; they had to find better cover than this. He asked her again where everyone was and she told him they were inside the villa. And so he pulled her to her feet by her hands, shocked at the blisters there. Then, zigzagging, he led her toward the terrace and up the marble steps that led to the swimming pool. When he reached the terrace, he paused for the briefest of seconds, wondering whether to continue on to the left or the right to get to the house, and then he heard a pair of German privates screaming for them to stop where they were and put their arms up. And so they did, and Marco was careful to spread wide his fingers so that even in the dark the fellows could see he was unarmed. Both soldiers' eyes were wild with fear, and one was waving his Karabiner rifle at them.

"We live here!" Marco told them in German. "Our house!" he added, pointing up at the villa.

For a long second the two men watched them. And then, when another shell blew apart three of the cypress trees that columned the exterior stairwell, one of the soldiers ordered them inside, prodding them at gunpoint through the loggia and the living room and into the kitchen. Inside, the second private switched on a flashlight and waved it across the room.

And there, huddled on the floor, Marco saw his family. His wife. His children. His parents. And, leaning against one of the counters, he saw also a Lee-Enfield rifle. A British sniper rifle. He wondered what in the world it was doing here, but then lost track of it when Massimo and Alessia threw themselves upon him, the children oblivious to the German soldier who was pointing a gun at their father and their aunt.

Francesca thought about when she was happiest. She sat with her head against Marco's shoulder, the side of her face buried against his skin where his neck met his chest. She had unbuttoned the top buttons of his shirt because she needed to touch him and hear his heart beat. Alessia was curled up on his legs and Massimo on hers. The children weren't sleeping, but in the intervals when the shelling ceased—the air still charged and the stench of gunpowder a fog that wouldn't lift—she thought they might be dozing. They were so tired. They all were. Her ears were ringing from the cannonade. Her thighs were sore; her knees were weak.

But Marco was home and she sighed against him, recalling the litany of firsts she had shared with this man and how happy he made her. First kiss. First embrace. First time they made love. First baby. Second. Nothing, she decided, made her really happy but Marco and Massimo and Alessia. That was it. That was all in the world that she really needed, and that was what this war had taught her. Let the walls come tumbling down around them, let the estate become a lifeless moonscape—a massive necropolis filled with the Fascist artifacts of a cruel and stupid regime. Let the vineyards and the olive grove burn. Let the Medici mirrors crack. So long as she had this man and these children, all would be well. The war would end, the fires would burn themselves out.

She kissed his sternum. She felt his arm around her pull her even closer against him. Through the window she watched the flares and the phosphorous white chrysanthemums, and she told herself they were only fireworks and no one was going to die. At least no Rosatis. At least not Marco and Massimo and Alessia.

❧

In the morning the shelling stopped, and Antonio stood before the kitchen window and gazed out at the ruined grounds of his estate and assessed the damage. He heard, among other things, the raspy *kowk* of a tern, and he glanced at the sky to see if he could spot the bird. He watched the soldiers emerging from their firing pits, squinting like old men at the sky; others sat, exhausted, their heads in their hands, beside the howitzers. There did not seem to be many wounded, but he really had no idea what was occurring on the other side of the house. The villa itself, however, seemed to have been spared. But he couldn't be sure: neither he nor his family had been allowed to leave the kitchen.

By the light of the morning, he honestly couldn't decide whether he was angrier at the damage to his property or at the degradations his family was enduring. His wife, a marchesa, peeing into a pot in front of her grandchildren, as if they were all peasants. It was appalling. The children were hungry and, worse, thirsty. Without electricity, they had no water at the villa, and they weren't allowed to retrieve some from the well, even though the fighting had, for the moment, subsided. He overheard a German sergeant telling two privates that if the British didn't attack that morning—and the sergeant said he didn't believe that they would—Captain Muller might abandon the big guns and allow them to try to fight their way north to Arezzo, where they could rejoin Colonel Decher and the rest of the division. Antonio recalled all the wine that Decher had drunk here. On the terrace outside this very window. Down the marble steps and beside the swimming pool. Now, it seemed, Decher actually had combat responsibilities. The man's dangerous and stupid little prayers had been answered. What an architect was doing in combat was beyond Antonio. It made as much sense as his son Marco mining beaches and then repairing roads.

He felt Marco beside him, and his son's presence cheered him. It reminded him of what was really important. Even this nightmare would soon be over. He put his arm around his son's shoulders.

"Tell me something," Marco whispered.

You made it. You're here, was all he wanted to say. *And soon they'll be gone. The Germans. This time forever. Either they'll surrender or they'll leave. But we, the Rosatis, will have endured.* Instead, however, he said simply, "Anything." In the corner, Francesca and the grandchildren were dozing. His wife and Cristina were awake but dazed.

"How could you allow the partisans to hide here?" Marco asked him, his voice an urgent whisper. In the night Antonio had told his son about Enrico and his men and the dying girl, but it had been difficult to share many details amid the shelling and the riot of emotions the family was experiencing. There was the terror as the Germans and the British dueled with mortar fire and artillery, and it sometimes felt as if the stone walls of the villa were going to collapse upon them, and yet there was also the children's—and Francesca's—undeniable delight that Marco was home.

"I had no choice," he told his son. "They just . . . appeared. And then suddenly the Germans were here, too. We never thought they'd be coming back."

"You know they'll kill us all, even my children, if they find them."

"How will they find them? Why would they go to the tombs?"

Marco gently pulled Antonio's hand off him and took a step back. He pointed at the gun that was still leaning against the wall. "You know what that is?"

"A rifle, obviously."

"It's a British sniper rifle."

"No."

"What did you think it was? A rake? A fencing foil?"

"I thought it was German. I assumed one of the soldiers left it here."

"No. One of the partisans left it here."

"God," Antonio said, shaking his head. "We have to hide it. The Germans must not have noticed it last night in the dark. They will today."

"Yes," Marco said. "They will. Even I spotted it when I got here, in just a flashlight beam." He retrieved the rifle and began to survey the kitchen.

"Under the stove, maybe," Antonio suggested. "Maybe if you angle it, it will fit."

Marco nodded. He was about to crouch and slide it under the oven when they both heard footsteps. Marco glanced at the doorway and registered the presence of a German officer, his arm raised and a pistol in his hands, but that was all: instantly, the quiet in the kitchen was destroyed by a single gunshot. Marco dropped the rifle and collapsed onto the tile floor, a marionette whose strings had been cut. Suddenly Francesca was awake and screaming *No, no, no!* and she fell upon her husband, oblivious to the children, who were standing over their parents, the two of them shrieking as well. Antonio saw in the entrance the German lieutenant who had shot Cristina's horse. He thought the bastard's name was Bayer, but he really didn't give a damn what the fellow was called. He threw himself at the soldier, fully expecting either to kill him or die trying. Bayer, however, swatted the marchese with the back of his hand—his right hand, the one holding the pistol—sending him spinning against the wall. Then the lieutenant grabbed a handful of his shirt and lifted him up onto his toes.

"Are you crazy?" he asked the marchese. Then he took his gun by the barrel and slammed the grip into Antonio's cheek so hard that even over the weeping and howls of Francesca and the children, the family could hear the bone break.

☙

By the time Vittore got to the radio station where Giulia was a secretary, the three Fascists who worked there with her were outside in the street tossing papers into a metal barrel and burning them. He nodded and started toward the building to find Giulia, but one of them, an announcer and writer named Carlo, stopped him and asked, "Have you heard anything? How close are the Allies?"

"I'd think you'd know a hell of a lot more than I do," he told Carlo. The fellow was really nothing more than a toady propagandist, but one would have thought the puppet government would have kept him apprised of the party lines and half-truths (and complete fabrications) he was supposed to broadcast.

"They don't tell us anything anymore. The last transcript we got was yesterday morning."

"God, aren't you a reporter? Ask some questions!"

"I was a reporter before the war," Carlo said, shrugging. "Now I just rewrite what they send me. I correct grammar and tone down the more obvious lies."

Vittore shook his head and opened the door, but he saw Giulia coming down the stairs from the station, a crate in her arms. He took it from her. Inside it was a plant, her purse, and a pair of shoes.

"I thought it would be more papers you needed to burn," he said, and he kissed her on the cheek, a reflexive gesture that struck him as unexpectedly normal under the circumstances. She was wearing a green dress and a pink scarf around her neck. She looked strangely festive.

"There's almost nothing left upstairs," she said.

"Why the dress?" he asked. "It's one of my favorites."

"I didn't know if I'd get to go home."

"So you wanted to be well dressed if you wound up a refugee?"

She paid no attention to his question and instead asked him the same thing Carlo had: how close were the Allies?

"Why does everyone think I would know when the Allies are going to get here?" he muttered, more bemused than annoyed, as they paused beside the men and the bonfire in the barrel.

"Because you're wearing a uniform," said Carlo.

"I spent the morning putting tinfoil and wool around frescoes. I just finished sandbagging a statue of Perseus. I'm not exactly commanding the Hermann Göring Division."

"My mother is terrified," Giulia said to him. "I want to go to her home, not mine. Is that okay?"

"Of course it is. It's fine."

"Is it true we're going to blow up the bridges over the Arno?" Carlo asked.

Vittore nodded grimly. "Yes," he answered. "I think it is."

"See?" the radio announcer said. "You do know things."

Vittore put the crate under his left arm and wrapped his right arm around Giulia. "Your mother will be fine. This is a liberation, not an occupation."

"That's awfully treasonous talk, Vittore," Carlo warned him, but it was clear that he wasn't serious. He knew which way the wind was blowing.

The bullet had pulverized Marco's left scapula and shoulder, and he was sweating profusely from the pain. He was trying to shield his family from the agony he was experiencing. But as he lay on his side, he didn't think he was going to die. At least not yet. Already Francesca was slowing the bleeding with a tablecloth she was pressing hard against the wound. Clearly the bullet had missed the major artery there. Marco was in fact more worried about his father, who had been knocked out for perhaps a full minute after the blow to his face. Now Antonio was awake and woozy, his left cheek and eye turning whorls of purple and black. He had spat two of his teeth into his hand and folded them into his handkerchief.

Marco looked back and forth between his parents and the lieutenant, who was standing just outside the doorway and waiting for someone or something. He had slung the British rifle over his shoulder.

"Maybe we still have some aspirin somewhere," Francesca said, and she smiled down at him.

Marco tried to focus. Aspirin should be the least of his issues. They were going to have to explain that gun. "The rifle," he whispered. "In a minute they're going to ask you about it."

"Shhhhhh," she said. "You can't worry about that."

He tried to lift his hand and place it upon hers, but searing, white-hot needles instantly stung him, causing him to wince, cry out, and drop his clenched fingers back onto the tile floor.

"It's okay," Francesca told him. "Shhhhhh."

But it wasn't okay, it wasn't okay at all. "You need to tell them it's my gun," he murmured softly. Over her shoulder he saw Alessia looking down at him, her face sad and scared and worried. He smiled at his little girl, at her big, wide eyes, and motioned with his chin so Francesca would note the child's presence. His wife turned around and called for Cristina, who at the moment was helping her mother tend to Antonio. But Cristina took her niece by her shoulders and steered her to the long wooden prep table the cook had used, underneath which Massimo was curled in a ball, shivering and sucking on his pinkie.

"You will have to explain the gun," Marco continued, his voice barely audible, but he had to be sure the lieutenant didn't hear him. "Say I had it with me when I got here last night. The private who found me? For all we know, he's dead. For all we know, he's in a trench on the other side of the estate."

"They'll kill you. I will never say that."

"They won't kill me," he lied. "But they will kill us all if they think we're hiding partisans."

Behind them he heard the sound of jackboots on the stone in the entry hall, and a moment later he saw a German captain, two privates trailing behind him. Bayer saluted, showed him the sniper rifle, and said, "He's over there."

The captain crossed the kitchen floor, and for a brief second his eyes and Marco's met. Marco tried to read them, but they were expressionless.

"You speak German?" the captain asked him.

"I do. I was a captain in the Italian army."

"Good for you," he said, and then he kicked Marco hard in the stomach, the toe of the boot knocking the wind from him and causing the pain in his shoulder to move like a tsunami up his neck and down his spine. He hurt so much that his vision grew fuzzy, and for a long moment he was only vaguely aware of his wife and his daughter screaming. Slowly, however, once again he was able to focus, and he gritted his teeth.

"You showed up last night, I hear," the captain said. "A deserter?"

He shook his head. The pain was making him tremble, and he tried to rein in his movements. He didn't want this officer to think he was quivering with fear.

"Then what? A partisan?" He pointed at the rifle Bayer was holding. "Is that your weapon?"

Before he could answer, he heard his mother. "Captain Muller," she began, her voice pleading, "you know us! Colonel Decher knows us! Some of the other landowners might be hiding partisans, but not us! Not us, you know that! You billeted your officers in this very house!"

Muller rubbed his eyes. Outside they heard the sounds of the soldiers talking almost casually and opening their ration kits in the lull; overhead they heard airplanes.

"This is my son!" his mother begged. "This is Marco!"

The captain regarded the marchesa. Then he motioned for Bayer to hand him the rifle. He inspected it briefly. "Your gun, yes or no?" he asked, looking down at Marco.

Marco nodded, but at the same time Francesca was telling Muller, "It's not. It's not!"

So Muller squatted beside Francesca. He glanced once at the rifle stock. Then he said to Marco, "Tell me what someone has cut into the gun. Two initials. If you can tell me, I'll believe it's yours."

There was nothing to say. Nothing to say at all. He had no idea, and he was in too much pain even to manufacture a guess.

"That's what I thought," Muller said when Marco remained silent. He rose to his feet and ordered Bayer and the other two soldiers over to him. He told them to roll Marco onto his back, his shoulder be damned, and pull his arms out like wings. Marco yelled like a gored animal when they spread his arms. Then the captain grabbed Francesca behind her neck by the collar of her blouse and dragged her away from her husband.

"Watch your hands," he said to his soldiers. "You, hold him closer to his elbow, not his wrist." He unlatched the safety and inspected the rifle once again. "A cheekpiece and a telescopic sight. Nice, very nice. But I won't need either for this shot." Then, at point-blank range, he shot a hole through the palm of Marco's right hand.

⚜

Once Vittore had escorted Giulia to her mother's apartment in Fiesole, he hitched a ride back into the center of Florence on a German army truck filled with empty crates. He asked the private driving the vehicle what was going to fill them, but the soldier was evasive. Still, Vittore imagined that within hours they would be packed with artwork and antique furniture some German general or SS officer was commandeering.

He hopped off the truck near San Lorenzo and started back toward the Uffizi. It had taken almost as long to drive as it would have to walk, because the roads were clogged with German military vehicles and staff cars. No one knew if the Allies would arrive in two days, two weeks, or even a month. The Nazis weren't expected to put up much of a fight south of Florence, but they were still building their defensive line to the north. It was possible—likely, even—that a rearguard action might grow more intense as they tried to delay the Allied advance.

When he reached the museum, he expected he would have another protection assignment waiting for him, another fresco or statue to entomb. Instead, however, he found Lorenzetti in the office they shared, packing a small satchel with a few books and some clothing that the scholar apparently kept at the Uffizi.

"What's this about?" he asked Lorenzetti.

"It's time for me to go underground," the fellow answered.

Vittore looked around to make sure no one was within earshot. "You're joining the partisans?" he inquired, honestly unsure if he had heard Lorenzetti correctly.

"God, no. The last thing I want is to get myself killed in the last days of this appalling war. By underground, I meant hiding. You should do the same. Maybe go back to that beautiful estate of yours and hide in the olive press. The Germans must have left by now."

Vittore leaned against the credenza and peered out the window behind Lorenzetti. The sun was reflecting off the glass of the buildings across the way. He thought of Giulia's bosses burning their papers. And yet the real Florentines did not seem on the verge of panic—only the Nazis and Blackshirts and collaborators. And did he fall into any of those categories? Of course not. Despite his uniform. Nevertheless . . .

"I won't ask where you're going."

"No. Please don't," Lorenzetti agreed. Then he handed Vittore a piece of paper with an official-looking seal and said, "Decher left us each one of these before leaving. Yours is on your desk." Vittore saw that it was an order from the colonel. The expert on Donatello and bas-relief was being told to report immediately to a combat unit being formed in Arezzo. "I told you, we are supposed to become cannon fodder."

Vittore put the paper down. "When was the last time you fired a gun?"

"Training camp."

"Me, too."

"And Decher? He's used to commanding the likes of us, not real soldiers. I tell you, he'll get everyone killed."

"You think he's that inept?" Vittore asked.

"I do. I also believe he's arrogant. And it seems to me that ineptitude and arrogance are a bad combination in battle. Dangerous."

"Cowardice is, too."

Lorenzetti raised an eyebrow. "In my case, we won't find out now, will we?"

Vittore picked up the dress dagger on the desk. It was about a foot long in its black scabbard and had a Roman eagle on the handle. Lorenzetti used it as a paperweight. "As you know," he told Lorenzetti, "I don't think much of Decher either. I never have. But my father rather likes him. And I've always thought my father had good sense."

"Your father misjudged him. I worked with Decher more closely than you. I know what he really thinks of your family."

Vittore fingered the tip of the blade, waiting. When Lorenzetti said nothing, he told him, "Go on."

"Your sister is beautiful but an inappropriate lover for his adjutant. Your sister-in-law is beautiful but should have her tongue cut out. Your mother is beautiful but too concerned with the peasantry. And your father is a fool who makes good wine but little else. He was lucky to be born rich."

"Was Decher the one who suggested that the Villa Chimera was a good spot for the howitzers? For Captain Muller's battery?"

"Of course he was." Lorenzetti shook his head. "I'm sorry."

"I think I suspected as much."

"The bright side?"

"I'm waiting."

"His adjutant will never be your brother-in-law. I wouldn't worry about that. Friedrich Strekker is the sort of eager young cripple who will be proud to die for the fatherland. Once the Germans are north of Florence, your sister can fall in love with a handsome Italian poltroon."

"Like you."

He put up his hands. "Like me—but not me. I promise."

"Will I see you again?"

"Of course you will. After the war. I will descend on your family's estate and avail myself of all its glories. The wine, the olive oil. The pretty girls at the parties. But you, my friend, what will you do?"

He thought of the orders he had waiting for him. "I guess I'll report to Arezzo."

"Even after what I just told you about Decher?"

He shrugged. "I didn't say I'd be of much help."

※

The gunshot was nearly deafening in the kitchen, and the bullet ricocheted off the floor and chipped plaster off the wall above Cristina. "Stop it!" she screamed. "He's not a partisan! You just saw it wasn't his gun!"

"Just shoot her, too," Bayer said. "She's pretty, but loud."

"No," Muller said to no one in particular. "I agree, I don't think he's a partisan. But I do think this. I think all of you are hiding them here, somewhere." He waved his finger at the adults before turning toward the marchese, who was sitting, stunned, against the wall, one hand on his rapidly swelling cheek. "Where are they, Antonio?"

Antonio took his fingers away from his face and tried to speak. But the inflammation and his ruined mouth savaged his German the first time he tried to form words.

"What's that, old man?" Muller asked. "You sound insane."

Antonio took a breath to gather himself. "I will tell your commander what you are doing," he said slowly, forcing out each syllable with care. "Colonel Decher and I are friends."

Muller rolled his eyes. "Of course you are."

"You cannot treat us this—" the marchese continued, but Muller kicked him hard in the side, the way a few minutes earlier he had put his boot into Marco.

"We're surrounded by the fucking British Army! I'm not going to get shot in the ass by partisans! I asked you a question. Where are they? Where the fuck are you hiding them?"

None of the Rosatis said a word, and so Muller raised the rifle once again, aiming it now at Marco's chest. Her brother was, much to Cristina's horror, still conscious, and so she found her eyes darting between Bayer and Muller and then to the two privates who had accompanied Muller into the kitchen and were restraining Marco. Unaccountably and unreasonably, she realized she was looking to them for help. She focused on the younger of the pair. He couldn't have been more than eighteen; butterfly-shaped splotches of blood from the palm of Marco's hand dotted his uniform sleeve. And yet he met her gaze and his sheer boyishness gave her the hope that somehow Captain Muller—his commanding officer—wouldn't actually finish off her brother. He wouldn't. This couldn't be happening.

"Please," she heard herself pleading, her voice little more than a murmur.

Muller glared at her, and the private looked away. The captain shook his head in disgust. "Please what?" he asked her.

"Spare him," she begged. "Spare us."

"Then tell me, goddamnit! Where the fuck are they? Now!"

She might have told him. Deranged by terror and loss and simple exhaustion, the abyssal descent into compromise, she found herself murmuring the answer in her head and trying to understand what would happen if she said the words aloud. In her mind's eye, she saw the captain pulling down his gun. Ordering his men to the tombs. And then . . .

Then what? Would Muller bother to ask her or her parents why the partisans were here on their property? And if he did ask, would he listen when one of them explained that the partisans had arrived the night before and there was nothing—nothing at all!—the family could have done? After that, would the Germans just exit the kitchen and leave them alone?

"I've had enough!" Muller snapped when she remained mute. Before he fired, however, Francesca yelled for him to stop. She fell at his feet and wrapped her arms around his legs.

"They're in the tombs!" she cried.

"The tombs," he repeated.

Francesca looked up at the soldier, nodding frantically. "Yes, yes—the Etruscan tombs! They're all there—they're all down the hill! If you don't know where the tombs are, I can show you!"

"Lieutenant?" Muller asked.

Bayer shrugged. "I know where they are. The entrance is by the cemetery."

"Good," Muller said. Then he glanced down at Francesca. "Thank you. Thank you very much."

She was weeping, but her tears only annoyed him. He arched his eyebrows and pushed her away with his boot, pressing the hobnailed sole into her neck and chest. She started to crawl back toward Marco, but one of the soldiers pinning her husband shooed her away. "Both of you, stand clear," he said to his men. Then he brought the British rifle to his shoulder one final time, pushed the black muzzle between Marco's teeth, and fired.

1955

SERAFINA JOGGED AROUND the loggia, and it was impossible not to imagine the statue of Venus that Cristina said had once stood atop the fragmented base. There were the goddess's gently curved arms, her slender hips, her petite, perfectly formed ears. The smooth, unblemished skin along the neck. Serafina envisioned the wisteria that had scaled the pergola before the war had come to the estate, and the children splashing in the swimming pool. She saw the olive grove in the midst of the harvest, the nets on the ground and the ladders against the trees. The farmhands, Ilario perhaps, amid the branches. She saw the cattle and the sheep and the horses. She heard the animals' bells. She pictured the lion's head of the chimera, the monster baring its teeth, its mane resplendent and wild in the summer sun.

But she also found herself picturing the Nazis on the terrace, some in black SS uniforms, Antonio's red wine in their elegant crystal glasses. The marchese entertaining them with his stories. She heard the sound of the Germans' laughter and their boots on the marble.

And she recalled the mushrooms. The Etruscan paintings. The mustached face of the British doctor who had saved her life.

Up ahead, Serafina saw Cassini's coffee-colored beret on the top step beside one of the columns of the Roman temple the Rosatis had built to anchor their family cemetery. She paused just beyond the path to the tombs and then, when she heard nothing, walked as far as the edge of the cemetery. There she stopped again and stood perfectly still on one of the marble slabs along the wall of cypress trees.

"Luciano?" she called out finally. "Cassini?"

A pair of swallows darted out from beneath the cornice and flew, almost playfully, over her head and beyond the Etruscan vault. But otherwise there was no response. And so, carefully, she reached inside her purse for her Beretta and flipped off the safety.

※

When Paolo didn't find the vehicle with Vittore's family on his way back into Monte Volta, he detoured to the village's small police station. He was furious with himself. He had the sense he had been too cavalier, convinced the madman struck only when he had one of the Rosatis alone. It seemed now that he was mistaken. At the station he alerted the lone officer on duty to the make and model of the missing automobile and asked the young fellow behind the desk to call the police in the neighboring towns about the missing car.

It was almost ten minutes later, on his way back to the villa, that he noticed the grass. He cursed himself once again, because he should have spotted it on his way into town: a patch of flattened brush beside one of the switchbacks on the hill that descended from Monte Volta into the narrow valley that separated the villa from the village. His eyes should have been on that side of the road even on his way into town; it was the direction in which the Rosati funeral car would have been driving. But he was so focused on keeping his own car on the pavement that, pure and simple, he'd missed it.

Now he parked the Fiat half on and half off the thin road, just about where the weeds and wildflowers had been crushed by tires, and climbed from his car. He peered down into the ravine and there it was. There they were. At the bottom of the gorge, easily sixty or seventy meters below him. The vehicle was overturned, a turtle upside-down on its shell, tires for feet, but right away he counted the people outside the dented metal and it seemed that everyone was alive. The only question was Tatiana, because she was in Giulia's arms, pressed against her mother's chest. But Giulia's body language suggested relief, not despair, as she walked back and forth beneath the shade of a beech tree, and the detective took this as a good sign. Meanwhile, Vittore was squatting on his haunches and talking to Elisabetta, and he seemed to be examining her arm. She was sitting upright in the tall grass and broom, crying, which Paolo found reassuring. And the police officer who had been driving? He had trudged perhaps halfway up the hill and was pressing a handkerchief hard against his forehead as he limped. He was putting little weight on his left leg.

"Here I come!" Paolo called to him as he began his way down the steep incline, careful not to tumble over the rocks and roots that hid beneath the grass.

The driver paused and waited for him.

"Is everyone okay?" Paolo asked the fellow when he reached him.

"I think so," he answered. "The older girl's arm is broken. Maybe her foot, too."

"And the baby?"

He shrugged. "She seems fine. Too little even to be scared. It was Elisabetta and her father who got the worst of it."

"Vittore doesn't look hurt."

"You can't see the side of his face from here. It's a pretty bad cut."

"And you?"

The officer pulled the handkerchief off his forehead. There was a long gash just above his eyebrow, but already the bleeding was starting to slow. Still, a welt that might soon rival the size of a bird's egg already was forming. "I lived."

"You might have a concussion," Paolo said.

"I know. And I've done something to my ankle."

"A sprain?"

"I guess."

"What the hell happened?"

"That road is ridiculous. It's meant for oxen and donkey carts, not automobiles."

"No one sabotaged your car?"

"No."

"And no one tried to run you off the road?"

He seemed to think about this. "Maybe I should tell people someone did. Maybe I should tell you that."

"But it was just a bad road."

He put the handkerchief back against his forehead and winced. "That's right. It was just a very, very bad road. I'm from Rome, where we have modern roads."

Paolo imagined him failing to navigate the tight turn and had to rein in his annoyance. In all likelihood, the man had been driving too damn fast. Poor Giulia. The other night she was climbing down a bedsheet with that little girl in her arms because a guard had left her for grappa. Now? This idiot before him had pretended he was racing in the Mille Miglia and nearly killed her and her children. Her husband, too. "I'm going to talk to the family," he said finally. "I'll see what Vittore wants to do about the burial. Can you make it back to the road?"

"Yes. I'll be fine."

"Good. Flag down a car. Go to the villa and tell everyone what happened. We were all starting to get worried."

"I think that little girl and her father need to go to the hospital."

"I think you do, too."

"Then maybe I should go to the village instead and get a doctor for the Rosatis? I could call for an ambulance."

"Let me talk to Vittore," Paolo said. "You just get to the villa, okay?"

"Okay."

"I'll be right behind you," he added, and then he continued down the hill to the family. As angry as he was at the officer, he was far more relieved that Vittore and his wife and children were alive. Never before had a car accident—a *mere* car accident, even one this needless and stupid—made him happy.

A pillar of sunlight fell through a hole in the roof of the villa, and the thrum of voices—her aunt, the priest, the villagers who were there for her mother—began to recede for Cristina. She crossed the gravel driveway to the front steps of the house and stood there for a moment, lost in a memory. Once more she was holding in her hands her niece's cloth dolls and the red and gold napkins that would become the gowns of Renaissance princesses. She gazed back at the small crowd and told herself that her brother and his family had to be fine, if only because the sheer logistics of killing or kidnapping them between the village and the estate seemed unmanageable. She reminded herself that they were being escorted by an officer with a gun. As her eyes wandered among the moldering ruins of her childhood home—the gardens, the terrace, and of course the villa itself—she recalled the thousands of hours she had spent beside the swimming pool. Slowly, almost like a sleepwalker, she walked to the edge of the hill and gazed down on it, the pool now but a cracked and dry cavity, weeds stretching up toward the sun through the tile. Still, she saw herself there in a white bathing suit and a towel. A German soldier in a gray-green uniform, his eyes a hyacinth blue. She reached for the stone at the center of the necklace he'd given her years and years ago and pressed it against the top of her sternum. Against her heart. She almost never wore it when she was going to see Vittore because it annoyed him: he said it meant she was still dreaming of a man long dead, but she knew he was also angry because Friedrich had been Decher's adjutant and a German. But she wore it today. How could she not? She was returning to the place where Friedrich had given it to her.

For months after the war had finally ended, she had expected him to return to her. For most of 1945. It wasn't until Christmas

Eve that she had finally lit a candle in his name. It was at the Duomo in Montepulciano. Her mother had stood beside her when she had set fire to the wick and then together they had knelt. Now her breath was a little short with grief for Beatrice. She was thirty years old, and she had lived with her mother every single day of her life. Even when, over the years, she had spent the night with a lover or with Francesca in Florence, the next day she had always gone home to the marchesa. She wiped her eyes and longed for stupor and shock—to feel only hollow inside—because it seemed whenever she was alone she cried.

She glanced back and saw that her aunt was chatting with the villagers and farmhands who had come to watch the caskets being lowered into the earth, and so she started down the hill toward the pool. She just kept walking. She imagined herself a woman walking off a cliff. She moved gingerly along the terrace, careful not to trip among the fragments and debris, and then she surprised herself and continued past the pool. She gazed at the brush that had overtaken the olive grove, at the copse of trees at the edge of the vineyard that were rising amid the stanchions that had once shouldered grapevines. Wild sunflowers were spreading along the knoll where the cattle had grazed. In the months after the war, all manner of squatters and refugees had tried to live on this land. The family hadn't had the energy to run them off. Eventually they had all left on their own.

She paused before the foundation for the barn. The walls, shaken by the shelling that had rocked the estate for days, had collapsed. Even without the frame, however, Cristina knew exactly where the horse stalls had been. Where her beloved Arabella had slept. She stood for a long moment by the spot where the animal had been killed and where she had held Friedrich's pistol and contemplated shooting a trio of German soldiers—everyone but her lieutenant. Then she knelt over the earth where she and her parents had buried the horse. As shallow as the grave was, it had never, as far as she knew, been disturbed. It was an almost indistinguishable mound now, a ripple among the vast swells that rolled out from the barn in all directions.

When she rose, she brushed the grass off her knees and listened. She heard neither birds nor planes. She didn't hear any vehicles back at the villa—no tires on the gravel, no car doors slamming shut—and so she continued on, veering off onto the tufa path. She honestly wasn't sure whether she was going to the Etruscan ruins or to the cemetery, but they were so close it really didn't matter.

It was a few minutes later, when she stood on the ground where once she and Francesca and the children had picnicked, that she remembered something: somewhere amid the ancient and the modern dead were supposed to be two detectives. Some fellow named Cassini and Serafina, who had gone after him. She wondered where in the world they were now, and despite the summer heat felt the hairs rise up along the back of her neck.

1944

DECHER STOOD ALONE and gazed down into the pit. He was aware of the summer sun on his back, even through his uniform tunic. The bodies, he saw, were bleeding out through their white blouses and red-check work shirts, turning the dry Tuscan dirt into mud. Pig slop. The dark eyes on many of the corpses were still open.

Enraged, he'd barked his orders in a voice that was manic and shrill, commanding his men to bayonet these idiot peasants, and his men had obeyed. They'd been as furious as he was, and not a soldier had even hinted that it would have been better to simply shoot the Italians. The partisans were cowards, and this was the only way to rein them in: kill their neighbors, kill their families— their mothers and fathers and children and friends. Were any of these civilians related to partisans? Decher had absolutely no idea. But that didn't matter. The Allies were pushing north through Italy and seemed poised to break out from the Normandy beach-head in France. The Russians were nearing Warsaw. This was no time to allow the massacre of four German officers to go unpunished. The rule was six to one, and Decher had been ordered to round up twenty-four civilians. At some point one had slipped away—escaped. And that was the straw that had led Decher to order the remaining twenty-three to be bayoneted as they stood with their backs to the mass grave they had dug at gunpoint here at the edge of the olive grove.

He felt the sweat running down his spine and puddling just

above his belt in the small of his back. God, he hated this country. Loathed it. Then his eye caught something moving in the pit and he stared a little more carefully. Fingers. A hand. It was moving like a wounded, dying spider up and along the black fabric of . . . that fucking village priest's cassock. It was the fucking village priest's hand. The bastard wasn't quite dead and his eyes were open, and for a moment he and Decher stared at each other as the priest's fingers reached and then rested upon the large gold cross that lay flat against his still-beating heart.

Beside him Decher felt a presence, but he didn't want to take his eyes off the priest. It was a contest, and he wouldn't lose to this bastard. Turning away would be an admission of guilt, and he would not feel guilty. This priest and his traitorous peasant parishioners had brought this slaughter on themselves.

"Sir?"

Decher recognized the voice. It was Lieutenant Reinhardt.

"Sir," Reinhardt said again, "should I gather a detail to bury the bodies, or would you prefer we have other peasants do it?"

He ignored the lieutenant and, without taking his eyes off the priest, unsnapped his holster and removed his pistol. Finally he had to blink so he could clear his eyes and focus. But then he raised the Walther, aimed it straight at the priest's forehead, and fired. The body spasmed from the violence of the gunshot, and instantly a black hole appeared that almost matched the color of the cassock. Decher lowered his gun and then, much to his surprise, felt his stomach lurch the way it had that time he had ridden in an airplane and abruptly it had fallen a thousand feet in an air pocket. He put his hand to his mouth, a reflex, because he knew he was about to be sick.

"Sir?"

He glanced once at the lieutenant, started to nod that he was fine, he was fine. But he wasn't. He fell to his knees and vomited at the edge of the pit.

"This heat," Reinhardt murmured. "It gets to all of us."

Decher spat and looked up at the young officer. At his obedient blue eyes. Reinhardt was a powerful, heavyset young man who understood that the German nation was fighting for its life. He was, Decher decided, everything that Strekker wasn't, and he thought to himself, *Thank God Strekker isn't here.* He shuddered when he thought of what Strekker would have said about all . . . this. He probably would have to shoot the sanctimonious cretin for desertion if he ever showed up.

No, he wouldn't shoot him. Because Strekker hadn't deserted. He wasn't the type. He was either dead somewhere on the road between here and the Villa Chimera—he imagined the vehicle he was in being strafed by the RAF—or working his way north as best he could. Strekker would have a legitimate reason for his absence.

"Before you bury them," he told Reinhardt finally, "blow up the bodies."

"Excuse me?"

"Put some explosives in the pit and blow them up. Bury whatever's left."

The lieutenant seemed to contemplate this idea. Then he shrugged and yelled at two privates to round up some charges they could bury among the bodies.

🦂

Francesca and Alessia were screaming on the kitchen floor, their wails biblical, but Massimo was merely whimpering against his grandparents' legs. Muller took Cristina by her arm and dragged her outside. She expected him to stand her up against the wall of the villa and shoot her as well, but she was too numb to care. Really, why go on? What was the point? *Just be quick,* she thought. *Please, dear Lord, let this all be quick and over soon.*

"I beg you," she heard herself mumbling, "spare the children." Out here, Francesca's and Alessia's howling was muted, but only slightly.

"Do the partisans have more than rifles?" he asked, ignoring her question.

"I don't think so," she said. "But I don't know for sure."

"How many are there?"

She tried to think. "Five? Six? No more than six. And two are wounded—and one is dying."

"All men?"

"No. Four men, two women. And it's one of the women who's dying."

"Fine. You're going to lead us to the tombs and make sure that my men aren't ambushed on the way there. You're going to walk down there right now and take them some food," he said, and he let go of her arm so he could massage his neck and his shoulder. Then he yelled into the house for Bayer and the other soldiers to join him.

"We don't have any food," she said meekly.

He shook his head, annoyed. "I'll give you some field rations. Say you stole them."

"I stole them," she repeated without emotion.

"That's right. Then just walk to the tombs. I'm going to take seven or eight men with me and follow you. No doubt there will be at least one partisan as a lookout. He will stop you. While you're talking to him, we'll kill him. Then you'll continue into the ruins and we'll kill the others. Do this and yes, we'll spare the children."

Bayer and the two soldiers who had been inside the kitchen came up beside them.

"Give me your field rations, Bayer," Muller said.

When the lieutenant paused, Muller rolled his eyes and told his men the plan. "Also," he added and pointed inside the villa, an afterthought, "tell someone to shut those two up."

Friedrich spotted the limbs—arms and legs and feet, the feet in some cases bare and in others still clad in shoes—and the clothing draped on the olive tree branches. Based on the fabric and the footwear, these weren't the reeking vestiges of soldiers; these weren't the sleeves and the shoes of Germans or Brits. They belonged to peasants, he decided. Peasants. Maybe partisans. And then he saw a woman's head in the grass beside one of the trees like a big rock, and even though he knew there were women among the partisans, he guessed this was a reprisal.

The command was in chaos as the division tried to assemble and move farther north. The remnants of an armored column— the troop carriers and half-tracks and trucks—were struggling to gather themselves, and amid the stink of diesel fuel, tired, unshaven men were packing their gear as quickly as they could. Others were tying olive branches to the roofs of the vehicles. Friedrich knew well how close the British were. It was possible they were already behind them, cutting them off as he stood and surveyed an army in retreat and this nightmarish fruit among the olives.

He saw a private who managed to look both haggard and plump sitting on the hood of a jeep. The fellow was pressing a last pair of socks and a brick of cheese into his haversack as Friedrich approached him. "Where is Colonel Decher?" he asked.

The private started to answer, but then they heard the sound of incoming shells and almost in unison dove to the ground beside the edge of the grove. The explosions sent them rolling, and Friedrich was reminded of the horrific moment in Voronezh when the building collapsed all around him and he lost his right foot. Pebbles and dirt rained down upon them both, but Friedrich realized he was fine. He had jostled his wooden foot when he had fallen fast and hard to the earth, but nothing more. He sat up and adjusted the straps. The private was looking at him, and Friedrich couldn't decide whether the fellow was wide-eyed with awe or with disgust.

"I asked you where the colonel was," he said evenly to the soldier. On the other side of the jeep, perhaps twenty or twenty-five meters distant, a soldier was hurt and screaming for a medic.

"He was just here, sir. I'm sure he's nearby. He wants us on the road now."

Friedrich waved his arm at the pieces of the dead in the midst of the olive grove. "What happened there?"

"We had to execute some of the villagers."

"A reprisal?"

"Yes, sir."

"But why are there body parts in the trees?"

"The colonel had us blow up the bodies in the pit before we covered them up."

Friedrich shook his head. Decher was an idiot. Did he really think blowing up the bodies would either hide the evidence or make it easier to bury the victims? He couldn't believe the man had been given a combat command. Besides, at this point in the war, any reasonable person had figured out that reprisals made no sense. There was a logic to revenge; there was a satisfaction to revenge. But killing innocent civilians? It never worked. All it did was make the men against you vow to fight harder.

"Were you part of the execution squad?" Friedrich asked.

The private shook his head. "Thank God, no. But I saw a minute of it from that hill—but only a minute. I couldn't watch. The villagers were bayoneted."

"What?"

"The colonel ordered them killed by bayonet. I'm telling you . . ."

"Go on, Private."

The private looked around, as if he feared someone were listening. "Never mind, sir."

"Tell me," Friedrich said. "I promise, you can."

"Well, if we have to surrender—and the rumor is we're already surrounded—everyone who was part of that detail is a dead man. When the British get here, they'll hang everyone who was a part of the squad. Or maybe they'll bayonet them."

Friedrich reached for a door handle and pulled himself to his feet. In the distance he heard airplanes approaching. He leaned against the jeep and thought of how hard he had worked to stay ahead of the British and reach the division. And for what? Clearly this private felt it was over. *When the British get here.* In his opinion, the Germans weren't likely to make it much farther north. And of course he was right. It was over for these men, it was over for the army, and it was probably over for Germany. Everyone knew it but Hitler. All a person had to do was look at a map. And the Germans deserved it. Men like Decher. Soldiers like Muller and Bayer. They all deserved it. He thought of Cristina and wondered what would have happened if he had stayed with her at the villa. Waited for the British to arrive and surrendered. Or, better still, hidden somewhere on that estate until the combatants had found other ground on which to duel. He saw himself working with Vittore to rebuild the olive press in the autumn. Making love with Cristina on a blanket in the sloping grass above the Etruscan tombs. Having coffee in a piazza in Florence in the last warm days of fall.

"Get down!"

It was that private. Friedrich turned and saw the soldier leaping once more behind the vehicle, but already the planes were upon them, three American Mustangs, and one was diving at them, its machine guns nearly as loud as its engine, and then the jeep was exploding in a deafening roar of white-hot flame and daggerlike shards of steel and glass. His last thought as he felt himself rising, rising, rising, the air sucked from his lungs in the blast? Cristina had so loved to watch the planes as they'd flown high above the Crete Senesi and the Villa Chimera.

Decher crawled his way through the high grass between the still-burning half-tracks and the blackened shells of the jeeps, his pointed elbows pickets in the soil. He heard the cries and moans of the wounded and wondered briefly if he was the only one still breathing who was uninjured. He was, he realized, terrified. He had never experienced anything like this, the planes swooping down upon them like hawks, the men on the ground with absolutely no way to defend themselves. A part of him couldn't believe that he had ever craved combat, and his initial thought now was to get the hell out of here. To stay alive. Slowly, however, a woozy bear awakening from hibernation, he was coming to his senses.

There were plenty of others still alive and unhurt. Had to be. But the British would be here soon. He had to rally the survivors and get them all on their way to Arezzo. Gingerly he rose to his feet and gazed around him. He saw two dead soldiers beside the smoldering husk of a jeep, and one—and he had to look twice to be sure he was seeing this correctly—looked a lot like Strekker. He jogged over to the pair and stared down at the face. Sure enough, it was the lieutenant. He stood there, transfixed by the sodden mound of entrails beside the fellow. All that had once been inside Strekker had spilled out onto the grass. It was as if his uniform tunic were a cardboard box that had grown waterlogged and useless in a flood. The fellow's eyes, mercifully, were shut. Decher leaned over and saw that the soldier's trousers were ripped and the leg that should have ended in a bone-white shaft of wood ended now above the knee, the pants a sodden red rag. The prosthetic, he guessed, had either been blown into thousands of tiny splinters or been reduced to a negligible pile of ashes somewhere. He spied a blackened metal buckle, but that was the only trace.

In the distance he thought he heard vehicles. He stood up and brought his field glasses to his eyes, but he didn't really need them. Working their way up the tortuous switchbacks that marked the hill were three British tanks—Churchills—a column of dust from the dirt road obscuring them only slightly in the summer heat. He had to get his men moving, he thought. They had to hurry. He glanced back at the olive grove and the parts of the dead in the trees. He wasn't quite sure what he'd been thinking when he'd had the peasants bayoneted, and he wasn't quite sure what he was thinking now. The problem, perhaps, was that he hadn't been thinking; he had been furious, appalled at the way this country was awash in cowards and partisans and traitors. An Italian was either spineless or treacherous. As a race, they were as bad as the Jews. Nevertheless, the method of execution had been a mistake—and a profound one. Even his own men had been appalled and (if he was brutally honest with himself) ashamed. And while he tried to convince himself that those soldiers were too weak to understand the dictates of total war, most of them were combat veterans. He knew in his heart that he was the one who was in over his head.

And so, with the sound of the approaching Churchills growing louder, an idea—tentative, inchoate—began to form in his mind. Just in case (though just in case of *what* was also chimeric and vague), he reached under his shirt for the aluminum oval that was his dog tag and ran it between his forefinger and thumb. Moving quickly, his eyes darting around him to be sure that no one was watching, he removed his cap and pulled the ID over his head and dropped it into his pants pocket. Then he squatted and lifted Friedrich Strekker's skull with his left hand and slipped off the lieutenant's dog tag with his right. When he had it, he let the corpse fall back onto the ground and slipped his old adjutant's tag around his own neck. He emptied the young man's pockets and picked the prosthetic buckle off the grass, hurling it as far away as he could. Then, as if saying good-bye to a close childhood friend, he left his pay book in Strekker's tunic and his kit beside the body.

When this war was over—and, sadly, it would be soon—he would find a way to straighten this out. He would concoct an explanation. But perhaps with the two dog tags he could be Strekker as long as necessary and then Decher when it was time to go home. The main thing he had to do now was ensure that if the Brits caught him, he wasn't saddled with the blame for this monstrosity and shot against the stone wall of some villa or—because, as the Rosatis might say, this war was slipping fast into Dante—an olive tree.

1955

SERAFINA STOOD WITH her back flat against the tufa wall, the entrance to the underground tombs four feet to her right. She held her breath for a long moment, listening. She thought she heard movement inside there. Cassini? Maybe. But she wasn't confident enough to call out to him now. She hadn't seen the beam of a flashlight or the flickering halo of a cigarette lighter or match. The idea crossed her mind that it was an animal. A boar, perhaps. A feral cat. No, not a cat. Cats are silent. In the trees on the hill just above her, she heard birds taking flight. She knew what her instincts were telling her: something was wrong. Someone was inside, and it wasn't her fellow detective from Florence. Or, if the detective was inside, he was already dead. And so she resolved to wait right where she was, at least for the moment, and see if anyone or anything emerged from the opening. She raised her pistol and focused. She thought she could smell the mushrooms, but she honestly wasn't sure if this was merely her mind playing tricks.

She couldn't have said for how long she stood like that, head turned, eyes on the entrance, gun drawn—two minutes? three?—when she felt movement above her and to her right. She was just looking up when she saw him, leaping down from the embankment a dozen feet above her, falling upon her, and chopping his arm so hard into hers that she lost the Beretta as together they tumbled to the dirt. She tried to breathe, but the wind had been knocked from her. Reflexively she started to extend her right arm to find the gun, but she couldn't raise it far enough; the scar tissue might just as well have been concrete, and the pistol remained inches beyond her reach. Still, she struggled, rolling so she could claw for the gun with her left hand, but by then it was too late. He was on top of her, on her back, wrenching her arm up toward her shoulder blade. She stopped trying to seize the pistol and instead used her free hand for leverage to push with all her strength against the grass to try to topple him off her.

And, surprising herself, she succeeded. But he still had a gun and now she didn't. He rolled away from her and stood up, gazing down at her, his chest heaving from exertion.

Serafina thought that she might have said aloud the single word *You,* but she honestly wasn't sure.

He looked older than when she'd seen him last. A lot older. Certainly more than eleven years older. But still she believed that she might have recognized him if she had passed him on the street in Florence, and—in context—she would have known him for sure in a small village such as Trequanda or in the woods of Mount Amiata. And, obviously, here. The last time they had been together had been in Monte Volta—*right here in Monte Volta*—and she had been in and out of consciousness. And, blessedly, mostly out. Yet still she had identified him instantly, even though she had assumed all these years that he was dead. A lean face beneath thick eyebrows and hair—ash blond, even now—that was no longer the boyish mop it had once been. It was thin, his forehead high. He looked wan, a little dissolute, but she knew the pattern of stubble that ringed that hard jaw and the way his gaze more times than not blended impatience and passion. He had always been intense.

She would have asked him why, but she knew the answer. She had understood the moment she had realized who it was who had attacked her here at the entrance to the tombs. The Rosatis had told the Germans where the six partisans were hiding. Where she was hiding. And then Muller and his small execution squad had killed Enrico's wife, Teresa. His brother, Salvatore. The only reason they hadn't shot her, she guessed, was that they had seen she was dying, and dying in serious pain, which probably made her death all the more pleasurable for them. Who knows? Maybe they even thought she was already dead. And yet somehow he had survived. She couldn't imagine how.

"You're alive," she said simply.

Enrico nodded. "I am. And you are, too. Thank God."

"So . . . you're not going to kill me?"

He looked down at the gun in his hand and considered the fact that he was pointing it at her. It almost seemed to surprise him. "No," he answered. "Not unless I have to. And even then, I'm not sure I could."

She motioned at the tombs. "Is Cassini in there? Is he dead?"

"Is that his name? The detective from Florence? Yes, he's in there. Chloroformed and bound. But he's alive. I only want the Rosatis. That's all. I want this to be . . . clean." He smiled. "Remember, my father was a physician."

She thought to herself, *Yes, yes, of course he was. It's why you knew how to keep me alive after the firefight. It's why you know now how to extract a human heart.*

He looked at her approvingly. "I thought I saw you last week. You were on a street corner with another detective—that Paolo Ficino fellow. But then I thought, not possible. Not possible at all. You were killed with everyone else inside there." A realization came to him and he nodded. "You changed your name," he said.

"I did."

"Serafina, right?"

"Yes."

"Clever," he observed. "And you're a detective. Imagine."

She tried to keep her eyes soft; she focused on Enrico but used her peripheral vision to explore the world beside him. Around them. She needed a weapon, and he was standing between her and her pistol. The gun was sitting in a patch of stone perhaps a dozen feet behind him.

"Where have you been?" she asked.

"The last night? The last week? The last year? Last night I actually slept in my car."

"The last . . . decade."

"Most of it? A POW camp in Pskov. You've never heard of it. It's in Russia. It wasn't the worst of the camps. I got lessons in communism. Can you imagine? There's an irony. Who knows? Maybe they thought I was a monarchist or a republican. Anyway, it was hard to be a communist by the time I left. Still, I only lost thirty pounds there. And I never even got typhus." He shrugged. "They repatriated me two years ago. When I had my health back—which took some time—I looked up the Rosatis."

"How in the name of God did you survive the massacre in there?" she asked, motioning back at the tombs. "How did you wind up in a Russian POW camp?"

"I wasn't in the tombs when the Germans came. I was over there," he said, rolling his eyes and pointing toward a meadow. "There used to be an irrigation canal. I was trying to get us water. I was trying to get you water. We were constantly boiling rags and cooling rags and putting them on your back and your side. Then I heard the shots. They were muffled because of the cave walls, but I knew what I was hearing. I knew what was happening. By the time I got there, you were all dead. You, too, I supposed. Christ, it was awful. I held my Teresa for I don't know how long. Her body was growing cold when I finally left. I went through the olive grove. The vineyard. I went into the valley because I knew the Germans wanted the high ground. I was . . . delirious. Devastated. I really wasn't thinking. And so, somehow, before the Nazis even made their last stand, I was behind their lines. In the midst of them—but not by design. That wasn't my plan—I wasn't going to try to sabotage anything. I was trying to get to the British or the Americans or the French. I don't know anymore. But suddenly the Germans were everywhere, so I hid in a work detail on the road to Arezzo. Italian soldiers who'd been disarmed by the Germans and reduced to slave labor."

"Like Marco Rosati," she said.

"I guess. But they shipped us all to the Apennines to build trenches and bunkers and antitank ditches before I could get away. And then, the night before a group of us were going to escape, we were put on a train and sent to Germany. Again, slave labor. And, worst of all, the Eastern Front. Maybe that's redundant. By then the Eastern Front and Germany were practically the same thing. Anyway, I was on the Oder River. At one point some SS thugs handed us winter coats and boots. I was grateful, I really was. But then they gave us rifles instead of shovels and told us to go stop the Russians. They said they'd be behind us if we even considered trying to run away. So instead we surrendered to the Russians. Fifteen of us. Maybe sixteen. I can't remember."

He grinned sheepishly, and she was reminded of how charismatic he had once been. And how cold-blooded. Perhaps he did take pride in being a doctor's son, but she recalled well how easy it had been for him to order an assassination. Then, of course, he had been a patriot. But executing the Rosatis today, ten years after the war was over? This was just murder. This was nothing more than revenge.

And he will have to kill me, too, she thought. *Maybe he doesn't want to, but how can he not, since I know what he's done—what he's planning to do?* Any moment he was going to circle back to this hard reality and, as much as it pained him, pull the trigger.

"I'm sorry about your ear," he said suddenly. He looked at her more closely. "And your neck."

She nodded.

"Your back? Is it . . ."

"Yes," she said. "It is. The right side."

He seemed to think about this—to recall the dying girl she had once been. He was still strangely moved by their reunion, by the fact that she, too, had managed against all odds to survive. He had absolutely no idea that twenty or twenty-five meters behind him, standing perfectly still, was Cristina Rosati. Serafina guessed that she must have wandered down to the family cemetery while everyone else was waiting for the car to arrive with her brother and his family. Her expression was somewhere between bewilderment and shock, and Serafina knew that she had to distract Enrico. She needed to speak, to say something, to give Cristina the chance to turn and slink away—to escape the madman who wanted to cut out her heart. And so Serafina started to tell him more about her back and the British doctor who had saved her life, but she hadn't spoken long before she saw that Cristina was neither edging backward nor running away. She wasn't retreating at all. Clearly she recognized Enrico, too. Clearly she remembered the night she had led the German soldiers to the tomb. Serafina could see in her eyes that Cristina knew this was not merely the partisan leader who once, long ago, had come to the Villa Chimera desperately looking for help; this was also the man who was exacting revenge on her family.

And now the woman had seen the Beretta on the rock and was slinking toward it on cat's feet. So Serafina described for Enrico what she had felt so long ago when she had first looked in a mirror at the hospital and gazed, transfixed, at her neck and her ear, and how she had felt a jarring riot of relief that she was alive and sadness that her family—her real family as well as her replacement family, people like Enrico and Teresa—was dead and she looked like . . . like this. Not an ogre. Not a monster. But forever scarred.

And then, her eyes still soft, she watched the marchese's daughter, a woman roughly her age who just the other day had found her own mother dead on a hotel room floor and seen her sister-in-law's heart in an ashtray—who had witnessed her family's torture in a kitchen in a once magical villa up the hill from where they were now—pick up the Beretta, spread wide her legs for purchase on the tufa stone, and shoot Enrico Tarantola in the back.

*

Hours and hours later, in the night, Paolo Ficino and his wife stood in the doorway to their daughter's bedroom in their apartment in Florence and watched the sheet atop their teenage girl's shoulders rise and fall almost imperceptibly in the moonlight. The child was a little more than half Serafina's and Cristina's age. Paolo had awoken first and come here, not precisely a vigil but a small, simple quest for reassurance. His wife had joined him a minute or two later. He thought now of his scarred detective and the marchese's daughter and the row of cedars that lined the path between the Rosati cemetery and the ancient Etruscan burial chambers.

In Rome, Vittore and Cristina Rosati sat in almost absolute silence at his dining room table, a single light on, while Vittore sipped a half glass of vermouth. He had planned to mix a Negroni, but it was two in the morning and that seemed like too much work. Giulia and the girls were sound asleep, even Elisabetta with her arm in that cast, the three of them in his and Giulia's bed. There really hadn't been room for him there anyway, he decided. Besides, he was never going to sleep tonight. Apparently his sister wasn't either. He had assumed she was out like a light in his older daughter's bedroom. She wasn't. He noticed that she was wearing one of Giulia's nightgowns. He rubbed his temples with his fingers, and with his thumb felt the bandages and gauze along the side of his face. It would be days before the swelling would go down. He thought of the moment that afternoon when the car had rolled off the switchback and, in the front passenger seat, he had felt helpless, unable to shield or embrace either Tatiana or Elisabetta. Thank God they had been fine. Yes, Elisabetta's arm was broken, but it wasn't a bad break, the doctor had said. And her foot was only bruised.

He looked up at Cristina and with the umbilicus of siblings sensed instantly what she was thinking. Not the precise details, not the particular images. But the lines around her eyes were all grief, and he knew that behind them was a memory of Massimo and Alessia. Their nephew and niece. Vittore had walked away from the war and found his way back to the Villa Chimera two days before Massimo had stepped on the land mine. He and Cristina had known instantly what it was that day in 1944, but for a moment he, at least, had deluded himself into believing that an animal had set off the explosion. It was just after three in the afternoon, and the two of them were working together to drape a piece of canvas across the cavernous hole in the villa's living room wall—the remnants of the family were still trying to convince themselves that they could rebuild their lives in Monte Volta—when they heard the dull bang. It was more of a pop, Vittore thought now. But then Francesca had come racing through the house like a madwoman and they had followed her out onto the terrace. There, down near the tombs, was a single stray plume rising black and still against the late summer sky. By the time the three of them had reached the children, Massimo was dead, his body ripped into small pieces—a leg here, a foot there—and Alessia was unconscious and dying. He had run with her in his arms back to the villa while Cristina had tried to restrain their sister-in-law; her howling would live on in his ears for months. But there had been no help and nothing to do for the girl at the house. She'd died within minutes. That night both Vittore and Cristina had feared that Francesca would kill herself.

"May the worst that Elisabetta and Tatiana recall from this summer be a car accident and a cast," Cristina said, breaking the silence.

"Tatiana? Who knows what toddlers remember?" he said, and he finished his vermouth. Then he stood and went to the window. From there he said, "And Elisabetta is like Alessia. Afraid of nothing."

"Can I ask you something?"

"Sure."

"Did you ever grow to like Friedrich at all?"

"No. You know that."

"Even after—"

"No," he repeated, cutting her off. "Never." He knew how she would have finished the sentence, because they had had different versions of this conversation so many times in the past. He turned around to face Cristina and leaned against the window frame. "Now that you know for a fact he's gone, will you please stop carrying that torch?" he asked. "Now that Mother's gone, will you start living your life?"

She considered arguing that she did not know for a fact that Friedrich was gone. No one did. She considered reminding him that although she had lived with their mother, she had lived her life. Instead, however, she went to him and bowed her head against his chest—a peace offering.

"It really is just us now," she said, her voice melancholic and tired.

"I know," he agreed. "I know." He put his arms around her and rubbed her back. If someone on the street had gazed up at them in the window, he would have presumed they were lovers, reuniting after a quarrel.

Which was precisely what someone in Florence would have surmised if he had glanced up at Serafina and Milton that moment on their terrace in Florence. From across the river, they might have spied the woman on a wrought iron chair, most of her weight on her left side. This time it was the man whose head was bowed. He seemed to be studying something on the insides of her thighs, or he—the two of them—might have been contemplating something far more intimate. From across the Arno, it was hard to say, and an onlooker was likely to have looked away, just in case.

And if he did, he would have missed this: a sudden small phosphorescent burst from a match as it rained heat and light upon the woman's bare skin.

NO, I DID NOT DIE when Cristina shot me. Obviously. I'm here, after all. The bullet shattered a rib and punctured a lung. But it was enough. One moment I was rather enjoying my reunion with—and she chose her name well—Serafina, and the next I was on the ground struggling for breath. And then I was looking up at the two women.

I was in Russia when Italy outlawed capital punishment in 1948. Only high treachery against the republic can get a person hanged by the state. Can you imagine? I cut the throats of two women, nearly decapitating one, and exhumed their hearts from their chests. And still they have no plans to execute me.

So here I am. Yet again a survivor. They tell me I will be here as long as I live.

We'll see.

Nevertheless, it is not unpleasant. Trust me, an Italian prison is infinitely more tolerable than a Soviet POW camp.

Once Serafina even came to visit. We spoke of our families. My beloved Teresa. Her brothers. We spoke briefly of the Rosatis.

It's clear that Serafina has a greater well from which to draw forgiveness than I. I reminded her that Francesca and Cristina had sentenced her to death, too. The Germans could just as easily have shot her when they murdered my wife and my brother. But she insists the family hadn't a choice. Not true. We always have choices. Isn't that what Dante teaches us?

I really have become quite the Dante scholar: "There is no greater sorrow than to recall our time of joy in wretchedness."

Serafina may think I'm a crazy person, but I'm not. She has her scars, too—and not only the ones I saw when she turned her head and her hair fell aside. We are both living out our lives in a Purgatorio. The difference? I arrived from the Paradiso, once young and married and so in love. But Serafina, she who was born alone in a fever dream of fire? She whose very skin is a tapestry of loss? Serafina, of course, arrived from the Inferno.

Acknowledgments

In 2004, Michael Barnard, owner of Rakestraw Books in Danville, California, put a small, remarkable memoir in my hands: *War in Val d'Orcia,* by the marchesa Iris Origo. The book chronicled life on her sun-drenched Tuscan estate when the nightmare of the Second World War rolled like a tsunami across her and her husband's lands. Michael urged me to read the memoir because my wife and I were about to visit our good friends Greg Levendusky and Pam Powers at the modest Italian *podere,* or farm, they were endeavoring to rebuild at the edge of the village of Montisi. Their new home was not far from the corner of Tuscany where Origo had once straddled two eras: she was a noblewoman, an anachronism even in 1943 and 1944, but at the same time she and her husband were pioneering landowners who modernized their property and tried to improve the lives of their tenant farmers. Origo was also a gifted writer, and her book fascinated me.

Meanwhile, I was mightily impressed by the way that Greg and Pam had restored the old Tuscan farmhouse and revived the land, and by the simplicity of their world in Montisi.

So in so many ways my thanks for this novel have to begin with the late marchesa Iris Origo and with my good friends.

I am also, however, profoundly grateful to Z. Philip Ambrose, professor emeritus at the University of Vermont. Although Professor Ambrose and I both live in northwestern Vermont, we first met at a summer choral concert at Sant'Anna in Camprena, an abbey perhaps six kilometers from Montisi. It is indeed a small world: six degrees of separation will always trump million-to-one odds. I was hoping Professor Ambrose could help me with my Etruscan history. He did that, but he was also an invaluable guide through the fictional village of Monte Volta and the experience of rural Italian civilians in the Second World War.

In addition, I want to thank a pair of physicians, William Charash and Marc Tischler. Dr. Charash, division chief for trauma, burn, and critical care surgery at Fletcher Allen Health Care in Burlington, Vermont, provided insight into Serafina Bettini's burns and how she might have been kept alive and then treated in 1944. Dr. Tischler, a cardiologist at Fletcher Allen and the director of the echocardiography laboratory there, helped me to understand the state of open-heart surgery in the 1950s and how a serial killer might extract a human heart. Both physicians are also associate professors at the University of Vermont College of Medicine.

Laura Renzi Goodyear was my all-important feet on the ground in Italy, researching there and explaining to me what parts of the investigation the Florence *polizia* might have handled and where the carabinieri might have fit in. (And big thanks to Krista Patterson Jones for suggesting Laura.) She was a spectacularly good researcher, and I am deeply appreciative. I used much of what she taught me and, I confess, disregarded other historical details. In any case, all credit for the minutiae in the investigation that are accurate goes to Laura; all blame for the liberties goes to me.

Thanks also to Jeremy Julian and Allegra Biery, with Northern Trust, for helping me understand the work of an American banker in Florence in 1955.

There were a great many books that were helpful, in addition to Iris Origo's memoir. Among them was Douglas Preston's and Mario Spezi's riveting and unforgettable *The Monster of Florence*. It is, like all of Preston's work, absolutely terrific—but it also allowed me to follow an actual investigation. Rick Atkinson's powerful *The Day of Battle* helped me learn the specifics of the fight for Sicily. (In addition, I found the epigraph for this novel in his extraordinary history.) And two wonderful novels inspired me and took me back to Italy as I was writing this story: Olaf Olafsson's *Restoration* and Mary Doria Russell's *A Thread of Grace*. Both novels are haunting and beautiful and brilliantly capture what life might have been like in Italy during the Second World War. Moreover, Olafsson's fictional Tuscan villa is downright magical.

Big thanks as well to Jane Gelfman and her staff at Gelfman Schneider—Cathy Gleason and Victoria Marini; to Arlynn Greenbaum at Authors Unlimited; and to Todd Doughty, John Fontana, Suzanne Herz, William Heus, Judy Jacoby, Jennifer Kurdyla, Jennifer Marshall, Sonny Mehta, Beth Meister, Anne Messitte, Roz Parr, Russell Perreault, John Pitts, Andrea Robinson, Bill Thomas, and the whole wondrous team at the Knopf Doubleday Publishing Group. And, of course, enormous thanks to my editor there, Jenny Jackson, who is grounded and smart and insightful, and capable of walking me in off the ledge when characters die or I need to delete three-thousand-word scenes. Without question, these are the attributes a writer needs in an editor.

Finally, I am so blessed to be married to Victoria Blewer. She, along with our wise-beyond-her-years daughter, Grace, read this book at different stages. The two of them always offered their suggestions in a fashion that can only be called diplomatic.

I thank you all so, so much.

CLOSE YOUR EYES, HOLD HANDS

A heartbreaking, wildly inventive, and moving novel narrated by a teenage runaway, from the bestselling author of _Midwives_ and _The Sandcastle Girls_.

Close Your Eyes, Hold Hands is the story of Emily Shepard, a homeless teen living in an igloo made of ice and trash bags filled with frozen leaves. Half a year earlier, a nuclear plant in Vermont's Northeast Kingdom had experienced a cataclysmic meltdown, and both of Emily's parents were killed. Devastatingly, her father was in charge of the plant, and the meltdown may have been his fault. Thousands of people are forced to flee their homes in the Kingdom; and Emily feels certain that as the daughter of the most hated man in America, she is in danger. So instead of following the social workers and her classmates after the meltdown, Emily takes off on her own.

A story of loss, adventure, and the search for friendship in the wake of catastrophe, _Close Your Eyes, Hold Hands_ is one of Chris Bohjalian's finest novels to date—breathtaking, wise, and utterly transporting.

www.ChrisBohjalian.com

Doubleday